MURDER

CROSSED

HER MIND

Also by Stephen Spotswood

Fortune Favors the Dead

Murder Under Her Skin

Secrets Typed in Blood

MURDER CROSSED HER MIND

A PENTECOST AND PARKER MYSTERY

STEPHEN SPOTSWOOD

DOUBLEDAY   *New York*

www.doubleday.com

DOUBLEDAY and the portrayal of an anchor with a dolphin are registered trademarks of Penguin Random House LLC.

Book design by Maria Carella
Jacket design and illustration by Michael J. Windsor

Library of Congress Cataloging-in-Publication Data
Names: Spotswood, Stephen, author.
Title: Murder crossed her mind / Stephen Spotswood.
Description: First Edition. | New York : Doubleday, [2023] |
Series: A Pentecost and Parker Mystery ; book 4
Identifiers: LCCN 2022057883 (print) | LCCN 2022057884 (ebook) |
ISBN 9780385549288 (hardcover) | ISBN 9780385549295 (ebook)
Subjects: LCGFT: Detective and mystery fiction.
Classification: LCC PS3619.P68 M86 2023 (print) | LCC PS3619.P68 (ebook) |
DDC 813/.6—dc23/eng/20221208
LC record available at https://lccn.loc.gov/2022057883
LC ebook record available at https://lccn.loc.gov/2022057884

MANUFACTURED IN THE UNITED STATES OF AMERICA

10 9 8 7 6 5 4 3 2 1

First Edition

To my mother, Margie Spotswood,
my very first fan

Remorse - is Memory - awake -
Her Parties all astir -
A Presence of Departed Acts -
At window - and at Door

—EMILY DICKINSON

CAST OF CHARACTERS

WILLOWJEAN "WILL" PARKER: Second in command to famed detective Lillian Pentecost. She might stumble, but she always comes up swinging.

LILLIAN PENTECOST: The finest mind in New York City. She's made a lot of enemies over the years, and one of them is finally closing in.

PERSEVERANCE BODINE: A retired recluse with a Kodak memory. What did she know that made someone want her to disappear?

FOREST WHITSUN: Headline-grabbing defense attorney and Ms. Pentecost's newest client. Though not for long if he can't lay off the backseat detective work.

THE RESIDENTS OF THE BAXTER ARMS: A collection of mothers, mechanics, and malcontents. Do they count a murderer among their number?

AGENT T. S. FARADAY: One of J. Edgar's shadowy minions. He'd frisk his own mother if he had one.

JOHN BOEKBINDER, CLARK GIMBAL, AND KEN DEVINE: The heads of the high-priced law firm where Bodine used to work. She knows all their secrets. Was one of them worth killing for?

LEONARD TEETERING: The humble owner of a small-town five-and-dime. Is that all-American mask hiding a Nazi spy?

DONNY RUSSO: A vicious member of mob middle management. He's got a big collection of knives and he'd like to stick one into Will Parker.

LIEUTENANT NATHAN LAZENBY: Pentecost and Parker's favorite homicide cop. But their association has come back to bite him.

ELEANOR CAMPBELL: Highlands housekeeper to Pentecost and Parker. Not afraid to browbeat a world-famous detective or two.

HIRAM LEVY: Holding down the night shift at the medical examiner's office. Dignified caretaker of the dead.

MAEVE BAILEY: The former Madame Fortuna—speaker to ghosts, seer of the future. Never met a mark she couldn't fleece.

MURDER

CROSSED

HER MIND

CHAPTER 1

I thought I knew what pain was.

I was wrong.

I've been punched, kicked, stabbed, strangled, bitten, and burned. I even got electrocuted that one time.

Nothing compared to this.

I was shaking, covered in cold sweat. There were screams in the distance. My torturer had his back to me, fiddling with something on his table of abominable devices. He turned toward me, a mouthful of yellow teeth peering out through that terrible rictus of a grin.

"Only a little ways to go now."

"You said that three little ways ago," I snapped.

"Every time you move, I have to stop," he said around the stub of a cigar. "You're lucky the line work is as smooth as it is."

"You're lucky I haven't kneed you in the teeth."

That was no joke, considering where he'd had his face planted for the last twenty minutes.

"I told you. The inner thigh is a sensitive area."

"I don't need you to tell me that, Bernie."

"All's I'm saying is if you wanted less pain, you could have put it on your bicep or your behind," Bernie said. "But you didn't and now here we are. I've got customers waiting and all I gots left is the red of the rose. You think you can grit your teeth and play statue for ten minutes more?"

I was lining up a comeback, but I bit it off. The tattooist didn't deserve my abuse. He was doing the job I was paying him for. Gifting me a permanent reminder of an old friend and a closed case.

"All right," I said. "If I can sit through *Maid in the Ozarks* I can sit through this. Fire up your engines."

Bernie propped his smoke on the table next to his inks, then flipped a switch. The needle in his hand began to buzz—a wingless hornet with a metal stinger. He leaned over me and the needle touched down high on the inside of my left thigh.

I tried breathing, I tried grinding my molars, I tried mentally reciting poetry.

I felt a Funeral, in my Brain,
And Mourners to and fro
Kept treading—treading—till it seemed
That . . . something something *. . .* Ah, shit.

No good. Even Dickinson won't stick when you let a metal wasp tread where only lovers usually linger. The needle was piercing me at a rate of four dozen pricks a second, the red ink of the rose mixing with the red of my blood so I didn't know which was trickling down my thigh.

Then I remembered what Ms. Pentecost said about her more painful multiple sclerosis flare-ups.

"Ignoring it is impossible. I can't make it go away, so I won't try. I give it exactly the attention it deserves, and not an ounce more."

Since she was a woman of exceptional sense, as well as the most sought-after private detective in New York City, I figured she must know a thing or three. The least her faithful assistant, Willowjean "Will" Parker, could do was take a shot at emulating her.

I stopped trying to ignore the pain. I let it wash over me.

Just let it be. And while that didn't make it much better, at least I stopped twitching.

I took my eyes off Bernie and his needle and looked through the propped-open door to the boardwalk, the sand, and the bluest ocean you could ask for. At least on that Tuesday afternoon in early September 1947. A breeze shouldered its way through, and for a brief moment the smell of ink and sweat and Bernie's rancid cigar was pushed aside to make way for salty Atlantic crispness.

I needed to find a thermometer and take a note. This was the perfect temperature. At least for New York City.

Because I've never been one to sit and jaw about the weather, my mind quickly wandered elsewhere. I thought about Miss Holly Quick, with whom I wouldn't have minded spending a Coney Island afternoon. The season had just ended, so the crowd had thinned out. Not so vacant that we could have canoodled together on the sand, but at least we wouldn't have had to stand in line for the Cyclone.

But Holly wasn't a roller-coaster girl, and besides, she'd left town for a monthlong vacation at a cabin in the Catskills.

I corrected myself. Not a vacation, a writing refuge.

She was struggling to find an ending for her book, which was scheduled to be published in the spring, and thought a month away from the city would do her good.

She'd ridden up with Marlo and Brent Chase on Saturday. The married couple were her friends, lovers, and editors, in that order. The cabin belonged to Marlo's family, which is how a pulp-magazine writer could afford a month away.

I hadn't been thrilled that Holly was out of pocket for all of September. Even less thrilled to learn she'd have to walk the better part of an hour to a general store to drop a nickel if she wanted to call me. Then there was the fact that Marlo and Brent were staying with her until Thursday. To settle her in.

"Not a bad euphemism," I'd told her when she laid out the plan. "I settled in two or three times last night; I'm exhausted."

Holly dropped her chin and gave me that look from over the top of her glasses—the one I was starting to know a little too well.

"Is this going to be a problem?" she asked. "Because I thought we'd been through this. Jealousy is not an attractive outfit on you."

"I'm not jealous," I said. "I'm envious. I just wish I was the one settling you in."

"I asked you."

"I know."

"You can still come."

But I couldn't.

Even if I could tear myself away from the office, I had the feeling that the arrangement the four of us had figured out would start to show its cracks if we were all bunking in the same cabin.

Holly suggested I come up later in the month after Marlo and Brent had gone, but I'd nixed that, too. Again saying that there was too much to do at the office. Backed-up paperwork and filing and this and that—thinking back on how I had prattled on, she must have known I was stitching up an excuse.

Lying on my back, listening to the buzz of the needle and the roar of the ocean, I wondered why I'd said no. A few weeks away sounded great. A few weeks away with Holly even better. Why had I begged off?

I took my mind by the chin and forced its gaze elsewhere.

Pentecost Investigations was between cases at the moment. There was the Tillman affair and the Vaughan murder. But both of those were in various states of getting wrapped. I'd deposited our outstanding checks that morning, bringing the business bank account up to mid-five figures. That should easily get us through the spring, even after taxes.

I also deposited my own paycheck, which would allow me to take a stroll through the fall fashions at Macy's without worrying about pinching pennies.

But not all our active cases were on the books.

There was Olivia Waterhouse, who had more or less taken up permanent residence in our life. However, after surfacing dramatically last spring, the fraudulent anthropology professor, blackmailer, and almost certainly killer had disappeared beneath the waves, leaving nary a ripple.

Not that we weren't searching the seas.

We were still trying to track down anyone who had been taken advantage of by Sunshine Services, Waterhouse's mock-up temp secretary company, which had offered dictation but provided extortion. Understandably, those victims—those who were still breathing—were hesitant to speak up.

No luck in luring any of the women who'd worked there to come forward, either. Even though we'd published notices in the papers offering cold cash.

Waterhouse engendered either fear or loyalty. Having been nose to nose with the woman, I was guessing a little of both.

And she wasn't the only thorn in my boss's side. There was also Jessup Quincannon, philanthropist and murder aficionado. Some people collect stamps. He collected murder memorabilia, along with the occasional murderer.

During a case last winter we discovered that he'd withheld information that might have gotten a killer caught sooner and prevented at least one body from hitting the ground. Since the body in question was employed by Ms. Pentecost at the time, she was taking it personally.

Which meant digging into Quincannon's life in the hopes of finding enough dirt to bury him. That wasn't easy. The man had money, and money bought you a lot of leeway. Especially when it was distributed in the form of bribes and campaign contributions to the city's high-and-mightiest.

But Ms. P was employing leverage of her own and managing to find some toeholds. There was the evidence-room sergeant who had been slipping Quincannon baubles from the city's bloodiest crimes. A letter from my boss to his got him canned. Then there was the councilman who—

"Done!"

"Already?" I asked.

Bernie snorted, then he took a cloth and wiped away the last of the loose ink and blood to reveal the finished tattoo: a rose wrapped around a dagger.

"So what do you think?" he asked.

I had scars and freckles aplenty but this was the first permanent mark I'd chosen for myself. That dagger was here for the duration. I'd be buried with it.

"The colors will even out as it heals," Bernie explained, taking my silence for displeasure. "Everything's swollen and pink right now. That's why the green leaves look kind of muddy."

I smiled.

"It's perfect," I said.

I don't know if it really was perfect. But it was just right. I pulled down my skirt, freshened up, paid up, got a quick speech from Bernie on how not to get my new tattoo infected, and strolled out onto the boardwalk. Dressed in a sweater-and-skirt combination, purse slung over my shoulder, I looked like a cookie-cutter coed taking advantage of the perfect September weather to air out her legs.

Ms. P didn't expect me back that afternoon, so there was no hurry. I slipped off my shoes and strolled down onto the beach, giving my toes a taste of warm sand.

A gust lashed in from the Atlantic. I had to choose between keeping my hair out of my eyes or keeping the handful of beachgoers from getting a view of my new tattoo. I chose the latter.

When the temperature hit triple digits in July I'd caved and visited my favorite barber. He'd lopped eight inches off my mane, so ponytails were out of the question for at least another couple of months. While my neck felt nice and cool, I now had to put up with frizzy red curls falling into my eyes.

I wasn't the only one taking advantage of the weather and the mostly empty beach. I passed a few other beachgoers, some walking solo, some in pairs. Up ahead, I saw one couple slip into the shadows under the boardwalk. I smiled and silently wished them a good time.

Seeing the pair of lovers, I found my thoughts returning to Holly.

We weren't exclusive, but that didn't mean we weren't serious. I'd spent more time with her than any five previous flings combined, and I wasn't bored yet.

So why'd I go digging for an excuse not to spend some time alone with her up in the Catskills? What was I afraid of?

Nothing, I told myself. I just didn't feel like going.

Really?

Really.

Back and forth like this for another twenty yards when a voice broke through my reverie.

"Get off me. No. I said no!"

The woman's cry was coming from under the boardwalk, where the pair of lovers had disappeared.

Over my five years working as Ms. Pentecost's leg-woman, I'd developed the terrible habit of running toward trouble instead of away, so I dropped my shoes and was kicking up sand before she got out the second "no!"

As I approached the shadows under the boardwalk, I slowed and reached into my handbag. My fingers slipped into the hidden pouch I'd had my tailor sew into the lining and found the grip of my brand-new Beretta. When you might be stepping into danger, it's always better to err on the side of armed.

But I didn't draw it.

Back in February, I had shot and killed a man. A righteous killing, at least so far as the City of New York was concerned. But there were a few officials who suspected the events that had led up to the killing weren't so righteous.

I hesitated at the thought of shooting two people in a calendar year, so I let my hand move from the grip of the .32 to a little treasure I'd recently ordered out of a specialty catalog—an eight-inch-long leather sap. The short blackjack was packed with sand and iron filings, making it incredibly dense. The flat beavertail end meant that, should it strike a skull, it was less likely to kill.

It still hurt like a demon.

More cries.

"No! Please, let go of me!"

On its heels, a man's voice. "Come on. Stop squirming. Why'd you come under here if you didn't want it?"

Sap firmly in hand, I eased around one of the massive wooden pilings and found the situation as advertised.

The woman—short, busty, with blond ringlets—was on her back in the sand. Her blouse had been torn open in a way that suggested it hadn't been voluntary. I could see only the back of the man—dark hair, jeans, work boots, and a leather jacket. He was on top of her, pinning her two hands with one of his while he used the other to fumble with his belt.

I set my bag down and snuck up behind them. With bare feet on sand, and the roar of the waves, stealth wasn't a problem.

In the movies, the hero would yell something like "Get your filthy hands off her!" I leave it to fiction to give bad guys a fighting chance.

I raised the sap over my head, cocking my elbow to get the right angle. It was then the woman saw me. Her eyes went wide and she started to say something. But not before I swung down, letting the flat of the sap connect with the back of the would-be-rapist's skull.

He collapsed, boneless, on top of his victim, who let out a groan and a muttered "Holy shit."

I rolled him off and helped her to her feet.

"Are you all right?" I asked.

"I think so," she said, doing up her blouse, which had remarkably retained all its buttons. As she did, I couldn't help but notice that she wasn't busty so much as well padded. Not that I'm one to judge.

"You know this mook?" I asked.

"No, he . . . he came out of nowhere."

Which was an odd answer because I'd seen the two go under the boardwalk together. I began to wonder if she was a professional. The blond ringlets didn't quite match her skin tone, suggesting a wig. And her makeup—all pinup lips and smoky eyes—was paired with some heavy pancake. Some of it had smeared, revealing the yellow of an old bruise.

It's bad etiquette to ask if someone's a prostitute, so instead I suggested, "Look, while he's out, let's get topside and see if we can track down a cop."

"No," she said, quick and firm. "I don't want any more trouble."

That nailed it. The mook was a john who decided he was owed a freebie.

"Okay, so no cop," I said. "How about we get out of here and—"

Before I could get the rest of the sentence out, the man lurched to his feet and charged. He must have been playing possum. Not entirely, though. His charge was slow and wobbly, and he dropped to a knee in the sand right before he reached me.

I sidestepped and let him fall. I raised the sap again, ready to put him out, but the girl grabbed hold of my arm before I could bring it down.

"No, don't!" she yelled. "Don't kill him!"

I tried to yank my arm away, but she was latched on tight.

Before I could explain that I wasn't planning on killing him, just gifting him with a serious goose egg, the man was on his feet and moving again. No chance to sidestep this time, and his shoulder hit me solidly in the gut, slamming me back into one of the wooden pylons. The impact drove the air from my lungs and the sap went flying.

The impact didn't do him any favors, either. He gave an explosive grunt and his feet slipped in the sand. He would have gone to his knees if he didn't have his shoulder wedged into my solar plexus.

I didn't give him the chance to recover. With his shoulder in my gut, his head was under my right armpit. I slipped my arm down the side of his neck, jackknifed at the elbow, and shot it up the other side. I brought my left arm over, grabbed my own bicep, and began twisting the noose.

The thug's excuse for a brain was suddenly starved of blood. By the time he realized what was happening, he was already going limp in my arms.

Out of the corner of my eye, I saw the girl pick up my blackjack.

"We won't need that," I told her. "But if you can slip his belt off, I can use it to tie his hands."

"Sure," she said. "I can do that."

She stepped toward us and reached in to grab his belt. Then she kept stepping, raised her arm, and brought the sap down on the back of my head. I had just enough time to appreciate her technique before I hit the sand.

The strike didn't put me entirely out. I was conscious enough to hear, though too stunned to do much else.

"Get up, you idiot." The girl's voice.

"Wha' happened?" The man's voice. Not as gruff now and a little slurred.

"I was gonna get rid of her and then you jumped up and went all gorilla on me."

"The bitch clobbered me."

"That's why I wrote a script for this. If you get surprised, you play dead and let me handle it, you dummy."

There was the crack of an open hand meeting flesh. Then

a second of silence before "I'm sorry I had to do that. But don't call me dummy, all right?"

A pause here. At least I think so. Time was mushy around the edges.

"Here's her bag," the girl said. "Let's grab it and go."

Shuffling, the sound of lipstick and change purse and assorted detritus colliding with one another. Then . . .

"Holy shit," the man said. "The broad has a heater."

Darkness.

CHAPTER 2

It took me a good two hours to get back to the Brooklyn brownstone that I call my office and home.

Very little of that time was spent unconscious. In fact, since I was able to track the sound of my muggers' feet crunching sand into the distance, I figured I was only dazed. Which is what I would tell my doctor the next time I saw him, since he had expressly warned me against any more "serious blows to the cranium."

I spent a couple of minutes waiting for the world to stop spinning and another doing an inventory of the situation. What had the thieves gotten?

My favorite purse. A single tear shed.

About ten bucks in assorted bills and coins. Bully for them.

My driver's license and my private investigator's license, issued by the State of New York. The latter I had a copy of, the former easily replaceable. Likely those would end up in the garbage.

The leather sap was gone. I'd have to dig out that catalog again.

Worst of all, they got my Beretta. I'd bought it to replace the Colt that had been confiscated as evidence by the NYPD last February. That one had never been returned and likely never would be.

I stumbled out from under the boardwalk and went to retrieve my shoes from where I'd dropped them. Then I started peering around for a cop. I saw a boy in blue at the far end by the rides and took five steps in that direction. I stopped before the sixth.

You really want to do that? a voice in the back of my head asked. Do you really want to bring the police into it?

I thought about that question. Why wouldn't I?

Well, first was the embarrassment of it. I hadn't only gotten jumped—I'd run straight into it like the world's bravest asshole.

Then there was the gun. But that was one of the firearms that I'd bothered to register, so that shouldn't be a problem.

Except it would. Registered meant it could be traced back to me. When, say, it was found in the hands of a pair of boardwalk muggers after they used it to rob a diner and shoot a waitress on their way out or something equally boneheaded and bloody.

I played out that little courtroom scenario in my head.

"Miss Parker, how did your gun come to be in the hands of a pair of cut-rate criminals?"

"Well, see, your honor, I was strolling along the boardwalk and I heard a yell and, well, long story short, they got the drop on me."

"They got the drop on you? On Lillian Pentecost's right-hand woman? On someone who has spent her albeit-brief career as a private detective trying to convince the world that she is every bit as tough as the next Tom, Dick, or Harriet, no matter the cut of her skirt? You were mugged? Like a civilian? A patsy?"

Cue the sound of reporters scribbling in the gallery.

Okay, so maybe the conversation wouldn't go quite like that. But I knew cops and I knew journalists. The former would love to take me, and by extension Lillian Pentecost, down a peg. The latter would be happy to print it.

I turned away from the flatfoot and began walking in the

direction of where I'd parked the Cadillac. I was halfway there when I realized that the tally of losses had been one item short: my keys.

I ran the rest of the way and was relieved to find the black sedan present and accounted for. I could have hotwired the thing, but that would have required getting inside, and the doors were locked. My set of picks were in a leather wallet under a false bottom in the trunk. Also locked.

I considered breaking a window, but someone might see and call a cop. Also, I'd have to pay to get the window fixed—out of my own pocket, of course—and while I liked to splurge on nice clothes and the occasional tattoo, I'd grown up tarpaper poor and didn't like to spend a nickel if it was neither necessary nor fun.

So I let the air out of all four tires just in case my assailants decided to go around the neighborhood matchmaking keys with car doors. Then, because New York cabbies aren't known to operate on the honor system, I went back to the boardwalk and scoured the ground for loose change. Bus fare.

Two changeovers and a ten-block walk later, I was trudging up the steps of the three-story brownstone that Ms. Pentecost and I shared as home and office. The sun was starting to disappear behind the buildings and the office lights were on. Through a gap in the curtains, I saw my boss at her desk, a look of consternation etched on her face.

Maybe I could sneak in, I thought. No use soiling her mood further. My hand was on the doorknob when I realized that, along with the car keys, the thieves had run off with my house keys as well. Given the number of enemies Ms. P had racked up over the years, I insisted on the door being locked when I was out.

So much for sneaking.

I rapped. I was sorting through witty remarks (*"Remember that article about crime in the city being on its way down. Well, let me tell you . . .")* when the door opened and I was faced not with my boss nor with Mrs. Campbell, our watchdog and house-keeper, but with a tall man in a well-cut navy pinstriped suit.

With his blond hair, blue eyes, and leading-man jawline, you'd probably call Forest Whitsun handsome. If you didn't know he was one of the city's leading criminal-defense attorneys and, by definition, a lying snake.

"Forget your keys, Miss Parker?" he asked.

"And my gun," I said. "But I didn't know you'd be answering the door."

He stepped aside to let me in.

"What sleazeball has you on the payroll this time? Don't tell me it's Don Milner," I said, referring to an embezzler we helped get locked up back in July. "I've seen his bank records and he can't afford you. Not anymore, anyway."

Whitsun chuckled, following me into the office. As I passed him, I caught an odd scent, something distinctly feminine, but I couldn't place it.

"I wouldn't take him on even if he could," he said. "I've seen the case file. This time I'm here as a client."

"*Potential* client, Mr. Whitsun," Ms. Pentecost clarified.

Whitsun must not have called ahead. My boss was sans tie and jacket; her shirt collar was unbuttoned and her sleeves rolled up; and her fingers were stained up to the second knuckle with newsprint. She must have been going through clippings in the third-floor archives when she'd been interrupted.

Her hair was still up, though, in its usual labyrinth of auburn braids punctuated by that single streak of silver.

"As I was explaining, I rarely do criminal-defense work," she was telling Whitsun. "And only then when I am sure, or at least reasonably sure, of the innocence of the accused."

"Yes, ma'am, you said. But this is a different kind of problem."

He took the chair opposite my boss while I settled in at my own desk—far more modest than Ms. P's oak slab but big enough to hold the essentials, including notebook and pencil, which I picked up, shorthand ready to go.

I crossed my legs and winced. I'd forgotten about the tattoo. I crossed my legs the other direction, winced again, and settled for two feet flat on the ground. Ms. P watched this, and me, with curiosity.

"Were there any difficulties on your errand?" Ms. P asked.

I tried a smile but got a grimace instead.

"Oh, just the usual," I said, leg throbbing to beat the band. Head pounding in counterpoint.

I wanted Whitsun to get on with it so we could turn him down and kick him out, and I could relate my boardwalk misadventure.

"Now, Mr. Whitsun," Ms. Pentecost said, settling back into the soft leather of her chair and folding her arms in her lap, "tell us about your problem."

Whitsun opened his mouth and stopped. The man had spun yarns in front of every hard-nosed judge in New York City. He could stand in front of a box of twelve men, each with a hanging rope in mind, and talk them into tears without sweating a drop.

But he'd never sat in front of Lillian Pentecost. Not like this. The word *intimidating* doesn't do it justice.

I'm not saying my boss makes a habit of frightening potential clients. I've seen washwomen and debutantes bare their souls and their secrets while sitting in that chair, trusting Ms. Pentecost to handle their goods with kid gloves.

But that was when she came into the conversation with sympathy. Replace sympathy with skepticism or, God forbid, dislike, and people sitting in that chair saw her differently.

Suddenly her wide mouth, lips pressed into a firm line, looked like it hid fangs; that not-quite-hawk nose grew into a beak; her cheekbones turned sharp; and the blue-gray of her eyes, glass and real alike, came to resemble the kind of sky people held firing squads under.

Did I forget to mention that the last time Whitsun and my boss had been in a room together she'd been in the witness box and he'd been explaining to a jury how she was an incompetent, disease-ridden, publicity-hungry shamus who wouldn't know a hoodlum from a handsaw?

"I think I should maybe start by way of an apology," Whitsun began, once he got his tongue working. "About some of the things I said during the Sendak trial."

I double-underlined the shorthand dot and strokes that meant "apology." I wanted to be able to find it quickly so I could savor it later.

"I don't think an apology is necessary, Mr. Whitsun. We were both doing our respective jobs, after all."

Translation: Yes, you do owe an apology. Better make it good.

Whitsun nodded. "I suppose you're right," he said.

I sighed. I was guessing the attorney was single.

"Although," my boss began, "I do wonder if your job extended to telling *The New York Times* that my multiple sclerosis had worsened to the point of cognitive impairment."

Whitsun's spine got a little stiffer in the chair.

"Now, I don't believe I said that."

"You heavily implied it," Ms. P snapped. "My disease was—how did you put it—turning suspicion into obsession?"

While her symptoms might add a couple decades on bad days—though I'd never seen her birth certificate, I was pretty sure Ms. P was only around the half-century mark—it had yet to impact her mental faculties, something I knew she lived in constant fear of. This made Whitsun's treatment of her during the trial particularly loathsome.

I never like to see a fight break out in our office. But I was in a foul mood, and I thought watching Whitsun called on the carpet would be a good antidote.

The attorney, to my surprise, took a deep breath, counted to three, and said, "You're right. I was playing some dirty pool there. I'm sorry that I went down that road and I sincerely apologize."

Ms. P gave him a considering look, then passed one to me. I shrugged.

"He seems sincere, but he gets paid big money to fake it."

Whitsun didn't exactly roll his eyes, but I could tell he wanted to.

"How about I tell you why I'm here? Then you can decide whether or not me being a no-good, dirty snake who provides his clients with the vigorous defense our Constitution requires should take precedence over a woman in trouble."

Those were the magic words. I'm not saying that all our clients were of the female variety, but they were more often than not. The world just seems to put its boot down a little more firmly on the fairer sex.

"Tell us about this woman," my boss said.

"Her name is Perseverance Bodine. Miss Vera Bodine," he said. "She used to be a secretary at Boekbinder and Gimbal. That's the firm I started with. I didn't leave under the best circumstances, but Vera and I stayed in touch. A while back, I started visiting her at her apartment about once a week. Well, every other week, at least."

Great, I thought. Whitsun was here to sic us on one of his girlfriends.

Ms. Pentecost must have thought the same thing.

"Miss Bodine is a lover?" she asked.

The look on Whitsun's face. Like he'd bit into a lemon.

"Jesus Christ, no! The woman is nearly eighty years old. She's a friend. I bring her groceries."

Whitsun glanced over at the drinks trolley.

"You mind?"

"Serve yourself," I said.

He got up and sorted through the bottles.

"Here's the heart of it," he said as he browsed. "Vera's a shut-in. She doesn't leave her apartment. Every other Monday

I bring her two weeks' worth of groceries. I knock, she opens. She usually won't let me in, so we stand at the door and chat. I stay a couple minutes to catch her up on my week. Then I leave. It's been that way for a while now. Except yesterday I got there and knocked and there wasn't any answer."

He finally settled on a Scottish whisky sent to us from one of Mrs. Campbell's kin. He poured three fingers, sipped off one, then poured two more. Properly fortified, he sat back down.

"I've been afraid of the day that was going to happen. I mean, Vera's older than my grandparents when they passed. I was the only person she ever saw, so it was likely gonna be me that found her. She'd given me a spare key. For emergencies, she said. I guess she figured I'd be the one finding her, too. So I let myself in."

The snake paused, taking a sip.

"What did you find?" Ms. P prompted.

"Nothing. The apartment was empty. She wasn't there."

He said that last bit like it was a grand reveal, and I don't think we gave him the reaction he was hoping for.

"Look—I can't impress enough how Vera never goes anywhere."

"Was she physically impaired?" Ms. P asked.

"It wasn't physical. It had just gotten too much for her. The city, the people. The world. The farthest I ever saw her go was the lobby of her building to get her mail."

"Were there signs of a disturbance in her apartment?"

"Not that I saw. But . . . it's hard to tell. You'll understand when you see her place."

"Did she have a telephone?"

"She did."

"Perhaps she did have a medical emergency of some sort and called a physician."

Whitsun was shaking his head before she finished.

"I thought of that. Her doctor's office was closed for Labor

Day, but I managed to get him at home. He hasn't talked to her since he stopped by for her yearly checkup in March. He told me she was healthier than a woman half her age. I phoned up half the hospitals in the city to make sure. Nothing. Even called John Boekbinder to see if he'd heard from her. No dice. That's when I started knocking on doors asking if there'd been any kind of commotion. The ones who answered said they didn't see anything. I called the police, but they wouldn't take it seriously. Useless!"

He drained his glass and glanced back to the trolley. He wavered for a moment, then set his glass firmly on the end table.

"I stayed there last night. In case she came back or there was a phone call or . . . I don't know . . . whoever took her brought her back. Dawn came and still nothing, so then I started sorting through my options."

"How'd we end up first on your list?" I asked.

He laughed, but there wasn't a lot of humor in the sound.

"Don't flatter yourself, Parker. You didn't even make the top ten," he said. "There are plenty of detectives I've used who I thought about calling. It's only . . . The men I've worked with are competent enough to confirm an alibi or get enough facts to crack a witness, but . . . this could get complicated."

As loquacious as he'd gotten, it still felt like Whitsun was skirting around something. Ms. P was of the same mind.

"Mr. Whitsun, you seem convinced that there has been some sort of foul play. You talk about 'whoever took her.' Yet there are any number of likelier possibilities. What makes you think that Miss Bodine is in trouble?"

The defense attorney turned his eyes up, like the answer could be found in the painting hanging on the wall behind my boss's desk: in the yellow of the field, the gray branches of the massive tree, or in the blue of the dress worn by the woman sprawled beneath it.

I thought maybe he had seen something in the painting,

because when he brought his eyes back down, there was the smallest smile on his face.

"Because she knows things," Whitsun said. "Things that a lot of people would like to get their mitts on."

"People such as whom?"

"Well, there's a few auto executives, a steel magnate, half of Wall Street. Oh, and Nazis. I shouldn't forget the Nazis."

That's what the smile was for. Because he figured he had us hooked.

He was right.

CHAPTER 3

"I wasn't always in criminal defense," Whitsun began. "It's messy and ugly. Worst of all, it doesn't pay very well. At least that's what the brass at Boekbinder and Gimbal always impressed on me.

"I'd managed to wangle a spot there right out of law school. There wasn't a student in my graduating class who wouldn't have stabbed me in the back for that job. Their client list includes some of the richest men in the country. Big businesses—real household names. If you did well there, showed them you had what it took, you were set for life."

As he continued, his voice took on a little bit of a drawl, something he employed purposefully in court. Jurors gobbled up that good ol' boy act, and he either came by it honestly or just couldn't help himself.

"I don't mean to toot my own horn, but I did pretty well. I wanted the partners to notice me, and they did. John, especially. He's the managing partner. He brought me in as one of his assistants. There were two of us. Me and Ken Devine. We'd sit in on meetings, take notes, write briefs. The yeoman's work.

"That's where I met Vera. She was John's personal secretary. Practically glued to his arm. There for every meeting; listening in on every phone call. Except she never took notes.

There would always be another girl on hand for that. At first I thought she and Boekbinder were—well, were lovers. He was married and she was in her late sixties, he in his fifties. But I'd heard he was capable of fooling around, and I didn't see what else he was keeping her on for."

Whitsun laughed, then got up and refilled his glass. Only two fingers this time.

"I feel ridiculous thinking about it now. That the only explanation I could come up with was that they were jumping in the sack. I told Vera that—this was after she retired—and she laughed her head off."

He sat back down and sipped his whisky.

"It was her memory," he explained. "She has the most remarkable memory."

"How remarkable?" Ms. Pentecost asked.

"First time I saw it in action, we were in a meeting with a crew of lawyers from a big company. You wouldn't recognize the name, but if you own a radio, they probably made the transistors. They were buying a controlling interest in— You know what? It doesn't matter. All that matters is that at some point one of the lawyers on their side cites this point in finance law. Real obscure. But he says it with confidence, so I took it as truth. So did everyone else. A couple seconds later, Vera taps on Boekbinder's shoulder, whispers to him.

"Then he looks at the other lawyer and says, 'I think you're wrong. The law actually states' . . . and so forth. The other lawyer says, 'No, I think you're mistaken.' Boekbinder gives Vera a nod and she recites it verbatim. Like she had the book open in front of her. The other side caves on that point, and it results in a couple million dollars in the plus column for our clients.

"That's when I discovered what Boekbinder actually kept Vera around for. She remembered every word said in every meeting. And she hadn't read every lawbook in the office, but she'd read enough. Didn't matter if she read it last week or last decade. Perseverance Bodine never forgets anything. Ever."

Whitsun inserted a dramatic pause here, like he was expecting this revelation to awe us. He was out of luck. I'd spent five years working with a traveling circus and sideshow. I'd met memory wizards before. Apparently, Ms. Pentecost was familiar as well.

"Was she a trained mnemonist, or did this ability come naturally?" she asked.

"I've never heard that word out loud before, but I know what it means," Whitsun said. "As far as I know, Vera never had any training. She didn't use tricks. She said she was born with it. Noticed it when she was a little girl. Everything since she was about two years old is still up there."

I tried to imagine it. Having every single thing that ever happened to me rattling around in my skull, even the bits I wanted to toss. Not to get dramatic, but it sounded like a little corner of hell.

"I can see how such an ability would be very useful," Ms. P said admiringly.

One person's hell is another person's useful. The third floor of the brownstone was given over entirely to notes, clippings, and case files. If my boss had Vera Bodine's memory, we could clear all that out and put in a conservatory. Add a few more skylights, get some plants.

"That one instance got our clients a couple million extra," Whitsun said. "Probably a hundred thousand of that trickled down to the firm. She'd been at Boekbinder and Gimbal for over twenty years. From 1919 until she retired in '41. You can do the math."

I did, and came out with Bodine earning her employers a seven-digit payday throughout the course of her career.

"I hope she got a big Christmas bonus," I said.

"I never saw her paycheck, but she never complained to me," Whitsun said. "By the time I left, we were close enough that she would have."

Ms. P shifted from port to starboard in her chair, and I saw her give a less-than-subtle glance at the Swiss clock on the bookshelf. Multiple sclerosis is a bitch of a disease. When it's not punishing you for moving too much, it's flogging you for sitting still too long.

"So how did you two become so chummy?" I asked, wanting to move things along. "And where do Nazis fit in?"

If Whitsun was annoyed at the prodding, he didn't show it. He'd had enough judges tell him, "Get on with it, counselor."

"I was at the firm for about four years. It took me three and a half to realize I wasn't happy," Whitsun said. "Most of the work was finding ways for big companies to become bigger companies. There's good money in that, but, God, it was boring.

"I think Vera saw how I felt. She started making a point of passing a few words with me. Asked how this or that case was going. At some point she started asking if I'd ever considered criminal law. She said I had the personality for it, which I took the wrong way at first. She explained she meant I was friendly and I thought more about people than property.

"One morning I come in, there's a copy of the *Times* on my desk with a headline circled in red pencil. The Father Carlyle murder. I knew it was Vera. She always had a red pencil tucked behind her ear, even if she never took notes. I went and asked her what was the deal. She said she thought it was a shame about what happened to Mr. Bannon's son. She never said, 'Forest, I think you should represent him.' But she wasn't being subtle about it."

If you read a copy of *The New York Times* in 1938, you probably heard of the Father Carlyle murder and the reasons why the father of a choirboy decided to beat a priest to death with a candlestick.

"I brought the idea up with Mr. Boekbinder," Whitsun said. "He was skeptical. It wouldn't pay. Also, there was the look of it. A firm's lawyer representing a priest killer. It was suggested that I resign my position—temporarily, of course—and go at it solo. Boekbinder said my spot would be waiting for me when the case was over."

I knew the rest of the story, at least as far as the case was concerned. I'd read up on Whitsun prior to the Sendak trial. I'd wanted to know who was going to be taking potshots at my boss.

Whitsun offered his services to Paul Bannon, who accepted them with no small desperation. What followed was an extended battle waged in the press, which laid the runway for a two-month marathon of a trial. Whitsun ended up losing. He didn't have much of a chance to begin with. But at least he got his client twenty years instead of the chair.

It cemented the myth of Forest Whitsun, a "real-life Perry Mason," who wanted nothing more than to champion the causes of underdogs everywhere. Or at least underdogs who could pay his fee.

What I didn't know was that it had been his second choice.

"After the case was over, I went back to Boekbinder and Gimbal like I'd planned," he said. "But John told me he thought it was better if I—how did he put it?—'followed the path you've chosen for yourself.' Really, though, I think Ken Devine talked him into ditching me. With me gone, he became John's protégé. I heard he made partner in record time."

So Whitsun rented an office, hung up his sign, and proceeded to get his dimpled chin featured on front pages left and right.

"Once things settled, I gave Vera a call. I'd heard she'd retired and I wanted to thank her for shoving me out of the nest. I went over to visit her. She lives on the top floor of this little place on West Thirty-eighth. I offered to take her out to dinner, but . . . she said she didn't do restaurants anymore. Ur . . . Anyway, she seemed to be doing all right. Mostly we talked about my cases. She said people deserved to have a fair shake in the justice system and she was proud I was the one providing it."

Whitsun rested his elbows on his knees and studied the rug. Like a little kid in the corner, thinking about what he's done.

"I should have gone back," he said. "I knew she didn't have any family. She wasn't working anymore. But things were jumping at the office. I called her a couple times to check in. Then the war kicked off and I spent a few years with the JAG Corps defending deserters. Spent most of 1945 and '46 getting my practice back on track. Didn't think about Vera again until last Christmas. I wondered whether she had anyone to celebrate with. So I showed up at her apartment with a couple pies."

Whitsun paused here. He found a speck of something on his tie and bought himself some time scraping it off with a fingernail.

"She wouldn't even open the door at first. I thought something was wrong. I threatened to kick it down. Finally she let me in. The place . . . It was a mess. Newspapers and magazines stacked to the ceiling. Towers of empty milk bottles. Big heaps of clothes and—God, everything you can imagine. I asked her how long things had been like that and she wouldn't say, but it must have taken a few years to pile up. First thing I did was go shopping for her. She hadn't been to the grocer in weeks. All she had was canned soup and powdered milk.

"It wasn't because she didn't have the money. It was that she didn't like to go outside anymore. It was all changing too fast, she said. She felt safer in her apartment.

"So I went shopping and stocked her refrigerator and offered to help her clean up, but she didn't want me moving things. Eventually she told me what she'd been up to during the war. Who had made her like that."

"Made her?" Ms. P prompted.

"Yeah," Whitsun said. "It was the goddamn FBI."

Which is, I'm excited to say, when the Nazis finally entered the picture.

CHAPTER 4

According to Whitsun, who heard it from Bodine, one day in March 1942 the retired secretary got a knock at her door. That startled her because she didn't get a lot of knocks. It was a pair of men in matching suits and badges who introduced themselves as agents of the Federal Bureau of Investigation. After a call to the local Bureau office to establish their bona fides, the old woman sat the two men in her kitchen, made up a pot of coffee, and heard their pitch.

Turns out the Bureau had a file on her. Any law firm that worked with the kind of high rollers that Boekbinder & Gimbal did was bound to come under some scrutiny. Enough people knew of John Boekbinder's secretary and her amazing memory trick that she ended up drawing the Bureau's notice.

They said they had a job for her, but they wouldn't say what. Only that it could play a vital role in the safety of the country. The kicker was that she'd have to move to Washington, D.C., for the duration. First to undergo a battery of tests to make sure her memory really was as amazing as advertised. Then to do whatever job they'd thought up for her.

She declined. She told them she'd be happy to help however she could, but her traveling days were done.

The agents insisted. She refused. End of meeting.

The pair returned twice more over the next few weeks. Same pitch, same plea. Same answer.

Bodine felt bad about it. At least that's what she told Whitsun. But not so bad that she was willing to uproot her life.

A week after the last failed attempt, she got another knock. It was a new agent. He didn't introduce himself, but Bodine had the sense he was a couple of pay grades above the others. She said if he was there with the same pitch, he could save some time and turn right around. He said not quite.

Cut to the kitchen, pot of coffee, the two sitting across the table. The agent reached into the inner pocket of his suit jacket, pulled out a photograph, and slapped it on the table.

"Take a look at that," he said.

It was a woman in a daring two-piece stretched out on a beach somewhere. She was leaning back on her elbows, smiling at the camera. The agent only gave Bodine a three-count to see the photo before snatching it back.

"What kind of dog was it?" he asked.

"Excuse me?" the old woman said.

"What kind of dog was on the veranda over her right shoulder?"

Bodine answered without delay.

"It was a terrier. A white one. I think the breed is called a Westie. And it was her left shoulder."

"The man walking it? Describe him."

Bodine had to give it only a moment's thought. "Tall, slender, dark hair, a thin, dark mustache. He's wearing a white or very light tan suit and a Panama hat. There seems to be some graying at the hair around his ears. That and the way the dog is straining at the leash. It makes me think he's on the older side. He can't quite keep up."

The agent nodded. "How long can you keep those details in your head?"

"Forever," Bodine said. "I will die with that man and his dog still filed away in my memory."

Then the agent told her about the job.

Whitsun paused here to sip his bourbon, leaving Ms. Pentecost and me on the edge of our respective seats.

"Come on," I blurted. "What was the gig?"

He shook his head. "She wouldn't tell me the details. She said she'd signed a paper and sworn an oath, and she took both seriously. All she would tell me is that it had to do with locating Nazi spies in the United States."

"That's it?" I asked. "That's all she said?"

"That's all she said."

"How did her memory help hunt Nazis?"

Whitsun shrugged. "Hell if I know. Believe me, I pressed her on it. Vera can keep a secret when she wants to."

"She told you nothing else?" Ms. P asked.

Whitsun thought about it.

"Just that whatever the FBI was having her do, it was important enough that they came to her," he said. "She said the agent came by every couple weeks. She'd do whatever it was he was having her do, then he'd leave."

"Did she tell you the agent's name?" Ms. P asked.

"She said he never gave it. Not once. Showed her the badge, but no ID. Sounds like a real gem. Even a month in, he was still playing games with her. Testing her."

"How do you mean?"

"She told me how one day as he was leaving he asked if she remembered the photograph he'd shown her. She said she did. Then he asked her what the woman on the beach was missing."

"Missing?"

"Her toe," Whitsun said. "Vera told him she was missing the smallest toe from her left foot."

"Did she say how long this arrangement continued?" Ms. P asked.

"From March 1942 until the summer of 1944. Then the

son of a bitch just cuts her loose," Whitsun growled. "Tells her not to breathe a word of it. Still doesn't give her his goddamn name."

Whitsun rearranged himself in his chair, didn't like the result, tried again, then finally stood up. Our office is good for four steps pacing in any direction. With his long legs he managed it in three.

"This agent is in there once, twice a month for two years. He must have seen how the work was affecting her. What her apartment was getting like."

"You think her work with the FBI resulted in her hoarding?" Ms. Pentecost asked.

"Of course!" Whitsun shouted. "Nazis and spies—all that pressure. What did they expect? I'd really like to get my hands on that guy."

He stood behind his chair and gripped the back, like it was a stand-in for the FBI agent's neck.

"Please, Mr. Whitsun." Ms. P gestured for him to retake his seat. Reluctantly, he did. "You reunited with her last December and found her unwell. She was hoarding. Her agoraphobia—if that's what it is—had limited her ability to care for herself. You bought groceries for her. Is this when you started visiting her regularly?"

He nodded. "At first every week. Then when I saw that she was okay—I mean her apartment was a mess, but she was safe and healthy—I kind of let it slide to every two weeks."

"Did her . . . condition . . . change?"

"It certainly didn't get better," he said. "Eventually she stopped letting me in. We'd talk at the door. I think she was ashamed of how things were. I mean she *is* ashamed."

The tense trouble showed how worried he was. He was *hoping* Bodine was only missing.

I was hoping we were near to wrapping up. In addition to my thigh, my head was starting to throb as well. I knew if I felt around under my curls, I'd find a goose egg where the black-jack had hit home.

"So, for eight months, you play delivery boy, check in on her every other week, then you show up yesterday and she's gone," I said, trying to hasten things. "That ever happen before? That she's not there?"

I could tell Whitsun resented answering questions from someone whose name wasn't on the door, but he took it like a champ.

"No. Never."

"She never talked about taking a vacation? Going to visit her long-lost sister in Albany?"

"She never went *anywhere,* Miss Parker," Whitsun declared. "And as far as I know, she has no family."

That certainly wasn't true. Humans didn't sprout up out of nowhere. But I got the point, so I moved on.

"Anything out of the ordinary happen recently?"

"Like what?"

"Like did she say, 'Hey, I was looking out the window the other day and thought I saw a Nazi strolling by'?"

Whitsun and my boss gave me identical looks.

"It's an honest question," I said. "Whitsun here is saying she wouldn't go out on her own. That leaves foul play. I'm wondering if she had a hint it was coming."

Ms. Pentecost stood and made her way to the drinks trolley. The first step was a wobbly one, but she regained her balance by the time she got her hands on her bottle of honey wine.

"Her glibness aside, Miss Parker is not mistaken," she said, pouring herself a glass. She didn't bother measuring in fingers. She just kept it from going over the rim. "Though I'm reluctant to assume foul play this early, the question stands: Has anything changed in Miss Bodine's behavior or demeanor in recent weeks?"

I don't know if it was the phrasing or that Ms. P's suits cost more than mine, but this time Whitsun took the question seriously.

"I spent a lot of last night sitting in Vera's place thinking about this. There's two things. One large, one small," he said. "The big thing is, several weeks back, she gave me a call at the office. Wanted to talk to me about a case she'd read about on the front page of the *Times* that morning. Julia Fennel. You know it?"

We did. Part of my job was to go through the daily rags and clip out articles of interest. Fennel's murder was of interest, though it had only been front-page news for a day before sinking deeper into the paper, overtaken by newer, sexier horrors.

Julia Fennel was an assistant director at the Museum of Modern Art, an expert in the kinds of paintings that look like mush to me. She was thirty-three, blond, and the kind of beautiful that Maybelline would love to crush into a powder and sell by the ounce. It was likely her photo that scored the case its one day of top billing. It certainly wasn't the complexity of the crime.

On Monday, August 4, she had been found dead in the bedroom of her Midtown apartment by a co-worker who was wondering why Fennel had missed a museum soiree the night before and now wasn't answering her phone. The room had been ransacked, her jewelry box emptied, and her skull opened to the air with the blunt end of a framing hammer.

The police put out feelers for the jewelry, and one of the stolen pieces—a gold bracelet with her initials engraved on the inside—was turned in by a pawnshop owner in Queens. A local carpenter and handyman, Nicholas Ramirez, had come in the same day the body was found and traded in the bracelet for $150.

When the cops picked up Ramirez, he said that he'd

been in the apartment the week before doing a job for her—doubling the size of her closet. That's why his prints were all over the place.

As for the bracelet, he told the cops that Fennel had been short of cash and used it to pay him. A bracelet worth about seven times what the pawnshop owner had handed over and ten times what the closet-expansion job was worth.

Oh, and why had the closet been left unfinished? the cops asked. Fennel had paid him for the job, after all.

He said when he came in Saturday morning to put on the final touches, she'd changed her mind. With the project nine-tenths done.

The police had the case wrapped in four days flat. Just in time to make the Friday morning papers, which framed it as a banal three-act play starring a dead damsel and a dumb crook.

Nobody was buying Ramirez's story. Not the cops, not the reporters, not the district attorney, who was fitting him to ride the lightning. Nobody except maybe Vera Bodine, who apparently read about the not-so-grand guignol and got right on the phone to Whitsun.

"She said he was getting a raw deal," he told us. "That I'd be perfect for the case."

Ms. Pentecost took a long sip of wine.

"Did you consider taking the job?" she asked.

"Absolutely not. My calendar is full. Besides, it's a lead sinker. I told her that on the phone. She pressed the issue again the last time I saw her. That was August eighteenth."

"What did you tell her?"

"Same thing. I think my exact words were, 'If I'm going to take on a sure loser, I at least want it to pay.'"

"How did she react?"

His face told us before his tongue did.

"She wasn't happy. She . . ." He had to corral his lips to get the words out. "She said she was disappointed in me. That I . . . uh . . . I was thinking too much about money. I said I wasn't doing this job for the fun of it and . . . I don't know. She said something, I said something. Then I left."

He slumped back in his chair, chin tucked to his chest.

"That was the last time I talked to her," he said. "I figured I'd make up for it next time I saw her. I picked her up a cheese-cake from Veniero's. She loves their cheesecake."

Whitsun was sitting so low in his chair I worried he might slither off. When I first found him standing at the door, he'd seemed his usual high-gloss, fully waxed self. Now the veneer was gone. He looked like a man who'd had a sleepless night and was staring down the face of another.

Suddenly he righted himself in the chair and forced the brightness back into his eyes.

"Look, I think that's as much of the background as you need. Time is short. She might . . . I don't know. Will you take the case? Will you help me find her?"

Ms. Pentecost took another sip. Slowly. I don't know if she was really thinking it over or was doing it to infuriate Whit-sun. Probably the former. Lillian Pentecost isn't petty.

She leaves that to me.

"What was the small thing?" she asked.

"What?"

"You said there were two changes in Miss Bodine's behav-ior. One large, one small. What was the small one?"

"It's not anything, really," Whitsun said. "She'd seemed a little worried the last time I saw her. Preoccupied. Even before I told her I wasn't biting on Ramirez."

"Did you ask her what was the matter?"

"I did," he said. "She said . . . she said she must be starting to get old. Because she'd misremembered something."

"Did you ask her what?"

He shook his head. "No," he said. "I wasn't really paying attention to that. I was worried how she was going to take the Ramirez news. I know what you're thinking. Senility. But she was still sharp. Sharper than most of the lawyers I know. Something happened to her. Someone did something. I know they did. I don't have time to sit around anymore. Now, will you take the goddamn case?"

CHAPTER 5

We took the goddamn case. I wouldn't have spent three chapters on it if we hadn't. We're all busy people here.

Because this was a missing person, not a murder, there was a ticking clock involved. If Bodine had been snatched, she might at that very moment be having the screws put to her. By who and for what was anybody's guess.

If Whitsun was telling it straight and she had a noggin full of high-power contracts and Nazi trivia, the sky was the limit.

Even though the hour hand had barely swung by the seven, we went right to work. We sent Whitsun ahead, asking him not to enter the apartment building without us.

Once he was out the door, I turned to the task of explaining to Ms. Pentecost why I had to knock on our own door and why we would be heading to Vera Bodine's place in a taxi rather than the Cadillac.

When I had first arrived back at the office, the plan was to give my boss the short and not-so-sweet of my boardwalk adventure. But as I sat there listening to Whitsun, part of my brain had been working on second thoughts.

Why bother Ms. Pentecost with my mugging? We were about to take on a new case to go on top of Quincannon and Waterhouse and whatever other plates she had spinning in that mind of hers. There was nothing she could do other than provide sympathy, and I didn't need any of that.

I could track down a couple of boardwalk bandits on my own.

"It was probably some kids. Saw a nice car, thought they'd mess with someone's day," I said, after telling her how I'd discovered the Caddy with four flats. "Then I'm on the ground making sure they didn't slash them and my keys slip out of my pocket and fall down a grate. A real Marx Brothers afternoon."

"That's very unfortunate," she said. "Please call for a cab. I'll go inform Mrs. Campbell of our plans."

I dialed the cab company and asked them to send a car around, then ran upstairs to my room. I slapped a bandage on my still-swelling tattoo and downed a couple of aspirin to quell my throbbing head. Then I swapped my college-coed ensemble for something more professional: a gray two-piece in light wool over a sleeveless blouse in robin's-egg blue.

I dug out my second-favorite purse and filled it with my third-best wallet packed with some spending money, spare keys, my replacement PI license, and the Browning Hi-Power.

Because I was the sort to have a backup lock-pick set, I added that as well. When you're planning to search an apartment, you don't want something pesky like a locked drawer to get in your way.

My hat collection had been growing, and I picked a dusty-blue fedora with a gray band and a tight brim. I took a moment to admire the results in my bathroom mirror.

Getting mugged might have dulled my pride, but everything else looked sharp.

Properly outfitted, I went back downstairs. I walked into the kitchen to find Mrs. Campbell pointing a meat skewer at our employer and looking like she might use it to check if the city's most brilliant detective was cooked through.

Our housekeeper is not an unimposing woman. She's barrel-chested and broad-shouldered, and the only prim thing about her is her cap of gray curls. Picture a taller Gertrude Stein and you're halfway there.

I caught the Scotswoman mid-tirade.

"—told me when you skipped lunch that you'd make up for it at dinner, and that's the only reason I let you be. Here you are skipping dinner, too. You know what the doctor said last time he was over. If you don't get to eating regular, you're only going to have more weeks like that."

The week she was referring to occurred at the tail end of July. There had been a heat wave that coincided with a hunt for a multiple rapist. That, combined with my boss's tendency to skip meals when deep in a case, had ratcheted up Ms. P's multiple sclerosis symptoms and landed her a prescription for eight days of bed rest.

At least it was supposed to be bed rest. She still managed to get down the stairs to the office or up the stairs to the third-floor archives on a daily basis. Though a bruise on her hip that I glimpsed when I was helping her change one night suggested that she'd taken at least one tumble without telling anyone.

Since then, she'd been very disciplined in doing the exercises and stretches her doctor prescribed and hadn't had a major flare-up since. But the threat of a bad day was always on the horizon, and Mrs. Campbell knew that as well as anyone.

Ms. Pentecost had her mouth open for a rebuttal but the housekeeper turned her attention and her tirade on me.

"And you! You know what the doctor said. Don't go saying you'll stop somewhere later. You always take her to some dingy diner. I don't know if grease sets off her symptoms, but it certainly can't help."

I held up my hands, patting the air like I was calming an angry dog.

"How about this. While we wait for the taxi—we are sans automobile at the moment—I help you put some sandwiches together. Is that ham hock in that pan?"

The housekeeper nodded, giving her prim curls a single, determined bounce.

"We'll cut some bits off that, slap on some of that Cheddar

I like, add some tomato and lettuce for color, some mustard, throw them in a paper bag, and I'll watch her eat it in the cab on the way there. I'll tip the cabbie extra in case of crumbs."

Mrs. Campbell turned her glare back to my boss, then back to me.

"You make sure she eats every bit."

Ms. Pentecost knew when she was outnumbered.

Ten minutes later I was nestled in the back of a cab heading over the Brooklyn Bridge and watching my boss chew. While she might have resented the mothering, she was halfway through her second sandwich before she reached her limit.

I tucked the remainder back in the paper bag, which went in my purse next to the gun. Half a ham sandwich and a heater. Wonder what a purse snatcher would think of that.

I spent the rest of the ride pondering.

Not about the case. I figured my boss had that covered. About how I was going to track down my boardwalk Bonnie and Clyde, recover my belongings, and restore my dignity.

Their act was pretty slick. I was guessing I hadn't been their first audience.

But a mugging was still a mugging, no matter how you dressed it up. Snatch and grabs are low risk, but also low reward. Half the time the cash is spent within the hour, either at a bar or on a needle.

This pair didn't feel like addicts. Too calm, too prepared. The girl was in disguise—a padded bra, probably a wig. She'd mentioned a script. It wasn't spur of the moment.

If this pair was setting up shop in Coney Island, they would have attracted attention. The police might have them on their radar.

I didn't want to officially involve the police, but I knew enough cops I could pose the question to and not have them pose too many back.

I was still making my list when we arrived at our destination. Time to put Bonnie and Clyde aside and get to work.

CHAPTER **6**

Vera Bodine's apartment building stood on the ever-shifting border separating the high-rises of Midtown from the warehouses and light industry that stretched out to the Hudson River. The skyscrapers were winning that particular tug-of-war, swallowing up the modest apartment buildings that had previously dominated the neighborhood.

Bodine's building had stubbornly held its ground. Consequently, the narrow four-story was surrounded on all sides by towering behemoths. Like a toddler lost in a department store.

If the tenants had ever had a view worth paying for, they were now stuck with concrete and steel and maybe a glimpse of Irene from accounting working late. The rent must still have been coming in, though. The stoop was clean, the brick was bright red, and the alleys that ran down both sides of the building were free of garbage.

So was the sidewalk out front, which is where we found Whitsun, keys in hand, tapping his foot impatiently.

I looked at what was chiseled above the front door.

"The Baxter Arms?" I said. "Somebody had aspirations once upon a time."

I was rightfully ignored.

The lobby was also well kempt. Green and white tile that was only a little chipped and a row of brass mailboxes set into one wall. Fifteen of them. Three on the first floor, four on the rest.

Barely half had labels, though. The building might have been holding its ground, but apparently its tenants weren't.

Bodine was in #401. The top floor.

No elevator, so we followed Whitsun up the stairs. At each floor I peeked out into a long hall that cut down the center of the building. Two numbered doors on each side and one unnumbered one at the end of the hall. A broom closet, maybe?

About as standard as small apartment buildings came. The only surprising thing about it was that it was still standing at all.

When we reached the top floor, Ms. Pentecost asked, "You said you knocked on her neighbors' doors. Did that include those on this floor?"

Whitsun shook his head. "The other apartments on this floor are empty. Have been since I started visiting her."

So much for a quick and easy witness. Whitsun fitted his key into the lock of #401, then paused.

"Look," he said. "How she kept her place . . . I don't want you judging her."

"I assure you, Mr. Whitsun, we are not in the habit of judging people on how they keep their homes," Ms. P told him.

He was not assured. If anything, he recommitted to his frown. But he stepped aside and let us enter.

I don't know what I had been picturing. Clutter. Disarray. Grime.

I was not prepared.

Ms. P and I had to turn sideways to sidle through the short hallway, which had probably been meant to accommodate an end table and a coatrack. Instead, there were stacks of cardboard boxes from floor to ceiling on either side. I glanced in the boxes as we passed and saw empty coffee tins, light bulbs, spools of thread, hand tools, and at least one packed to the brim with Kewpie dolls, their wide plastic eyes staring out at me through the box's half-open lid.

Beyond that gauntlet, the apartment split into two directions. We went left first. Without Whitsun announcing it, we might not have recognized the room we entered as a kitchen. Nearly every square inch was covered. Piles of newspapers and magazines towered in the corner; boxes of canned goods were scattered around the floor; heaps of dish towels covered the countertops.

There was a narrow alley on the floor that allowed access to the stove and cupboards. One of the kitchen chairs was empty, as was a small square of space on the kitchen table—barely big enough for a single plate. The one window in the kitchen had a view of the side of an office building and let out onto a fire escape.

We did an about-face and carefully made our way to the living room.

It would have been considered spacious once upon a time. There was a small fireplace on one wall, flanked by bookshelves. I counted three plump chairs and a sofa. Or at least the shapes of them. They were covered in coats and scarves, boxes with labels in faint pencil that read things like GOOD COATS, SCRAP PANS, and KEEP PLATES? although most of the labels had been crossed out and replaced half a dozen times.

Then there were the books. They filled every inch of the bookshelves and were stacked floor to ceiling against the walls, the towers of tomes bending like Atlas under their own weight. I glanced at the spines: *Three Guineas; I Am a Fugitive from a Georgia Chain Gang!; Black Reconstruction in America 1860–1880; The Little Prince.*

If there was reason, it didn't rhyme.

Even the fireplace had been conscripted for storage and was packed solid with what looked like ten years' worth of phone books.

And there was the smell. I'd started breathing through my mouth as soon as we walked in, but it still crawled up my nostrils.

I could pick out fried eggs and stale beans; mildewing wallpaper and crumbling books; damp wool and old carpet and everything else that seeps into the pores of any old apartment over time. But smothering it all was an overpowering floral reek, something that I immediately associated with little old lady. It was the scent I'd noticed on Whitsun back at the office.

I hadn't been able to pin it down until we squeezed through the next doorway into what I assumed was Bodine's office or sitting room. Sitting on the edge of the rolltop desk that had been rendered useless by the sheer tonnage of paper atop it was a small white linen bag tied closed with string. A sachet—filled with a fistful of dried lavender if my nose could be trusted.

I had a very faint memory of my grandmother keeping one in her delicates drawer. One.

Now that I'd seen the sachet on the desk, I noticed them everywhere. They were sitting in corners, perched on top of bookshelves, and there was one on every windowsill.

Instead of scrubbing, Vera Bodine had laid down a lavender stink that, in my opinion, was worse than all the other odors combined.

I recommitted to breathing through my mouth.

In the office, along with the desk, was a mahogany console that held a radio and record player. That, at least, was relatively clean. Sure, there was a three-foot stack of records on top, but the turntable was clear.

The armchair in the middle of the room was clear, too. That, along with the crumb-covered plate on the floor beside it, revealed a woman who would sit eating gingerbread cookies and listening to her records or the radio.

An empty can filled with cigarette butts told me this was where Whitsun had spent the night waiting for Vera to return.

Next was the bedroom. It was, if you can believe it, the worst of the lot. Half the room was taken up with stacks of clothes and old furniture. There had been a structural collapse in one corner—a landslide of sweaters and pillows. There was a window in here as well, but it was half-obscured by a wardrobe.

The bed itself was nearly covered in coats and blankets and God knows what else. A narrow cavity in the middle showed where Bodine slept. She must have started at the foot of the bed and wedged herself in every night. The lavender smell was so thick in here it almost had substance.

One last door led into the apartment's bathroom. I expected to find the toilet being used to store shoestrings or buttons or who knows what, but apparently that was another place Bodine drew the line.

Vera Bodine's home was like an old heart, its arteries so clogged and constricted it could barely do the job it was built for.

How did anyone live like this?

I must have said that out loud because Whitsun answered.

"I don't know. I kept offering to come in and help clean it out. She told me she made do. That it wasn't really that bad."

Not that bad? You could barely turn around. I had to squeeze into a corner just to let Ms. Pentecost into the bedroom. I brushed up against the wardrobe and the pile of detritus stacked on top began to wobble.

The whole room seemed to wobble. Like at any moment the walls could come tumbling down and smother me. Whitsun was standing in the doorway, blocking the only exit.

The flowery stench was unbearable. It was like a fog, swimming down my throat and settling like sludge in my chest.

Ms. P put a hand on my shoulder.

"Would you mind going back to the kitchen and pouring me a glass of water?" she asked. "While you're there, see about that window leading to the fire escape. We'll want to know if it was possible to gain entrance that way."

I squeezed by her and Whitsun and retraced our path, keeping my eyes aimed straight ahead. In the kitchen, I went right to the window. It clearly hadn't been cracked in a while, and it took a couple of hard tugs to open.

I took a deep breath of clean air to push out the sludge. Then I climbed over the sill and onto the fire escape.

I leaned on the rail and listened to the throb of my pulse slow from a mambo back to a steady waltz. I whispered a string of curses at the bank of windows across the alley.

I liked to tell Ms. Pentecost that I wasn't claustrophobic, I just got antsy when I didn't have a clear path to an exit.

"Think about it," I had told her. "I ran away from home right into a traveling circus. It makes sense that I'd chafe at a cramped floor plan."

But I'd admitted to Holly one night—this was after I told her I always liked to sleep with the bedroom window open—that Ms. P was probably right. Tight spaces made me panic. A switch flipped in my brain and kept me from thinking straight.

I told her a story about my father and the root cellar and a long, dark night that seemed to last an eternity.

Holly.

I wondered where she was at that moment. Knowing her, she was probably sucking on a Chesterfield and typing away, oblivious to the world around her, trying to figure out how her hero—a disgraced P.I. with a twice-broken nose and a dark past—was going to get out of the pit he'd dug for himself.

There was a thump behind me, and I turned to find my boss's head sticking out the window.

"Did you really want a glass of water?" I asked.

"Not particularly."

"That's good. I wouldn't trust Bodine's glassware."

"What surfaces I could see appear to be clean," she replied. "And the bathroom has been scrubbed in the not-too-distant past. Miss Bodine's home is not filthy. Merely . . . cluttered."

"Cluttered?" I exclaimed. "That does not even come close to doing this place justice. I've never seen anything like it."

"I've come across hoarders before," my boss said. "Frequently there's a compulsion involved. Or a mania of some sort. I'll have to ask Dr. Grayson."

Grayson was Ms. P's psychiatrist. She'd met her through Holly, who was also a patient of the good doctor's. Which meant that Dr. G was probably getting an earful about me from two different sources, and if you think that didn't put a knot in my guts, you have severely overestimated my self-esteem or underestimated my curiosity.

"Mr. Whitsun located a photograph of our subject," Ms. P said. "It's from when he visited her before the war, but he says her appearance has not changed much."

She passed the photo out to me.

It showed Whitsun smiling and kneeling next to the kitchen table. Seated at the one chair was a small elderly woman in a flowery housedress with a pair of cat's-eye glasses hanging around her neck from a beaded chain.

It was hard to gauge size, since she was seated, but she looked tiny. Maybe five feet tall. Not quite emaciated, but on her way there. The skin on her face was loose, her cheeks falling down into jowls that blended with the loose flesh around her neck. There was a bump on her nose so prominent you could have mistaken it for a roller coaster.

She would have been ugly if it hadn't been for the smile. It was big and wide and made it clear that she was happy Whitsun was there.

"She looks like a nice lady. Who took the picture?"

"Mr. Whitsun had a timer attached to his camera," Ms. P explained. "It allowed him to set it and pose before the exposure was taken."

"So what's first on the agenda?" I asked. "The cops, the Nazis? The FBI? I have a suggestion about the latter, by the way."

"I think, perhaps, we will start with her neighbors," Ms. P said. "Mr. Whitsun spoke only to a few, and his questions were perfunctory. It's not quite eight o'clock. Most of them should be at home."

I looked over her shoulder at the mountains of newspapers and boxes and cans and wobbly walls.

"I can conduct the interviews myself," she added. "Mr. Whitsun can accompany me."

That snapped me out of it.

"You think I'm letting you go knocking on a bunch of strange doors with only a lawyer for protection? Start digging a tunnel. I'm coming back in."

CHAPTER 7

The interviews with Bodine's neighbors went in the file verbatim, but I'll stick to the highlights, such as they were. For the most part, we kept things swift and simple. After all, we were a trio of strangers calling on folks at their home post-dinner, pre-bed. Also, there were fourteen apartments to get through and we didn't want to hit midnight before we were done.

Scratch that—not fourteen. Only seven occupied apartments, as it turns out, not counting Bodine's. Three on the third floor, two on the second, two on the first.

The structure of each interview went like this:

Do you know Perseverance Bodine?

When was the last time you saw or spoke to her?

Have you noticed any changes in her behavior recently?

Have you noticed any strangers in the building?

Have you noticed anything out of the ordinary at all?

There were variations and follow-ups and so forth, but that was the gist of it.

We led with the fact that Bodine was missing and that we'd been hired to find her, and that usually paved the way.

Since the rest of four was vacant, we went down a flight and started on three.

In #301 we were greeted by an elderly man who barely

spoke English. Ms. P had a handful of languages under her belt, but Polish wasn't one of them. After some hand signals, we got the most basic of our questions across.

No, he didn't really know Bodine. No, he hadn't seen her recently. Lots of head shakes. Lots of shrugs. Then some pointing at his ear and then at the ceiling.

He'd heard her moving around.

"When was this?" Ms. Pentecost asked. "Yesterday? Monday?"

He knew that much English, at least, and croaked out, "Yesterday."

Whitsun poked his head into the conversation. "That was me. He heard me moving around."

"Sunday?" Ms. P asked, pointing to her ear, then at the ceiling.

He nodded.

"Saturday?" she asked.

He thought for a second, then nodded again.

"Saturday," he croaked. "Thursday, Friday, Saturday, Sunday. Yesterday. All days."

We left him to his dinner of pierogis and some kind of pungent soup and moved down the hall.

At #302 we discovered a city bus driver with a face like a sour lemon, who kept checking his watch. Like he was three stops behind schedule and we were holding him up. We'd caught him in the middle of some electrical project. A bundle of snipped wires was sticking out of his shirt pocket and he was holding a screwdriver.

"Last time I saw her was maybe two weeks ago," he told us, tapping the screwdriver against his teeth as he thought. "I was coming in, she was going out. At least I think it was her. I get her and the new bitty in 102 confused."

"When was this?" my boss asked. "The date, if possible?"

The man snorted and rolled his eyes but did the math.

"It was still daylight out, so I didn't work the extra shift, which means it was a Monday. Monday two weeks ago, maybe five o'clock."

"Are you sure this was Vera Bodine? From the fourth floor?" Whitsun asked.

"Like I said. It could have been whatshername from 102," the man said. "Actually, it probably was 102. 'Cause I never saw the woman upstairs go out. And this woman I passed was dressed up. Skirt, jacket, and all. The woman upstairs was always nightgowns and sweaters."

"So it wasn't Vera?"

"Look, I was beat, and one old lady is the same as another. If she looked like Rita Hayworth I would have stopped and studied her. Now, if you don't mind, the Yankees game is on and my radio is busted because the electrical socket burnt out with the cord still in it. This whole goddamn building is falling apart!"

He closed the door in our face before we could thank him.

"Useless," Whitsun grumbled as we moved to the next apartment. "Doesn't know one woman from another. Monday two weeks ago is when I last saw Vera. I'm damn sure she didn't have plans to go anywhere."

In #303 we found Del and Barbara, a Negro couple on the far side of middle age. Their only child had gone off to college in Atlanta and they were in the midst of packing to move house to the West Coast.

"I've got a cousin who can get me a job in the carpentry shop at Warner Brothers," Del explained. "With Joseph down at Morehouse, there was no reason to stick around here anymore."

"The rent's good," Barb said.

"Hasn't gone up a cent in years," Del added.

"But it's not as nice as it was," Barb said.

"Absolutely," Del concurred. "The boiler failing. Pipes leaking. The people just aren't—well, they aren't as friendly as they used to be. And then there are the rats."

"Oh, God, the rats! We actually found one in our kitchen. Our kitchen!"

"I think they're squirming under the alley door and up the back stairs."

"It's always locked. No one uses it."

"I've heard them moving through there at night."

"Holidays will be more difficult. For Joseph, I mean. Us being in California. He'll have to fly to visit."

"He'll be fine, though. He said he'd dogsled if it meant spending Christmas in Hollywood. Anyway, what were you asking about again?"

Their double act had my eyes vibrating, but I got it under control enough to repeat that we were looking into the disappearance of Miss Bodine from upstairs.

"Have you seen or spoken with her recently?" Ms. P asked.

The pair put on identical pondering looks.

"Not for a while," Barb said.

"She's pretty quiet. Keeps herself to herself," Del added. "I've passed maybe ten sentences to her all the years we've lived here. It's not that kind of building, though. Everyone keeps to themselves, for the most part."

"I've talked with her a bit more than that," Barb said. "The last time was I guess about a month and a half ago? I saw her in the lobby when I was picking up my mail. I asked her if she was thinking about taking the Danberry Group's offer."

"The Danberry Group?" Ms. P asked.

"They're a company buying the building. Or trying to buy it? I'm not entirely sure," Barb said. "Back in March they sent letters to all the tenants offering three hundred dollars if we moved out by the end of the year. The Sandersons took it first. They were in 202. They moved in June. And the Ritchies just across the hall. They left at the end of July. But I think they were moving anyway. And the old man in 103. I can't remember his name. He moved last week."

"That three hundred was the shove out of the nest we needed," Del declared. "The nest being empty now, and all."

Whitsun shouldered his way to the front.

"What did Miss Bodine say about the offer?" he asked. "Was she thinking of taking it?"

"Oh, I don't think so."

"You don't think so because she said as much? Or are you surmising?"

"Well, neither. I mean . . . What I mean is she didn't know about it. The offer," Barb said. "She said it was the first she'd heard of it."

"Why wouldn't she have gotten the offer as well?" Whitsun asked.

"I have no idea."

"Anything else?"

"Anything else what?"

"Did she say anything else?" If I was a prosecutor I would have objected on the grounds of badgering.

"She said . . ."

"Yes?"

"She said she was going to talk to a lawyer. She said she didn't think it was right. Pushing people out like this. But . . . it's not really pushing. Not if they're paying us and we want to go. And we do."

Whitsun opened his mouth to lob another question, but Del stepped between them.

"I think you should leave," he said firmly. "I'm sorry Miss Bodine is missing, but that's all we know. We have packing to do."

I could tell Ms. P wanted to grab Whitsun by the scruff of the neck, but she settled on taking his arm and leading him away, leaving me to do the thanking.

With that accomplished, I found Ms. P down the hall giving Whitsun a lecture on interview etiquette.

"—hired us to do. Which includes canvassing her building for possible witnesses."

"Look, Pentecost. I'm not exactly wet behind the ears. I've thrown a million questions at a thousand witnesses. I know what I'm doing."

I waded in.

"Your witnesses were on the stand. They had to answer or plead the Fifth. They got peeved at you, they couldn't kick you out and lock the door."

Whitsun was squaring himself up for another round, but Ms. P beat him to it.

"We have nothing, Mr. Whitsun," she declared. "No clues, a vague chain of events, no evidence a crime of any sort has been committed. All we know is that a woman who reportedly never leaves her apartment is not currently there. The police were correct when they refused to investigate. There is, at the moment, nothing to work with. So I would appreciate it if you allowed me to do the job you hired me to do without interference."

That little speech apparently worked. Whitsun smoothed out his shirt and his ego and nodded at her to lead the way. On the way down to the second floor, I took stock of Whitsun. In addition to looking tired and frayed, he was now practically trembling with impatience.

"Listen," I said, "at least we know Bodine was in her apartment and moving about as late as Sunday."

Whitsun made a noise from the step below me.

"You don't believe him?" I asked.

"Eyewitnesses are spotty," he said. "And earwitnesses? Who knows? He's old and he doesn't speak the language. He'd be terrible on the stand. And that bus driver saying he saw her going out? Vera didn't go out. That's the whole point. He must have gotten his old ladies confused."

He paused at the landing.

"I don't like this real estate thing, though," he added. "Someone trying to get the tenants out. Probably hoping to force the owners to sell. She was going to talk to a lawyer, but she never said a word about it to me. I guess she could go back to Boekbinder and Gimbal. But why talk to them when I was seeing her every week? Every other week."

He sounded hurt. Why hadn't she come to him if they were friends, like he said? I didn't have an answer.

While I figured the chances of Bodine leaving under her own steam far outweighed her being taken, I disliked this new angle as much as Whitsun. Manhattan real estate seemed a clearer and more present danger than Nazis.

There was no answer at #204 and the Sandersons had moved out of #202, or so said Del and Barb. Ms. Pentecost knocked anyway and got silence as confirmation.

I took the opportunity to check the unnumbered door at the end of the hall. On the way up I'd spied it and thought broom closet, but there was one on every floor, and who needs that many brooms? Then I remembered what Del said about the rats and the back stairs.

I tried the knob but it wouldn't budge. And there was no lock to pick. I knocked and was rewarded by a muted echo.

Whitsun came up behind me.

"I know what you're thinking," he said. "That she went that way and maybe had an accident. But it's always locked."

"You're sure?"

"That's what Vera said when I asked about it. The only way you can get into it is from the back alley. I don't think it's ever used except when repairmen need to lug up equipment. So they don't scuff the main stairs."

I don't like to take a lawyer's word for anything, so I made a mental note to confirm that for myself, and we moved on.

At #203 I got excited for a second. The man who opened the door wearing nothing but a too-small undershirt and a pair of boxers had a face that looked like it had been used as a punching bag. He also had a .38 hanging from the coatrack next to the door.

While Ms. P was going into her spiel, my hand slipped into my purse, moving the ham sandwich aside to get to the Browning. Then I recognized the gun as a Smith & Wesson Model 10—standard issue for the NYPD. A little more over-the-shoulder spying and I saw blue trousers and a pressed uniform draped over a chair.

Sergeant Grady perked up for half a moment when he discovered the great detective Lillian Pentecost was working a missing person's case in his own building. His mood took a turn when we said Miss Bodine had been missing for barely a day. He let loose a string of profanity, including a noun-verb combination I'd never heard before.

"I work the night shift. My alarm clock doesn't go off for another hour. I was dead asleep," he moaned.

"Look," he added. "The woman's not missing, she's wandered. Check the churches. Old folks who go wandering always end up at church. Especially broaaah."

I think he was going for "broads" but his jaws got away from him and he sucked in a yawn.

"Sorry about that. You mind if I try and catch whatever winks I've got left?"

Ms. P squeezed in one last question before letting him go back to sleep.

"Have you noticed anything suspicious around the building? Especially anything that might concern Miss Bodine?"

Grady scrunched his battered mug up into a thinking face. Suddenly his eyebrows shot up.

"Oh, yeah, I forgot about that."

Our eyebrows rose in solidarity.

"Forgot what, Sergeant?" Ms. Pentecost asked.

"She woke me up. Miss Bodine did," he said. "Just like you

three. Knocking on my door because she had a—how did she put it—a professional question to ask me."

"And what professional question was this?" Ms. P asked.

"She wanted to know who to talk to if she wanted to report a crime."

CHAPTER 8

There was no holding Whitsun back.

"What crime?" he demanded.

"I don't know," Grady said. "She didn't say."

"What do you mean she didn't say?"

"I mean she didn't say."

"You didn't ask?"

"Of course I goddamn asked," Grady told him. "That's the first goddamn thing I did. I asked, 'What crime are we talking about, Miss Bodine?' She said she wasn't sure."

"She wasn't sure? She wasn't sure what the crime was? Or that one had been committed? Which was it?"

"I don't know."

"You don't know?"

"She didn't goddamn say which," Grady growled. "She said she wasn't sure. She was being all quiet and whispery. Like she was embarrassed to be asking. I said, 'Why don't you tell me about it and I can tell you what you should do?' She waved me off. Said she was probably imagining things. Apologized for waking me up. She went on her way and I went back to sleep."

"You went to sleep?"

I thought Whitsun was keyed up enough to actually put hands on Grady, so I took a step between them.

"When was this?" I asked.

"I don't know. Maybe two weeks ago," he said. "Yeah, that's it. Two weeks ago, Monday. That was the night patrol brought in those six drunk coeds from Wisconsin. Puked all over the floor. God, what a mess."

"Did you follow up?" Whitsun asked.

"Follow up? I was dead to the goddamn world when she came knocking," Grady said. "I didn't even remember until now. Besides, she admitted she was imagining things."

"She said she was *probably* imagining things."

"Listen, buddy," Grady said, hitching his thumbs into the waistband of his boxers like it was a gun belt, "you would not believe the things people bring to me. Old folks, especially. The Polish guy upstairs? His shower stopped working last month. He thought it was a problem for the law. Woman who lives two doors down from the precinct? Stopped me when I was heading home. Said she thought somebody was creeping up on her stoop and warming her milk bottles. Not stealing them, mind you. Warming them. There's a mystery for you. Go solve that one, city's greatest detective."

Grady realized he might have made one quip too many and unhitched his thumbs.

"What I'm saying is old people get confused."

"Vera Bodine did not get confused," Whitsun declared.

Grady's punch-beaten brow grew a couple new creases. "Hey, where do I know you from?"

I didn't know if Whitsun had ever had Grady on the stand and I didn't wait around to find out. I grabbed Whitsun by the back of his collar and yanked him out the door, this time leaving Ms. P to do the genuflecting.

"Can you believe that?" Whitsun asked. "An elderly woman knocks on his door asking for help and he forgets. Forgets!"

"Take a breath, Whitsun."

"Jesus Christ, the cops in this city."

I was hoping Grady hadn't heard that and was pushing

Whitsun toward the stairwell when a voice called out, "Is there a problem?"

A bespectacled head was poking out of #201. The hand holding the door open was grasping something metallic and black and for a second I thought it was a heater. Then I looked closer. Not a gun. A caboose.

After we reassured the man that there was nothing wrong, we gave him the usual speech. By then Ms. Pentecost had smoothed Grady's feathers and sent him back to catch whatever winks he had waiting.

The man invited the three of us in.

Really, I think he just wanted to show someone the model train set he'd laid out in his living room. It wasn't a small affair, either. Furniture had been pushed away and at least one rug disposed of for the project.

He saw me noticing and explained, "It runs better on a hard surface."

I listened for the sound of children, but didn't hear any. If he wasn't embarrassed to be a fortyish man with army-issue specs and a beer gut caught playing with toys, I wasn't going to be embarrassed for him.

"I didn't know her very well," he said to our question of whether or not he knew Bodine. "Enough to say hello. My wife knows her a little better."

He attached the caboose to the end of the line of cars.

"Is your wife at home?" Ms. Pentecost asked.

"Rhoda is on a birthday cruise. Four weeks! She went with a college friend because the city wouldn't give me the time off. 'Rodney,' they said, 'you're indispensable.' Though they don't pay me like I am. I repair subway cars. When they break down in a tunnel, I'm the one they call who goes in and gets them running again. Like today. Eighth Avenue was backed up to heck and back because of a busted R9. But I got underneath that sucker and got her going."

Rodney paused, as if he expected applause.

"Anyway," he continued, "Rhoda's off in the Caribbean and I'm playing bachelor. That's why I get to bring out this beauty. When the wife's away, the boys will play, right?"

He chuckled at what was clearly a well-worn joke. When we didn't join him, he turned back to his trains.

"She doesn't really know the woman very well, though. We were sometimes getting each other's mail. The box for 401 is right above 201. Rhoda was always bringing her mail up. Homemade cookies, too. Rhoda likes to bake."

"I don't suppose one of those pieces of mail involved a letter from the Danberry Group?" Ms. P asked. "The real estate concern that's offering money for tenants to leave by the end of the year."

Rodney's eyes lit up.

"You heard about that, huh?"

"I have."

"I don't think we got any letter for her like that. But she did ask Rhoda about it a little while back. Asked if we were taking it."

"And are you?"

"We're really thinking about it," he said, fiddling with a control box attached to the tracks. "B and O is hiring folks in Jersey City. Better vacation time with them. And there's a house over there that's real nice. Has a garage where I could keep this set up all year."

He flicked a switch. There was a spark from the panel, and the train lurched forward and began circling.

"When was the last time you yourself saw or spoke with Miss Bodine?"

Rodney looked resentful that we were interrupting his playtime.

"Oh, gosh, I don't know. Three weeks?" he said. "I was leaving for work and she was headed out to go shopping."

"Shopping?" Whitsun asked. "You're sure it was her. Not the woman downstairs?"

"Of course I'm sure," Rodney said. "I saw her a few times that week. I remember because I'd never seen her out of the building before. I didn't think she ever went out."

"When was this?" Ms. P asked.

"I guess it would have been the second week of the month. All in the morning. Seven o'clock or so."

"And how do you know she was going shopping?" she asked.

Rodney shrugged. "She had a grocery sack."

He adjusted something on the controls, and the train sped up.

"Did you speak to her?" Ms. P asked.

"A little. She asked after Rhoda. That sort of thing."

"You haven't seen her since?" I asked.

He shook his head.

"Sorry."

We went through the rest of the list. Did he see any suspicious people? Did Bodine have a beef with anyone in the building?

Nothing.

We tried to nail down the dates of when Rodney had seen her, but the best we could do was the week of August 11–15. He'd seen her at least three mornings that week. He didn't know which three, but two were back-to-back, and not Friday because he was off on Fridays. And he had spoken with her only the once.

We left him to his locomotive and proceeded to the ground floor. On the stairs, I asked Whitsun about the scowl on his face.

"I don't trust him," he said.

"Rodney the train guy? What's not to trust?"

"He's too cheery."

He was probably disgruntled because it meant that Vera wasn't as housebound as Whitsun believed, suggesting that maybe he didn't know his friend as well as he thought he did.

I kept this to myself, figuring Whitsun wasn't in the mood for such keen insight into his psyche.

Only three apartments on the first floor and #103 was recently vacated, according to Barb. We knocked anyway, just in case. Nothing.

However, #101 was answered by the world's smallest fighter pilot.

"What's the password?"

"Those are some nice goggles there, ace," I told the boy. "Is the ranking officer at home?"

The towheaded guard did an about-face and screamed, "Mom! People are here!"

A woman emerged from the kitchen, one arm wrapped around a baby girl, the other holding a pot of something. She was managing to keep the former from toppling while stirring the latter with a wooden spoon.

Martha Watson and her husband had been in the building for less than a year and had returned only last week from a monthlong trip to California to visit her parents.

"I wanted them to meet Sarah Jane, and they hadn't seen Cody since he was four. He's eight now. And frankly I wanted to get out of the apartment before Gene went away again. He works for the War Department. They've had him flying all over the last couple years."

The long and short of it was, the Watsons had been absent for most of August, and she couldn't remember the last time she saw Vera Bodine.

"It's been months. Maybe since the beginning of summer or longer."

I saluted Commander Cody on the way out. He presented his tongue and blew a raspberry.

So much for military discipline.

The woman who greeted us at #102 wasn't a blue-hair; she was brunette with a healthy dose of gray, done in a frizzy bob that spread out like a pith helmet. She was a good twenty years younger than Vera Bodine. I guess to the bus driver in #302, every woman older than Rita Hayworth was a fossil.

We gave our speech and she hesitantly let us in. She introduced herself as Mrs. Diane Murphy, a retired schoolteacher and recent widow.

"I only moved here in June," she said. "I still need to fill the place out."

She wasn't kidding. Her living room consisted of a battered armchair and a folding table where she took her meals, if the plate of watery spaghetti was any indication. There were a few boxes scattered about, as well as a small metal cage with a handle on top.

She saw me notice it.

"That's for Mr. Whiskers," she explained. "Or it was for him. He's gone missing. I left the front door open. Stupid of me. He'll come back, though. Probably off chasing rats."

She smiled, but it looked fake and fragile. Like she was still trying it on for size.

We asked her the usual lot, but came up empty. She hadn't received an offer to move out, but she hadn't been there long. No suspicious activity around the building. No strangers lurking. She'd never even laid eyes on Vera Bodine.

"I've heard about her, of course," Murphy said. "I was chatting with the woman on the second floor. Can't remember her name. I think her husband does something with trains. This was shortly after I moved in. Anyway, she said that the woman on four has the floor to herself and she never goes out. Said she thought she was something of a hoarder. That maybe the rats people have seen around were her fault."

"I've never seen any rats near her apartment," Whitsun said.

"Oh, well. I don't know. I've never met the woman. But I do hope she's all right."

As a final question, I asked if she remembered leaving the building two weeks ago dressed in a nice jacket and skirt. She would have passed the charming bus driver in #302 on her way out.

She looked genuinely confused.

"Oh, no," she said. "I haven't had a reason to get dressed up in a while."

On that cheery note, we left. The hour hand on my watch was about to kiss the nine.

In the lobby, we had a brief, contentious conversation about what to do next. Whitsun was all for action.

"Every minute we waste is a minute we won't get back."

Which sounded great as the capper to a closing argument, but useless as far as actual direction was concerned.

"While that is true, there is little else that can be done tonight," Ms. P patiently explained. "Businesses are closed; phones will go unanswered. It's better to sleep while we can and reconvene at first light. By then I'll have a better idea of how to proceed."

Whitsun paced and ranted some, but eventually agreed to meet us back at the apartment building first thing in the morning. However, he wasn't calling it a night.

"I'm going to take that idiot sergeant's advice and go check the churches."

"Was Miss Bodine a religious woman?" Ms. P asked.

"I didn't think she was, but who knows? What else am I gonna do?"

"Maybe say a prayer or two while you're there," I added.

He made a face but I heard him mutter, "Maybe I'll do that," as he walked out the door. He made a turn and headed up the street in search of our missing woman or God or both.

I don't think it spoils much to tell you that he found neither.

CHAPTER 9

Before we bade farewell to the Baxter Arms, I ran around to the back of the building to check the rear stairwell. I hadn't wanted to do it while Whitsun was there, on the off chance we discovered Bodine lying at the bottom sporting a broken neck.

The alley separating the building from the much taller one behind it was wider but grimier than the ones running along the side. In addition to the windows of the first-floor apartments, I found a steel door set directly in the center of the building, lit by an overhanging electric light that looked like it could have been installed by Edison personally.

As promised, the door was firmly locked. It was a good lock, too. It took me a solid seven minutes to open it and cost me one bent pick and a snapped skeleton key.

No Bodine at the bottom or at any of the landings farther up. I checked the doors on every floor and, yes, they were locked and could be opened only from the stairwell side.

My curiosity sated, I went back around front to join my boss.

"No luck. Which I guess is good luck, since the alternative would have probably been a dead old lady," I said. "Now let's see what we can do about finding a cab to Coney so we can pick up the car."

Ms. Pentecost and I had a routine where, on the drive back

from interviews and autopsies and the like, we would strike up a running conversation on what we'd learned and what we should do next. Now, I trust a good taxi driver to mind his business and keep his ears shut to backseat gab. But the good ones look a lot like the nosy ones, and even the best cabbies get their curiosity piqued when they hear words like "missing" and "Nazi."

So we stayed mum as I directed the cabbie to the side street in Coney Island where I'd left the sedan. The only chatter the driver was privy to was Ms. P's inquiry as to whether I still had that half a ham sandwich. I said I did and passed it over and she thanked me.

Thrilling stuff.

The Caddy was right where I'd left it, tires flat as pancakes. I used my spare key on the trunk and pulled out the pump. The cabbie offered to give us a hand—for a fee, of course—but I declined. He made a crack about how my dainty lady arms weren't up to pumping four tires from flat. I tried out that new phrase I learned from Sergeant Grady and he responded in kind and sped off.

While I started reinflating the tires, Ms. P took a seat on the curb and we sorted through the case, such as it was.

The problem, as I saw it, was simultaneously a lack of evidence and a surfeit of leads. I explained as much to my boss.

"The possibilities get my blood going, too," I said, pumping away. "You've got big business at her law firm. Hunting Nazis with Hoover's boys. Then you've got these real estate folks looking to coax tenants out. Probably wanting to buy cheap, tear it down, and build a big office building. That's serious money. Could be the owner of the building wanted to sell and Bodine threw a monkey wrench into the works."

Up, down, up, down with the pump. Really getting my knees into it.

"Of course, that's assuming foul play," I continued. "You know what they say about assumptions and asses. All we've got is an empty apartment and an elderly woman who, looking at the state of her place, has a few screws loose. Whitsun says she was a shut-in, but hell if she isn't getting around. We've got her leaving the apartment, three, four days, at least. And what the hell was happening on the eighteenth? She's waking up Grady to report a maybe crime, slapping Whitsun's wrist for not taking on Ramirez, then going out somewhere in her Sunday best. Shoot—Ol' Cauliflower Ears might be right. Vera could have gotten confused and walked out. She might be at a church or a police station right now, sipping a cup of hot chocolate and trying to remember her name."

Usually Ms. P is on her toes with a conversational volley. All I got was silence. I looked over to my boss. She was picking apart the last bit of crust from the sandwich, rolling it into balls and letting them fall into the gutter. Presents for the earliest pigeons.

I gave her the benefit of the doubt that her brain was working and waited her out. After half a minute, my patience was rewarded.

"Let us assume," she began, "that some form of foul play has occurred. Not because it's likely. In fact, the scenario you describe is more probable. If that is the case, Mr. Whitsun will find her tonight, or she will turn up at either a police station or a nearby hospital. That would, of course, be the most preferred outcome."

She pushed herself up from the curb using her cane, then began a slow counterclockwise stroll around the car. After half a circuit, she stopped using the cane for balance, laid it across her shoulders, and draped her hands over it, like a woman in the stocks going for a constitutional.

"However, we have been hired to investigate this incident, and we have certain specialties. Ones that go beyond calling hospitals and knocking on church doors."

One of those "certain specialties" being foul play. Frequently, though not always, of the fatal sort. I gave the first tire a kick. It could have been firmer, but I just needed to get it twelve blocks to a service station that had a pump that wasn't Parker-powered. I moved on to tire number two.

"Okay," I said. "Throw out the adage about asses and assumptions. Are we assuming kidnapping or are we assuming murder? And does it matter?"

"Only insofar as speed is concerned," Ms. P said, never pausing her circuit. "Kidnapping means that Miss Bodine is still alive, and that may change if we tarry. So we'll assume kidnapping and that we are working against a clock."

I was pumping away again, which did not make for the smoothest thinking. But it was my boss's brain that got people to write all those zeroes on the checks.

"As you've already observed, we are not without avenues to pursue," Ms. P continued. "Our first port of call should be the offices of Boekbinder and Gimbal. Hopefully we can convince them that there is some urgency and they'll be willing to talk about cases Miss Bodine was privy to that might have drawn attention so many years later. Then there is the matter of her apartment building. She told her neighbor that she was going to speak to a lawyer. If it wasn't Mr. Whitsun, it was likely someone at her old firm."

That made sense. We could kill a lot of birds by chucking a rock at Boekbinder & Gimbal. Though I didn't hold out hope of cracking anything open. Lawyers weren't too forthcoming, no matter how many clocks were ticking away.

I judged the second tire inflated and moved on to number three.

"We will also need to consider the murder of Julia Fennel and the case against Mr. Ramirez."

"You think Bodine was onto something?" I asked. "That she was sure Ramirez was innocent because she knew who was guilty?"

"That's certainly a possibility."

"If she knew who had done it, why not tell Whitsun? And how would she know? The woman never left her apartment. Or almost never."

"I don't know," my boss admitted. "When a crime is committed, we must always ask the question 'Why now?' What precipitated Miss Bodine being taken? The Ramirez case is relatively recent."

How would a shut-in get information about a killing? Did she see something? Overhear something? Come across something on one of her jaunts? Trouble usually starts close to home. I started mentally sorting through her neighbors. Maybe one of them killed Julia Fennel and . . . And what? Happened to mention it to Bodine in passing?

I filed Ramirez under our to-do list beneath grilling the partners at Boekbinder & Gimbal.

"Okay, that's her former employer and her most recent obsession taken care of," I said. "Are we going to ignore . . . the FBI and . . . Nazis? Because . . . Hang on."

I stopped pumping and leaned against the Caddy to catch my breath.

"Because I know I read . . . too many pulp stories. . . . I know that. . . . Or it might be the patriot in me . . . but it seems . . . if we're listing ways a woman might intersect with trouble . . . meddling with Nazis should be at the top of the list."

Ms. P strolled around to my side of the car and leaned next to me.

"We should certainly pursue it," she said. "But extracting information from the FBI is tedious under the best of circumstances. Since we are operating under the assumption that time is of the essence, I suggest we place Miss Bodine's work with the federal government at the bottom of the list, at least for now. Also, why don't we call for a tow truck to take the car to the service station? This is needlessly exhausting."

Because I'd gone with the "teenage vandals" story, I couldn't explain to her that these flats were a problem of my own making and that pumping was part of my penance.

Instead, after my lungs settled, I told her, "It's not so bad. Besides, it gives us a chance to chat in the fresh air, and I refuse to spend a dollar on a tow truck when I don't need to."

I didn't want her interrogating that too closely, so I swerved the conversation.

"While I agree with you that the FBI can be—what word did you use? Tedious? That is the politest way of saying 'shit-heads' I've heard in a while. Anyway, I agree with your assessment. However, I'd like to draw your attention to how Bodine described this nameless agent: arrogant, shifty, paranoid. Doesn't that sound like a particular federal so-and-so we know and don't love?"

I was, of course, referring to one Mr. T. S. Faraday, an agent assigned to the New York City office of the FBI with whom we'd danced in the past. Ms. Pentecost was shaking her head before I hit the last question mark.

"I have quite a bit more experience with the FBI than you," she said. "Those qualities—the arrogance and refusal to share information—could describe many of the federal agents I've encountered. There are several hundred assigned to New York City. The likelihood that Agent Faraday was the one tasked with handling Miss Bodine is remote."

It wasn't often that I knew more than my boss, so you'll have to forgive me if I let a somewhat smug grin spread across my face.

"While it is true that arrogance and secrecy are a hallmark of Hoover's boys, and you have a longer history with them than I do, I have certain experience that you do not that makes me almost certain it's Faraday we want to talk to."

"What experience is that?"

"I've seen his girlfriend without her shoes on."

CHAPTER 10

By the time we got back to the brownstone, it was nearly eleven and my arms were wet noodles. But we made the drive there on four firm tires. I flopped into my desk chair while Ms. P made straight for the third-floor archives where she would likely spend a few hours perusing old cases and new curiosities.

She didn't appreciate it when I said things like, "Please do not exhaust yourself. Your multiple sclerosis does not always care about your second wind." Luckily, as de facto office manager, I'm also in charge of keeping appointments.

"Don't forget we're meeting Whitsun first thing," I said. "I imagine his first thing comes several hours earlier than yours."

"I will keep an eye on the time," she assured me, almost certainly hearing the concern behind the concern. "Are you still determined to make your approach tonight?"

"I am. Like you said, we have to assume the worst. Treat it like we're on an episode of *Winner Take All*."

She didn't listen to that particular show, but she understood context clues. She wished me luck and then continued up the stairs. I paused to listen to the familiar tap-thump of feet and cane. Once I was sure she was safely on her way, I picked up the phone and dialed a number.

I could barely hear the guy on the other end and he could

barely hear me, but eventually he managed to catch my question.

"She goes on at midnight!" he screamed into the receiver.

I shouted a thank-you, hung up, and hurried upstairs to my bedroom, where I started sorting through the contents of my closet. Where I was heading, my suit wouldn't do. Besides, my shirt had grease stains on the cuffs and the whole outfit reeked of lavender.

I settled on a tight black cocktail dress with a conservative hemline balanced by a daredevil neckline. Daring enough that I'd blend, but not so flashy that I'd draw eyes. Not that that was really much of a concern. I'd have to get pretty creative to draw attention at the White Clover.

There was a time, the elders have told me, when there were joints all over the five boroughs where two men could cuddle in a corner or a couple of ladies could take a turn around the dance floor without fear of being booted or billy-clubbed.

Somewhere in the early decades of the century that changed. People of influence—those with a firm grasp of decency but a much looser grip on compassion—decided it was time to clean up these havens of sin and vice. One by one, clubs and bars were shuttered and their regulars forced to do their drinking and cuddling at home, out of sight of the prim-and-proper public.

The war provided a bit of a pause. Who gave a crap what the queers were up to when there were Nazis to be killed?

But once the war was over, the city finished the job it had started. That no-sign place in the East Village where I once saw Tallulah Bankhead necking with a waitress? Gone. That basement club in Harlem where I'd danced cheek to cheek with a blonde who put the femme in fatale? Boarded up.

A couple years prior, my friend Hollis Graham said something to me that I never forgot:

Nails that stick out get hammered down.

At the time, I waved him off. Now I could see it. The start of it anyway, and maybe worse to come.

All of that wasn't necessarily running through my head as I walked past the no-neck bouncer guarding the door. But typing about it now, the irony is not lost on me.

What irony? you ask.

The White Clover was one of the few pre-existing joints that had kept its doors open. The reason? The mob.

They had a piece of the club. Not a controlling interest. That kind of operation would come later with places like Club 82. Here the mob was a minority concern—enough to keep the place breathing a few years longer than its neighbors.

They did that by paying off the cops when needed. When a raid was inevitable, they'd get advance word and tell everyone to lay off the lewd and indecent acts. Like two men holding hands and so forth.

There was plenty of that tonight. Even though it was midnight on a Tuesday, the place was packed. Mostly men, but a few curious ladies. It wasn't spacious, and half the real estate was taken up by the bar and the stage, where at that moment a blond drag queen in an evening gown that was more rhinestones than fabric was butchering the last verse of "I'll Walk Alone." She was accompanied by a pianist, who, if his ears were working, probably wanted to be put out of his misery.

Between the smoke and the caterwauling, my headache had come roaring back. The inside of my thigh wasn't feeling all that great, either, and I quickly scanned the crowd, in a hurry to find my mark and retreat somewhere quiet.

It didn't take long to spot him.

Going back to the irony of the joint. If you wanted a double dose you need only have followed me to that table in the back and the man nursing a Manhattan. Agent T. S. Faraday.

An FBI agent at a gay bar owned by the mob.

He had nabbed the shadowiest corner in the place, but I'd seen him close up and in daylight and I don't know why he bothered hiding. He could have had his photograph in the dictionary under the entry NONDESCRIPT.

Medium height, medium build, hair brown, eyes brown, suit brown, face symmetrical but not so much that you'd notice. The only thing that marked him as anything other than a Fuller Brush salesman was the relationship between him and the room.

Those flat brown eyes—and I'm not knocking the shade; mine are the color of mud—never stopped moving. If a fly happened to wander in the door, Faraday would have clocked it. If he could have, he'd have frisked it for a weapon and wired it for sound.

So I knew he'd seen me as soon as I walked in, but he wasn't used to me in a dress, so it wasn't until I was halfway to his table that his eyes widened in recognition. Not pleasure, just recognition.

I slid over a chair from an adjacent table and sat down next to him.

"How's it going, Faraday? Hunting Commies?" I made a show of looking around. "That guy over there's wearing a red necktie. Want me to distract him while you bug his cocktail umbrella?"

No response from the very special agent. Utterly expressionless, he kept his face turned to the stage as the rhinestone blonde put a stake through the heart of Dinah Shore and took her bow. The only clue that he'd heard me at all was the vein throbbing on his forehead.

"No need to play coy," I said. "This is purely business, not pleasure."

"It's never a pleasure with you, Parker," he said, still refusing to look at me. "What did I tell you and your boss last time we talked?"

"You told Ms. Pentecost that she should retire and take up knitting and never call you again," I said. "While my boss has neither retired nor embraced needlepoint, we haven't dialed your number in over a year. So when I realized we had to break the fast, I thought it best to do so in person."

"You thought wrong," he said. "Now scram."

"This doesn't have to be painful. Besides, all I'm . . ."

But I'd lost his attention. For real, this time. Every ounce of it was being poured out for the figure stepping onto the stage.

I wasn't offended. You wouldn't be, either, if you'd ever seen Rosa Rivera, sometimes known as Rosie Red or Raring Rosa and for a brief stint during the war as Rosa the Riveting, during which she performed her closing number with two dozen lit sparklers tucked into her bosom.

Big brown eyes that were anything but nondescript, lips custom-shaped for a microphone, cheekbones you could cut your finger on. All of it framed by shoulder-length pitch-black waves that you would bet good money was a wig and you would lose.

And all that was before your eyes dipped below her chin.

The black velvet number she was wearing that night didn't have a single rhinestone, but her physique did its own sparkling. Sure, her bust might have been structurally enhanced but the rest of the hourglass was legit, and at five foot ten she had legs that most Rockettes would strangle their mother for.

And the girl could sing.

When you think of me
I get hot.
When you look at me
I get hot.
When you walk with me,
talk with me,
dance with me,

drink with me,
sing with me,
swing with me,
I get . . .

The crowd finished the line for her.
"Hot!"

Ain't nothing gonna cool me off
but
yooooou

While Faraday watched Rosa, I watched him. I always thought of the FBI man as the coldest of fish. It wasn't that he was hard-hearted. He'd removed the organ entirely—tucked it away in a safe-deposit box somewhere.

Whenever I saw him with Rosa, I had to re-evaluate.

I glanced down at his ring finger. For as long as I'd known him, Faraday had been conveniently, if not happily, married, and Rosa was his mistress. Over the summer I heard a whisper on the grapevine that he and his wife had split. The bare finger suggested it was true.

The romantic in me hoped it was because he wanted to spend more time with Rosa. The detective in me figured the wife found out.

I didn't plan on asking.

I felt sorry for interrupting his moment, but time was of the essence. I put my mouth against his ear and whispered, "Perseverance Bodine is missing."

He grimaced.

"Am I supposed to know who that is?"

As fun as the denial dance could be, my card was full.

"You probably shouldn't have used a photo of Rosa to test-drive Bodine's memory," I said. "Not many nine-toed bomb-shells have their snapshots carried around by FBI agents."

Faraday wasn't slow. It took him only a second or two to realize I had him.

"Call me tomorrow," he said.

"Why put off tomorrow what we can talk about tonight?"

He looked at me, then back to the stage, then back to me.

"Yeah, I know you have a more exciting program planned for your evening, but I'll make it quick," I said. "You tell me what you were up to with Bodine and I'll skedaddle and leave you and Rosa to play interrogator and reluctant witness. I've always pictured her as the interrogator, by the way. Do you use the cuffs? I've heard you really have to watch out for chafing. Some folks—these are friends of mine—use a silk scarf, or sometimes wool when silk got hard to come by, and—"

He spat out a word I'll do you the favor of censoring.

"Fine," he said. "*After* her set."

I was okay with that. The girl could sing, after all.

I flagged down a waitress to see if I could get a hot coffee and a couple of aspirin. It was shaping up to be a long night.

CHAPTER 11

An hour later the three of us—Faraday, Rosa, and me—were sitting in the living room of her apartment around the corner from the club. It was a dingy one-bedroom on the third floor of a six-story walkup, but Rosa had done what she could to make it home.

The sofa and pair of overstuffed chairs were soft and in matching shades, even though they were likely thirdhand. The curtains covering the room's single window featured hand-stitched flowers. A tattered square of red silk was draped over the lamp in the corner, giving everything a pinkish glow. The result was more oceanside sunset than bordello.

The happy homemaker was stretched out on the sofa. She'd ditched the black velvet in favor of a fluffy pink bathrobe. Her showgirl legs were propped up on one arm of the sofa, feet crossed, revealing nine toenails done in a shade of midnight blue.

Up close, I could see the scar where the littlest piggie of her left foot used to be. It wasn't clean, but bullets rarely are. She told me the story once: how her father had done it when he learned that the child he had thought was his firstborn son was going by Rosa now.

"I got lucky," she'd said. "He was aiming at my head, but he was so drunk he tripped over the cat and shot my foot instead. Ruined a perfectly good pair of suede boots."

Lying on her back as she was, with her head cocked over the side, she offered me an upside-down view of her features, but I could still read the amusement. Watching Faraday watch me watch him: he in one chair, me in the other, both of us trying to look casual.

I thought I was having more success. He was still wearing his jacket. He hadn't even loosened his tie.

I'd just finished summarizing the Bodine situation—her disappearance, Whitsun's concern, how we knew she'd been hunting Nazis for the FBI.

Faraday didn't even pretend to give it any thought.

"I can't talk about an ongoing investigation."

"You ended the project. The war's over."

He shrugged. "There are always loose ends. Unresolved questions. You know that, Parker. Cases are never *really* over. Besides, it's a national security issue. It's top secret."

"Your grocery list is top secret," I spat back.

"I wouldn't trust you and Pentecost with that, either. Every time I open the paper, I see your boss's name in a headline."

I nodded, as if I were giving him the point. Then I came back with, "You know what would make a good headline? 'Little old lady helps FBI hunt Nazis, goes missing, feds hang her out to dry.'"

He didn't leap out of the chair, but he braced his legs for it.

"Pull some shit like that and the big man will put you on his personal to-do list. That is not a place you want to be."

I was skeptical about how many teeth that threat had. Hoover's reputation as a boogeyman seemed overblown to me. But better paranoid than sorry.

"Of course we won't do that," I assured him. "Ms. Pentecost and I have what are called ethics. You can look it up in the dictionary later. However, Whitsun knows all about Operation Kraut-Hunt or whatever you called it. As a defense attorney he and ethics are not always on speaking terms."

Faraday sank back in his chair and stewed. He was in a real bind. After all, the man made paranoia a way of life.

Not surprising, considering what would happen if his overlords found out he was with Rosa. I'd heard the State Department had started using Truman's loyalty program as a way to weed out homosexuals from the federal rosters, and it probably wasn't planning to stop anytime soon.

They'd be going around with a color wheel, and any marriage with even a tinge of lavender would be getting worked over. And here was Faraday, freshly single.

He could argue that Rosa was as much a woman as anyone else shopping in the ladies' section of Macy's, but that wouldn't hold water with the feds. He'd be plucked out along with the rest of the undesirables.

Yeah, I was leveraging this fear and, no, I didn't feel great about it then and even less so recounting it now. At the time, I told myself the ends justified the means and besides, Faraday would have done the same to me, given an excuse.

Which is probably how a lot of souls get bartered away over time. In rationalized, bite-size pieces.

On the couch, Rosa sighed and turned over onto her stomach so she could look at her boyfriend right side up.

"Come on, Teddy," she purred. "The old lady is missing. You told me you liked her. That she reminded you of your abuela."

Faraday squirmed, either at being outnumbered or in annoyance at Rosa for letting it slip that he had feelings. And a grandmother, apparently. I'd assumed he'd been cobbled together from melted-down badges and redacted reports.

"Fine," he finally said, wrenching his face back to something resembling neutral. "What do you remember about the Duquesne Spy Ring?"

"Not too much," I admitted. "I was still with the circus. I didn't read many newspapers."

"Let me jog your memory."

Faraday started talking. While he told the tale, Rosa went to the kitchen and retrieved some beverages. Gin for herself and her beau, a Coke for me.

Faraday explained how the Duquesne Spy Ring had been big news in the months leading up to the attack on Pearl Harbor. A group of Nazi spies and German sympathizers based right out of New York City. Their plan was to collect information on the U.S. military buildup and send it back to the fatherland via shortwave radio. The idea being that the information would be used in the future for sabotage and assassinations and general villainy.

That never happened, because the FBI got a toehold in the organization—including control of the Long Island–based shortwave transmissions—and rolled up the whole ring. Or so they thought.

"There were suspicions there was a second ring," Faraday explained. "Maybe a backup in case something happened to the Duquesne lot."

The reason for that suspicion was that the U.S. had picked up other shortwave messages—also based somewhere on Long Island—going out months after the Duquesne ring fell.

"They stopped after Pearl Harbor," Faraday said. "Maybe they'd finished the job. Maybe they got word we were hunting them. I don't know. But we were pretty sure there were still some German sympathizers running free."

That's where Bodine came in. Every couple of weeks Faraday would bring over a box of documents. Immigration papers, newspaper articles, photos of church socials and family picnics, pictures of German military officers and students graduating from German universities. Hundreds of photos. Thousands of documents.

Bodine's job had been to go through each and every one and find connections.

"I had her focus on the Bund to start with. That seemed like the ripest field to go picking."

The German American Bund, Hitler's fan club in the

United States, was outlawed in 1941, but had been plenty active before then, especially in New York. In 1939, twenty thousand of them had rallied at Madison Square Garden. I remembered seeing the pictures: a dark mass of people pressed against a stage decorated with a giant picture of George Washington flanked by swastikas.

The Bund fell apart soon after, and its members spent the war with their lips sewn shut. At least if they knew what was good for them.

Bodine combed through photos from the rally along with a dozen other Bund events. She made connections between faces that had been caught sieg-heiling and men who, a little while later, were members of town councils or filling out the rolls of local police departments.

She made other connections, too.

The immigration documents from one man described a birthmark that mirrored one in a photo of a teenager graduating from a German university. Different names, but more than enough in common to suspect they were the same person.

A woman in a photo from a church social was wearing the same sweater as a woman photographed entering a basement apartment in some unnamed German city. Bodine couldn't match the women, but she was sure the sweater was the same because of the unique pattern.

That kind of thing.

Faraday spent what free time he had following up on her leads.

"Any luck?" I asked.

"Only the bad kind," he said. "Don't get me wrong, I found plenty. Connections between this and that person and officials in Germany. So-and-so went to school with Himmler, things like that. It all went in one file or another. Maybe to get used for leverage later. That sort of thing happens. But if there were ever any arrests, I wasn't the one making them."

He took a slug of gin and shook his head.

"By summer '44 the shortwave from Long Island had been quiet for over two years. My bosses figured whoever it was had packed up and left. They pulled the plug on the thing, and I let Bodine go."

Two years spent working an operation and nobody behind bars for his trouble. That must have had Faraday steaming.

"So you're telling me that all that time Bodine never found a real Nazi spy?"

"Is that what I said?" Faraday asked.

I thought about it.

"No," I clarified. "You said there were no arrests. So there was somebody you liked for it, but you couldn't prove it."

"There were a bunch of somebodies."

"Any one body in particular?"

Faraday made eye contact with Rosa and nodded his head toward the bedroom.

"Really?" Rosa asked. One word, but she put an edge on it. "She can hear but I can't?"

"She's . . . Well, she's in the game. And . . . you know . . . I want to limit your exposure."

Blessedly, Faraday stopped talking. Maybe he noticed how Rosa's eyes had narrowed. Like she was sizing him up for his funeral suit.

"Fine," she said, swinging her feet from couch arm to floor. She stood and gave her robe a demure little tug. "I will be waiting in the bedroom. Unexposed. You're free to join me. If you think I can be trusted."

Faraday watched as she walked into the next room and shut the door. Like a condemned man keeping an eye on his executioner.

"You're gonna pay for that later," I said.

Dread was replaced with displeasure.

"Stick to the subject, Parker."

"Gladly. Bodine fingered someone and it turned out to be something more than nothing."

"Leonard L. Teetering."

"Sounds like he should be selling whoopee cushions out of the back of comic books."

"You're not far off," Faraday said. "He owns a five-and-dime in Danville. That's on Long Island, in case you're wondering. I think he carries whoopee cushions."

"How does Mr. Teetering fit into this?" I asked.

All of a sudden, Faraday pushed himself out of the chair and hurried to the window. He didn't move the curtain, but rather shifted his head so he could peer through the gap. While he checked for who knows what, he continued.

"Bodine matched a photo of a group of German soldiers—officers, actually—taken in Belgium in 1914 with one of a library ribbon-cutting in Danville in 1938," he said. "Specifically, she matched a nasty scar on the hand of one of the men."

"Neat trick," I said. "So what was the problem?"

"The scar was all we had to go on. The photo of the German officers was water-damaged. You can't see the man's face."

"Tough break."

"They got tougher."

"How do you mean?"

"A few years back, Teetering was putting a back porch on his house. Got clumsy with the power saw. Took off his left hand."

I hazarded a guess. "The one with the scar?"

"Yep."

"That was convenient."

"Yes, it was."

"Did you take a run at him anyway?" I asked. "Show him the pictures?"

He took his eye away from the curtain and pointed it at me.

"Never showed him the pictures. I don't like sharing evidence if I don't have to. But I took a run. His story never changed. Leonard Teetering, born in Cuyahoga County, Ohio.

Birth certificate to match. Parents deceased. Never married. A perfectly pleasant small-town Joe scraping out the American dream one bag of penny candy at a time."

I blinked. I'd never known Faraday to wax lyrical. I sipped my soda and kicked the tires on his tale.

"Any way Teetering could have found out about Bodine?"

Faraday shook his head. "No chance," he said. "I never let him know what we had on him. Never showed him the picture. I was going to take another go, but then my superiors sent down the order to end it."

I didn't believe in leakproof operations, so I assumed there must have been at least a little chance Teetering had discovered how the FBI had sniffed him out. But I didn't feel like getting into a fight with Faraday over loose lips.

I posed the question I knew Whitsun would want me to ask.

"All that time you spent with her, did you notice her behavior change?"

"She was already a shut-in when I got there, Parker. That's not on me," he snarled. "The woman wouldn't even come to the office. I had to bring everything to her."

I decided to press it.

"What about her apartment? How she was living? Any changes there?"

I'd never seen a fed show shame before. Thought they had it trained out of them. I was wrong.

"I talked to her about it, all right?" Faraday said. "I asked her if things were okay. If she needed somebody to come in and clean for her, maybe. But it wasn't all that bad. Not when I saw her last."

"It's bad now."

Faraday slammed the glass down on the coffee table. Gin sloshed onto scarred wood.

"Well, that's not my goddamn fault, all right?" he snapped. "The woman was plenty savvy. Savvy as anyone I ever met, your boss included. And a patriot, to boot. You know why she was doing it? She said it wasn't fair that all these good men were off risking their lives while people back home calling themselves Americans were looking to stab them in the back. I didn't force her to do a damn thing."

Playing the blame game was getting me nowhere good, so I asked my last question.

"Did she ever ask about the people she was fingering? About whether anything came of it?"

"Every once in a while," he said. "She never pushed it."

"What are the chances she tried to follow up on any of these loose ends on her own?"

Faraday laughed. It sounded alien coming out of his mouth. Like a dog trying to whistle.

"The woman was a shut-in. Where's she gonna go?"

Which was the question we'd started with. We were still no closer to an answer.

CHAPTER 12

I left Faraday to try and unruffle Rosa's feathers. I paused in the door to politely request he send over copies of the two photos Bodine had matched. He agreed, if only to get me out of the apartment. Rosa had cranked up a phonograph and the sounds of *La Traviata* were drifting from under the door of the bedroom.

I think forgiveness was on the menu.

Back behind the wheel of the Caddy, I checked my watch. Two-thirty. I wondered if Holly was still awake. She kept Pentecost hours, so it was possible.

I thought of her tucked away at her borrowed desk in her borrowed cabin, three hours away and unreachable by phone. The wave of loneliness blindsided me.

If she'd been in town, I might have called her, seen if she was still up, gone to her place and told her about my seemingly endless day. Coney Island felt like a lifetime ago.

She'd listen and smoke her cigarettes, then tell me how it all reminded her of this story or that, and she'd ask to see my new tattoo and I'd tell her it was still sore, but she'd promise to kiss it and make it better.

For a few seconds I actually considered turning the Caddy toward the George Washington Bridge. Three hours there, give her a peck, three hours back. I'd be home in time for our meeting with Whitsun.

I came to my senses.

"Jesus Christ, Parker. Show up in the middle of the night, and she'll think you've lost your goddamn mind," I murmered to no one.

I shoved the loneliness down where it wouldn't do any damage. Shortly after that I parked the Caddy in front of our brownstone. I had a stray thought as I walked up the steps.

There was a pair of muggers still out there who had keys to my boss's car. Therefore, they also had keys to the front door of the brownstone. I'd have to start putting the chain on at night. And if I didn't get those keys back soon, I'd have to get the locks changed. How was I going to explain that to the boss?

Speaking of, I glanced up before going inside. A light was burning on the second floor.

I stopped in the kitchen to see how well I knew Mrs. Campbell. Pretty well, as it turns out. An extra sandwich was sitting on a plate on the kitchen counter, neatly wrapped in wax paper. Since my boss hadn't claimed it, I did. I ate it at the kitchen table, cleaned up my crumbs, then swung by my desk to grab a notebook and went upstairs.

I knocked softly at Ms. Pentecost's bedroom door.

"Come in."

I found her lying in bed, a copy of some foreign novel propped open in front of her. She'd taken herself apart for the evening. Her suit had been traded for a nightdress; her intricate braids were dismantled, leaving her hair to tumble down her shoulders in waves of auburn and silver; and her glass eye was sitting on the nightstand, nestled in a white linen handkerchief she kept there for that purpose.

The eye was a new one, and she'd been test-driving it for the last week. She reported that it was a better fit than her previous models. The side that faced her skull was a better mold, she said. I regretted to inform her that the blue was a couple degrees farther off from her natural color. She said that didn't bother her and explained that there was actually a condition where people had two different-colored eyes, and she gave it a name but I had stopped listening by then, and I'm not looking it up now.

She tucked a bookmark into the novel and closed it.

"I didn't know you spoke German," I said.

"I don't. This is Dutch. Which I don't speak, either. I can read some of it, but not without assistance."

She gestured to a second book open on the bed beside her—a Dutch-to-English dictionary.

"I've got a stack of Chandlers in my room. You would probably pooh-pooh them as lowbrow, but at least you don't need a whole other book to enjoy them."

She did not dignify my suggestion.

"Were you successful?"

"I was. Do you want the rundown now or in the morning?" I asked.

"Now, please," she said. "Mr. Whitsun called. He had no success finding anyone who has seen Miss Bodine. I suggested that our first step be a conversation with her former employers. He was able to reach John Boekbinder at home, and has arranged for a meeting with him and Mr. Gimbal at nine."

Which meant playing rooster for Ms. P around seven, since it took a while for her to get presentable. Exactly the kind of job I'd wish on my worst enemy.

I sat down in the armchair by the window.

"All right," I started. "The short version is, yes, Virginia, there are Nazis in the U.S. Or Nazi, singular. Maybe. The long version is . . ."

I took her through Faraday's story. I kept it short. I left the color of Rosa's nail polish for my typewritten notes. As I talked, I found myself twitching the curtains aside and looking out. Nothing there but the usual landmarks.

Apparently, paranoia is contagious.

"So what do you think?" I asked my boss when I was finished. "If we're still working under the assumption that something untoward has happened to Bodine, does this put Nazis higher or lower on our list of suspects?"

Ms. P gave that a couple seconds' thought.

"It would seem lower," she said. "Nothing came of this domestic spy-hunting project. Also, there's little chance Miss Bodine's involvement was known. Removing her at this late date achieves nothing."

I concurred and told her so. It was an interesting story, but when it came to actually finding our missing mnemonist, a waste of an evening.

"Not a waste," Ms. P said, reclining on her mountain of pillows and closing her eyes. "If nothing else, it tells us about Miss Bodine. About her character. And the contradictions within it."

Ms. P loved her people and their character and contradictions. I gave her a ten-count, then asked the obvious.

"What contradictions?"

No answer. Ten seconds had been too long. The genius was asleep.

I switched off the light, tiptoed out of the room, and swiftly followed suit.

CHAPTER 13

The offices of Boekbinder & Gimbal occupied most of the fifteenth floor of an office building east of Bryant Park. We found Whitsun pacing the sidewalk in front, paper cup of coffee in one hand, cigarette in the other.

He'd showered and changed, but shaving hadn't been on the agenda. His eyes were more blood than blue.

As I wedged the Cadillac into a parking space, I saw him look pointedly at his wristwatch.

"It's only nine-oh-five," I said as I hurried around to the other side and helped Ms. P extract herself from the plush leather. "If you knew what it took to only be five minutes late, you'd kiss my feet."

Instead of puckering, Whitsun stomped out his butt, tossed his coffee in a garbage can, and gave a nod to the man in the maroon suit stationed by the entrance.

"Good morning, Frankie."

The grandfatherly-looking doorman smiled and nodded back as he held the door for us.

"Mr. Whitsun. Long time no see."

And we were in.

During the elevator ride up, we had about twenty seconds to chat. Or we would have if Whitsun hadn't monologued.

"I went in a spiral out from the apartment. Hit every place that was open. Mostly churches. A couple of bars. There's an all-night diner on Thirty-eighth. Nobody'd seen her. Nobody recognized her. When I got home, I went back to calling precinct houses. Nothing. But, you know, if she wandered in during the day, they're not going to tell the night shift. They'd just—I don't know. Ship her to a hospital or Bellevue. I called there again. And . . . um . . . I started trying numbers at the morgue. No luck. Though I guess I didn't really want to have any there."

We were spilled out into a reception area that smelled like new floor cleaner and old money. A secretary who was about ten minutes out of high school escorted us down a narrow hall to a spacious corner room whose furnishings consisted of a single long table—walnut, if I know my hardwoods. Rows of windows on two sides gave a pigeon's-eye view of Bryant Park and the metropolis beyond.

There were two men in the room, one young, one old. The younger one was seated at the far end of the table. The older one was standing at the window, sipping from a coffee mug and admiring the view. He turned when we came in, smiling when he saw Whitsun.

"Forest!"

Whitsun stepped forward, hand extended.

"John."

Grip, shake.

"It's good to see you. It's been a while."

Whitsun's former boss wasn't what I expected. I'd pictured someone with white hair and bird bones with a weak chin and a stuck-up nose. But if I had to pick one adjective for Boekbinder, it would be "ruddy."

Most of his hair had indeed gone white, but he still had a full head of it. His features were pleasantly patrician in a Spencer Tracy manner. Everything was relatively firm and centered around a pair of dark eyes that seemed to be operating fine without spectacles. He looked like the kind of man who played tennis and didn't have to rely on people to let him win.

There was a round of introductions and handshakes.

"You remember Ken Devine, of course."

The younger man at the table approached, hand extended.

If Whitsun was movie-star handsome and Boekbinder was patrician ruddy, Devine was downright pretty: wavy black hair, dark eyes sparkling behind long lashes, delicate fingers that could still give a good handshake. But the smile he gave us was anything but easygoing. It looked carefully chiseled, and when it touched Whitsun, cold as granite.

"Forest."

"Ken."

Gunslingers in three-hundred-dollar suits.

Boekbinder must have recognized the tension, because he took Forest by the shoulder and drew him over to the table.

"Let's all have a seat while we wait for Clark," he said. "How are you doing these days? I haven't seen your name attached to any big cases lately. Then again, I stick to the business section."

"I'm building up the practice," Whitsun said. "Big cases make for good publicity, but they eat up a lot of time."

"I'm sure they do," Boekbinder chuckled.

"Not much money, either, I imagine," Devine said, smile still carved in place.

"Decent enough," Whitsun replied.

"I heard you took on the Sendak case pro bono."

"The mayor asked for a favor," Whitsun said. "You don't have to worry about my paychecks, Ken. I'm not starving. Besides, at least I don't have to sit in line to have my name on the firm's stationery."

Whitsun smiled when he said it, but it was clear he was jabbing at old wounds. If he hit anything, Devine didn't let it show.

We took our seats. Whitsun, me, and Ms. Pentecost on one side of the walnut slab, Boekbinder and Devine on the other.

Once everyone was settled, my boss took the lead.

"I assume Mr. Whitsun informed you why we wanted to speak with you."

Boekbinder animated his pleasant features into a frown.

"He only said it was personal and urgent. I assume it has something to do with Vera Bodine, since he called my home on Monday asking if I'd heard from— Ah, Clark! Come on in. We've just started."

A man was standing in the doorway—Clark Gimbal, I presumed. He proved that not every lawyer needed to double as a magazine model.

He was probably five years younger than Boekbinder but, unlike the managing partner, Gimbal looked every minute of his age. Gray, sallow skin; stringy black hair scraped into a comb-over that didn't quite do the job. Either his maker had decided to skip the shoulders or he'd misplaced them somewhere.

Gimbal had the posture of a man who'd spent his life hunched over ledgers and rarely came up for air.

"What's this about?" he asked as he shuffled in. "I'm putting the final touches on the Gibson Manufacturing contract and— Oh, hello, Forest. It's been . . . I don't know how long. What's going on?"

Boekbinder looked to Whitsun for the answer.

"Vera has gone missing," he said, then briefed them on events to date.

Boekbinder and Gimbal appeared concerned. Devine just looked confused.

"So what?" Devine said. "She's a grown woman."

"You don't understand, Ken," Boekbinder said. "You haven't seen her since she retired. She's become something of a recluse."

Ms. P jumped on that.

"So you have been in contact with Miss Bodine. Was it in a personal or professional capacity?"

Gimbal subtracted a few degrees of bend from his spine.

"I'm afraid that's privileged information," he declared.

I was about to point out that he'd basically tipped us that the answer was professional when Boekbinder saved me the trouble.

"Look, Clark. It's Vera. You know she wouldn't up and leave. Certainly not for two days. I think we have a duty to her as our client as well as a former employee—one who made some important contributions to this firm, I might remind you."

Gimbal threw his hands up. "It's your call, John."

I had the feeling it was John's call a lot.

"After she retired, we continued to handle all of Vera's legal affairs," Boekbinder explained. "Everything from drafting personal legal documents to overseeing her investments."

Whitsun looked confused.

"Investments? What investments?"

"Some stocks, bonds. And the building, of course."

All three of us raised a finger to ask for clarity, but Whitsun got there first.

"What do you mean the building? What building?"

"Why, the Baxter Arms," Boekbinder said. "I assumed you knew. She bought it outright back in 1940."

"How the hell did she manage to do that?" Whitsun asked.

"She invested wisely," Boekbinder explained. "With some help from the firm, of course. She was looking to retire and didn't want to rely solely on her pension. I think she also—well, she liked the idea of choosing who her neighbors were. There were some rumblings that the building was going to be sold. Vera put in an offer and they accepted. Gimbal managed the deal."

"It was really an excellent bargain," Gimbal said with pride. "Many thousands under what they were asking."

"What would the building be worth now?" Ms. P asked.

"Oh, quite a bit more," Gimbal said.

"Have there been any offers?"

Gimbal looked at Boekbinder, who gave him the nod.

"Quite a few over the years," he told us. "I've counseled her to sell a number of times. With the profit, she could buy a home anywhere in the city."

So our elderly shut-in was worth a bundle. I didn't know real estate. I had maybe two grand in my checking account. Less, once I paid my tailor. I was guessing a Midtown lot was six figures, easy.

"Were you aware there's been an effort by a real estate concern, the Danberry Group, to empty the building, I assume as a way of forcing a sale?" Ms. P asked.

Boekbinder looked confused, but Gimbal nodded. "Vera called a while back and told me about it. Paying money to tenants to move out. It's a common tactic."

"Did Miss Bodine need the building to be occupied? To survive there on her own, I mean?" Ms. P asked. "As I understand, she has not increased the rent in several years."

"I don't know," Gimbal said. "She's very . . . mercurial when it comes to how much she charges tenants. Consequently, every cent of it goes directly into taxes and upkeep. Utilities. Things like that. I'm not sure what her savings are like. If there were no rent coming in at all, I don't know how long she could stay there."

"Who else knows that Miss Bodine owns the Baxter Arms?" Ms. P asked.

"No one," Gimbal assured us. "She didn't want her neighbors to know she was their landlord. We set her up with a management company that handles several other apartment buildings in the city. Everything goes through them—rent collection, applications, repair requests, any complaints."

"Have there been many complaints?" Ms. P asked.

"I'm not sure," he said. "I'll have to call the management company."

"I would appreciate it if you would."

"What are you thinking?" Devine asked. "That somebody

found out she was their landlord and what? Did something to her because their rent was too high? That's ridiculous."

"People have done worse for less, Ken," Whitsun said. "You'd know that if you came down out of the castle once in a while."

Devine leaned in for a retort but Boekbinder cut him off.

"Clark—did Vera say anything about anyone bothering her? Any tenants?"

Gimbal shook his head. "She didn't say anything to me. I think she would have called if there had been any trouble."

"What about the Negro family? There was some bit of trouble with them, wasn't there?"

Gimbal thought for a moment before saying, "That was right after she bought the building. And I think it settled itself."

"There was a problem with a family?" my boss prompted.

"Some people didn't like that Negroes were allowed to move into the building," Boekbinder explained. "Although of course they didn't know it was Vera who approved it."

"Were there threats?"

"Nothing like that," Gimbal said. "Just some letters to the management company."

"I would like to see those as well, if you don't mind," Ms. Pentecost said.

Again, Gimbal looked to his fellow partner, who gave the nod.

"Anything we can do to help, Miss Pentecost," Boekbinder said.

He was getting the title wrong, but at least he had the deference down pat.

"When was the last time you saw Miss Bodine?"

"I haven't seen her since she bought the building," Gimbal said. "Not in person, anyway. All our communications have been telephonic."

Ms. P nodded then looked to Boekbinder.

"I spoke with her late in the spring. May, I think. It was

concerning her will, which I'm afraid is definitely confidential," Boekbinder said.

"And you, Mr. Devine?" she asked.

"I haven't seen her since her retirement party," he said.

"You never visited her apartment?"

"Why would I? She was a secretary. Yes, her memory was very impressive. But it was little more than a party trick. I don't see—"

"We all loved Vera," Boekbinder said. "She was part of the family here. She probably knew more about the law than any lawyer I ever met."

"Knowing the law and knowing how to implement it are two different things," Devine retorted.

"You always treated her like shit, Ken," Whitsun said, not quite under his breath.

The way the other three lawyers reacted to the vulgarity, you'd think their former co-worker had dropped a piece of the substance onto the waxed walnut.

"What the hell does that mean?" Devine demanded.

"I mean you treated her like a flunky."

"I did no such—"

"You had her do your Christmas shopping, for God's sake!"

"That was the firm's shopping. For staff and clients."

"John asked you to do it and you dumped it on her. Had her running around for a week."

"She was a secretary!"

Boekbinder patted the table in front of him.

"Now, boys, boys. Settle down."

The "boys" in question settled, but both looked ready to dive back into the ring at the first bell.

"You'll have to excuse them, Miss Pentecost," he said. "Ken and Forest have always butted heads. Strong rivalries breed good lawyers, is what I always say. Though, Ken, you're going to have to learn to hold your temper when you're managing partner."

Whitsun sat back in his chair.

"*Managing* partner?" he asked, looking from Boekbinder to Devine and back again.

"That's right," Boekbinder said, smiling. "My wife's finally getting her wish. I'll be retiring this fall. Ken will be taking on most of my clients, though I'll be staying around as a consultant. Beginning in the new year, it will be Boekbinder, Gimbal and Devine."

"But what about Clark?" Whitsun asked.

We all looked at the aspiring hunchback.

"Oh, no, no, no," Gimbal said, raising his hands as if to ward off a blow. "I'm perfectly content where I am, thank you."

Whitsun looked at Devine and shook his head.

"I guess backstabbing really pays off, huh, Ken?"

"Oh, don't be jealous, Forest," Devine said, ruining his pretty face with a nasty smile. "I thought you were happy defending priest killers and arsonists and—what was that one last spring? That's right—the woman who drowned her baby. The sanitarium instead of Sing-Sing. You must be very proud."

Whitsun leapt out of his chair, and for a moment I thought he was planning to dive across the table. From the look on his face, Devine must have thought the same thing.

Instead, Whitsun snarled three words, one of which was a lot stronger than "shit," and walked out of the room.

We all listened to his footsteps as they receded down the hallway. My boss was the first to recover.

"Mr. Whitsun has had a difficult few days. He's very worried about his friend."

"Of course," Boekbinder said.

"It's hardly his fault," Gimbal added. "Ken baited him."

Devine shrugged.

"What can I say?" he said. "I can't abide hypocrites. We all remember what he was like when he was with the firm. I'll tell you what. All this worry over Vera. I wouldn't be surprised if he had some kind of ulterior motive."

"What might that be?" Ms. Pentecost asked.

Another shrug.

"Who knows? All I know is that the man is ruthless. He called me a backstabber, but he's the one who would have put a knife in his mother's back to nab a client. I doubt his years of slumming have changed that."

I expected the other two lawyers to object, but apparently all three were in agreement on that point.

"Does anyone mind if I get back to work?" Devine asked. "I've got to get the associates prepared for that meeting."

Boekbinder nodded, and the younger lawyer stood up and walked out.

"Now, Miss Pentecost," Boekbinder said, "is there anything else?"

Both he and Gimbal looked anxious to get back to work themselves. Or back to staring wistfully out the window, in Boekbinder's case.

My boss gave it a good ten seconds' thought, then said, "One final question. Are either of you aware, in your capacity either as Miss Bodine's lawyers or as her friends, of anyone who might wish her harm? Or of any situations that she might have been involved in that would put her in danger?"

Befuddlement wasn't a good look for high-priced attorneys, but Boekbinder and Gimbal tried it on for size anyway.

"Ken phrased it poorly, but he was correct. Vera—for all her gifts—is a retired secretary," Boekbinder said. "One whose life . . . Well, her life is quite limited. As are her interests. So, no, I know of no one who would wish her harm."

"She was very kind," Gimbal said. "When she worked here, I mean. Always sticking up for the other staff. Making sure everyone got the raises they deserved. That if someone was ill or—well, there was that one girl who . . . um . . . She was in a family way. Vera made sure she had a job here when she was . . . um . . . ready to come back. She was always very keen on making sure everyone was treated fairly."

Boekbinder clasped his hands in front of him on the table.

"If you take nothing away from this meeting, know this: Vera was more than my assistant. She was my friend and confidante for many years. I will help you in whatever way I can, within the constraints of the law, to find out what happened to her. If any ill has befallen her, she deserves someone of your caliber seeking the truth."

It was a good speech, delivered with an open, honest face. But the delivery boy was a lawyer. So if you're wondering whether to believe him or not, find a coin and flip it. That's what I planned to do.

CHAPTER 14

Outside we found Whitsun pacing circles on the sidewalk, his hands shoved so deep in his coat pockets I thought he'd punch right through. The doorman was giving him a look like he didn't know whether to call for a cop or a priest.

He stopped spiraling when he saw us.

"Did they give you anything else? Anything useful? God, Devine is a piece of work. Can you believe I used to call him a friend?"

He tilted his head back, counting floors until he got to fifteen. But all he got was an eye full of morning sunlight bouncing off the windows. He looked away, blinking.

"You know he spent the war right here? Doing some kind of public relations thing for the army, but really he was working for the firm. Clawing up the ladder."

He injected that last bit with some venom, but I knew envy when I heard it. Devine was being handed a silver platter that, in another world, could have been Whitsun's.

Maybe he still thought it should have been his.

Whatever was going through his head, he must have realized he was waxing maudlin. He gave a full-body shake, pried his hands out of his pockets, and flipped back to the first page.

"So, really, did they give you anything?"

I shook my head. "Nothing to write home about."

"What's next?" he asked. "Visit hospitals? I'm not sure they took me seriously on the phone. We can start with the one on Fifty-ninth. What's its name? You know the one I mean. Then we can move out from there."

My boss took one breath. Two. Three. Once Whitsun managed to keep his feet still for two seconds running, she asked, "When was the last time you slept, Mr. Whitsun?"

"Uuhhbrrrrrrr . . ." is my best crack at spelling the sound he made as he tried to come up with a number.

"Did you sleep last night?" she asked.

"Well, no, but I—"

"I doubt you slept well the night before, at Miss Bodine's apartment."

"I got a couple winks in."

"Then what's next is that you go home and sleep."

"I'm perfectly capable of—"

"Of picking a fight in a law office?" I threw in. "You're down to one cylinder and it's starting to grind."

He began to argue, but quickly realized he was up against a united Pentecost and Parker wall, and that's not something for the weak-hearted to scale.

"I guess I could head home, get some shut-eye. Just an hour or two. I know missing-person cases. I know time is . . . um . . ."

There were a lot of words I could have handed him. Instead, I used my digits to wave down a cab. I shoved Whitsun into it, coaxed him into saying his address out loud, then sent him on his way.

"If I had a buck for every minute I've had to spend convincing some man he should take a powder and let us do our job, I could retire," I told my boss as we walked to the car.

Ms. Pentecost didn't comment. We both knew she'd probably be a goddamn millionaire.

———

As for Whitsun's question regarding what we do next, the answer was pretty obvious. Vera Bodine spent most of her life in her apartment. It's where she disappeared from and, if there was a clue as to where she'd gone, that's where it would be.

As to whether we would find it, that was another story. I could toss an average-size New York City apartment in under two hours. A little more, if they had a lot of books to flip through.

But Perseverance Bodine didn't live average. I couldn't even begin to estimate how long a search of her joint would take. Days? Weeks? A month?

She'd been missing for going on three days, or so said her downstairs earwitness. More than that and things got dicey as far as finding her in good health. We might not have time to do a full search.

Also, I had at least one other ticking clock to think about. The two muggers and my missing gun.

They'd had my piece for about seventeen hours. Which was plenty of time to sell it, shoot it, or toss it. Two people scamming for coin weren't likely to pick door number three.

Shooting it would be bad. Selling it might be a bit better, if it were a pawnshop. More likely they'd sell it direct to somebody who needed a pistol. When you bypass the gun shops for an under-the-table deal, it usually means you're not shopping for a fashion accessory. You're looking to pull the trigger.

Thanks to Midtown traffic, I had a few minutes to think about my next steps. I had calls to make and, because I had chosen the path of deceit, I needed some privacy to make them. Which was why, as we approached Vera's apartment building, I suggested to Ms. P that she get a head start while I run back to the brownstone for vittles—my employer had yet again skipped breakfast—and to catch up on the office work that was an essential part of the duties I got paid for.

"I won't be more than an hour plus travel time," I said. "There's some bills that need paying, and I'm sure Mrs. Campbell will appreciate knowing we're keeping your stomach and health in mind."

It was dirty pool, but it worked.

Once parked, I walked Ms. P up to the apartment and got her settled in the kitchen. I suggested she do a quick once-over, but she nixed it. Her intent was to start at one end of the apartment and oh so slowly make her way to the other.

"We have no idea as to exactly how Miss Bodine arranged her possessions," she explained. "Going about the job piecemeal will be pointless until I have some sense of her order."

I was skeptical that there was any order whatsoever to the place, but I wished her well.

"Watch out for avalanches," I warned as I walked out the door.

By the time I got back to Brooklyn it was nearing lunchtime. I caught Mrs. Campbell in the act of pulling a roast chicken out of the oven.

"Any chance of turning that into something more portable?" I asked, explaining that the boss would be out of pocket for the afternoon and needed sustenance. She said she'd lop off some choice bits and wrap them to go. As I was present and accounted for, I tore off the legs, put them on a plate, and went to my desk.

Between bites, I pulled out my address book and made a list of numbers. Most of them belonged to precinct houses in and around Coney Island, but I threw in a few private operators and a couple folks from the district attorney's office.

An hour later, my dialing finger was sore, the chicken was nothing but bones, and I was no wiser than when I'd started. None of the cops I talked to had run into my muggers. Neither had the PIs. The district attorney's office had nothing on the record fitting their modus operandi.

Which meant my pair were very smart or very new. I was

betting on new. How smart could you be if you'd been rel-
egated to robbing people under the boardwalk at Coney?

It was a rhetorical question, but I was about to get an
answer anyway.

I was going through my contacts again, looking for anyone
I'd missed the first time around, when the phone rang. I was so
sure it was Holly calling from the Catskills that I snatched up
the receiver like it was a winning ticket at Belmont.

"Hello?"

A man's voice came through the line.

"Miss Parker?"

I deflated.

"Speaking."

"This is Bob Nebalt at First National."

It took a second, but I placed him. He was an assistant
manager. I'd passed a few words with him and knew him
barely well enough to say hello whenever I stopped by to make
a deposit.

"Hello, Mr. Nebalt. How can I help you?"

"Well, I was wondering if you wanted more checks for the
business account as well as your personal one," he said. "Diane
forgot to ask. You'll have to forgive her. She's new."

My first reaction was confusion. As far as I knew, the business checkbook was full, as was mine. My second reaction
started as a chill at the small of my back that quickly clam-
bered up the full length of my spine.

"Um . . . no, I think we're fine on business checks," I said,
stalling for time as I got my brain working. "Thank you so
much for calling to make sure."

This is what my brain was doing. Taking another mental
inventory of my stolen purse.

The first time around, I'd stuck to the obvious losses:
money, licenses, firearms, and such. I hadn't thought about the
sundries that I shove in there over the course of a day. Like
deposit slips.

On my way to Coney yesterday, I had swung by First National and deposited a handful of checks from clients, as well as my own twice-monthly paycheck.

With one of those and my ID, you could pull a scam or two. But you'd have to show your face. My face, actually. And since I was at First National at least twice a month, they knew me from Eve.

"Bob, could you do me a favor?" I asked.

"Of course. Anything at all," he schmoozed. Nebalt was excellent at schmoozing, which is why he got the second-biggest desk at the bank.

"I've been running ragged and I neglected to write down the transactions I've made in the last week. Could you remind me of them? I'd hate to drop a remainder somewhere."

"Not a problem, Miss Parker. Just give me a moment."

There was the sound of shuffling papers.

"Let's see. On Tuesday—yesterday—you deposited three checks into the Pentecost Investigations account and one into your personal account. These were for—let me see . . ." He gave some numbers that tallied with mine. If everything was kosher, then that's where things should have ended. But he kept going.

"Then of course this morning you withdrew five hundred dollars. This is from your personal account. Does that correspond with what you have?"

"Yes, it . . . it corresponds," I lied. "By the way, what time was I there this morning?"

"The time?"

"Yes," I said. "So I have it for my records."

The question made me sound like a ditz, but we were good customers, so Nebalt was kind enough not to point it out.

"Well, you were here right at opening. Nine a.m."

So when I was sitting down with the gentlemen of Boekbinder & Gimbal, I was also at First National withdrawing half a grand.

"One last thing," I said. "I could have sworn I asked you a question this morning. Something about interest rates. Do you remember what it was?"

"Well, no. We didn't actually exchange words." I heard the confusion in his voice. He must have thought I'd gone utterly scatterbrained. "As far as I know, you only spoke with Diane."

"Right. Diane. The new girl."

"But I did wave, if you'll remember," he added. "I was at my desk assisting a client."

"Right. How could I forget?" I exclaimed. "Now, let me try and remember. Did I go there first or the swim club? What was I wearing?"

"What were . . . you wearing?" Nebalt echoed back.

"Yes. What was I wearing?"

I pitched the question as straight as I could, and he answered in kind.

"Well, I think it was trousers and a jacket. Gray pinstripes. And a hat. A cap, actually. I noticed that because it wasn't your usual fedora. Does that . . . Is that helpful?"

"Very," I said. "Thanks so much. I'll keep an eye out for those checks. They're coming to the office, right? I didn't give you another address?"

"No, no. They always go to the address on the account. It's standard policy. Security, you understand."

I told him I did and thanked him and hung up. I paused for a few seconds to give my mouth time to catch up with my brain. Then—

"Son of a bitch!"

CHAPTER 15

The drive back to Bodine's apartment gave me time to try out some more creative curse words. To say I was pissed would be an understatement.

I was also impressed.

When I'm trying to sort through a crime, I sometimes think about how I'd go about it. Let's say I had a woman's purse with all the paraphernalia that had been in mine, and I wanted to squeeze out maximum juice.

First thing I'd do was look her up. For most women, this would involve a bit of legwork, but not if the mark in question was one Willowjean Parker. She had been in the papers, after all. Not as much as her employer, but enough. She tried to keep her picture out of the rags, but a couple had slipped in.

And since her PI's license was in the purse, not to mention a few business cards, I would know exactly what stories to go hunting for in the newspaper archives of my local library.

I thought about the few moments of contact I had with the female half of the team. The blond hair that didn't quite match the skin tone, the padded bust, the shift in her voice after the game was blown.

This girl thought she was an actress. If I were her—and I trusted my performing chops—I'd then go shopping. I'd spend some money on a decent suit. Too shabby and it would stand out. Then splurge on a red wig that I'd curl and cut to fit.

After that, I'd case the bank. There was no time left to do that yesterday. So this morning, I would have staked the bank out before opening and watched the employees as they arrived. I wouldn't be able to know which teller was the least experienced, but I could make a guess as to which was the youngest. Youngest usually meant newest.

I'd wait for the morning rush, when citizens were hurrying to finish their errands before heading to their jobs. At its very busiest, when the lines were jam-packed, I'd head in and pick the new girl's lane. Diane.

I'd be polite but rushed. I had business that needed tending to and required cold cash to do it.

"Diane, hi, I have an account here—two accounts, actually, but I'm talking about my personal one. I've run out of checks but I have my account number and my identification . . ." And so on.

Wave back to Bob Nebalt when he waves at me. Look—Bob knows me. We're all friends here. Then hurry out the door five hundred dollars the richer.

Some adjectives came to mind. Inventive. Detail-oriented. Most of all, audacious.

That little con had taken serious chutzpah and not a little bit of restraint. Chutzpah to walk in there and claim my name, and restraint to go for only five hundred. Much more and it would draw attention.

And there was nothing keeping them from pulling the same con again. Not if I was keeping quiet about what had happened.

Another string of curse words. I needed to nip this in the bud and I needed to do it quick.

I'd gotten that far and no farther when I pulled up in front of the Baxter Arms. I grabbed the cloth sack from the passenger's seat. In it was a carefully wrapped chicken breast and a bottle of milk.

"I'm back and I come bearing gifts," I called out as I entered the apartment. There was a muffled answer from the kitchen. I squeezed around the corner and found Ms. Pentecost sprawled out on the floor, legs akimbo. I dropped the sack of food and ran to her.

"What happened? Did you fall?"

She waved me off.

"No, no. I'm down here on purpose." She gestured to the stacks of opened letters that she was hip-deep in. "It seemed the most comfortable way to sort through things. Though I expected to be a bit further along by now."

Saying "I told you so" is considered rude, especially when you're talking to a genius. But I got the opportunity so rarely that I couldn't help it.

"This is what I meant when I said you should do a once-over rather than dig until you hit bedrock," I told her. "We could have a battalion and it would still take us a week to even find the floorboards, much less check them for secret hiding places."

"On the contrary," my boss countered. "There is a semblance of order here. The strata progresses linearly. For example, while there are a few copies of other newspapers on the top, the rest of these seem to be a long-running subscription to *The New York Times* and are stacked in order. The correspondence is organized the same."

"Anything lascivious?" I asked. "Please tell me our septuagenarian eloped."

"Unfortunately it's comprised almost entirely of bills. Mostly ones sent on from the apartment management service. If there is personal correspondence, it's stored elsewhere. However, she has annotated many of these invoices. Noting the rising costs of electricity; of maintenance and repairs, and so forth."

"So our old lady is worried about money."

"Or at least aware that it should be a concern," Ms. P said. "Regardless, it shows she has not lost her secretarial acumen.

She has an eye for details. And for order. As I said, these were all stacked chronologically. Not a single invoice misfiled."

"You're saying there's a method in the mess?"

She nodded. "I am."

"Does this order give us any hint to what happened to her?"

"Not as of yet, no," she said. "Now, will you please help me up? I need to use the facilities and there's nothing I can use to support me that won't collapse."

I reached two hands down and pulled her up. She immediately lurched, falling into my arms.

"My foot's asleep," she explained.

After a few wobbles, she got fully upright.

"How long have you been sitting there?" I asked.

"How long have you been gone?"

Great, I thought. Cross-legged on cold linoleum was not a good way for Ms. Pentecost to spend two hours.

"How about I take over for a while?" I said as she made her way to the bathroom. "You can take a cab back to the brownstone, prop your feet up. Put your brain to work."

"I'm perfectly capable of continuing. I only need to splash some water on my face and stretch my legs."

Stubbornness wasn't a side effect of multiple sclerosis, as far as I knew. I believe she was born with it.

"I wasn't going to mention this," I said, "but Mrs. Campbell had some words to say about you crawling around in a muck pile like this. That it was something she might need to mention to your doctor."

She glanced over her shoulder with a look that wasn't quite fear but was a distant cousin.

"Maybe I will go home for an hour or two," she said. "If only to ease Eleanor's mind."

She edged into the bathroom and closed the door.

While she attended her business, I attended mine. Which required a telephone.

I'd spied a stack of old Bakelites in one corner of the living room, but upon examination it seemed those were only for show. Eventually I spotted a bit of telephone cord and followed it to the phone, which was tucked under the sitting room's one available chair.

I dialed the brownstone. When Mrs. Campbell picked up, I told her there had been a change in plans and to expect our employer shortly. Then I dialed a cab company and asked them to send a car around.

Soon after I hung up with them, Ms. P opened the bathroom door. She dislodged a bath towel that had gotten tangled around her cane and started smoothing out the creases in her suit.

"If we're going to spend any amount of time here, I'm afraid we will have to organize Ms. Bodine's lavatory. Did I hear you speaking with Mrs. Campbell?"

"Also calling you a cab. Which should be here by the time we navigate the stairs," I said. "I'm going to keep your lunch pail for my own enjoyment. I might get peckish and I'm scared of looking inside the icebox."

I'd hit the end of that little monologue before I noticed the look on Ms. P's face. Curiosity and concern.

"I understand how this sort of confined space may make you uncomfortable," she said. "There's no reason you need to do this alone. You could come back to the office with me and we could begin again later together."

I shook my head.

"You know as well as I do there's a clock ticking. And we have no idea where the hands are. Somebody should be here going through the place."

"We could call Mr. Whitsun," she suggested. "Provided he is somewhat rested, he does have some experience in—"

"Hell no," I said. I don't make it a habit to interrupt the smartest woman in the city. Only when she's talking nonsense. "First, I've been in more cramped quarters than this. My first six months with the circus I shared an eight-by-ten trailer with two spec girls and a three-legged terrier. Second, you'll need mittens in Hades the day that I let a client, much less Forest Whitsun, do my job for me. Third . . . is pretty much the same as first. I'll be fine. If I get antsy, I'll open the window."

She let it go, and seemed to come to terms with calling it an afternoon. But as I walked her downstairs, she got that look again.

"Are you sure you're all right?"

Some of what I'd been worrying about must have leaked onto my face. For a moment, I considered telling her. The mugging, the gun, the scam at the bank. It would be painfully embarrassing for half a minute, but then I'd have two minds working on the problem. And one of them would be Lillian Pentecost's.

"Fit as a fiddle," I said instead.

I don't know if she took it for truth, but she didn't ask again.

The cab was waiting outside, as promised. I eased my boss into it, gave the cabbie the address and an extra buck to make sure she made it in the door, and was about to slap the roof to send him on his way when she poked her head out the window.

"Call immediately if you find something."

"Don't worry. I have the number memorized and everything."

I slapped.

The car sped.

I went back upstairs to wander the labyrinth.

CHAPTER 16

And wander I did.

Ms. P's technique of starting in one spot, digging to the bottom, then moving to the adjacent spot hadn't worked. Besides, I didn't have the patience for it.

I mean, I'm possessed with a liberal dose of the stuff. Put me on a stakeout and I have the patience to play statue in a car seat for as long as needed.

But in that case I know what I'm waiting for. In this one, it was a snipe hunt. We didn't even know if the clue we were hunting existed.

So I wandered.

I picked through the newspapers in the kitchen and the magazines piled under the bathroom sink. I flipped through the packets of envelopes Ms. P had dug into and peeked into the drawers of the rolltop desk. I went diving into mountains of old clothes heaped in the living room, taking the time to pull each and every pocket inside out. I made a pile of the scraps I found and went through them when I was finished. A hundred handwritten receipts. A thousand balls of lint. Seventeen mints still in their wrappers.

Maybe one of those was a clue, but a clue to what? Hell if I knew.

I'd been working for a little less than an hour when I started to get that suffocating feeling again. Part of it was the tight space, but some blame could be laid at the feet of all the lavender sachets scattered about, the combined odor of which seemed to grow thicker the longer I was there.

I didn't want Ms. P to come back to find me passed out in a pile of old nighties, so I took five on the fire escape. It was midafternoon and the building across the alley was bristling with activity.

I watched workers move from desks to filing cabinets to water coolers. A few looked my way, curious about the woman hanging her heels off the fire escape. Maybe envious they couldn't do the same.

I waved. No one waved back.

Someone on a lower floor lit up a cigarette, and the smoke made its way skyward and up my nose. I was pretty sure it was a Chesterfield. Holly's brand.

Can a heart have a charley horse?

I shook my head in disgust. She'd barely been gone a week, and already I was pining. How pathetic is that?

Sure, Holly was special. I'd had a handful of folks I could call friends. Another handful I'd label as lovers. But few I could call both.

But pining leads to distraction, and that can get you in trouble.

Besides, I was sure Holly wasn't pining for me. For one, she had her writing. When she got a typewriter in front of her, the rest of the world might as well exit stage right.

And she had Marlo and Brent there for one more night if they stuck to schedule. I didn't think they'd stay longer. They'd promised to take over the weekly visits with Holly's mother at the nursing home as soon as they got back. It was the only way Holly had agreed to leave the city, and she wouldn't want her mother to go another day unattended.

I'd offered to assume that duty, but according to Holly, I unsettled her mother. Maybe it was because the second time we met, I ended up shooting a man.

Go figure.

Still—the three had one more night on the bearskin rug.

Was I jealous? Was that it?

I poked at that a few times, but eventually came to the conclusion that if there was jealousy in the mix, it was a minor ingredient. While I didn't plan to spend any time in the sack with Brent and Marlo, the pair were nice enough and I knew they loved Holly. She was safe with them.

I looked at my watch. My five-minute break had turned into fifteen. Time to get back to work.

Keeping the kitchen window open in an attempt to air things out, I moved on to the sitting room, where I flipped through the leaning tower of records, resulting in several near-topplings but no revelations.

After the sound of the traffic and the wind, the silence of the apartment felt like I had cotton balls plugged in my ears. I took one of the records—Vivaldi—put it on the Victrola, and flipped the switch.

As the silence was replaced with the sound of strings, I moved into the bedroom. The floral stink was truly overbearing in here, but the window was painted shut so I'd have to grimace and bear it.

I tried under the bed first, but it was packed to the brim with shoeboxes, which, surprisingly enough, seemed to all contain shoes. At least the first five did, and that was a big enough sample for me.

I looked at the narrow open space on the bed where Vera Bodine had spent her nights. I had this mad, fleeting notion that I should lie down there, close my eyes, and see if that would help me think like our missing woman. But it was too much like a coffin, and I'd sampled that sensation already.

By then the smell had gotten too thick and my head was starting to swim again. I started moving back toward the kitchen and the fire escape, and was halfway through the sitting room, when I stopped.

I had noticed something.

I didn't know what I had noticed, I only knew there was something I had seen and had missed.

Over the years working as a private detective, I've learned to pay attention to those sensations. It's saved my life on more than one occasion.

I slowly turned and retraced my steps to the bedroom, going slow, eyes taking in every detail.

Same mess. Same junk. Nothing new.

I sat down on the edge of the bed.

"You're losing it, Parker," I said, punctuating the sentence with a sigh. To sigh, I had to take a deep breath. It was on the inhale that I caught it.

The smell.

Lavender, absolutely. Mildew, sure.

Something else.

I made my way around the bedroom, this time leading with my nose.

Where I grew up, our house was bordered on three sides by fields. Consequently, we got our share of field mice, especially in winter. Some had the decency to spend a few months in the walls, stealing the occasional scrap of bread before debarking in the spring.

More than a few died.

I always seemed to notice the smell first, and it was my job to track them down. My dad called me his "little hound dog," which was probably the nicest compliment he ever gave me.

Young Willowjean thought it was fun. A game. This little girl walking from room to room, sometimes crawling with her nose pressed against the floorboards.

Hunting death.

That's what I did at Bodine's.

I got to the pile of clothes and pillows against the wall, the one that had suffered a collapse. I nudged the pile some and revealed the corner of a hope chest. I shoved the rest of the clothes off until the lid was clear and the hinges were unencumbered.

I opened it.

I was immediately punched in the face by a wave of flowers and rot. I looked down through watery eyes. At first, all I saw were sachets, dozens of them.

Then, peeking up through the white linen bags, I saw the curve of a hand; an elbow; a slice of cheek, the skin gray and wrinkled.

The clock stopped.

"Hello, Vera."

CHAPTER 17

You may be under the misapprehension that, being a detective, I stumble on bodies all the time. In fact, it's rather rare. By the time Ms. P and I are invited to the party, the body is usually already at the morgue.

Rarely do I find them in situ.

Okay, yes, I had gotten up close and personal with a corpse that was dumped at our back door the previous winter. But I hadn't been the one who discovered it and it was put there specifically for us to find, so that doesn't really count.

The point is that this was a rather unique situation. Made even more unique by the fact that I had the body to myself for as long as I wanted.

The cops weren't on their way. No one was going to come busting through the door. I was alone with a murder victim and I had all the time in the world.

I was assuming murder at this point because I didn't think Vera crawled into a hope chest and covered herself with sachets.

First, I went to the front door and triple-checked that it was locked. No use taking chances.

Then I went to the kitchen and rummaged until I came up with a pair of rubber gloves. They weren't the best fit, but they would do.

Then I went back to the chest, knelt down in front of it,

and started removing the sachets and placing them on the floor around me. I wanted a better look at the corpse, but I was conscious of leaving an errant fingerprint. I didn't want the police to get confused.

Once I had the body mostly uncovered, I gave it a close once-over.

Even if I tripped over a corpse every day of my life, I don't think I'll ever get used to it. Being in the presence of a person who until recently had been laughing and crying and breathing and chatting with friends and thinking about what to do for dinner.

Until someone decided they should stop.

In the presence of a human devoid of its humanness, you become very conscious of how much of us is just bone and meat.

That was especially true in the case of Vera Bodine. I wasn't a physician, so I wasn't qualified to estimate a time of death, but I knew it was a hell of a lot longer than a few days.

So much for our downstairs earwitness.

She was curled on her side, but what I could see of her face was barely recognizable from the photo Whitsun had brought us. The entire body was swollen, bloated. She was dressed in a nightgown and a hip-length wool sweater. The nightgown had maybe been white, but was now stained gray with whatever leaks out of the human body after death. The sweater was black and hid the stains nicely.

The smell was indescribable, so I won't even try.

Let's just say that the chicken I'd had for lunch was threatening an encore.

I got my stomach in check and did the best examination I could without actually moving the body. The corpse was in such a condition that I worried trying to move it would cause something to . . . well, to fall off.

The Vivaldi had come to an end, so as I looked her over, I filled the silence.

"All right, Vera. What are we looking at here? Is that a scrape on your knuckle? Hard to tell. Everything's a little red. Maybe you fought back, huh? . . . I'm not seeing any blood on your nightdress. I think this one's ready for the rag bin, by the way. Hope it wasn't a favorite . . . No obvious wounds, but who knows what you have on the downside of you . . . Okay, I'm going to move your hair a little. Just a little. I don't want it to . . . to come off . . . Huh . . . That looks like it could be a dent. Okay, now I'm going to see if there's anything in your pockets here. Hope you don't mind."

Our friend Hiram, who got paid to spend his nights with corpses, said that he talked to the dead while he was examining them as a way of acknowledging their continued humanity.

I was trying to keep my nerves and my guts under control.

As gingerly as I could while wearing heavy rubber gloves, I opened up the small breast pocket of the nightgown and slid in two fingers. I felt something crinkle.

A clue?

No, a candy wrapper.

The sweater had nice big pockets on the hips. Since she was lying on her side, I had easy access to the left one. I reached my hand in. Nothing.

I should have left it at that. But when you've got three spins of a wheel, it's hard to stop at two.

I leaned over and slid my hand down between the body and the side of the chest, moving aside the remaining sachets as I did so. Doing so put my face immediately over the body. Breathing through my mouth wasn't doing it anymore, so I held my breath and hoped I wouldn't pass out on top of a corpse.

After some awkward fumbling, I located the pocket and gave it a gentle tug to get it out from under her. The tug got the pocket free, but it also caused her head to loll toward me, and suddenly I was face-to-face with our victim, except her eyes didn't look like eyes anymore. They were swollen and green, like any second they would burst, spraying me with—

I fell back, landing hard on my tailbone. The pain was the only thing that kept me from fainting. I took a deep, shuddering breath.

Then I took another one, held it, and went back in.

My mother didn't raise a quitter.

With my eyes looking firmly away from the corpse's, I slid my hand into the now-accessible pocket and felt around. My fingers clamped on something. Gently, I pulled out a long, wet rectangle of paper.

A clipping, maybe? From a newspaper?

It was hard to tell. It had been soaking in whatever gravity was pulling out of the former Vera Bodine and was now stained a dark, uniform gray. Whatever had been printed on it was utterly obscured and it was threatening to revert to pulp in my gloved hand.

"If this turns out to be the *Times* crossword, I'm going to be real disappointed, Vera."

I carefully set the clipping aside and went about putting things back as I'd found them. I didn't dare try and shift the head back, but I replaced the sachets, distributing them as best as I remembered.

I wrapped the clipping carefully in a handkerchief. Then I took it into the kitchen, emptied the grocery sack of Mrs. Campbell's thoughtfully prepared lunch, and placed the evidence inside.

I walked outside to the Cadillac and put the sack in the hidden compartment in the trunk where I kept things that I didn't want the authorities to stumble across.

I do not advocate tampering with a crime scene. I certainly don't advocate walking off with evidence. There's a lot of activities that I don't advocate but sometimes participate in and you're just going to have to come to terms with that.

With that done, I went back to the apartment. Once inside, I dialed a number.

"Pentecost Investigations" was the reply. "How may I help you?"

"You know, we've really got to come up with a slogan," I said. "Something short and catchy. 'Mysteries managed at a reasonable rate.' 'Crooks collared or your money back.' Something like that."

Ms. Pentecost made a sound that I'll interpret in retrospect as approval.

"Did you find something of interest?" she asked.

I'd already used up my supply of witticisms, so I gave it to her straight: the smell, the hope chest, the body, the search, the soiled paper. She didn't interrupt and didn't chastise me for frisking a corpse. She had only one follow-up question.

"What did you do with the gloves?"

The reason she asked was obvious. If the cops found the gloves, they'd suspect that I went rummaging. Which tells you everything you need to know about Ms. P's philosophy regarding the authorities: what they didn't know wouldn't hurt us.

"I put them in the sack with the clipping," I told her.

Another grunt. This one definitely of approval.

"Who should I call first, Whitsun or the cops?"

"The police," she said. "I'll phone Mr. Whitsun. Though I'll advise him not to go to the scene."

Smart. Since he got paid to get crooks off the hook, Whitsun wasn't exactly an NYPD favorite.

"When was the last time you ate?" she asked.

"Two chicken legs a couple hours ago."

"You might consider eating something else."

She knew as well as I that time spent with the police when there was a body involved was counted in hours.

"I think whatever I put into my stomach now is going to come right back up," I told her. "Anything I should leave out?"

A pause as she gave it some consideration.

"The FBI."

That would have been my answer, too.

"Be sure to give Whitsun the same instructions when you break the bad news."

"I will," she said. "Good luck."

She hung up. I tapped the receiver switch to get an operator and gave her a number. It was time to inform the authorities.

CHAPTER 18

Actually, I informed the authority. Singular.

Specifically in the form of one Lieutenant Nathan Lazenby, who had my vote as best homicide cop in the city. It had been a while since I'd last spoken to him, and it was almost pleasant to hear his gravelly baritone coming over the line.

"What do you want, Parker?"

"Oh, so many things," I said. "Something to permanently get rid of unwanted freckles; some high heels you can actually run in; a good knish. It'll start getting chilly soon. Don't you love a nice hot knish in the fall?"

He said some words that the *Times* would not have seen fit to print.

"Also, I would dearly love your presence—and probably a half dozen of your fellows, including some of the boys from the crime lab."

"Why would you like that?"

"Because that's who you usually invite when there's been a murder."

There were more questions and some answers and a bushel more swears, and it ended with me giving him the address and him giving me the command of "Don't go anywhere. Don't touch anything."

I promised him I wouldn't. The touching had already been done, after all.

———

The first officers arrived in about ten minutes. They looked at the state of the body and the apartment and decided not to touch a damn thing until the big guy got there, which he did about fifteen minutes later.

Lazenby had the physique of a stevedore, the mind of a Jesuit priest, and the wardrobe of a man who had family connections in the Garment District. All of his suits tended to run in shades of gray, with that day's straddling the line between gunmetal and granite. I wondered if they charged extra for the fabric required to stretch across his hulking shoulders and around his expanding middle.

Though, to be fair, his middle seemed to have contracted a bit since the last time I'd been close enough to examine him. Also, his black and gray beard had been trimmed to the point where I could almost make out the shape of his chin.

"Looking sharp, Lieutenant," I said as he squeezed through the entryway. "Taken up calisthenics?"

"Like I need to invent a reason to jump around. Where's our body?"

Lazenby doesn't waste words or time. I led him to the bedroom and the woman waiting for him. The other officers had fled that room pretty quickly, so we had the place to ourselves.

Lazenby knelt by the hope chest as I had, pulled a pencil from his breast pocket, and used it to knock aside some of the sachets to better reveal her face.

"It's hard to tell, but I'm pretty sure you're looking at one Perseverance Bodine, called Vera by her friends. Last confirmed sighting of her a little more than two weeks ago, but she stayed to herself, so that doesn't say much."

"You touch the body?" he asked.

"I did not," I said with a straight face.

The little *v* shape between his eyes suggested that he didn't believe me. It wasn't that I was a bad liar. As a rule, Lazenby doubted everyone until proven otherwise.

He grunted and pushed himself to standing.

"I'm going to have our crime-scene boys called. The medical examiner's office, too, so we can get someone out to confirm death, as pointless as that might be. Then you and I are going to go outside and have a chat about why we found you with a corpse and what you and Lillian Pentecost have to do with it."

I could have done a lot of parsing of the word *found*, but I gave him a pass. He barked some instructions to one of his sergeants, who I pointed in the direction of the working phone. Then Lazenby and I descended the three flights to the street.

People had emerged to poke their heads into the stairwell and watch the parade of police: the Polish gentleman, whose ears weren't as good as we thought; the model-train enthusiast; the night-desk sergeant. Grady nodded at Lazenby, who nodded back. Then he looked to me.

"I guess she wasn't at a church."

I shook my head. "Afraid not."

He grunted and went back into his apartment.

Out on the sidewalk, it was approaching quitting time and the office buildings around us were beginning to fling out their human ballast. Lazenby led me into the alley below Bodine's fire escape, where we had a modicum of privacy.

"All right," Lazenby said. "Make it quick. And don't leave anything out."

By ignoring the second instruction I was able to manage the first, giving him the generalities—minus the Nazis—in a little under ten minutes.

When I was finished, he had me go through it again, this time probing for weaknesses.

"Why did Whitsun come to you after only a day? Did he suspect she'd been killed? Did Pentecost?"

"What made you go to her old boss first?"

"Why was she on Whitsun about the Fennel murder?"

I batted about .500 on his questions. He had just asked me to run through everything a third time when one of the officers came hurrying around the corner toward us.

"Lieutenant, we've got a situation. Some guy's trying to get into the apartment. Says he knew the victim. He's not taking no. Talking about suing everyone in sight."

Lazenby and I followed the officer back upstairs, where we found Whitsun going nose to nose with three NYPD officers. So much for Ms. P's advice to stay home.

"You say she's dead, so maybe she is, maybe she isn't. It wouldn't be the first time the New York City Police Department got something wrong. This is private property. I have a key and permission from the resident to be here. Do you?"

I didn't know how many winks Whitsun had managed to get, but it wasn't enough. Also, he'd apparently slept in his suit. He looked more like a Bowery vagrant than a member of the bar.

When Lazenby put his slab of a hand on his shoulder, Whitsun whirled.

"You! I should have known."

Lazenby nodded. "Yes, Mr. Whitsun. Me. What did you call me the last time I was on the stand? I think it was 'a lumbering cog of the penal system more interested in enhancing my own reputation than making sure the people I arrest are actually guilty.' I might have misquoted you a bit, but I think that was the gist of it."

I saw Whitsun's response ignite behind his eyes. I stepped out of Lazenby's shadow and snuffed it out before it burned both of us.

"It's true," I told him. "Vera's dead."

He opened his mouth, but nothing came out.

"She was dead long before we started looking for her. There was nothing you could have done."

I heard footsteps behind us and turned to see a cluster of men from the crime lab. I recognized a couple of them from the previous winter, when they'd had reason to crawl around the backyard of the brownstone. One of them had a camera slung around his neck and the others carried cases of varying sizes.

"Good luck, boys," I told them. "You're gonna need it."

Lazenby ushered Whitsun aside so his men could get in. Whitsun followed them with his eyes, but made no further effort to try to get into the apartment. The reality of the situation had finally hit home.

"Mr. Whitsun?" Lazenby said. "Counselor?"

Whitsun blinked. "Yes?"

"I'd like you to come down to the precinct and give a statement. Tell us about your relationship with Miss Bodine. The events of the last few days."

Whitsun gave the request a full five-count and then said, "No, I don't think so."

The response surprised me. Not Lazenby, apparently.

"I can get a material witness warrant," he said calmly.

"Then get it," Whitsun snapped. "In the meantime, I won't be walking into a room with you or any other police officer. Not without a warrant and not without my own attorney present."

I tried to talk some sense into him.

"I understand not wanting to get cozy with the cops, but Lazenby's one of the good guys. If he's going to find out what happened to Vera, he's going to need your help."

Whitsun grinned, but there was no joy in it.

"Come on, Parker. You can't be that naïve. There are no good cops. There's crooked cops and then there are cops who look the other way."

Whitsun squeezed past Lazenby and headed toward the stairs.

"I'll be seeing you with that warrant," the lieutenant said.

"I'll be waiting."

Great. With Whitsun clocking out, the police were left with only one person to fill in all of the blanks.

It was going to be a long night.

CHAPTER 19

It was such a long night that it threatened to become an early morning. There was more questioning at the apartment and a stretch of time spent watching Lazenby direct the crime-lab boys. Usually he wouldn't stick his nose in, but Bodine's apartment was such chaos that there were arguments as to how to proceed.

After that was done, we went to the station where he settled me in a windowless room that had too many light bulbs and smelled like flop sweat.

I won't go into detail about the following six hours. There was a deluge of questions; some time with a typewriter hammering out the events of the past two days; and a whole lot of sitting alone in that room while Lazenby disappeared to coordinate with his men working the apartment.

Just north of midnight, Lazenby judged that I was squeezed dry and gave me a ride back to the Caddy, which was still parked in front of Bodine's place. By then the police had called it a night and the building was dark and silent.

As I got out of the unmarked sedan, Lazenby had a few last words for me.

"Tell Pentecost to talk to her client," he said. "We're gonna get him in a room one way or another. It won't look good if we have to drag him there."

"I'll pass on the message for her to pass on the message," I said.

He sped off.

I was about to pop the trunk on the Cadillac to check on the lunch sack and purloined evidence when I noticed some furtive movement in the alley by Vera's building.

Or at least it had aspirations of being furtive.

"I think you're gonna need to work on your stealth, Commander."

Cody uncrouched and came to the mouth of the alley. He didn't have the goggles, but their imprint was still circling his eyes and nose. He was wearing Superman pajamas and a pair of boots he could have fit into three times over.

"I'm not an expert on bedtimes," I said, "but I bet it's past yours."

"Sarah Jane cries a lot," he said. "Mom falls right back to sleep but it takes me forever."

"So you decided to sneak out and go skulking?"

"I'm hunting rats!" he said, reaching into his back pocket and proudly displaying a slingshot.

"Nice sidearm," I said. "You using quarter-inch shot?"

His eyes lit up. A girl who spoke his language.

"I ran out," he told me. "So now I'm using these."

He held out his other hand to show me half a dozen lug nuts.

"I found these lying around the hall," he said. "They don't fly as good, but it won't matter if I get close enough."

"You get close enough a lot?"

He shrugged.

"Not really. If I could get into the back stairs, I bet I could get close," he said. "My mom's heard them moving around in there at night. I've heard squeaking, too. When we're at home? It's kind of muffled, but I figure that's where they've got to be hiding. I'd go in there and hunt them and kill them, but it's locked."

I hadn't seen any rats when I'd run up the back stairs the

evening before, but I didn't tell him that. Let tiny heroes have their dreams.

"You think if I asked the landlord, they'd let me in to kill them?" he asked, looking up at me with big, serious eyes.

"What's your beef with rats?" I asked.

"They're vermin," he said, probably trying out the word for the first time. "I don't want them to come in and bite Sarah Jane. They'd really hurt her."

I didn't particularly care for children, but I was considering making an exception.

"How about this," I said. "I'll give the landlord a call and make your pitch. If you go back inside and at least pretend to sleep."

He gave the proposition careful consideration before blessing it with a single, solemn nod. I walked him to the front door.

"No more midnight rat hunting," I told him as we stepped into the lobby. "Not for a while."

He nodded. Then he looked down at his feet and traced a circle on the green and white tile with one boot-clad toe.

"Is the old lady you were looking for dead?" he asked. "When I got home from school, the police were here, and I asked and my mom said she was sick but I don't think there would be all the police if she only had to go to the hospital."

I nodded. "Yeah, she's dead."

"Did somebody . . ." Something stopped him from finishing the question. Maybe it was too big, even for an eight-year-old Pied Piper.

"It's nothing you have to worry about," I said.

I could tell he didn't quite believe me, but that's all right. I didn't quite believe me, either. I watched as he went back into his apartment. Then I went out and sat in the Caddy for twenty minutes, staking out the front door. Just in case he was counting to a hundred before sneaking out again.

He didn't. And I left.

CHAPTER 20

The more serious the crime, the slower the investigation.

There are exceptions. Kidnapping comes to mind. Mainly because if that's not solved quick, the chance of recovering the victim alive goes downhill fast.

In this case, the adage held true. When Perseverance Bodine was missing, we were working against a clock. When her clock stopped, so did ours.

Or maybe it didn't stop, but it certainly wasn't ticking quite so loud anymore.

Thursday was quiet. No calls from the police asking Ms. P to come in for a statement, though there was nothing she would have given them that I hadn't.

Plenty of calls from the press, however. They didn't have the story for the morning papers, but had picked up on it by the time the evening editions hit the stand.

SHUT-IN FOUND SLAIN, STUFFED IN TRUNK

HOARDER DEAD FOR DAYS IN CHEST

PENTECOST SNIFFS OUT BODY BURIED IN APARTMENT

How they got the "sniffs" right and the sniffer wrong, I don't know. Actually, I do. It's because when we started getting the calls from reporters, we gave the stock line of "It's a confidential matter."

It was confidential who hired us. Confidential how we ended up unearthing Vera Bodine. Confidential as to what leads we were following.

Actually, we didn't know if we were following up any, because by evening there was still no word from Whitsun on whether we were officially on the case.

Were we pivoting from missing person to murder?

Now, I know what you're thinking. So what if Whitsun didn't want us on the payroll anymore? There was no way Lillian Pentecost was going to let dead bodies lie.

But sometimes we did. Let murders go unmeddled with, I mean.

When Vera Bodine was missing, we were the best people for the job. Now that she was dead, Lazenby and his boys had the edge. They had the body and the evidence and the manpower to go through that junk shop of an apartment in days instead of weeks.

The only thing we had that they didn't was Bodine's work with the FBI. Maybe they would get that, too. Bodine might have jotted down a note or three. In the meantime, at Ms. P's instructions, we were keeping that detail to ourselves.

Another reason we didn't go full-bore on a case we didn't know if we were getting paid for is that we had other irons in the fire, and one of them was starting to get hot.

Just before dusk, as we were perusing the evening editions, the phone rang. The voice on the other end of the line was low, deep, and had that refined British quality that makes me think of black homburgs and walking sticks.

"May I speak with Lillian Pentecost, please."

"Who may I say is calling?" I asked in my politest private-secretary tone.

"This is Silas Culliver. Personal attorney to Mr. Jessup Quincannon."

"One moment, please." I put my hand over the mouthpiece. "It's Quincannon's pet shark. He wants a word."

Ms. P gave me the nod.

"I'm transferring you now, Mr. Culliver."

That was our fancy way of saying Ms. Pentecost would pick up the receiver at her desk and I'd put down mine. This time, though, I kept the handset to my ear.

If, as we suspected, Quincannon had kept mum on a murderer, it had led directly to Holly having a gun to her head and me having another dead body on my record. I had a stake in seeing Quincannon get what was coming to him.

"Mr. Culliver. How may I help you?"

"Ms. Pentecost. I believe you are acquainted with one of my clients. Mr. Jessup Quincannon."

That was cute. Not only asking if we were acquainted with him, but calling him "one of" his clients.

If what we'd learned was true, Quincannon was his only client. Culliver spent his days traveling around the country, sometimes even the world, bribing police and judges and the families of convicted murderers in an effort to add to Quincannon's ever-growing collection of gruesome souvenirs.

I'd never met Culliver, but his cultured syllables made me picture Basil Rathbone minus the charm.

"I am certainly acquainted with your client, Mr. Culliver," my boss said.

Ms. P could play polite with the best of them.

"I believe you have been making inquiries into certain aspects of his business and personal life," Culliver continued. "These inquiries have extended to indirect, or sometimes direct, interference. My client is concerned as to your motives. I must admit so am I."

Ms. Pentecost pulled the receiver away from her ear, took a deep breath, twisted her neck to the side and got a few pops out of the topmost vertebrae, then returned the receiver.

"Mr. Culliver, let's strive for candor. Otherwise this conversation will prove lengthy and fruitless," she said.

"Please, Ms. Pentecost. I appreciate a healthy dose of honesty."

"The aspect of Mr. Quincannon's life you refer to is his obsession with murder and those who commit it. The inquiries I have made are in regard to how he procures the material in his collection, his Black Museum, as it's generally known, and what crimes he, and by extension you, commit in order to do so. The interference you speak of amounts to a handful of calls to certain officials informing them that the bribes you have paid have not gone unnoticed. The suggestion that, should they continue, certain members of the press will learn about them as well. As for my motives, they are simple: the eventual cessation of Mr. Quincannon's activities. He disgusts me. He values death over human life, and as he is a man of wealth and influence, his values have a greater impact than those of most men. His obsession has driven him to shield at least one murderer from the police. I imagine it's not the first time. Should I discover evidence to support that theory, be assured I will use it. Is that honest enough for you, Mr. Culliver?"

I refrained from standing and cheering, but it wasn't easy.

When Culliver started talking again, his voice had changed. A new note had been added to that staid English tenor. It wasn't anger or outrage. It sounded like amusement.

"That was certainly refreshing, Ms. Pentecost," he said, and I could almost hear the curl in his lip. "And in this case, profoundly helpful. It clarifies what advice I will give my client as to his next steps."

"What will those steps be, might I ask?"

There was a chuckle from the other end of the line, and for the first time he broke character. There was something mean in that laugh. Like a little boy pulling wings off a fly.

"I think Mr. Quincannon will want that to be a surprise. Good day."

Click.

My boss set the phone down and sat back, staring at the device like it was a snake that had just sunk its fangs in.

"That was ominous," I said, hanging up my own handset. "I'm not fond of surprises in general. Especially ones arranged by Quincannon."

"I agree."

"What should we do?"

She shook her head. "There's nothing to be done except to stay our course. And be watchful."

I didn't need the resident genius to tell me that.

The call from Quincannon's pet viper was a spur in the rear to address my own personal problems. Namely, my two muggers. I didn't know what Quincannon had planned, but I didn't want to have my ass hanging out when it happened.

Friday evening, after dinner, I went up to the third-floor archives under the excuse of pulling clippings that might be related to Bodine: the Fennel murder; the Bund and various Nazi doings in New York; any mention I could find of Boek-binder & Gimbal.

Ms. P was spending the evening sitting behind her desk and taking a bite out of that Dutch book, so I had the third floor to myself.

If you haven't been to our third floor, imagine some lost basement room in the New York Public Library: rows of shelves packed with file boxes, each containing notes and clippings and assorted evidence. Some hints you aren't in a library might be the skylights; the ladder you can prop up to get to the roof; the articulated skeleton in the corner collecting dust; and the island of space in the center of the room with its massive Egyptian rug, comfy armchair, and a lamp I was told was Tiffany.

I spent the first hour doing what I said I would. I couldn't find much on Boekbinder & Gimbal. Didn't even know where to start, really. They turned their noses up at criminal cases, and that's what we, and by extension our archives, were dedicated to.

There was plenty about Nazis in New York, though. Too much, really, and most of it probably irrelevant.

Material on the Fennel murder was much easier to assemble, since it was recent and there was a limited amount. I reacquainted myself with the case—the beautiful art expert, the framing-hammer head wound apparently delivered with some amount of passion, the pawned bracelet.

Why did Bodine care? Did she simply feel sorry for Ramirez because he didn't have a snowflake's shot in hell of beating the charges? Or did the old woman know something?

I gave those questions five minutes of thought, then put it all in a folder for Ms. P to peruse later.

With that chore done, I turned back to the archives and to organized crime in the Coney Island area. The people in charge of enforcing the law hadn't come across my muggers. Maybe I'd have better luck with the folks who made a living breaking it.

I pulled as many files as I could find, planted myself in the wingback, pulled the string on the standing lamp, and got to reading.

Two hours later and I was ready to throw in the towel. It wasn't that there weren't clippings on crime in Coney, or about the fingers the mob had in this particular pie. There were plenty. The problem was, the criminals that got mentioned were the wrong sort. They were either the high-level gangsters who made headlines because they were the decision makers in the families. Or it was low-level guys who got scooped up doing this or that.

Kings and pawns. What I was looking for was a knight.

I needed someone who got around a bit, knew the neighborhood. Someone who had a wider view of goings-on around Coney Island, but wasn't so high up that he didn't know names and faces.

My eyes were sore and bleary from hours of scanning small print, and a little before midnight I called the search off. I put the files back where I found them, pulled the string on the lamp, and went downstairs to bed.

As I went about my evening ablutions, I tried to think. Who the hell did I know who'd have a finger on the pulse of the criminal scene in Coney?

I was midway through brushing my teeth when the answer came to me.

"Sub ud uh bith."

I wiped the foam off my chin and started making plans.

CHAPTER 21

The next day dawned and still no calls about Bodine, except those from the press. Which was well and good, since Saturday was our open house and we didn't have the time for it.

On Saturdays, anyone with a problem—specifically those who couldn't afford our usual fees—was free to "queue up and spill out their troubles," as Mrs. Campbell liked to say. If someone thought they had a dilemma that Lillian Pentecost was the solution to, they could show up and tell us their story. The line started moving at eleven a.m. and kept going from then until dinnertime, or when Ms. P hit her physical limit.

Sometimes we managed a ten-minute miracle, solving a pocket-size mystery before our guest could even get comfortable. Mostly, Ms. P dispensed advice, or in the case of legal difficulties, recommended law firms that took on indigent clients.

Around noon, I left my desk and went down to the basement, where a baker's dozen of women dressed in exercise clothes were waiting for me. The basement, like the archives, was one single, large space. Crates and boxes and assorted curiosities were piled around the edges, and one corner had been turned into a makeshift darkroom, but most of the center was taken up by a sprawl of old wrestling mats. There were also mats affixed to the wall to deaden the sound when I used the space as a target range.

For an hour every Saturday I gave whoever showed up a quick self-defense lesson, sharing some of the dirty tricks I'd picked up over the years. When I first started, I had maybe two or three regulars. Five years in, I had double-digit students, and sometimes that first number wasn't a one.

I told the women to warm up with some jumping jacks while I used the darkroom to change out of my suit and into athletic shorts and a ripped Brooklyn Dodgers sweatshirt.

"All right, ladies," I said when I came back out, "I've got a treat for you. It's a little move I picked up from a lady lion tamer. How'd you like to learn how to really spoil a rapist's day?"

Having been inspired by the scene my muggers had mocked up, I decided to demonstrate what to do if they were ever in that scenario for real—pinned to the ground by a man who was trying to take advantage.

I was in the middle of walking them through exactly how to snap the rapist's arms like a bundle of twigs when Mrs. Campbell called from the top of the stairs.

"Will! You're needed!"

I left the women to practice what I'd shown them and hurried up to the office. There I found my boss behind her desk and Clark Gimbal hunched in the seat of honor, briefcase in his lap. He looked startled when I walked in, then I realized I was still in my exercise attire.

"Sorry," I said. "We're pretty casual on Saturdays."

"Mr. Gimbal is delivering the documents we requested," Ms. Pentecost explained.

Gimbal coaxed an errant hair back into his comb-over.

"Yes, I . . . um . . . Considering recent events. Awful, awful, really. Vera dead. Murdered. It's . . . Well, I thought I should get these to you as soon as possible."

He popped open the briefcase and removed a few typed pieces of paper along with a bundle of letters.

"This is the tenant list," he said. "I believe it's up to date. I also have a list of phone complaints, as well as letters from tenants. It only goes back two years. I'm afraid the older ones have been discarded."

"That will have to do," Ms. P said. "Did Miss Bodine have any direct hand in the administration of the building? Did she ever see these letters?"

"No, no," Gimbal said. "I told the management company not to bother her with that. The only direct hand she had was in choosing who was allowed to rent an apartment and how much they were charged."

"Really?"

"Yes. I would call and read her the person's details—occupation, date of birth, and so forth—and she would say yes or no and suggest a monthly rent based on their circumstances."

"Did she turn many people down?" Ms. P asked.

"Oh, no," the lawyer said. "On the contrary, she very often said yes when I counseled otherwise. And the amounts she charged for rent were always too low by market standards. There was one gentleman—fresh off the boat, didn't even speak English. Very iffy proposition. She insisted we take him and charge him—oh, I don't remember the amount. It's in here somewhere. But it was far too little. Then there was the Negro family, of course. Bound to create trouble. But that was Vera. A soft heart."

"Yes," Ms. P said. "So I understand. Well, thank you very much, Mr. Gimbal."

That was Gimbal's cue to hand over the documents and scoot, but he seemed hesitant.

"So you are still investigating the case?" he asked. "I was wondering, since the police are involved now. I didn't know if Forest was still engaging you. Since . . . Well, he hired you to locate Vera and . . . unfortunately you have."

Usually, we don't comment on our clients. Not unless there's a warrant attached to the question. So I was surprised when Ms. Pentecost gave him a straight answer.

"It's true, Mr. Whitsun hired us to locate Miss Bodine and,

sadly, we have," she said. "We have yet to discuss what our involvement will be going forward. Mr. Whitsun has been somewhat distracted. Understandably so."

"Oh, yes, yes. Absolutely understandable," Gimbal said. "But . . . um . . . Well, since he has not explicitly hired you to investigate Vera's murder, I would like to do so. Hire you, I mean."

Ms. Pentecost cocked her head a few millimeters.

"By you, do you mean the firm of Boekbinder and Gimbal, or you personally?"

"Oh, myself. Personally, I mean. I can write you a check today. I assume you require a retainer."

He reached into his briefcase again and pulled out a checkbook and a pen, opening the former on top of the Baxter Arms documents.

"It's not that I lack faith in the police," he said as he fumbled the cap off the pen. "A fine institution. Made up of good, hardworking men."

The cap jumped out of his fingers and rolled across the floor. I played fetch for him.

"But being a—oh, thank you. Being a lawyer. Not criminal, mind you, but familiar with the course of such proceedings. I know how long these things can take. There was a break-in two doors down from me over a year ago. The police have yet to find the culprits. A year. It's really . . . I don't want Vera's death—her murder—to linger unsolved. I would like to . . . Well, to have it put to rest. The culprit found. As soon as possible. Now, for what amount should I make this?"

Ms. P studied him in silence for a few seconds before saying, "I'm very sorry, Mr. Gimbal. Until I speak with Mr. Whitsun, I'm still in his employ. At least as far as the matter of Miss Bodine is concerned. In the meantime, I could not in good conscience take money from you. As a rule, I try never to serve two masters."

He blinked twice, then very primly replaced everything in the briefcase and snapped it shut.

"Of course," he said. "Very sound. If Forest decides not to . . . um . . . not to keep you on the case, please let me know?"

"I will, sir."

"Excellent. Thank you."

Gimbal was up and halfway to the door before Ms. Pentecost said, "Mr. Gimbal? The documents?"

He stopped in his tracks.

"Oh, my goodness, yes. Of course." There was an ungraceful opening of the briefcase against his leg and an awkward fishing out of the papers. I stood and retrieved them, not trusting him to make the five steps back to Ms. P's desk without tripping over a loose thread.

"Again—thank you," he said. "And please call. I do want Vera's murder solved as swiftly as possible."

Once he was gone, Ms. Pentecost and I took a few minutes to debrief before returning to our Saturday duties.

"That was interesting," she said.

"Do you think he was trying to feel us out? See where the case is?"

"Perhaps. However, if he were, I would think he'd ask more pointed questions," she noted. "He seemed very uncomfortable being here."

A statement, but the question mark was implied.

"Maybe he's hiding something," I said. "Could be that's why he wants in on the Bodine case. Figures if he's writing the checks, we won't look at him as a suspect. Not that he is one. Or that anyone is definitively writing the checks at the moment."

I added, "It could also be that this is the first time he's taken the initiative in a dog's age and he has to relearn how to walk without Boekbinder holding his hand. What do you think?"

She took a deep breath and looked to the office door, behind which was a still-considerable queue.

"I think that, on the face of it, Mr. Gimbal is simply concerned that Vera Bodine's murder be solved as swiftly as possible. If anything lies beneath that face, we can't yet say."

That was a lot of syllables to state the obvious, but rationing had eased up, so she had them to spare.

I hopped back downstairs to finish my class on masher mashing, and Ms. P got the line moving again. That Saturday she took it all the way to the bell, and I ushered the last of our visitors out at 5:08.

By the time I stepped back into the office, my boss was already flipping through the letters Gimbal had dropped off along with the tenant list.

I grabbed the list and immediately made a second copy. I like to memorize names, and typing them out is the quickest way to do so.

#101   Gene Watson (DOB: 5/13/1921)
Occupation: naval officer
Martha Watson (DOB: 12/4/1919)
Occupation: homemaker
Children:
Cody Watson (DOB: 4/30/1939)
Sarah Jane (DOB: 3/9/1947)
Move-in date: 2/1/1947
Rent: $45 p/month

#102   Diane Murphy (DOB: 11/20/1890)
Occupation: none; widow with pension
Move-in date: 6/1/1947
Rent: $38 p/month

#201   Rodney Camper (DOB: 7/11/1909)
Occupation: train repairman
Rhoda Camper (DOB: 2/22/1912)

Occupation: homemaker
Move-in date: 7/1/1941
Rent: $45 p/month

#203   Erasmus Grady (DOB: 9/29/1901)
Occupation: police officer
Move-in date: 1/1/1946
Rent: $38 p/month

#301   Andnej Wocjik (DOB: 6/14/1868)
Occupation: tailor
Move-in date: 3/1/1944
Rent: $25 p/month

#302   Daniel Snejbjerg (DOB: 6/21/1913)
Occupation: bus driver
Move-in date: 9/1/1938
Rent: $60 p/month

#303   Delbert Johnson (DOB: 9/30/1899)
Occupation: carpenter; theatrical-set construction
Barbara Johnson (DOB: 4/12/1901)
Occupation: shop clerk
Children:
Joseph Johnson (DOB: 2/7/1929)
Move-in date: 11/2/1940
Rent: $40 p/month

"Erasmus. I wonder if the boys at the precinct house know that."

"What was that?" Ms. P asked from behind the letter she was reading.

"Oh, nothing. Just thinking how much I like Willowjean."

I grabbed the list of phoned-in complaints and half the stack of letters and began reading. Once I was finished and

Ms. Pentecost had caught up, we switched. There weren't all that many, and the process took us under an hour.

The complaints fell into only a few categories: the plumbing; the electrics; the rats; and various interpersonal issues with other residents, some more serious than others.

It seemed that the Baxter Arms was starting to come apart at the seams. There were three times as many complaints sent that past summer than in all of 1946. The pipes in individual apartments were constantly springing leaks, and the hot-water heater in the basement had failed twice.

Electrical outlets needed to be replaced, and hallway lights had decided to go on strike. Mr. Wocjik—who either could write English better than he could speak it or knew someone who could—had nearly taken a fatal tumble because all the lights had gone out in the stairwell.

Then there were Commander Cody's archnemeses, the rats.

They'd shown up around the Fourth of July and had been seen scurrying in the halls and squeezing under doors.

Which segues nicely into the personal-complaint portion of our program. At least two people—Del Johnson and Gene Watson—suggested the blame for the vermin should be laid at the feet of Vera Bodine.

Cody's father did more than suggest.

"You have somebody hoarding garbage, of course you're going to get vermin. The woman should be evicted."

Did Vera know about these complaints? I wondered. Gimbal said the management company handled everything, but might something have been said? To her face, maybe?

Also, how did Watson know Bodine was a hoarder? Was it common knowledge, or had he been inside Vera's apartment? The sheet listed him as a naval officer. I assumed aviator. His wife said he worked for the War Department.

Doing what? I wondered. Hunting Nazis? Was there any connection there with Faraday and the FBI?

I shoved those ideas to the side. I was trying to connect dots that might only be dust.

Despite Vera's getting blamed for the rat problem, she did not win the prize for least popular neighbor. Multiple letters had been sent complaining of Snejbjerg the bus driver, playing loud music, smoking foul cigars with his door open, and coming in at all hours making a ruckus.

The Johnsons had also sent a letter regarding a more serious complaint. At the end of July, somebody had slipped a typewritten note under their door. Del quoted it verbatim in his letter.

Some anonymous neighbor didn't like sharing an address with the Negro couple and strongly suggested they move before something unpleasant happened to their son. The anonymous writer specified the unpleasantness, but I'll refrain, thank you very much.

This must have been what Del meant when he said people weren't as friendly anymore.

He and Barb suspected Snejbjerg. He'd been surly to them when they first moved in, and had complained a number of times about their son running in the halls when he was younger. They'd thought things had calmed down, but the note suggested otherwise.

"Well, that's a whole lot of nothing," I said when we were finished. "I mean, there's plenty. But not much in terms of our murder investigation. Assuming we're investigating."

Ms. P didn't immediately answer. She was too preoccupied with putting the letters back in chronological order.

"I guess Cody's dad could have murdered Bodine because he blamed her for the rats. But leaving a corpse in a chest doesn't actually help with that, does it? Maybe it has something to do with the threat against the Johnsons. If it was Snejbjerg, I mean. Gimbal says he didn't bother Bodine with the complaints, but maybe she heard about it anyway. Inserted herself into the problem somehow. Is it a coincidence that Snejbjerg's rent is higher than anyone else's? Or is that Bodine's way of punishing him? Could he have found out she was his landlord? He's been there since before she bought the joint, so he's had the longest to figure it out. But I don't know. There's a lot of missing steps between anything in these complaints and Bodine's death. Or am I missing something?"

Ms. P looked up. "What was that? Missing what?"

Ah, I thought. My boss's brain had clocked out. Not an uncommon occurrence on Saturdays. Spend seven hours running a mental marathon and you'd be ready for a drink and a nap, too.

"I'm assuming we are done for the evening?" I asked.

"I think so, yes."

"Then I think I'll go out," I said. "Maybe catch a movie. Swing by the Famous Door and see who's playing."

"Have a lovely evening," Ms. P said, heading for the drinks trolley.

I told her I planned to, fetched my hat, grabbed the car keys, and headed out. Not to the movies, and certainly not dancing.

I had to go to Coney Island to interrogate an old friend.

CHAPTER 22

Actually, my destination wasn't quite Coney Island, but close enough that you could claim it. If you asked the rest of the city to be real quiet you could hear the rides going at Luna Park.

It was half of a shotgun-style house. The barrels had been split down the middle by a landlord looking to get double the rent for the same amount of work.

I'd seen uglier places, though. In the right light, it even looked picturesque.

The postage-stamp yard was surrounded by an honest-to-goodness picket fence. The fence was more gray than white, but it was the thought that counted.

As I pulled up, the door opened and a woman stepped out. She was dabbing tears off her cheeks with a handkerchief, but was managing to smile at the same time.

I let her get half a block, then got out of the car and walked up to the door. There was a small, neatly hand-painted sign secured above the mail slot.

MAEVE BAILEY, SPIRITUAL ADVISER

I had my hand up to knock when a voice called from inside. "Come on in, Will!"

I did.

I passed through a cozy sitting room and through a doorway blocked by a set of beaded curtains. Those are always fussy, but I managed to slip through without getting too many caught in my curls.

On the other side I found a trio of armchairs arranged in a circle. No windows, no paintings, a couple bookshelves, and a potted palm that I'm pretty sure was rubber. Most of the room's illumination came from a single pendant light hanging from a chain in the middle of the ceiling. Its frosted globe gave everything a faint, otherworldly softness.

That included the woman sitting in what was surely the comfiest of the three chairs. She looked decidedly different from the last time I'd seen her, standing on the edge of a circus lot watching the tents come down.

She had the same delicate features, the same henna-wash hair. She'd picked up a few more wrinkles, but still looked closer to sixty than seventy.

It was the outfit. She'd traded in her flowing silks, the oversize spectacles, and the heaps of spangly jewelry for a basic A-line in a red-rose print and a pair of round specs with thin gold frames. She'd kept a few of the gaudier rings, though.

"I'm sorry," I said. "I was looking for the one and only Madame Fortuna, but I seem to have stumbled onto her respectable suburban sister."

"Oh, shove it where you love it," she growled.

"Maeve, it is you!"

"Yes, it's me. For fifty-nine years now, that's all I've ever been."

"Fifty-nine?"

She shrugged. "More or less. Now give me a hug."

I leaned over and gave her a squeeze, then sat down across from her. The chair was still a little warm from her last client.

"How'd you know it was me at the door?" I asked.

"You think my whole game is bullshit? I could always feel when you were close by. You've got a very powerful aura."

I might have bought that when I first met her, but I wasn't fifteen anymore and a line of bunk had to be a lot slicker than that for me to swallow.

"You saw me out the window?"

She stuck her tongue out at me.

"I was showing Mildred out. Saw you pull up. Nice ride, big-city detective."

"It's a company car."

"Who cares? It's the show that counts."

Maeve knew a thing or two about putting on a show. She had been one of the longest-serving employees of Hart & Halloway's Traveling Circus and Sideshow. She'd lured the rubes into her tent with promises of seeing the future or soliciting the spirits and sent them out with a little hope, or comfort, or permission to do what they had been planning to do in the first place.

For a reasonable price, of course.

When the circus finally folded its tents for good, Maeve had done as she'd promised—come back to New York City and set up shop. Though it wasn't quite what I expected.

"Spiritual adviser? What happened to mystic and medium and all that jazz?"

"If I were working the boardwalk, I'd go that route. Draw in the tourist crowd," Maeve explained. "But there's already at least two operators working that game. An Italian grandma doing the medium gig and this Armenian girl doing palm reading and tarot. Tits out to here. She sneezes hard and she's gonna get a citation for indecency. I can't compete with that. Besides, do you know what the rent is on a beachfront joint?"

Maeve went off on a tangent about real estate and the price of a cup of coffee, but eventually got around to explaining how she'd settled on a more residential neighborhood, and with that choice came the need to change up her act.

"These days I've got to rely on repeat customers," she said.

"That means putting on the kid gloves. Feed 'em bread crumbs, but still make it exciting enough that they tell their friends."

"Okay, but what are you actually giving them?" I asked. "Like with Mildred. You talk with her dead husband? Tell her a trip to Boca is in the future?"

The old fortune-teller shook her head. There was the tiniest of jingles. She still had her bells woven in there somewhere.

"With Mildred, there is a dead husband. She lost him in the war. But I don't chat with him. Kind of the opposite. Mildred needs to get over it, get on with living. I do this whole thing about me seeing this dark specter of grief with these tendrils that tie her down, keep her trapped and unhappy. Then we talk about what's managed to cheer her up. Like getting a letter from her niece in Ontario. So I tell her, 'That letter burned away one of those dark tendrils. You should write her back and tell her how happy it made you.' Really what I'm gunning for is to get Mildred to plan a trip to Ontario. Can't bring that up yet, though. It's too soon."

It resembled the technique of a so-called spiritualist Ms. Pentecost and I had come up against a while back, except she used her game to weasel out incriminating information on her clients. This was like the flip side of that coin. A con game on the side of the angels.

Maeve stood up, knees cracking like wet firewood.

"Jeezum crow, the symphony of old age. Follow me into the kitchen. I've got another client in twenty minutes and I want to squeeze in a bite. While I'm eating you can tell me what you need."

"Who said I needed anything?" I asked.

"Because you're here."

I followed her through another door—this one made of wood rather than beads. We passed through a modest bedroom to the kitchen at the back of the house.

It looked like every kitchen in every shotgun apartment

ever: icebox and oven on one side, kitchen table, sink, and the window over the sink on the other. Cramped but cozy.

"Maybe I came over for a visit," I suggested while she opened the icebox and pulled out a plate covered by a tea towel.

"You've had the better part of a year to visit," Maeve said, putting the plate on the narrow strip of counter between icebox and stove. "Now you're here on a Saturday evening? Either you've come courting, and you know you're not my type—too short—or you need a favor or you're looking for information. One of those."

A Madame Fortuna with the edges filed off was still pretty sharp.

"All right, you got me. I was wondering if— What the hell is that?"

She'd taken the towel off the plate to reveal a slab of veiny gray meat.

"Haven't you ever seen boiled beef tongue before?" she asked, taking a knife and slicing off a few thin portions. "One of my clients owns a butcher shop. He brings me goodies. It's not bad. You should try it sometime."

She tossed the slices into an iron skillet, then smothered them in paprika and black pepper, which made me skeptical about how not bad it was. When she was finished, she fired up the burner and very quickly the tiny kitchen was saturated with the smell of sizzling meat.

"So what do you need from old Maeve?" she said, taking a fork and poking at the tongue. "Don't know what I have that you'd be in the market for. I'm fresh off forty years on the road, after all. Still getting my city legs."

She'd put her back to me and was talking a lot, which meant she was nervous. She probably thought I was angling for old dirt from Hart & Halloway. It was a little satisfying to surprise her.

"I want to know who you're paying protection money to."

The fork paused mid-poke, then started skewering again.

"I don't know what you mean," Maeve said.

"Okay, I'm going to forgive you for that," I told her. "Not only was it a lie, but it was a terrible one. Of course you know what protection money means. Shoot—even Big Bob had to pay up whenever we spent more than two weeks in a large enough city. Otherwise we'd end up with flat tires and shredded tents. Like you said, you've been here almost a year. More than enough time for whoever's running the protection racket in Coney to hit you up. You're not on the boardwalk, but you're close enough. Being a spiritual adviser, you are, and I mean no disrespect, a soft target for the mob. So I'll ask again. Who do you pay up to? I don't mean who does the collecting. I don't want the muscle. I want the guy who made the original pitch."

At no point during this monologue did Maeve turn around. She just kept shifting and shuffling the tongue around on the pan. My nose was detecting the first hints of scorched meat.

"You might want to take that off the burner," I said. "You can keep your back to me while you do it, though."

She took the pan off and turned to face me.

"What are you asking about all this for? Is Lillian Pentecost going up against the mob now?"

"I don't think even my boss would take a bite that big," I said. "A woman got—well, she got mugged under the boardwalk by a coed team. They used what they got from her purse to scam her bank. I doubt they're connected to the mob, but I can't see them working the area long without the local honcho hearing about it."

If I wasn't telling Ms. P about my boardwalk misadventure, I certainly wasn't spilling it to Maeve.

She turned her attention back to her meal, finding bread and mustard and arranging the slices of tongue into a sandwich. While she constructed, she talked.

"I see where you're going. Hoping this guy can give you a name or two. But . . ." She paused to do some slathering.

"I don't know if you'll get anything out of—well, out of the guy you want me to name. He is not a pleasant character. You approach him with your usual amount of tact and he finds out that it was me that sicced you on him? I've made friends in the neighborhood, but none that would take a beating for me."

Sandwich constructed, she joined me at the kitchen table. She took a big bite, chewed, swallowed, and managed not to dribble tongue juice and mustard all over herself, which is better than I could have done.

Then she gave me a real friendly smile and said, "But we're a pair of smart dames. I bet if we put our heads together, we could figure out a way to track down this pair without having to ask any wiseguys for help."

That smile and calling me a smart dame. If she hadn't been trying so hard, I might have gone right along with her. But I knew Maeve, and I knew her tics and her traps.

All that talk about being afraid for herself might have been true to an extent, but I also knew it was cover. She wasn't protecting herself, she was protecting me. Or at least she thought she was.

I used to think Maeve was the sharpest operator in the business. But in my years working with Ms. Pentecost, I'd come across sharper. With distance I'd come to see that Maeve's idea of protection usually boiled down to "Keep your head down and your mouth shut."

When you're talking about a traveling circus—two hundred pretty strange people moving from town to town—that's usually good advice. Except when it's not.

Like that time a mutual friend was murdered. The one I had a still-itching tattoo in remembrance of.

I was pretty sure Maeve fibbed right to my face during that case. If she really did lie, then that little omission got me almost killed three times. Four, if you count the firebomb, which I do.

Even though she was right that we could probably conjure up another plan, it would take time, and that was in short supply. Who knew when this pair might try for another bite at the bank-con apple?

Then there was my stolen Beretta. I'd seen enough plays to know what Chekhov said about guns. Eventually, it was going to go off.

I had to force Maeve to do the hard thing. Which wasn't easy.

"Look, Maeve," I started, "I know you don't like opening your mouth when you don't need to. Especially when it involves introducing friends to trouble. But I'm a big girl and I can take care of myself. This time around, don't you think it's easier if you just tell me the name?"

Maeve had a poker face like nobody I knew, but on "this time around" I saw it. Something at the corner of her mouth whispered that I was right. She had lied when Ruby was murdered.

I also saw that I had won.

She put her sandwich down and slid the plate away from her, no longer in the mood for eating.

"All right, kid. You want this, you've got it."

She told me a name: Donny Russo. Then she went on to explain why I should stay clear of him. When she was finished, I couldn't disagree. Anyone with a lick of sense wouldn't go within ten blocks of Russo.

Unfortunately, we're talking about me. Me and sense were occasional pen pals at best. By the time I said goodbye to Maeve, I was already making plans to meet the man.

CHAPTER 23

The planning continued on the drive home.

Donny Russo was mob middle management, but he liked to think of himself as an enforcer. And he liked knives. Maeve passed on some details that were gruesomely banal enough to be true.

The Westchester cops had an open warrant on him for assault. Apparently he'd walked into some bar upstate and gotten handsy with a waitress, and when somebody objected, he'd relieved the good Samaritan of two of his fingers.

A real charmer.

Maeve also said he seemed to have the protection business in Coney locked down tight. He might be a sadist, but he was a competent one.

Good.

That meant he was the sort who would notice if anyone started working the territory his bosses had put him in charge of. He'd notice and he'd take names.

The bad news was that approaching him would be like reaching out to pet a junkyard dog. And I had a fondness for all my fingers.

By the time I was walking up to the front steps of the brownstone, I'd come up with three possible plans and discarded each for various reasons. I was so wrapped up in my thoughts that I didn't see the figure jump out of the car across the street until it started dashing across the avenue toward me.

My gun was halfway out of its holster before I recognized who it was.

"Jesus Christ, Whitsun. Running out at a woman in the dark like that is a good way to get killed. What are you playing at?"

To his credit, he looked properly abashed. He also looked mildly sharper than he had last time I saw him. His suit was freshly pressed and his five o'clock shadow was only a couple hours old.

"Sorry, Parker. I've been sitting over there for a good half hour trying to decide whether to knock or walk away."

"Well, I've got a key, so let me present you with a third option."

I opened the door and yelled.

"I'm back! I've brought company!"

The shouting wasn't necessary. Dinner was done and Ms. P was back at her desk with her pair of books. She didn't seem surprised by our guest. Quite the contrary.

"Mr. Whitsun. Please have a seat. I was wondering how long it would take you."

"Take me?" he asked, settling into the usual client chair. "Take me to what?"

"To decide to hire us to investigate Miss Bodine's murder."

I sat down at my own desk. There was a freshly typed sheet of paper lying facedown on it, and my chair had been adjusted. I was guessing for someone about seven inches taller than me. I used two fingers to lift a corner of the paper and started reading. Meanwhile, Whitsun was trying to drum up some bluster.

"I think you're getting a little ahead of yourself," he said. "Firstly, I never said that's why I'm here. Secondly—"

"Mr. Whitsun, please let's skip the posturing. It's been a

very long day. Usually, I would have abandoned my desk hours ago. But I suspected that I might be hearing from you."

Whitsun didn't look like he was buying it. I wouldn't have, either, except I'd read the paper on my desk.

"All right, let's put aside the fact that I wasn't sure myself that I was going to walk in here until two minutes ago," Whitsun said. "The fact is I've been on the fence. Still am, if I'm being honest."

"Honesty, I'm told, is a virtue," Ms. P said. "Miss Bodine was your friend. You chafe at handing over the responsibility of investigating her death to anyone else."

"Exactly. I might not be the so-called greatest detective in New York City, but I'm no slouch."

"You are certainly not. However, the fact that you are sitting here means that you have come to the obvious conclusion. That you simply won't have the time to investigate Vera Bodine's murder."

"What are you talking about?"

The way Whitsun asked the question made me think he already knew the answer. Which was irritating, because I certainly didn't. Fortunately, Ms. P explained.

"After your—what was the word you used, Will? Tantrum? After your tantrum with the police, you spent some time considering your next moves. Where could you best direct your energies. It would have occurred to you rather quickly that the Fennel case is the one thread you are most capable of following. You've met with Mr. Ramirez?"

Whitsun, who for once was speechless, could only nod.

"You offered to represent him."

No question mark on the end of that sentence.

"How did you know all that?" Whitsun asked when he got his tongue working again.

Ms. P shrugged. "Because I'm very good at my job. Will? The contract."

I took the sheet of paper off my desk and handed it to Whitsun.

"That is our standard contract, with a few minor modifications," she explained. "Will, I hope you don't mind. I availed myself of your typewriter."

"Not at all," I said. "I put a fresh ribbon in yesterday."

We gave Whitsun time to read. The contract did the usual job of establishing an amount for our retainer—we were not giving Whitsun the family discount—as well as including a few bespoke provisions.

Namely, Whitsun would be informed daily by telephone of our progress. He would not, under any circumstance, try to horn in on the investigation.

Ms. P used much more elegant terms, but that was the gist. If Whitsun tried to play backseat detective again, we could dump him and his case and keep the retainer.

Considering his usual disposition, I expected Whitsun to haggle, but he reached over and grabbed a pen off Ms. P's desk.

"Maybe the stories about you aren't exaggerated, Pentecost," he muttered as he signed.

Then he pulled out a checkbook and wrote out the retainer. It wasn't so big that it required a comma, but it was close. He signed that without a quibble as well, then passed both contract and check to me.

"All right," he said. "That's that. Now what?"

Later that night, I would ask Ms. P how she pulled off her little bit of psychic prestidigitation. Turns out she and Maeve shared a bag of tricks.

"I saw Mr. Whitsun loitering in his car across the street. It was clear he was on the cusp of a decision," she explained. "It could only be whether or not to hire us to investigate his friend's murder. This likely meant that he knew his time and energy would be taken up elsewhere. Helping Mr. Ramirez could be interpreted as Miss Bodine's last request to him. He feels guilty about her death and the condition of her life before it, so he could hardly deny her. But to confirm, I called Rikers and identified myself as a secretary from the district attorney's office. I told them I needed to arrange an interview with Mr. Ramirez for Monday. I was informed that he now has private counsel. That was when I started typing the contract."

Remember when I said I'd met operators a lot slicker than Madame Fortuna? This is what I was talking about.

But that explanation was in the future. At that moment, we had our client and our case and the question before us: Now what?

"Now, Mr. Whitsun, you tell us about your meeting with Mr. Ramirez."

He opened his mouth, then snapped it shut.

"I can't do that," he said. "He's my client now. Everything he tells me is confidential."

"Oh, come on, Whitsun!" I exclaimed. "Stop picking nits."

"They're called ethics, Parker. Despite what some people believe, I happen to have them."

Ms. P looked about as frustrated as I was, but managed to keep it polite.

"I understand your dilemma," she said. "However, one of our obvious inquiries will be why Miss Bodine was interested in this case. That will mean investigating it. As we will be doing so as contracted representatives of you, any investigation into the Fennel case will be at your behest. You would be entitled to what information we uncover. I believe that makes your sharing information with us to be legally and ethically sound."

There was a little bit of haggling here, including some penciled-in revisions to the contract. At one point, Whitsun asked, "What happens if you find out my client is guilty? What happens then?"

"Then," Ms. P said, "we renegotiate."

With all the goddamn lawyering out of the way, Whitsun finally started talking.

"I wish I had more to give you," he said. "The papers got the story right for once. Why wouldn't they? Ramirez has been telling it to anyone who'll listen. He was hired by Julia Fennel to enlarge her closet. Which he did from July thirtieth to August first. He was supposed to finish up the next morning. Put up some trim, install some clothing rods. But when he showed up, she told him not to bother. She didn't want him to complete the job. He explained that it would only take about two hours, but she held firm. Said she wanted him gone. When he asked for his payment, she told him she didn't have cash and gave him the bracelet instead. Told him that should get him enough. He figured it for costume jewelry. They argued. She told him to take it or leave it. He took it. That was Saturday. On Monday, he went to Three-Ring Pawn and got a hundred and fifty bucks for it. Which, incidentally, is about a grand less than it's worth. If you read the papers, you know the rest."

The rest was not good for Ramirez.

First, there were the neighbors who heard him and Julia arguing over his fee. According to them, she practically screamed at him to get out.

Second, there was the framing hammer that had been used to kill her. It had been wiped clean of prints, but Ramirez was kind enough to identify it as his own. He said he left it behind in the rush when Fennel showed him the door.

Why wipe off the prints if he was going to botch everything else? you ask. Good question, and could be counted as a point in Ramirez's favor. But I'd seen murderers do less logical things when their blood was up, and so had the cops.

Third, there was the money. A wad of cash stashed under a false bottom in Fennel's nightstand. Only a hundred or so—pin money, probably—but that meant there was no reason for her to barter using her jewelry. She could have paid Ramirez outright.

All of this was why no private attorney was clamoring to represent Ramirez. No attorney until Whitsun.

"No offense, but this case looks like dogshit," I told him.

He sighed and sank deeper into his chair.

"The worst thing is, I bought the guy's story. I've met more than my share of crooks and I don't think he's lying."

"Are there any other suspects?" Ms. Pentecost asked. "A lover of Miss Fennel, perhaps?"

Whitsun shook his head. "God, I wish. I'd kill for a jealous boyfriend. I chatted with some of her colleagues at the Museum of Modern Art. As far as they know, she was unattached. Had been since she started working there seven years ago. Came to events alone. Never talked about boyfriends. Had offers from men, but turned them all down. One of the other assistants confided that she thought Fennel might be seeing somebody but was hiding it because . . ."

The defense attorney looked at me and blushed.

"Well, because she was—she might be having a relationship with a woman," he said. "That's apparently not unheard of in the art world."

That was interesting. I knew he'd dived into Ms. Pentecost's biography during the Sendak trial. I guess he dived into mine as well. Deep enough to discover who I like to two-step with.

"I assume you pressed Mr. Ramirez about any connection he might have had with Miss Bodine," Ms. P asked.

"At length," Whitsun said. "He's never heard of Vera. Never did any work at the Baxter Arms. I came at it from a bunch of different angles, and as far as I can tell there is not a single thing connecting them."

I waited for Ms. P to ask the next question, but she had her eyes closed. Considering it was the tail end of a long day, it was a coin flip as to whether she was deep in thought or nodding off. I took up the slack.

"You talked with the cops yet?"

Whitsun's lips curled into something close to a smirk. It wouldn't have looked good on Perry Mason and it didn't look good on him.

"They want to talk, they can get a warrant."

"What do you have against cops?"

"Well, let me see. They beat confessions out of suspects, especially innocent ones. They slow-march my clients through booking. They falsify evidence. They lie on the stand." Whitsun ticked off each item on his fingers. "Oh, and this is in addition to treating every defense attorney like scum."

"You think playing hardball is going to make them like you any better?" I asked.

"I think if I showed up on their doorstep on my knees, ready to answer whatever they wanted to ask, at the end of the day I'd still be scum," Whitsun declared. "I'm the one who puts them on the stand and shows a jury the thousand mistakes they made between the cuffs and the courthouse. I shine a light through the cracks in the system."

That sounded a little grandiose, but I couldn't argue with it. Couldn't argue and didn't want to.

The Swiss clock began chiming. After nine chimes, Whitsun looked at his watch for confirmation. He could have saved the trouble. We had an actual Swiss clockmaker in once a year to grease the cogs and make sure the minute hand wasn't dragging.

"I should go," he said. "I want to hit the ground running on Ramirez's defense. Including scheduling another bail hearing. His story may be dogshit, but without fingerprints on the murder weapon or eyewitnesses or blood on his clothes, I might be able to get him bail. If anything, I'm going to make the DA work for it."

Ms. P managed to rouse herself to stand and shake hands.

"We'll be in touch," she told him.

"Oh, I know," he said. "Once a day, or so says the contract. You'll notice that I'm not asking what your next steps are. Or how you're going to follow up on Vera's work with the FBI. I'm trusting you to do your job."

All that little speech got from Ms. P was a single nod. He didn't even get that much from me. But I was polite enough to walk him out.

"Whitsun might not have asked what's next, but I'd sure like to know," I said when I came back into the office. "My personal preference is to go back to Faraday. See if we can get any more on his supposed secret Nazi. I'm assuming that's why we kept Bodine's FBI work from the police. So we can use it to leverage Faraday if we need to."

Ms. P's lip twitched, which was as close to confirmation as I was going to get. She extended her arm, holding her hand outstretched in front of her. She'd been doing that more often. Gauging the symptoms. Like checking the gas in her tank.

Her hand was trembling, but only a little.

Satisfied, she retracted her hand and looked back to the clock.

"Our dilemma, such as it is, is that we have several avenues to pursue, but we are lacking some of the basic facts of the case."

I saw where her mind was heading and understood why she'd looked at the clock.

"The stars are out," I said. "I think that means Shabbat is over."

She nodded.

"Please call Hiram and arrange a meeting."

CHAPTER 24

Usually our chats with Hiram were held over a corpse, him being employed by the office of the medical examiner and our handy expert on all things dead.

This time it was held over poached eggs and toast.

That was what Mrs. Campbell served up for breakfast Sunday morning, along with half a dozen choices of jams and a carafe of coffee that looked sized to caffeinate the 101st Airborne.

As a rule, Sunday was our day off, Mrs. Campbell's included. Not because we held to the Christian Sabbath, but because if we didn't label a day as Do-Not-Touch, both Ms. P and I were likely to keep going until our respective batteries ran out.

All that's to say that, when it came to Sundays, we were expected to catch as catch can as far as grub was concerned. But when Mrs. Campbell heard Hiram was coming over, she refused to let us be in charge of feeding him.

"I won't have you serving Mr. Levy yellow rubber and burnt crumbs," she told us. "Not out of my kitchen."

So she adjusted her schedule, did the poaching and toasting and plating, and then ran off to make the rounds of the various organizations she volunteered for.

While Ms. P and I are known to talk shop between bites,

we put business on hold until we were down to the last of the toast and coffee.

It gave me time to get over the novelty of seeing Hiram in such a different environment: in daylight; not surrounded by white tile and stainless steel and dead bodies; and in a dark suit and tie rather than a white coat.

His height hadn't changed. He was still a smidge shorter than me. His beard was still tightly trimmed, his hands still delicate, nails clipped to the quick. His eyes were still small, dark, and piercing.

But sitting at our dining table, smearing marmalade on a corner of toast, he seemed spectacularly normal.

We passed the time with pleasantries. The health of his children and wife; the Dodgers' chances of going the distance; and how our mutual friend Sam Lee Butcher was faring in his role as orderly and unofficial student.

"I am trying to persuade him to become an actual student, specifically in the medical program at Howard University," Hiram explained. "I believe that not only would he gain entrance if he applied, but he would be able to do so on scholarship. However . . ."

"He needs convincing?" Ms. P asked, guiding a forkful of eggs mouthward.

"Having never graduated from high school, and having experienced such a . . . transient youth, he believes a university education beyond him. I've explained there are exams he can take. That his swift understanding of what I've taught him of anatomy and pathology suggest they would prove little challenge if he applied himself."

"His response?"

"Dubious."

I didn't know every chapter in Sam Lee's biography, but I knew enough to understand why he might be gun-shy about making any big changes. Like me, he'd spent his formative years working roustabout for a traveling circus. And, like me, he'd tripped face-first into good fortune and gotten a plum gig assisting a brilliant eccentric. He probably considered himself supremely lucky to have gotten the cards he was dealt and decided to stand pat.

My boss didn't see that, though.

"Ridiculous," she said. "The young man has an exceptional mind. Combined with his boundless energy and curiosity, he will likely thrive in any atmosphere where he is regularly challenged. If he continues to remain unconvinced, let me know. I'll have a word."

"I have hope that I will break through to him," Hiram said. "However, if I fail, I would appreciate it, Will, if *you* would speak to him."

"You think I'd be more convincing than the font of all wisdom here?" I asked.

"I think Samuel respects you. Even idolizes you. What you say to him as regards his own self-worth and self-interest matter deeply."

The notion that my words could make that sort of impact was intimidating. Frightening, even. I didn't want to have that kind of influence on anybody. I didn't say that, though.

"Sure," I told Hiram. "I'd be happy to have a chat with him. If he needs it."

I hoped that he wouldn't.

With the small talk and eggs and most of the toast gotten out of the way, conversation turned, as it is wont to do at the breakfast table, to the rate of decay of the human body.

"There are certain constants about a body's transformation after death," Hiram began. "Milestones that we can count on. You know, of course, about rigor mortis. It begins appearing approximately two hours after death, progresses throughout the body over the course of the next six or eight, lasts for another twelve or so, and eventually disappears. If the body is found quickly, this can help us estimate a time of death. However . . ."

He popped a corner of toast smeared with marmalade in his mouth, chewed, and washed it down with some coffee.

"However, when the body is not found quickly, it becomes much more difficult."

"This is the case with Miss Bodine?" Ms. P asked.

"It is. Though I have not had the pleasure of meeting her in person, I have kept my ears open, as you requested."

That was news to me. I looked at my boss.

"As you requested? When did you do that?"

"Immediately after you called informing me you'd found her body."

You can never accuse Lillian Pentecost of dragging her feet.

"As I was saying," Hiram continued, "I did not work on Miss Bodine personally. But I did consult some. I was able to make a few suggestions that cleared up questions the examiner had regarding the body."

"Questions about time of death?" I asked.

He tilted his head from side to side.

"Somewhat about the time. More about the curious circumstances following her death."

"Curious?"

"Yes. Regarding the milestones of human decomposition. Once rigor has dissipated, these markers are spread farther and farther apart. Over the next few days, the body begins to turn green, to bloat, and to leak from the mouth, nostrils, etcetera. This pressure can cause blistering and skin slippage. The abdomen may burst. If unabated, this process of active decay will continue for weeks as the body's tissues fully liquefy."

He slurped the last of his coffee and reached for the carafe.

"This is, of course, the most general of descriptions of decomposition," he explained. "Many factors can speed or impede the rate of decay."

"Factors such as the body being stored in a wooden chest?" I asked.

"Yes," Hiram confirmed. "The chest was dry—at least before the body was inserted into it. It was relatively airtight. All of this could have affected the decomposition process."

We were both waiting for Hiram to present some hard numbers, and apparently he could sense it.

"As I understand it, Miss Bodine was last seen alive approximately two weeks prior to her body being found. Is this correct?"

"That's the last eyewitness account," I said. "Not counting our earwitness, who I'm guessing was mistaken, considering the state of the body."

"Earwitness?"

"Her downstairs neighbor says that he heard Bodine moving around as late as last Sunday. That's three days before I found the body, in case you're counting."

Hiram frowned, and his fingers did a sort of pinch and pull with his beard.

"It's likely that Miss Bodine was dead the full two weeks, or nearly so. However, your earwitness—that's a very awkward word—might not have been mistaken."

I raised a finger.

"Hang on. Are you about to tell me that *Valley of the Zombies* was a documentary? That the dead can walk?"

"They can't walk, but they do occasionally get moved about," he said. "One of the things I was consulted about was postmortem lividity found on her stomach and breasts. Again, I did not see the body in person, but I was shown photographs. After a few suggestions made by me, it was determined that Miss Bodine had been lying dead on her stomach for several days before being moved to the trunk."

There was a five-count while I tried to squeeze that information into what we had so far.

"Okay, so hang on. Our killer whacks Bodine. Speaking of whacks, was that dent on her head the cause of death?"

Hiram nodded and reached for the last piece of toast.

"Yes. A single heavy blow from— Oh, does anyone else want this? No?" He took a bite and continued, somehow managing not to sputter crumbs while he did so. "The blow was from a rather heavy, dense object, I think. With a curved edge."

I tried to recall if I'd seen anything fitting the description at Bodine's but couldn't remember for all the clutter.

"Okay, so the killer whacks Bodine. Then what? Hangs around for two, three, five days. Then, when the smell starts to get bad, he shoves her in a trunk and fills it with lavender? It doesn't make any sense."

Hiram shrugged.

"As I regularly remind Lillian, I can speak to the what and the how. I cannot speak to the why."

Right. The why was our job. In importance it fell only slightly behind the who. I was pondering the motivations of our hypothetical murderer when something dawned on me.

"We've got two women now—Bodine and Fennel—who were both clubbed to death," I said. "Is that a coincidence?"

I'd directed the question at Ms. P, but Hiram fielded it.

"Julia Fennel? Again, she wasn't one of mine, but I assisted in the early stages," he said. "There was quite a bit more energy behind that attack. Multiple blows delivered . . . Well, you know I don't like to speculate on motivation, but it certainly seemed like something fueled by strong emotion. Vera Bodine, however, was felled by a single, clean blow."

He added, "Bludgeoning is one of the most common methods of murder."

That made sense. Not everyone habitually carried a knife or a gun. But just about anybody could pick up a hammer.

There were other questions, some from me, some from my boss.

Ms. P wondered what Vera Bodine weighed in at. The answer was barely a hundred pounds, which meant that anyone of moderate strength could have gotten her tucked away in the chest.

I asked if he'd heard any whispers from the police about how the excavation of Bodine's apartment was going. The collection of fingerprints and whatnot.

It was far outside an assistant medical examiner's remit, but Hiram liked to keep his ears open. This time, though, we were out of luck.

"The police, of late, are more hesitant to share details of their cases," he said. "I'm not sure if this is in general or specific to me. I'm sure it has not gone unnoticed by you that at no time over the last six months have I been assigned to a victim connected to a case that you were known to be working on."

It certainly hadn't gone unnoticed by me. There were a lot of murders in New York City, after all, and more than a few people slinging a scalpel for the medical examiner's office. A less suspicious sort could chalk it up to six months of bad dice rolls.

But we were the suspicious sort. It said so on our business cards.

"You think our relationship has become known by your superiors?" Ms. P posited.

"I think our relationship has always been known," Hiram corrected. "I think someone, somewhere, has decided to care."

That was concerning. Not only for us, but for Hiram. He wasn't exactly well liked among his colleagues. Partly because he preferred challah over hot dogs, but mostly because he was smarter than any two of his co-workers combined.

His job security came from nobody wanting to take his place on the night shift and from his willingness to work for two-thirds the pay of his peers. That last detail was why, after our questions had run dry and our goodbyes had been said, I handed him an envelope of greenbacks on his way out the door.

"Give our best to the wife and kids," I said as he tucked the envelope discreetly away in his coat pocket.

"To the kids, yes. To my wife, perhaps not."

"I don't know why she doesn't like us so much. We're very pleasant people once you get to know us."

"While she has resigned herself to my work with the dead, she does not like that you ask me to think so deeply about murder and murderers," he revealed. "She thinks you're a bad influence."

"Well . . . she has us there," I admitted. "Still, you can't tell me you don't enjoy it."

He smiled. Not the usual Hiram smile, but a big whopping grin.

"Will," he said, "it is simply the very best part of my day."

CHAPTER 25

With Hiram gone, I went right to my desk and added his fee to our expense report under "professional consultation." The eggs and toast I threw in for free. While I was doing that, Ms. P took her seat behind her own desk.

"That was illuminating," she said.

"If you consider *illuminating* a synonym for *confusing*," I replied, dotting the last *i*. "Why kill Bodine and then, however many days later, come back and shove her in the hope chest? I say come back, though I guess it's possible they camped out. In either case, killers usually don't like to spend so much time around their victims. At least not the sane ones. Please don't tell me we've got a kook. I don't know if I have the constitution for another nut."

Usually Ms. P will chastise me for using words like *kook* and *nut,* but this time she let me have it.

"No," she said. "There are rational reasons for our killer to spend an extended amount of time in Miss Bodine's apartment."

Ms. P knew I preferred to get to an answer on my own, so she gave me time while I pointed my brain at the question. You kill someone and stick around, or keep coming back, for days—weeks, even. Why? Someone might linger for five or ten minutes, maybe as long as an hour, if they were—

"He was looking for something!" I blurted. "Because

Bodine's apartment is what it is, the hunt took him days. So long that, eventually he—or maybe she, because Bodine was light prey—had to move the body because it started to get rank."

Ms. P nodded. "That is the most logical conclusion. At least with the evidence at hand. The question now becomes—"

"What was the killer looking for and did they find it?" I finished.

"If Mr. Wocjik was right, someone was in her apartment as late as Sunday. It suggests the search, if that's what it was, was ongoing."

"That's interesting," I said. "But they didn't come back Monday, because if they did, they would have run into Whitsun. So did they find something Sunday, or did they get to the door, hear Whitsun moving around, and scram? Also—does this move her neighbors up the list of suspects? Because we asked them if they'd seen any strangers about and got noes across the board."

All good questions and worth pursuing. But the big one now was what did a retired secretary, a shut-in hoarder, a woman who lived in a cage of her own making, have that was worth killing for?

"Perhaps it's time to take a closer look at your souvenir," Ms. P said.

"Souvenir" was our personal code for evidence that fell into my pockets at crime scenes. In this case, the clipping that had been soaked in our victim's internals.

It was so wet it was on the cusp of disintegration. I'd placed it in a safe spot near, but not too near, the furnace in the basement. There it had been slowly drying for several days.

"You think that's what the killer was after?" I asked. "Wouldn't he have frisked her pockets right off? That's the first thing I'd do."

Ms. P shrugged. "Murderers are not always thinking clearly. Now, is the paper ready?"

"I checked it this morning. I was afraid to touch it, but it looks pretty dry. It's still a black and gray nothing. I'm only assuming it's from a newspaper considering the sheer quantity of them Bodine had stacked around."

"Good," she said.

"Good?"

"Then my little experiment is unlikely to make it worse."

Her "little experiment" was something she'd been raring to try ever since she heard about it in some running correspondence she was having with a chemist in the U.K. Supposedly this genius had come up with a chemical solution that could dissolve organic matter while leaving inorganic matter relatively unharmed.

I was skeptical. So was Ms. P, but she was also willing to give it a go.

"You sure you don't want any help with this?" I asked as I walked with her down to the basement.

"It's dipping a piece of paper in and out of alternating solutions. I believe I can manage."

I took her at her word and set her up in the darkroom. I'd cleaned the developing trays to get rid of any dried traces of photographic compounds and laid out the bottles of chemicals I'd purchased at her direction.

I took a pair of tongs from the darkroom and used them to recover the newspaper clipping from its place by the furnace. It was dry and stiff, both sides covered with flaking bits of I don't even know what.

I brought it over to Ms. P and laid it on the darkroom's narrow table.

"Smart money says that thing disintegrates before you get to the second soaking."

"If that's the case, at least we will know not to employ the technique when we encounter this situation again."

I was hoping I wouldn't come across anymore gore-soaked papers in the future, but you never knew.

"What are your plans for the day?" she asked as she began filling up the first developing tray.

"I was thinking that it's time to start plucking at this Nazi connection," I said. "I made a call earlier and discovered that Leonard Teetering's five-and-dime is open from noon to five on Sundays. I have a hankering for some licorice and whoopee cushions."

"You will be circumspect."

A statement of fact, not a request.

"I'll have circumspect coming out both ends."

She made a sound that I took for approval, if not amusement.

"Now, I'll leave you to your sciencing. I'm gonna go put my eyes on a Nazi."

CHAPTER 26

Before I left, I got into costume and retrieved my props.

The costume was a long-sleeved white blouse and ankle-length skirt in a gray that wasn't far off from our soaked souvenir. I pinned my hair back into something less heathenish. My curls gave the bobby pins a run for their money but everything eventually held.

I accessorized with my dowdiest pair of Mary Janes and a pocketbook that looked big enough to fit a Bible. Instead of the good book, I filled it with a good gun, tucked neatly beneath the usual supply of handkerchiefs, mints, and assorted debris.

I checked myself out in the mirror. I could pass for a sweet churchgoing girl if you squinted a little. I decided to add a touch of lipstick and a whisper of rouge. I wanted to look God-fearing, not ghostly.

My final prop was a choice section from the Sunday morning edition of the *Times*. After dropping away for a couple days, the Bodine murder had bounced back to the front page. The reporter had somehow gotten word of Bodine's prodigious memory.

She was still an old woman who died alone in her apartment, but now she was an interesting old woman. Freakish, even.

I knew from my circus experience how much the world loves a good freak.

I was about to head out the front door when it occurred to me that I would be leaving Ms. Pentecost alone at the brownstone, the keys to which were in the hands of a pair of muggers–turned–con artists.

This had been on my mind all week. Previously, I'd shaken it off by telling myself the odds of my muggers trying anything were slim, and that Mrs. Campbell was always within shouting distance.

But now our housekeeper was gone for the day. And there had been something about listening to Hiram describe what happens to a body after it dies. Something sad and terrible and . . . inevitable.

You see, I had this habitual fear that one day I'd come home to find that one of Ms. Pentecost's enemies had broken in. She'd made a lot of them, after all. They'd broken in and . . .

Enough of that.

I threw the bolt and latched the chain, then I walked through the kitchen and out into our rear courtyard, grabbing the set of keys that lived on the little hook by the back door as I went.

On the far side of the small courtyard was the renovated carriage house where Mrs. Campbell spent her off hours. On either side were brick walls that ended well over my head, each inset with an iron gate that led to the alleys flanking the brownstone. I used the keys to unlock the padlock securing the one on the right, passed through, latched the padlock behind me, then strode up the alley and out to the car.

It mollified my fear, but it was a maneuver that I didn't want to become routine. I needed to fix this situation and fix it quick.

Luckily, I had the not-inconsiderable trek to Danville, Long Island, to spend pondering. Specifically how to approach

Donny Russo in a way that would let me leave with life, limb, and whatever information he had about my assailants.

By the time I pulled onto Danville's Main Street I had something resembling a plan. To call it fraught would be an understatement. It would take a metric ton of moxie and a pair of brass ovaries to pull off.

Luckily, I had both.

I parked on a side street well short of the five-and-dime. I didn't want Teetering to see me driving the Cadillac. The slick sedan didn't quite fit with the picture of a modest churchgoer.

I slung my bag over my shoulders, tucked the paper under my arm, and strolled the few blocks to Teetering's store. On the way, I made sure to fix my mouth into a pleasant smile and tried to think virginal thoughts.

A bell above the door announced my arrival into Teetering's Five & Dime. It was like I'd time-traveled back to when I was six or seven and I walked into the five-and-dime in my hometown. A dollar in one pocket to pay for my mother's order of fabric and thread, a pocket full of pennies in the other to blow on candy or a pulp detective magazine.

The store was a single, long room with half a dozen rows of shelves containing anything and everything you needed for small-town living. There were tools and canned goods, plastic army men and windup animals, dress patterns and spools of thread, light bulbs, replacement glass for hurricane lamps, pencils and notebooks, and at the back, along with the cash register, a glass case of penny candy.

There were a handful of customers in the store. A pair of old ladies also made up for church were sorting through the dress patterns; a middle-aged man in overalls was trying to decide between two hammers; and a trio of little girls stood in front of the candy case, pointing fingers and tossing numbers at the man behind the counter, who was picking out sweets a penny's worth at a time.

He was doing the picking one-handed, his left arm ending short of his shirt cuff.

Teetering.

I paused at a rack of comic books, keeping one eye on the colorful covers and the other on the man ringing up the paper bags filled with licorice whips and candy cigarettes.

He was on the shorter and heavier side, with a perfectly round head that didn't quite have enough hair to cover it, though he didn't bother with a comb-over. Instead, he made up for it with a mustache that Poirot would have been proud of.

He had an ankle-length green apron tied around the neck. From what looked like an infinite number of pockets sprouted pencils, pens, a notebook, a ruler, and whatever else an on-the-go shopkeeper needed. He sported a pair of spindly, wire-rimmed glasses that looked like they might have come free from the Salvation Army. But the eyes behind them seemed sharp enough.

I watched as he expertly punched out the girls' purchase on the cash register.

"That all comes to seventy-nine cents, ladies."

Was there a hint of a German accent hiding behind the vowels, or was I imagining things?

There was some distress among the girls as they laid out their coins on the counter. Apparently they were short.

"Ah—I forgot the Sunday schoolgirl discount," Teetering said. "That brings the total to seventy-four cents."

The girls clapped and smiled and ran off with their candy while Teetering scooped up the coins with his one hand. As he did so, his eyes came up and met mine. I quickly looked away and busied myself with examining the subtle difference between *Action Comics* and *Adventure Comics*.

The old hardwood boards of the floor announced his approach.

"Can I help you find something, miss?"

I went with a mix of delight and ditheriness.

"Oh, I don't know," I said, turning to find him standing a hair too close for comfort. "I'm visiting my cousins in South-ampton and they have a son—he's just turned ten, you know, and I missed his birthday. I know he reads these things, but I honestly have no idea which ones he might like."

"Ten-year-old boy, you say." Teetering started flipping through the comics. "Well, anything with Superman is always popular. Captain America, as well."

"I worry that these sorts of things will stunt his learning. I mean, it's not really reading, is it?"

Teetering thought for a moment, then bent down to the lower shelves and picked up a copy of *The Rio Kid*. On the cover, a cowboy in a brilliant blue uniform was kicking over a poker table and firing his pistol at whoever was on the other side.

"These are collections of short stories. There are some pic-tures, but only a few."

He handed me the magazine and I looked at it with muted alarm.

"Oh, but this looks so violent, doesn't it?"

Teetering tilted his round noggin from side to side.

"I suppose, yes. I don't think it's any more violent than the Westerns children see at the movie house or listen to on the radio."

I shook my head in dismay at the state of the American soul.

"It's just awful. You'd think there would be enough vio-lence in real life that we wouldn't have to make it up. I mean, look here." I pulled the paper out from under my arm and put the headline about Bodine right in front of his face. But not so in front that I couldn't see his reaction.

"This poor woman killed in her own home. Can you believe that?"

It took Teetering a second to realize it wasn't a rhetorical question.

"No, no. It's awful," he finally said.

"It really is awful." I was starting to wish I'd worn a string of pearls so I could clutch them. "My brother fought in Europe, and do you know what he said to me? He said that at least the violence there made sense, you know? Because they were fighting the Nazis. Those monsters deserved everything they had coming to them. But something like this . . ." I shook the paper in his face. "There's no sense to it at all. What kind of person does this? Walking into an old woman's home and clubbing her to death? I mean, really."

Was there something in Teetering's face during that little monologue? I was about to dive into the next chorus when the shopkeeper made a show of looking over my shoulder.

"I'm afraid I have to help a customer, miss. But if you have any more questions, please let me know."

He walked purposefully over to the middle-aged farmer who was still trying to decide between two near-identical hammers. Did he pull the ripcord on the conversation because of his secret guilt over being a Nazi, a murderer, or both? Or did I make my good Christian girl a little too sweet to stomach?

I spent half a minute looking through the magazines before shaking my head in disgust and walking out.

I went back to where I'd parked the Cadillac, but instead of hopping in, I kept going for two more blocks, made a right, another right, a left, and ended up in front of a small Craftsman house bordered on one side by a stand of trees and another by a fence nearly as high as the roofline.

Teetering liked his privacy.

Which was good for me, too. It meant there were only a handful of neighbors across the street who had a direct view of his front door, and I was hoping they were all at church, or wherever Danvillians spent their Sundays.

I walked up to the door confidently, knocked, waited,

knocked again, reached into my bag, found what I was looking for, then dropped my bag to the ground.

"Oops."

I kneeled down to pick it up, gave a quick look behind me
to make sure no one had come wandering down the sidewalk,
and went to work on the front door with my set of picks. I had
the door open in well under a minute, which said less about
my skill and more about Teetering's cheap lock.

I quickly stood up, looked around again, knocked again,
then tried the door. I acted surprised when it opened, then
stepped inside.

"Mr. Teetering. It's Laura from the Salvation Army!"

I closed the door behind me.

All of that rigmarole was so that if there were eyes on me,
I was giving them a more plausible scenario than a strange
woman picking their neighbor's front door. One that wouldn't
have them phoning the police.

Not that I planned to stay long enough to get caught.

I wasn't tossing the place. This was solely a sightseeing
visit. I wanted to get a sense of who Teetering was when he
was at home. I didn't expect to find a shrine to Der Führer in
his closet, but I wouldn't slap lady luck away if she decided to
get fresh.

It was your standard two-bedroom bungalow: living room
facing the street, kitchen, short hallway leading to bedroom,
bathroom, second bedroom turned into office. The house
wasn't anything to write home about, and I won't write much
about it here, either.

Teetering went for wallpaper over paint, enjoyed overstuffed couches and chairs, and had a thing for birds. Paintings
and photographs of birds were the house's main decorative
theme. I touched nothing in his office. I didn't open a single
drawer.

If Teetering was a Nazi—and not just any old Nazi
but someone who'd been tasked with covert intelligence

gathering—who knew what kinds of little telltales he'd left in place? Not all of them were as obvious as an eyelash pasted over the seam of a drawer.

I did a full tour, saving the kitchen for last because it was the least likely to be interesting and if I needed to skedaddle early, I wouldn't mourn missing it. When I finally got to it, I discovered that the door that I thought led to a pantry actually opened on stairs that descended into darkness.

I felt around for a light switch. Nothing.

Did I remember to bring my little flashlight? Nope.

Did Teetering have one ready at hand? Nein.

Did I start making my way carefully down into the darkness anyway? Oh, yeah. I'm that breed of moron.

An image came into my head. That down in the basement Teetering kept a re-creation of the 1939 German American Bund setup at Madison Square Garden, but in miniature. A painting of George Washington flanked by a pair of Nazi flags. Stacks of pamphlets urging the U.S. to let Europe settle its own business. A list of everything Hitler had gotten right.

That was quickly replaced by grimmer thoughts.

I'd seen the photographs of Dachau. I'd read the descriptions of what had been found there. I paused and breathed deep through my nose.

Soil and rot, but the rot of old potatoes rather than the stink of the grave.

My feet finally landed on a packed dirt floor. There were two tiny windows on either side of the room, both set high up in the wall, their light almost entirely obscured by dust on the inside and weeds on the outside.

I could make out dim outlines in the darkness. A large, free-standing cupboard, some shelves along the wall, a long, flat table that I discovered only because I bumped my hip into it.

I stretched out my hand and felt carefully along the table. A rough wooden handle. A jagged strip of metal.

My mind was leaping ("Ah, this is where he dismembers his victims") when my fingers closed on the unmistakable shape of a screwdriver.

This is a man who built porches himself. Of course he'd have a workshop.

I was heading back toward the stairs when the hair on the nape of my neck stood at attention.

I stopped. I suddenly had the very clear sense that I wasn't alone in the basement.

You're spooking yourself, I thought.

Except I didn't say that out loud. Because I didn't really think I was spooking myself, and I didn't want to ruin my hearing.

Was that breathing mine? Or someone else's?

As I listened, my hand crept into my purse, fingers moving aside notebook and handkerchief in search of a pistol grip.

I nearly had it when a hand latched on to my shoulder and a voice whispered in my ear.

"What do you think you're doing?"

CHAPTER 27

Every couple weeks one of my students asks, "Why do we have to practice the move so many times even after we've got it down pat?"

And every couple of weeks I give my standard answer: "You want to know it so well you don't have to think about it. Because when you need it, your brain probably won't be working. You want your muscles doing your thinking for you."

My muscles realized my attacker was too close. I didn't have the space to draw my gun, turn, and fire. Instead, my muscles reached up with both hands, grabbed the wrist of the arm connected to my shoulder and pulled.

I loaded the guy up on my hip and was about to flip him when suddenly his weight was gone and his other arm was snaking around my neck.

Instinctively I let go of the first arm to attend to the one wrapped around my throat. I spread my fingers out and dug into the soft flesh beneath what Hiram was kind enough to once identify for me as the radius.

I bent my knees and dropped my elbows to my hips. The man grunted in pain and his grip around my throat loosened. Sensing daylight, I dropped down and spun, getting out from under his grip. Somehow I'd managed to keep ahold of my bag and I had my hand in and the gun halfway out when a flashlight clicked on.

The attacker held it under his chin, pointed upward. It took me a moment to recognize the horror-show face.

"Faraday?" I gasped.

I was gasping because my lungs had gone the way of my heart—up my throat and off to Poughkeepsie.

"Jesus Christ, Parker. You almost tore my arm off."

I wanted to say that if he hadn't turned the flashlight on in time, I'd have very possibly blown his head off, but that was too many words, so I opted for "What? . . . How?"

"What am I doing here? Keeping you from being a complete idiot. As for how—"

He pointed the flashlight at the far back corner. It illuminated a set of concrete steps leading up to a slanted basement door.

"I would have gone to the front door and yelled and knocked and pretended to drop my purse, but I thought I'd be smart," he said.

By then I'd recovered my full complement of the English language, and I used it to let him know what he could do.

"I agree," he said. "How about both of us do that, and we do it using the basement steps here. That way the neighbors won't see our little tea party."

We emerged in Teetering's backyard, which was bordered on one side by the wooden fence and on the other two by trees. The house had a back porch that looked newer than the rest of the building. After lopping off his hand, Teetering had eventually gone on to finish the job.

Faraday closed the basement doors, then did something complicated with a length of fishing line strung through the narrow gap in the doors, and managed to re-latch them from the outside. He yanked the line off, then took a handkerchief out of his pocket and wiped the handles free of fingerprints.

"I'm assuming you didn't rearrange any furniture," he said.

I didn't dignify that with a response. Instead I asked, "What the hell are you doing here? Are you following me?"

"Don't flatter yourself, Parker."

I decided to take that for truth. He didn't get here by tailing me. Which meant . . .

"You're watching Teetering. Why? I thought you said the case was done. You took your run at him and came up empty."

He looked away, staring out at the trees, like he was worried there were squirrels eavesdropping.

"These cases are never over," he said. "You know that."

That was true. It was also bullshit.

"It's because of Bodine. You're worried she's dead because she helped you."

"Maybe I'm worried a secret FBI investigation is going to end up on the front page. Did you ever think about that?" he snapped. "I'm surprised you and your boss haven't spilled it already."

"We don't go telling tales to the press for fun."

He harrumphed.

"Yeah, your boss'll probably hold on to it in case she wants something from me."

That was exactly how I'd interpreted things, but I wasn't going to tell him that. Also, I'd used anger to deflect difficult questions enough times that I recognized the tactic when I saw it.

"I'm not buying it," I said. "If this was a cover-up, you'd be spending your time wiretapping reporters or nosing in on the police investigation. You wouldn't be staking out Teetering. I think Rosa was right. You liked Bodine. You're worried you might have been responsible for her death."

His eyes turned away from the tree line and fixed on me. For a split second I could see it. The guilt.

The Tin Man had a heart, after all.

Then the shutters snapped shut and it was back to the cold, flat gaze of a fed.

"Let's get out of here," he said. "Teetering is supposed to be at work until five, but who knows."

We slipped out through the alley between house and fence and walked naturally but swiftly toward where I parked the car.

"What does your boss think?"

I nearly tripped over my Mary Janes. Faraday asking me for a lead? Satan must be selling ice skates.

"You should stop by the office and ask her yourself."

Faraday let out one of those cold, humorless barks.

"Right. That's what I'll do. Get seen standing on Lillian Pentecost's doorstep."

"Then I can't help you. Like I said, I don't tell tales out of school."

We'd arrived at the Cadillac. I half expected Faraday to hop in the back seat, but I saw him glance at a battered sedan half a block away.

"Anything you're specifically curious about?" I asked. "I can deliver the question to Ms. Pentecost, since you don't want to be seen courting."

I expected more wisecrackery. Instead, he pitched it straight.

"One thing I'd like to know is what the killer was looking for."

"Looking for?"

"You don't hang out with a corpse for days on end unless you're hunting. And there were a lot of places to hunt in that apartment."

Faraday knew about what had turned up in the autopsy, and he'd come to the same conclusion we had. I must have shown surprise on my face.

"You see, Parker, I can keep an eye on Teetering and nose into the investigation at the same time."

That was the thing about Faraday. In some ways, he was

almost a caricature—the paranoia, the needless cloak-and-dagger. Then I remembered that he was as much an operator as my boss. One with a healthy dose of cunning and a lot of resources to draw on.

"What do *you* think the killer was looking for?" I asked.

Faraday looked up and down the street. The only person in sight was a boy in short pants dislodging a stick from the chain of his bicycle. Faraday X-rayed him, decided he wasn't packing, and answered the question.

"Maybe the killer thought Bodine had written something down," he said. "Notes about her work with us. Names. Places. That sort of thing."

"Did she write things down?" I asked.

Faraday shook his head.

"Not in my presence. I told her absolutely not to. But . . ."

But she was a civilian. Faraday didn't trust civilians. Or other feds. Or detectives, animals, small children, etc.

"You worried the killer found it? These notes she might have made?"

"Actually, Parker, I'm more worried he didn't."

He was concerned that the notes detailing Bodine's work with the FBI were still somewhere in the apartment. The apartment that the police were in the process of searching.

"Be nice if someone caught the killer quick, then," I mused.

No answer. Not even a nod.

Sensing the conversation was at an end, I opened the door and hopped into the driver's seat.

"Say hi to Rosa for me. I'll send Ms. Pentecost your best."

Faraday didn't stick out his tongue, but I could tell he wanted to.

He started toward his car and I turned the key, put the Caddy in drive, and was halfway to the corner when I had a thought. I flung the sedan into reverse and managed to hit neither cars nor Faraday as I backed up down the street.

I rolled down the window.

"I know the mob isn't real high on Hoover's to-do list at the moment, but . . ."

"What do you want?" he growled.

"A tiny little favor. Trust me. It'll be painless."

CHAPTER 28

It took me three rattles of the front door before I remembered that I'd latched and bolted it. I went through the alley to the gate, wondering how I was going to explain this bit of vaudeville to Ms. P.

Luckily, I didn't have to.

I found my boss still in the basement, splayed out on the wrestling mats. She was barefoot, pant legs rolled up to her knees, with every button on her blouse undone, and dripping with sweat.

I'd have been alarmed, but I'd spent enough time in my little closet of a darkroom to know what was what.

"Madame, your Maidenform is showing."

"It gets exceptionally warm in there," she said, without even bothering to lift her head my way.

"We should install some form of ventilation."

"Soon as I get a day off, I'll string up some ductwork," I said. "So was it worth it?"

"See for yourself."

She gestured toward the furnace, where the square of paper was lying, pinned flat at the corners by some loose bricks.

"Don't pick it up. I fear that the drying process likely made it brittle."

I went over and peered. I swore under my breath, but apparently not under enough.

"You don't approve?"

"It's blank," I said, examining the paper, which was now the color of over-creamed coffee. "I mean, yeah, whatever you did took out the . . . um . . . the organic matter. But it took the ink along with it. At least that's what I think. I'll have to get a magnifying glass to make sure."

Behind me, Ms. P pushed herself to her feet, wobbled, then put a hand against a pillar to steady herself.

"I've already examined it under a magnifying glass," she informed me. "The only thing visible is the circle."

"Circle?"

She wobbled in my direction.

"Look closely," she said, reaching into her pocket and pulling out a penlight. "The bottom right quadrant."

I took the slim chrome light, got down on my hands and knees, and clicked the button. I swung the tiny bright beam to the bottom right of the paper, then got my nose as close as it would go without touching.

There was an impression in the paper—an oval. The paper had been so stained that it hadn't shown up before.

"Bodine circled a word," I said. "Or a bunch of words."

The impression didn't look like a single pencil line, either. Bodine—assuming it was her—went around the words a bunch of times.

"Whatever this was, she really didn't want to forget it."

I thought about what I'd just said.

"That's funny for a woman who supposedly never forgot a thing."

"I thought the same," Ms. P said. "Which suggests the emphasis wasn't for her benefit."

She'd circled the word for someone else. Whitsun? Faraday, maybe? And what word? What article? Was it even from a newspaper? There were a hundred newsletters and magazines, even comic books, that got printed on cheap pulp.

I voiced all this to Ms. P while she went through the process of rebuttoning her blouse and retrieving her footwear.

"All very good questions," she said, meaning she didn't have the answers, either. "There is also the issue of relevance."

In other words, did this have anything to do with anything? Or did Ms. P waste her Sunday getting a chemical high for nothing?

"Probably not what the killer was hunting for," I said, more to myself than Ms. P. But she was the one who answered.

"Why is that?"

"A newspaper article—assuming that's what it is. Bodine circles a word and gets whacked for it? It would have to be a hell of a word. Frankly, I'm leaning more toward Faraday's theory. He says hello, by the way."

She motioned for me to continue, and I went into a summary of my excursion, ending with Faraday's concern that Bodine might have written down details of her work with the FBI.

By the time I was through, we were both at our respective desks enjoying a refreshing beverage—milk for me, several glasses of water for her.

Her first question was: "Mr. Teetering displayed no reaction when you showed him the paper and the headline about the murder?"

"None," I said. "But if this guy's been living a lie for years, he's going to be real good at hiding his feelings."

"It was a worthwhile gambit, if only for your discovery that Agent Faraday is taking a personal interest in this case."

I tried out one of those thoughtful *hrrmmmms* that my boss is fond of.

"Yes?" she said.

"Faraday's talk about headlines got me thinking about

how Bodine's memory trick earned her another front-page slot. Most of the cops on the case aren't going to know that kind of esoteric—I think that's the right word—esoteric victim biography. I suppose the reporter could have picked it up at Boekbinder and Gimbal. But why go hunting there? She's been retired for years. Basically, there are half a dozen sexier crimes to fill up column inches with."

Though she does not play, my boss has an excellent poker face.

"Your conclusion?" she asked.

"My conclusion is that Roberts at the *Times* owes us another favor."

She let me have her most modest of smiles.

"It seemed the thing to do," she said. "The story was fading from view. Miss Bodine's memory provides an additional aspect of sensationalism. Having the murder remain on the front page will hopefully provide added stress for the murderer. Perhaps goad him or her into making a mistake."

"It's also a warning shot across the FBI's bow," I noted.

She nodded. "True. Though that was before I knew that Agent Faraday was emotionally involved in the case."

"I didn't think he had it in him."

"Everyone has pressure points, Will. No matter how much they would like us to believe otherwise."

So, yeah, if you're ever wondering where I got my sneakiness from, look no further than the woman who signs my checks.

Soon after, Ms. P decided that we should treat the rest of our day off as intended, and announced her intention to spend the next hour in a hot bath.

"Good luck getting that chemical smell out of your hair," I told her. "I recommend vinegar. If that doesn't work—scissors."

While she soaked, I sat, going backward and forward over my plan for the next day, wondering if I could trust Faraday to hold up his end.

After an hour of this, I gave up. Faraday would come through, or he wouldn't. The plan would go off, or it wouldn't. I would walk away with the information I was looking for, or . . .

Or I might make the front page myself. And not in a good way.

Monday morning saw me sitting at a hole-in-the-wall diner sipping coffee and watching the men filing in and out of Suilebhan's Pool Hall across the street. Suilebhan's (pronounced "Sullivan's," according to Maeve) was located in a less-than-reputable corner of Brooklyn, sandwiched between a dry cleaner's and what had once been a grocer's until somebody put a torch to it.

Before going to bed, I'd told Ms. P I'd be spending the morning running errands. She didn't question me and said she didn't plan to be up and about until noon, if not later. While she'd managed to get the smell out, hunching over trays of chemicals for multiple hours had done her in.

"Do not," she told me, "wake me for anything less than an emergency."

"If the firemen have to carry you out, I'll tell them to do it quietly."

I looked at my watch—10:25.

Time.

I took a last sip of rancid coffee, slapped a quarter on the table, and walked out of the diner. As I crossed the street, I had a little time to reconsider every wheel and cog of the plan.

I was reconsidering my costume, for one. I'd considered going the damsel-in-distress route. "My name is Lucy-Loo and some scoundrels have done me wrong!" Except I didn't gauge

Russo as the type to help damsels. Distress would be like blood in the water to him.

Also, while I'd never met Russo, I'd rubbed up against enough New York wiseguys that it's possible he, or someone else in that pool hall, would know me on sight.

So my costume for the morning was Will Parker, right-hand woman to the famed detective Lillian Pentecost. It included a ladies' frontier-style suit in tan twill. The high-waisted, tapered trousers and cavalry-inspired jacket with its big shoulders made me feel like a gunslinger jangling her spurs toward a rat's-nest saloon.

So did the Baby Browning I had tucked into the custom holster at the small of my back. And if I could have fit a bigger gun under there without a bulge, you better believe I would have.

I also reconsidered the linchpin of this plan. It required that Faraday stick to a script, and I think you know by now how iffy that proposition was.

More than anything, I reconsidered not telling Ms. Pentecost what I was about to do.

As I was getting dressed that morning, I thought about walking across the hall and waking her up. Telling her the whole thing, from boardwalk to bank to my chat with Maeve.

I actually had my hand raised to knock on her bedroom door. But I stopped.

What was I looking for? Comfort? A scolding?

This was my mess to clean up. Ms. P had enough on her plate.

So I walked across the street alone. Not quite high noon, but it might as well have been. Though there wouldn't be a gunfight in the cards. Not if Faraday could follow orders.

"Yeah," I muttered as I put my hand on the pool-hall door, "this is gonna go swell."

I swung the door open and stepped into darkness.

Okay, not exactly darkness, but certainly dimness in the extreme. It was an aesthetic choice that worked for Suilebhan's, which didn't have much in the way of eye appeal. Not much appeal for the other senses, either.

There was the sound: the clatter of pool balls paired with the clink of glasses and the rough laughter of men.

The smell: cigarette smoke, sour beer, the tang from the jar of pickled eggs sitting open on the bar, and the layers of human sweat that had soaked into the floorboards and the felt of the pool tables over the decades.

Finally, there was the feel of the place: like I was stepping into a cave where something hungry was hiding.

I was certainly attracting a lot of eyes. There was the bartender, a hefty guy with a mop of white hair whose lumpy features looked like they'd been shaped by a sculptor who was all thumbs. There was the pair of men at the nearest pool table. They were old enough that the pool hall might have been built around them and at no point during that time had anyone asked them to change their clothes.

There were the people sitting at the bar, who were exactly the sort you'd expect to find sipping whiskey and beer at 10:30 on a Monday morning. I was pleased to see I wasn't the only female in the joint. There was a woman at the farthest barstool—a fiftyish bottle blonde whose fire-engine dress provided the only color in a gray-and-grime landscape.

I clocked all of these characters before focusing on the rearmost pool table and the two men standing behind it.

The pair looked right at home at Suilebhan's. But at the same time, they didn't belong. Their suits were too slick, their haircuts too sharp; both had a healthy flush to their faces, like their livers weren't planning on sputtering out at any minute.

I caught them mid-tableau.

The guy on the left, the one I'd seen walking into the place only a minute before, was handing an envelope to the guy on the right. Mr. Right took the envelope, used his thumb to rifle the bills inside, then tossed it into a carryall that was sitting on the pool table. It looked very full.

As I walked toward them, Mr. Right gave a nod, said something I couldn't catch, and Mr. Left turned and hurried toward the door.

We passed each other and I caught the beads of sweat scattered across his forehead. He was a member of the crew. The count was right. But he was still sweating.

That's because Mr. Right was Donny Russo, and from everything Maeve had told me, there was nothing right about him.

He looked straight enough: mid-thirties; inoffensive features; wearing a double-breaster in Carolina blue wool that probably fell off the back of a truck. The only two standouts were his eyes and his size.

His eyes were a brilliant green that might have been called "emerald" if the word "acid" wasn't sitting there.

As for his size, he barely topped five feet and not in a fireplug kind of way. More like a ballet dancer. I'd call him petite, but never to his face.

That's because of the knives. Russo liked knives. Maeve had really driven that point home, pun absolutely intended.

"He doesn't just use them to kill, either," Maeve had said. "He marks his territory. Lot of guys who crossed him have scars. Some girls, too. The girls, especially. There's this story I heard about a hooker he was with. Said something about his height. Nothing rude, but that didn't matter."

Maeve told me the story. I won't repeat it here. Just because it's taken up permanent residence in my brain doesn't mean I have to infect yours.

I knew the kind of man I was walking up to. In fact, I was kind of counting on it.

"Mr. Russo? Donny Russo?"

I got a sulfuric soak as his eyes washed over me, top to bottom, lingering in all the usual places.

"Who's asking?"

"My name's Will Parker. I work for Lillian Pentecost. The private detective? Maybe you've heard of her."

I held out a business card. He took it and set it on the felt without a glance.

"Maybe I have. What's that got to do with me?"

"We're working a case, and we think you might have information that could be of some help."

He laughed. It was shrill and high. Cackling, almost. Like a hyena.

"Get outta here," he said. "I'm doing business."

"Sharing this information—it might be mutually beneficial. That means it would help you as well as—"

"I know what it means!"

The anger flashed like sunshine off a chrome bumper. Harsh, blinding, then gone.

I could feel the room's eyes on us now. When he'd told me to get outta there, it hadn't been a polite suggestion. It had been a command. I had ignored it. Then I'd compounded the issue by insulting his intelligence.

Now everyone was wondering what he was going to do.

He glanced around the pool hall. He could feel the eyes, too. He reached into his coat pocket, and I tensed.

Going for a knife already?

He pulled out a tube about the size of a roll of mints. He untwisted the cap, pressed it to his nose, and took a great whiff before tucking the tube back in his pocket.

Benzedrine inhaler. Great. The guy was an amphetamine junkie.

"Listen, red," he said, lips curling into a leer. "How about you and I go in the back? You can show me some of those benefits. You do a good job, maybe I'll tell you what you want to know."

Another laugh. This was a cue to the other men in the room to chuckle along with him. Which they did, because they knew what was good for them.

This wasn't the first time I'd been made that kind of offer. Usually I'd respond accordingly. But I needed Russo to hear the pitch first, so I ignored the leer and the laughter and threw it.

"A Jack-and-Jill team working the boardwalk. Snatch-and-grab with some theatrics. The guy is in his twenties, dark hair, brown eyes, maybe five-seven. Big black mole on his left cheek. The girl comes off younger, but she's big on costumes, so it's hard to say. My bet is you've run into them."

With each word, Russo's eyes went a little more flat, a little more dead. I didn't even know if he was registering what I was saying. All he knew was that this woman standing in front of him, after being told to leave, after being told she'd do better work on her knees, was going right on talking.

And everyone in the room was watching it.

"I'm guessing this pair didn't get the nod from you before they started picking off beachgoers. In fact, I'll bet they're on your list of dumbass crooks who are bad for business. If we took them off the board, we'd be doing you a favor."

There was a pause here. Russo just stared at me. No acid in his eyes now. They were as cold as cold can get.

Then he smiled. A hyena smile to match his hyena laugh.

"A favor? That's what you figure?"

I nodded.

"You and your boss, you think about my business a lot? How you can help me?"

I didn't nod this time and he didn't wait for one.

"You think I can't handle my territory? That I can't take care of some little punk and his uptown whore?"

Bingo. He knew them. Now I just needed Faraday to come through. I glanced down at my watch. I thought I was subtle, but not subtle enough.

"You got somewhere to be?" Russo asked.

"No, it's only—"

He was fast. So fast I didn't know what happened at first. I had to dissect the move later.

He swept his right leg behind my knees while grabbing my throat with his left hand. His leg pulled one way, his hand shoved the other, and suddenly I had my back on the felt.

I didn't know where the knife came from, either—a six-inch stiletto that I didn't see until its tip was pressing into the underside of my chin.

There were gasps and shouts around the room and then silence. Everybody held their breath, myself included.

Here's the thing about knives. They're not as deadly as guns. A whole lot harder to use effectively, too.

But they're scarier. Ms. P once referred to it as "the primal fear of having your flesh parted."

That was half the point of flashing a blade. The fear.

I was feeling it. I'd told Faraday 10:30 on the nose. That deadline had come and gone.

My plan was falling apart fast.

"Where do you get off thinking you can come in here asking questions?" he said, leaning over me, one hand on my throat, the other on the knife. "Come in here sticking your nose into my business. Your pretty little nose."

I thought about Ms. Pentecost. Back home, still asleep. Was she going to wake up to a phone call from the hospital? Or the cops asking her to come identify a body?

I wished I'd told her where I was going.

I wished I'd gotten to talk to Holly.

He moved the knife away from my chin and pressed it against the underside of my nose.

"Maybe it's not so pretty. I'm thinking maybe you'd look better without it."

He began to press up with the blade.

CHAPTER 30

"Donny, not in here."

That came from the lumpy bartender. Both I and my assailant glanced over at him, half cowering behind the bar.

"Don't tell me what I can do!" Russo screamed. "This place doesn't burn down because I say it doesn't burn down. You got me?"

The bartender must have got him, because he ducked entirely behind the bar. Russo's grip on my throat got tighter, but during the outburst the knife had drifted away from my nose.

He was also distracted enough that I was able to reach my hand behind my back, slip it under my jacket, and wrap my fingers around the Browning's grip.

I tensed, ready to throw my hips to the side, hopefully dislodging Russo and getting the distance I needed to draw. There was no way I wasn't going to get cut. That was a given. But if I moved fast enough, I could turn the gun on Russo before I got stabbed.

I was half a breath from putting my plan into action when a phone rang. It was the pay phone hanging on the wall at the back of the bar.

Russo froze. He waited for the ringing to stop, but it didn't.

"Florence. Go see who it is."

The bottle blonde at the bar slid off the stool, adjusted her skirt, and tottered over to the phone.

She picked it up.

"Yeah, who is it? . . . Yeah? . . . He's busy. . . ."

"Who is it, Florence!"

"It's Mack," she said.

"What's he want?"

She turned back to the mouthpiece.

"What do you want? . . . Yeah. . . . Yeah. . . . Okay, I'll tell him."

She turned to Russo.

"He says there's a raid coming."

Russo looked up, taking the blade away from my face entirely.

"The hell there is. Everyone's paid up."

Back to the mouthpiece.

"Donny says everyone's paid up. . . . Uh-huh. . . . Uh-huh. . . . Really? You're kidding."

"What's he saying, Florence?"

"He says it's not the cops, it's the feds. They got your name."

"My name? The feds? Which feds?"

"Which feds is it, Mack? . . . Uh-huh. . . . What? The vacuum cleaner people?"

"What's he saying? Vacuum cleaners?"

"What was that, Mack? . . . Oh, yeah, I get it." Away from the receiver. "Mack, he said it was Hoover's boys. But I only know Hoover from vacuum cleaners. What he meant was—"

"I know what he meant, Florence! The hell does the FBI want with me?"

As much as I hate to break into a good routine, I spoke up.

"It's gotta be drugs."

Russo looked back at me, startled. I honestly think he'd forgotten I was there.

"What did you say?"

"Word is the mayor doesn't trust the cops to get the job done, so he called Hoover direct. They've been partnering with the Bureau of Narcotics. Big bust in Harlem last night."

All of that was bullshit. What mattered was that it was plausible bullshit. It also mattered that, when I said drugs, Russo's eyes got real focused real quick.

Here's the thing about middle-management mobsters. They're low enough on the food chain that they never have enough money. But they're high enough up that they could be working some operations on the side without getting smacked down.

That was usually drugs.

The big problem for Russo was that while the New York cops might be on the take, and had little incentive to hold him on that outstanding warrant, the feds were another matter.

He called to Florence.

"Ask him when this raid is."

I almost blurted out. "It was supposed to be ten-thirty, damn it!" but I managed to keep my mouth shut.

"Hey, Mack," Florence said. "When did you hear the raid's happening?"

I don't know what Mack said because the answer came courtesy of the sound of screeching tires on the street out front. Russo leapt off me, the knife disappearing up his shirtsleeve.

The guy had a forearm rig under there. Good to know.

He grabbed the carryall and dashed toward the back door. I hurried after.

He kicked open the door and careened into the alley behind the pool hall. He turned left, saw what I assumed was FBI ruckus at that end of the alley, then dashed in the other direction.

He dodged around the bumper of the car parked in the alley and took about three steps before he skidded to a stop.

There was bustle at the other end, too. They weren't coming down it yet, but Russo's escape route was blocked.

While he was realizing this, I took the keys out of my pocket and used them to open the trunk of the Cadillac, which I had parked in the alley right before walking across the street and into the diner.

"You want out, hop in."

Startled, he turned.

"What?"

"I can get you out of here."

He looked at me like I'd just said I could leap tall buildings and was willing to take him with me.

"Think about it," I said. "They stop me, I show them my card. Nobody's searching Lillian Pentecost's car."

He walked toward me. I had to fight to keep my hand from reaching for my holster. Once he was within stiletto distance, he stopped.

"Why would you help me?" he asked.

"Because you're going to help me. I get you out of here, you tell me who the pair is working the boardwalk. Deal?"

That was the kind of reason he could understand. A self-serving one. It helped that the sound of shouts suddenly came from inside the pool hall.

"Deal," he said, hopping into the Caddy's trunk. I'd say "squeezed," but it was a big trunk. I could have fit three Russos and had room to spare.

"Keep quiet and still. And keep hold of this."

"This" was the jack from the trunk. I handed it to him. To take it he had to let go of the carryall. I snatched the bag and slammed the trunk shut.

Russo immediately began yelling and banging on the lid.

I banged back and hissed loud enough for him to hear.

"This is insurance," I said. "You'll get it back. But if you don't want to end up in a federal prison, shut it and shut it now."

He might have been a blade-happy psychopath, but he wasn't a stupid one. He shut it.

I hopped in the Cadillac, turned the key, and slowly pulled the sedan out of the alley. With my free hand, I grabbed a beret and silk scarf from the passenger seat. I slapped the former on my head, wrapped the latter around my neck, and rolled the window down.

As I nosed the car out onto the street, I leaned my head out the window and waved to the besuited man standing next to the unmarked sedan. He might as well have had a WE LOVE HOOVER button pinned on his lapel.

"What's going on? I came to pick my dress up from the dry cleaner's and suddenly all heck is breaking loose."

I pretended to just then notice the holster poking out of his jacket.

"Oh, my!"

He gave a reassuring smile and flashed his badge. "Federal Bureau of Investigation, ma'am."

"The FBI? In Brooklyn? My gosh. What's going on? Did somebody do something?"

"I can't really say, ma'am."

Apparently feds could smile if they thought they were talking to a pretty lady and not a nosy detective.

"Is it somebody dangerous? Should I be worried?"

"Not at all, ma'am." He leaned down and whispered conspiratorially. "It's the Commies."

I gasped, raising my hand to my throat to protect it from the rough hands of those dastardly reds.

"Commies?" I mouthed.

He nodded.

"We got word they were having a meeting. Bunch of union guys who were secretly reds. You didn't hear it from me."

He smiled and put a finger to his lips. I followed suit, gave him a wink, and eased the Caddy out onto the street and slowly drove off.

That agent seemed a little too excited to get into the union-busting business. But I'd told Faraday to make up whatever story worked, as long as Russo's name got thrown into the mix.

I wondered if Faraday would get in trouble when the raid fizzled. Knowing him, he'd set it up through a third party. Heart or not, one thing I knew Faraday believed in was self-preservation.

I made a point of hitting potholes and taking corners at speed, but I kept the sedan within five miles of the speed limit. This would not be a good time to get stopped by a cop.

While I drove, I revised my plan. I hadn't known about the bag of money. But now that I had it in hand, I figured I should put it to good use.

I made a stop at a hardware store for a can of lighter fluid.

Twenty minutes later, I pulled the Cadillac into a space across from 240 Centre Street. I got out of the car with the bag and set it on the sidewalk. I unzipped it, doused its contents in lighter fluid, and got out my lighter.

"How you doing in there, Donny?" I asked. "Nice and blended?"

"I am going to slice your face off, you little bitch."

"Now, don't be like that, Donny. I saved you from the feds. Which was awful magnanimous of me considering you were threatening to remove my nose at the time. Me and my nose, we don't always get along. It's a little puggish for my liking, and there are the freckles. But I'm real attached to it, regardless."

Some more compliments from the trunk.

"I'm sure you say that to all the girls, so I'm going to not take it personally," I said. "Before I pop open this trunk, I want you to take a big whiff. Stick your nose right up to the keyhole."

There was a pause and then . . .

"What the hell is that? That kerosene?"

"Lighter fluid, actually. Your bag of cash is soaked in it, and I've got my Zippo open and lit."

I gave him a second to digest that before continuing.

"Also, we're in a pretty public place."

I told him the address. That set off another round of invective.

"My point is when I pop this trunk, you should get out real slow. But not so slow you attract attention. Capiche?"

Another pause.

"Yeah, I got it."

A psychopath, but a smart one.

I unlocked the trunk and then took three quick steps back. I dropped the carryall to my feet, stuck a Chesterfield in my mouth (Holly had left a pack in the Caddy), and flicked the Zippo. To the casual observer, I should look like a dapperly dressed woman about to light a cigarette.

Now, if only no one noticed the mobster getting out of the trunk.

Russo followed direction perfectly, opening the lid just far enough to slip out. Then he was vertical, hat on head, the fingers of his right hand tucked under his jacket cuff in search of that forearm holster.

"Better keep the stiletto in its cradle," I warned him. "I might have to call for a cop. I could probably find one."

I glanced across the street at the white castle-like building that dominated the block, the headquarters of the New York City Police Department. Officers were filing through its doors, lingering on the sidewalk chatting, and hopping in and out of police cars. The whole place was swarming with boys in blue.

Russo took his hand out of his sleeve.

"What do you want?"

"I told you," I said. "I only want a pair of names."

"They're penny-ante. What the hell did they do that's got Lillian Pentecost on their ass?"

"That's our business," I said. "If they're penny-ante, you shouldn't make a fuss about giving them up."

His eyes wandered across the street and stayed there.

"If you're worried about getting labeled a snitch, don't be," I said. "As soon as I have those names, I forget yours. This ain't something that's going to end up with the cops, so no one's going to come asking."

He looked from police headquarters to the bag, then up and down the street. He might as well have hired a skywriter to plaster his thoughts across the September blue.

Can I grab the bag before she drops that lighter? Can I get away fast enough before I'm tackled by half a precinct worth of police?

I crouched down, holding the Zippo a few scant inches above the bag.

"I get any closer, the fumes are gonna catch," I warned him. "Tell me the names or this week's profits go up in smoke."

That apparently clarified his thinking. For the first time, I saw it in his eyes: fear.

These weren't his profits. They were his bosses' profits. Sure, it was probably only a few grand. They might forgive him. Give him a chance to make good.

But there'd be questions, and he'd have to explain how a woman had gotten the drop on him. This was a guy who would kill to save face and probably had.

"His name's Manny Casper. He used to hang around some of the boys. Hoping to be a player. Little momma's boy actually asked me if he could be made. Idiot."

"Manny wasn't mob material?" I asked.

"Manny could take a shit and miss the ground. Couldn't trust him to get anything right. He begged his way into being the driver on a job. All he had to do was drive. Nothing else. Halfway through the route, the idiot drops the keys down a sewer grate. Tried to hot-wire the truck and he flubbed that, too. Put me out five grand."

I thought back to under the boardwalk. That loping, clumsy run the man took at me. That paired nicely with the image Russo was painting of Manny Casper.

"What about the girl?" I asked.

Russo shrugged. "Some skirt he met at a club."

"You said she was uptown."

"Yeah, thinks she's an actress. Really, she's just another junkie whore."

"She's a junkie?"

"Heroin. I heard she's going around saying she kicked it. But once a junkie, always a junkie."

I didn't like the sound of that. A junkie meant my gun had probably already been sold. Or traded away in exchange for drugs. But could a junkie have pulled off that con at the bank? I didn't know.

"Where can I find Manny?" I asked.

"Hell if I know. I heard he moved out of his place weeks ago. Couldn't pay the rent. He and his bitch are probably holed up in a flophouse somewhere. I told him that five grand is coming out of his wallet or his hide. And the juice is running."

I figured he knew more than he was telling, but I'd pushed the envelope as far as it would go. Eventually some cop was going to wonder why that woman was crouched by a carryall, and why she was taking her sweet time lighting her smoke.

"Walk to the corner," I said.

"What?"

"Walk to the corner. Then I get in the car and drive off. You come, collect your money, we call it a day."

"How do I know you won't run with the cash? Or set it on fire?"

"You don't," I said. "But that's the deal. You got a getaway from the feds. I got my name. You get your money. A good soak in a tub will get the lighter fluid out. You don't like it, you can go right across the street and lodge a complaint."

Those green eyes splashed fire across my face.

"We're gonna meet up again one day," he promised.

I came up with three good retorts, but by then he was already on his way toward the corner.

I considered taking the money or dropping the Zippo. But a deal was a deal, and frankly I didn't want Russo on my back. I knew he'd show up sooner or later. I wanted it to be later.

I left the carryall where it was, got in the car, and drove off.

In the rearview, I saw Russo sprinting toward the bag.

I allowed myself a good laugh.

Suddenly the events of the last hour came rushing back. As soon as I could, I pulled over, opened the door, and threw up my coffee into the gutter.

CHAPTER 31

It had just struck noon when I pulled up in front of the brownstone. I was trying to figure my next steps in tracking down Manny Casper and his paramour. I wondered what the chances were that I could squeeze out a few more free hours before turning my attention back to the Bodine case.

Slim, as it turns out.

Through the front window I saw the top of a large head set on a pair of shoulders as wide as my torso was long.

Lazenby.

I walked into the office as casual as I could.

"Sorry," I said. "Errands took a little longer than expected."

I sat down at my desk and got a notebook ready to go. That's when I noticed that Lazenby was holding a mug of what looked like our good German lager. Accepting beer during working hours was out of character for the lieutenant.

Ms. P had apparently decided to start cocktail hour early as well. She was leaning as far back in her chair as the mechanics would allow and had a glass of wine cradled to her stomach.

"Is this business or social?" I asked.

My boss didn't answer at first. She was too busy giving me a look. I wasn't entirely familiar with this variety. It was a mix of motherly concern and sniper's glare.

Not for the first time, I wondered if Lillian Pentecost was a mind reader. I wiped a hand across my chin, checking for dried vomit.

She turned her attention back to Lazenby.

"It's business," Ms. Pentecost said. "The lieutenant was explaining how he has very little time for anything else these days."

From my desk I had an excellent view of Lazenby's face. It wasn't quite grim, but somewhere in that vicinity. Consulting my thesaurus, I'm going to go with *dour*.

"What's wrong? The mayor got you chasing burglars again?"

That was in reference to some rigmarole the prior winter. Despite specializing in homicide, Lazenby had gotten saddled with taking down a citywide housebreaking operation. A case that we had no small hand in helping crack.

Lazenby chuckled, but there was no humor in it.

"I wish," he said. "Anyway, I didn't come over here to air out my woes."

Which meant he was willing to share with my boss, but not with me. It was a reminder that Lazenby and Ms. P had history. One I wasn't always privy to.

"I need you to talk some sense into your client," Lazenby told her. "Whitsun won't give a statement. Says if we come in with a material witness warrant, he'll fight it. Clam up, drag it out."

"He places little trust in the police," Ms. P noted.

"Oh, I know. Let's be honest—he doesn't have many friends on the force, either. I don't care about that. I care about finding whoever killed Vera Bodine. Right now he's obstructing that investigation. From everything I can tell, he knew her best. I need him to talk to me so I can get a fingerhold on her life, establish patterns, get a sense of his history with her. What did she tell him? Did she have any conflicts with people? Why am

I listing questions? You know what I need. It's goddamn basic detective work."

He let the dust settle on his avalanche of words, then continued.

"It doesn't look good for him. Refusing to talk. He doesn't care, but he should. The other side of the coin is that Bodine's a priority because of the headlines. Once those go away, I'll get told to spend my hours on other cases."

He took a sip of his beer. It became a gulp, which became two. He pulled a handkerchief out of his pocket and patted foam off his beard.

"You know how many murders have hit my desk since Wednesday? Seven. That's not counting the accidental drowning that I'm pretty sure wasn't an accident. If it wasn't for the headlines and Bodine having money, she'd be at the bottom of the pile."

Last winter we had to work three murders at once. It had been exhausting, and we even had help for some of it. Seven, maybe eight, plus Bodine and whatever had been on his plate before she turned up?

I no longer wondered why Lazenby had accepted beer at noon. Now I was wondering why he didn't go for something stronger.

"What do you need from me, Nathan?" Ms. P asked. "If it's to convince Mr. Whitsun he's being an obstinate jackass, I'm afraid that challenge may be beyond me."

The lieutenant downed the rest of his mug in one gulp.

"I was thinking of something a little more involved."

Lazenby told us what he was thinking, and after some brief negotiation, Ms. P agreed. I made a call, then hopped into the kitchen to ask Mrs. Campbell to postpone lunch.

"All she's eaten today is half a biscuit and jam," our housekeeper informed me, adding something pungent to a pot of greens.

"We've got another guest coming," I told her. "As soon as they leave, I'll usher her right to the table."

"This guest need feeding?"

"It's a lawyer. As far as I know, they only eat their young."

Then I went back to my desk where I found Ms. P and Lazenby chatting about the case.

It was quite the dance, with neither wanting to give away too much information. The pair might have had a friendly relationship, but at the end of the day Lazenby wanted the NYPD to get the collar. And while Ms. P might respect Lazenby, that feeling didn't extend to the department as a whole.

This resulted in exchanges like:

"Even with all your men, the search of Miss Bodine's apartment must be quite challenging."

"We're making do."

"But you haven't found anything of interest?"

"I didn't say that." Pause. "Any suggestion on where we might focus?"

"I shouldn't hazard a guess."

There was also:

"The lavender sachets—I assume they're a rather commonly sold item."

"Every home goods store has them, and hotels buy by the dozen. But I've got a man on it."

"One man, over a hundred stores in the five boroughs alone."

"I can do the math, Lillian."

"Of course you can."

And then:

"What do you make of that grocery sack?"

"Which one is that, Lieutenant?"

"The one Bodine was seen carrying those times she left the apartment."

"Perhaps it was for groceries."

"None of the stores nearby knew her. Besides, I thought Whitsun did her shopping for her."

"I suppose she might have used it to carry something other than groceries."

"Thank you, I got that far on my own."

And most amusingly:

"Were you or your men informed of the times prior to these last few weeks that Miss Bodine was seen leaving the Baxter Arms?"

"What? No. Everyone told us they'd never seen her leave the building until this past month. They told you and Parker different?"

"No. But it's good to confirm that Miss Bodine's forays were new behavior."

Luckily, I wasn't expected to participate. I was still a little shaky from that morning's adventure. I kept finding my fingers wandering up to my nose, trying to rub away the phantom press of a blade.

It wouldn't go away, and every time I did it, I caught a whiff of lighter fluid. I needed a shower, a break, a breath.

I was about to excuse myself in order to obtain at least one of the three when the doorbell rang.

Breathing would have to wait.

CHAPTER 32

I opened the door to find Whitsun standing on the steps.

"Heading to the rodeo, Parker?"

"It's fashion, Whitsun. Pick up a magazine sometime."

"I'll stick to *Newsweek,* thank you."

I stepped aside to let him in. He rounded the corner into the office and stopped in his tracks. Lazenby had moved to the couch. That had been Ms. P's suggestion, the idea being that it would make the scene look more relaxed. Which I thought was silly. You could stick the lieutenant in an aloha shirt and the man would still radiate authority.

"What the hell is this?" Whitsun asked. "Parker told me you had news on the case."

"I do, Mr. Whitsun," Ms. P said. "But first, I would like to have a consultation."

"This is a goddamn ambush." Whitsun turned on his heel, but found the office door closed and me parked in front of it. "You think I won't go through you, Parker?"

"I think you'd try."

Whitsun knew enough about me to decide not to force the issue. Instead, he turned and aimed for the door to the dining room, where he could take the long way around to the front door.

As he passed, Ms. Pentecost stood and held out an envelope.

"If you leave, I must insist on giving you this."

Whitsun stopped. He was starting to look like a windup toy that kept hitting corners.

"What is it?" he asked, looking at the envelope in her hand but not taking it.

"My resignation, as well as a check for your advance."

"You can't do that. We have a contract."

"Which states that if I find any reason I cannot fulfill its terms, I will withdraw," Ms. P stated. "Your obstinacy is— Do not interrupt!"

Whitsun shut up. You'd do the same if you ever heard Ms. P use that tone with you.

"Your relationship with the police is adversarial. Mine is not. Not inherently so. Have I withheld information from them on occasion? Yes. Though I hope I have made up for that by providing equally useful information. The identity of criminals, for instance."

She and Lazenby exchanged a look. I had the feeling he was of the opinion that the scales remained unbalanced.

"In short, the police have manpower and resources that I do not, and so it behooves me not to impede their investigation. At least not for foolish reasons."

Once there was enough of a pause that Whitsun felt safe to talk, he asked, "You think I'm being foolish?"

"I think you want to find Miss Bodine's killer. I think the police are a useful tool to accomplish this," she said. "We are not in an interrogation room, and you may leave whenever you wish. It is far preferable to being served a warrant."

Whitsun thought it over, looked from the envelope still in Ms. P's hand to Lazenby and back again. Then he sat down and turned his chair to face the lieutenant. He looked at the clock on the shelf.

"You've got thirty minutes," he said.

I've talked about Lazenby's interrogation style before. He can be intimidating when he wants to be, but can also go at it soft. Like a father confessor. Coaxing out details, making the witness feel comfortable. So comfortable that they don't guard their tongue and let slip something they were hoping to hold close.

No slow coaxing here. Thirty minutes ain't much. Not for an interview involving a murder. Lazenby fired off questions hot and quick. His pencil dashed across the pages of a spiral notebook, but he never looked down at what he was writing. He kept his attention fixed on Whitsun the entire time.

What was her relationship with her neighbors? Did she ever talk about them?

Do you know of anyone with a grudge?

Why did Bodine have an interest in the Fennel case?

Do you know of anything else that might have been worrying her?

On that last, Whitsun answered, "No," with a straight face. We were still keeping the FBI out of it, it seemed.

There was more, but you get the idea. Lazenby had about seven minutes left of his promised thirty when there was a knock at the door. I abandoned my post to go see who it was. I used the peephole first, worried about a particular mobster who might not have appreciated being locked in a trunk.

It was one of Lazenby's boys. A sergeant I recognized from previous cases. I slipped the latch and opened up.

"Good afternoon, Sergeant. I'll tell your boss you're—"

Then he was barreling by me, followed by three other uniforms and a man in a mediocre suit. The uniforms I didn't know. The suit I did.

"Hey, what the hell do you think—"

By then we were all in the office and the officers were laying hands on Whitsun. Ms. Pentecost was on her feet, eyes wide with outrage. She and Whitsun both shouted something, but I couldn't make out either of them over Lazenby's bellow.

"Staples, what's the meaning of this?"

Detective Donald Staples held up a folded piece of paper.

Fair-haired, slender, and on the rugged side of pretty, the golden boy of the NYPD usually adopted an open, friendly face. All the better to lure suspects into a false sense of friendliness. Not today.

"I'm serving a material witness warrant for Forest Whitsun," he declared.

Whitsun reached for the paper, but Lazenby got to it first. He looked it over.

"Judge Creed signed this? There's no way he signs papers on my case without checking with me first."

Staples shook his head. "It's not your case anymore, Lieutenant."

Lazenby recoiled as if he'd been slapped. If he had the words to respond, he'd misplaced them. My boss lent him some.

"Detective Staples," she said, "Mr. Whitsun was complying with the lieutenant's request for an interview. If you insist on conducting it at a station house, he would be happy to make his own way there."

I don't know if "happy" was the word I'd reach for to describe Whitsun. If he tensed his jaw any more, his molars were going to shatter.

Staples didn't respond. In fact, he refused to even look in Ms. Pentecost's direction. Instead, he gave the uniforms a nod and they escorted Whitsun out. The defense attorney availed himself of his right to remain silent except for a quick side-mouth to me on his way out the door.

"Call my office. Ask for Pearl. Tell her what's happening."

Then he and the uniforms were gone. I turned to find Lazenby and Staples facing off in the middle of our office. The big man's hands were clenched into fists, knuckles turning white. If it came to blows, he was a clear favorite. But he kept his temper in check and his hands at his sides.

"You're taking my case away from me, Donald?" Lazenby asked.

"I'm not taking it, Nathan. It's been given to me."

Staples might not have been throwing punches, but that was a blow that landed.

"The commissioner doesn't think I can get the job done?"

"The commissioner . . ." Staples worked his jaw from side to side, like he was chewing his words into something easier to swallow. "He thinks you're being a little too accommodating."

"It's the headlines, isn't it?"

Staples threw up his hands. "Of course it's the headlines. You were dragging your feet. You should have had Whitsun in the box days ago."

"So that he could play dumb? Then run to the press with stories of police incompetence? You'd really have headlines then."

It was our office, but Ms. Pentecost and I might as well have been the wallpaper. If I thought they were going to keep it up, I'd have run for popcorn.

"So you interrogated him here? With them?" Staples said, finally acknowledging the private detectives in the room.

"It's a witness statement," Lazenby said. "I was getting it."

Staples laughed.

"Witness? How about prime suspect?"

That was news to everybody else in the room.

"What do you mean prime suspect, Detective? What is his motive for murdering Vera Bodine?" My boss had asked the question, but Staples directed his answer to Lazenby.

"We got hold of a copy of Bodine's will. She left the building to Whitsun, lock, stock, and barrel. I talked to some real estate folks. If he sold it today, he'd clear three hundred thousand, no sweat."

Staples paused to let that sink in. Then he piled on.

"He was the person closest to her, he had a key to her apartment, and he has the clearest motive. I mean . . . My God, Nathan. You know better than anyone how often the person who reports someone missing turns out to be the killer."

Yeah, Lazenby knew the numbers. So did we.

I watched as the lieutenant processed all this. He turned to my boss.

"Did you know about the will?" he asked.

"I did not," she said. "Nor, do I believe, did Mr. Whitsun."

Another laugh from Staples. I hadn't pegged Staples as cynical, but his laughter certainly was.

"You'll excuse me if I don't take your word for it."

The way he said "your" made me want to throw a punch myself, but I followed Lazenby's example and kept my hands holstered.

Staples turned to Ms. Pentecost, finally giving her his full attention.

"You want to know why the lieutenant is being taken off this case, look in the mirror. As soon as I heard you had a hand in this, I knew you'd try and interfere. Not this time."

He packed that last sentence with a lot of weight. He was referring to the murders last winter—the case where Holly came into our lives, the one listed in our archives as "The *Strange Crime* Killings."

Yeah, there was interference. If that's what you call keeping secret that three murders were connected and flat-out lying to Staples's face about it.

If he was looking for Lillian Pentecost to flinch, he was disappointed.

"I assure you, Detective," she said, "I want nothing more than to find Miss Bodine's killer and bring him or her to justice."

He studied her for a long moment, like she was standing in a lineup and he was deciding whether her face fit the crime. When the moment ended, he held out his hand to Lazenby, who looked confused until he realized Staples was asking for the warrant back. The lieutenant handed it over.

"Well, Ms. Pentecost," Staples said as he tucked the document back into his jacket pocket, "it's very possible we already have our killer."

Then he turned and left. He didn't spare me a single glance. Not even a nasty one.

CHAPTER 33

"I'm sorry, Nathan. I fear our relationship may have done you some damage."

At first I wasn't sure he heard her. The big man's posture had suffered something of an avalanche. His shoulders were slumped and his eyes were flat and distant. Then he shook himself and rebuilt some of his scaffolding.

"It's not your fault," he said. "You never twisted my arm. Donald was right, though. I should have hauled Whitsun in earlier. I only thought . . . Well, it doesn't matter. You didn't twist my arm."

He grabbed his jacket from the back of the sofa and slipped it on.

"I'd better get back," he said. "I doubt I'll be let in the interrogation room. But I'd like to get a look at Bodine's will."

"As would I," Ms. P said.

Lazenby paused in the midst of doing up a button.

"You should probably get it from somewhere else."

Ms. P nodded. He nodded back. Another nod to me and off he went.

I thought about seeing him to the door, maybe slip him a reassuring word, but I was fresh out.

Ms. P lowered herself back into her chair and let out a rattling sigh. She sounded like I felt.

"I'm officially putting Staples into my black book," I said.

"He's merely carrying out his duties," Ms. P noted.

"Sure, but look at the timing on that. He must have had eyes on Whitsun to know he was here, and he would have caught Lazenby's unmarked at the curb. He could have waited. Instead, he did it in a way that left the lieutenant with egg on his face."

She picked up the wineglass, swirled it, then peered at its contents like they were tea leaves.

"You should call—"

"Whitsun's office. Got it."

I got on the horn and asked the operator to connect me. A woman's voice answered and when I asked for Pearl she said, "This is Pearl." I told her what was up, she asked all the right questions, and she said she'd head to the precinct house to make sure he had representation.

So an associate, not a secretary. I hoped for Whitsun's sake he hired her for the strength of her law, not the length of her legs.

I hung up and swiveled my chair around.

"Okay, so I know what you told Lazenby, but are you really sure Whitsun didn't know about the will? Only real friend, sole beneficiary—makes sense she would have told him."

"When it comes to thoughts of mortality, we do not always do the sensible thing."

"That is especially vague, even for you," I told her. "All I'm saying is that we don't have any real reason to trust Whitsun. I hate to give credit to Staples, but he was right when he said—"

The phone rang.

"With the day I'm having, that'll be the IRS telling us we're being audited."

I picked up.

"Hello, Pentecost Investigations, Will Parker speaking. How may I help you?"

The voice on the other end was male, on the older side, and with a cadence that seemed oddly familiar, though I would have bet good money I'd never heard the voice before.

"Hello, you must be Willowjean."

"I must be, yes."

"I've always said that's an absolutely lovely name. Not that you shouldn't feel free to use the diminutive if you prefer."

"Thank you and . . . thank you?"

"Now, I'm sure you're very busy, but could you put Lily on the phone, please?"

"I'm sorry, did you say 'Lily'?"

Out of the corner of my eye I saw my boss's head jerk my way.

"Yes," the man on the phone said. "If she's available."

"May I ask who's calling?"

"Oh, I'm sorry, yes. Tell her it's her father."

Great—a crank call. I covered the mouthpiece with my hand and turned to my boss.

"I've got a guy on the line who—"

She was already picking up the handset on her desk.

"You can hang up now."

I was a little slow in complying, and she repeated, "Will. It's okay. You can get off the line."

I did.

"Hello? Dad? Is everything okay?"

If you've been following along with these narratives of mine, you know that Lillian Pentecost's life before coming to New York City wasn't so much an open book as a redacted pamphlet. A ways back she'd let it drop that she had a father and he had been a minister. From her use of the past tense, I'd assumed he was deceased. A false assumption, unless this was a very long distance call.

"Yes. . . . Yes. . . . When was this? . . . Are you sure? . . . When was the last time you saw it? . . . Ah. . . . Yes, I remember him. Did he describe this man?"

As she talked, she swiveled her chair around until it was pointed at the back wall and the painting hanging over her desk. She tilted her head, looking up at the tree and the field and the woman beneath it.

When she finally spoke again, her voice had changed. There was an undercurrent that wasn't there before.

Lillian Pentecost was angry.

"I'm sure it's fine, Dad," she lied. "No, no. Really. . . . It's probably some curiosity seeker. Or a common thief. Don't concern yourself. But thank you for letting me know. . . . Yes. . . . Yes, and I you."

She reached back and dropped the phone into the cradle, keeping her chair pointed at the wall and the painting. She was so stiff she was practically levitating in her seat.

For once, I left the silence alone. Ten seconds, twenty. After half a minute had passed, she suddenly stood, turned, grabbed her cane, and headed toward the door.

"I need to go out," she said.

I stood up.

"Alone," she added.

"Boss, I don't know what's going on but—"

"This is a private errand. I need you to stay here. We have too much going on to leave the office unattended."

I sat back down.

"Of course. Whatever you say."

I stayed seated while I listened to Ms. P walk to the front door. I stayed seated while she opened it, walked through, closed it. I even stayed seated as I watched the top of her head cross the office window, moving toward the corner in search of a cab.

Then I leapt up and hurried for the door.

CHAPTER 34

I don't know what she told the cabbie but he did not spare the horses. It was all I could do to keep up with him while staying out of sight and not running too many red lights in the process. When the cab dropped off the East River Drive and started moving north, I got an idea of where Ms. Pentecost was going.

A few minutes later I watched as the cab pulled away from a familiar residence in Washington Heights and Ms. Pentecost began walking purposefully toward the locked gates. During the drive I decided on my course of action, and it wasn't stealth.

I pulled the Cadillac right up to the curb and hopped out. Ms. Pentecost stared daggers at me, her finger hovering over the buzzer attached to one of the gateposts.

"I know, I know," I said as I walked toward her. "You don't want me here, but here I am. We can stand and bicker or you can resign yourself to the circumstances and yell at me later."

She pushed the buzzer.

A tinny, female voice came out of the intercom box.

"Who is it?"

"Lillian Pentecost to see Jessup Quincannon."

A pause of exactly three seconds and then—

"I'll be right out."

We looked through the gate, up the cobblestone walk, to the front door of what I suppose you'd call a mansion. I thought it looked more like a haunted house. A Victorian gargoyle squatting on top of a hill. Four stories of turrets and eaves and ornate flourishes. Like icing spread over a cake that had long been lost to the maggots.

"I don't suppose you want to tell me what this is about."

No answer from my boss.

"A hint will do. Just so I know where to aim when the shooting starts."

This was only half a joke. I still had my Browning tucked in the back holster. Usually this sort of comment would have garnered a wrist-slap response from Ms. Pentecost. Something along the lines of "Please try to keep the gunfire to a minimum."

All I got was more silence.

The front door opened and spat out a figure: a tall woman made even taller by high-heeled boots with lacings that crawled all the way up her calves. She was wearing a sleeveless white blouse and a black skirt that ended well above the level the town fathers would have signed off on. Her hair hung down her back in a long pitch-black braid, and the only color on her face was her lips, painted in a shade best described as "arterial."

Her beauty, like the house's, was a distraction.

Alathea looked like the kind of secretary who was hired to work on her back, but her job was to knock you on yours if the situation demanded it. She was Jessup Quincannon's bodyguard.

"Ms. Pentecost. Miss Parker," she said as she opened the gate for us. "Mr. Quincannon's been expecting you."

I didn't believe her. I hadn't even been expecting me. Ms. P didn't utter a single syllable as we followed Alathea up the cobblestone walkway toward the manse.

"Love the boots," I said.

"Thank you. They're custom-made. I can give you the name of the cobbler, if you want."

"Don't bother. I don't have the legs for them."

"I like the suit. I can't go in for the cavalry-style jackets. With my shoulders, I would resemble a football player."

And so forth.

If you didn't know me, you might mistake this for polite banter. If you did know me, you might think it was flirting. But if you knew both me and Alathea, you might see it for what it was: two dangerous women sniffing each other out.

We walked through the front door into the dark-paneled entry hall.

"Mr. Quincannon is with the collection," Alathea said. "We can take the elevator up."

She walked us to a small private elevator that must have been installed within the last seven months.

"Fancy," I commented.

"Several of Mr. Quincannon's associates are elderly or infirm," she said, directing a pointed glance at Ms. P's cane. "He wanted to make it easier for them to visit the exhibits. It would be a tragedy if anyone was injured. Speaking of which."

She held out a hand, palm up.

I reached back, pulled the Browning out of its holster, and handed it to her. She set it on a round lacquered table next to the elevator door.

I wondered if the table had been put there expressly for that purpose. Considering Quincannon's past guest lists, which included a parade of murderers, convicted and otherwise, I wouldn't have been surprised.

Despite being brand new and freshly oiled, the wood-paneled elevator creeped up two flights in the time it took most to do ten. So as not to rattle the bones of Quincannon's collection of ghouls, I presumed. Then the doors opened and Alathea led us out into the Black Museum.

Long glass-topped cases were filled with every type of curiosity: photographs and documents; mementos taken from the pockets of victims, weapons of every sort, some with the blood still on them, now dried to a black-red rust.

The walls were the same, with exhibits framed and pinned and hanging, all very evenly and artfully spaced. Some of the items that had been present when I was in that room seven months earlier were gone, replaced by new finds.

For example, the spot on the wall that had once featured a dress supposedly belonging to one of Jack the Ripper's victims, was now home to a car door, its sand-colored paint bullet-ridden and blood-flecked.

It had to be a fake, I thought. No way in hell was he getting hold of Bonnie and Clyde's car.

Still, money could buy anything, and Quincannon spent his commemorating murder, along with the men and women who did the deed.

As a fig leaf to inquiring authorities, nothing was labeled. Everything deniable. So if I wanted to know about that door, I would have been forced to ask its owner.

He was standing there waiting for us, but not alone. Next to him was a brick wall in a tweed suit: six feet and change, bald as a newborn, with a face like a Jersey steelworker.

I wondered who Quincannon had pissed off enough to necessitate a second bodyguard.

Quincannon whispered something to the man and received a whispered reply in return, then the mobile mountain turned and walked to the elevator. As he passed us, he nodded to my boss.

"Ms. Pentecost," he said in a voice fit to attend King George. "A pleasure to see you again."

He looked like muscle, but he talked like money. I knew that voice, too. This was Silas Culliver, Quincannon's pet lawyer. I couldn't have pictured him more wrong if I'd tried.

Whether my boss found seeing him a pleasure, I'll never know. She made a beeline for the man of the house.

"Where is it?"

Most people hearing my boss's tone would have started looking for the exits. Not Quincannon. He smiled with unabashed glee.

"Lillian," he said, "what a lovely coincidence. I was just thinking about you."

With my boss taking the lead, I had the opportunity to study our host. Despite being worth something in the eight figures, he liked to dress down: jeans and a white linen shirt open at the collar.

He was slightly north of seventy, with a full head of lacquered silver hair and the posture and complexion of a much younger man. You'd think evil would age you, but if anything, he looked even more full of vim and vigor than last time. I wondered whose neck he'd sunk his fangs into to get that rosy glow.

Unkind, I know. Anyone glimpsing him on the street might mistake him for the stately grandfather type. But I'd seen him with his mask off, and could still make out the leering sadist underneath. Ms. Pentecost repeated herself.

"Where is it?"

"Where is what, dear?" said the monster in the man suit. "You'll have to be more specific."

"Don't try me, Jessup."

"Oh, but it's so much fun. And so easy," he said, smiling even wider. "Well . . . sometimes it does require a bit of effort."

He walked over to one of the largest of the glass cases. Last time I had been there it had held a collection of knives and straight razors. Now it had only one "exhibit." It was a wooden painter's box, its compartments filled with tubes of oil paint and brushes whose bristles looked as stiff as a blade. The inside of its lid had been used as a palette, every inch of its surface covered by pools of dried paint.

I'd never seen it before in my life. At the same time, something about it tugged at my memory.

Ms. P stood over the case, staring down, her face indecipherable.

"I'm torn, really," Quincannon said. "Space in my collection is limited. I'm wondering if it's foolish to dedicate an entire case to one exhibit. Especially one that has only a single murder attached to it. Or is it two? It's unclear. There was a fire, it seems. Many of the records were lost."

My boss reached out her hand and pressed her fingertips against the glass.

"This does not belong to you."

I thought my boss's voice was cold before. I was surprised the glass of the case didn't frost over.

"Oh, I assure you, my dear, it belongs to me. I paid good money for it."

"You stole it from my father's property."

I'd heard what spiders sound like when moving en masse, and that's what Quincannon's quiet laughter reminded me of.

"I certainly did not," he said. "I haven't left the city in months."

"But you paid someone to," Ms. P countered. "To remove it from the . . . from his toolshed."

"I think that would be very difficult to prove," Quincannon said. "As would verifying the provenance of the piece."

I was looking at the dried paint on the lid when it suddenly clicked into place. The colors. The yellows and ochres. That very specific shade of blue. I could match each shade with a color in the painting above Ms. Pentecost's desk.

The one of the woman under the tree. The one without a signature.

"If you feel compelled, you are more than welcome to try," Quincannon was saying. "In court. In public. Of course, to do so, you'd have to talk about what this set of paints represents."

Then he added, almost in a whisper, "You'd have to talk about what happened to your mother."

Ms. Pentecost snatched her hand off the glass like she'd been burned.

"Give it back," she said.

His smile grew even wider. Too wide. Like it was trying to wrap its way around his skull.

"Ask nicely."

Ms. Pentecost's composure broke then. Her bottom lip quivered. For a moment I was terrified that she was going to cry. I didn't want this man—this vile, vile man—to see that. To see her tears.

He'd love it. He'd lick them right off her cheeks.

No tears fell. What happened was, in some ways, so much worse.

"Please," Ms. Pentecost said. "Please do not put this on display. Please return it to me."

Quincannon's smile fell away. Like the wires at the end of his grin had been cut.

"I think not," he said. "I think I'm going to keep this right here. I might even make it the centerpiece of one of our salons. As a lesson. If you interfere in my affairs, I will certainly take a hand in yours."

We'd been snapping links in his macabre supply chain and, as Silas Culliver promised over the phone, here were the consequences. The payback.

I didn't understand it. This whole scene was like coming upon a sunken ship, with only broken fragments visible above the waves, the rest lost to the depths.

All I knew was that it was personal.

I was afraid that Ms. Pentecost would ask again. Would say "please" again.

I needn't have worried. My employer gathered herself. Raised her chin. Found a few spare inches in her spine.

"You think that this has been me interfering, Jessup? Sending a few letters to corrupt officials? Getting property clerks fired?"

She actually smiled. Just a small one. A grim one.

A hangman's smile.

"This has been nothing," she continued. "A pastime. Something to occupy my attention between things that really matter. But now . . . Now I see that's been a mistake. Like leaving a spider to build its nest in a high corner. I've let you sit here. Growing fat. No more taking swipes at your web. Now I think I will have to deal with you once and for all."

There was no quiver in her voice now. Unless you count the kind that holds arrows, and those were aimed straight at Quincannon's heart.

He heard it. So did Alathea, who I saw out of the corner of my eye, advancing a few steps to get a better angle in case she had to leap forward to protect her employer.

No need.

Ms. Pentecost turned her back on Quincannon and moved toward the elevator, cane pounding a death march against the floor. I hurried to keep up.

"Now, Lillian, there's no reason to—"

Ms. P stopped, turning so quickly I almost ran into her. Her face . . . I had never seen her face like that. I imagined that if anyone had, they weren't around to talk about it.

"If you ever . . . Ever! Come near my family or my friends again, I will put you in a grave myself."

Quincannon's mouth hung open. He didn't even try for words. Alathea had a pistol in her hand, a wicked-looking snub nose, and hell if I knew where she'd had it strapped.

Without waiting for a response, my boss turned back around, walked to the elevator, and stepped inside. I followed.

My last image of Quincannon as the doors closed was proof that, while he might have been pure evil, he had half a brain.

Because he looked afraid.

I made sure to retrieve my gun on the way out.

CHAPTER 35

The drive from Quincannon's back to the office took thirty-seven minutes. That's a long time to share the inside of a car in silence, but Ms. Pentecost and I managed it. She didn't look much like talking and I wasn't going to force it. At least not when all I could see of her was her profile in the rearview mirror as she stared out the window.

As soon as we walked through the door of the brownstone, Mrs. Campbell came steaming out of the kitchen.

"Will Parker, you promised," she snarled. "Right after your meeting you were sitting her down for lunch. Next thing I know, you're both up and gone."

"Something unexpected came up and—"

But she was already on to our boss.

"I've turned the last of the chicken into a pot pie. And I threw some tomatoes and greens into a pot. I know it's not your favorite, but you've got to keep your iron up."

Ms. P held up a hand. "I'm not hungry."

"Don't be daft. Half a biscuit won't do until dinner. You know what your doctor said about missing meals. So why don't you go into the dining room and have a seat and we'll see if you can't eat a wee bite? Just a bit of—"

"I am not a child, Eleanor," Ms. Pentecost snapped. "I do not need you to spoon-feed me."

She turned her back on the housekeeper and walked into the office.

Mrs. Campbell looked stung, but only for a moment. She'd been with Ms. Pentecost longer than I, and had witnessed our boss's full range of moods. Her face quickly firmed up and she gave me a nod.

"You better deal with it," that nod said.

I walked into the office to do just that.

Ms. P was at the drinks trolley, pouring a glass of wine. She filled it up high enough that it spilled over the side. She put it to her mouth, sipped off the excess.

"I would like to be alone, Will."

She phrased it like a request, but her tone said it was an order.

"I gathered that," I said. "But I've been told that it's good to talk about these things. Whatever the hell this thing is."

As I spoke, she took her glass behind her desk, went to sit, then changed her mind. Instead, she downed the wine in a single swallow and walked back to the drinks trolley to pour another.

"If you don't want to talk to me, maybe you should call Dr. Grayson," I suggested. "This seems like the kind of thing you keep a psychiatrist around for."

"I don't want to talk about it with anyone," she said. "Not right now. All you need to know is that it's personal and none of your concern."

Now I was starting to get angry.

"None of my concern? This is Quincannon we're talking about. He makes a threat and then follows through and I don't even understand what it means. I'm not stupid. It has to do with that painting hanging on the wall and apparently your mother and a murder. Maybe two. Quincannon didn't seem to know, but he knew a whole lot more than I do. Considering that whatever he throws at you might go awry and hit me, I think you owe it to me to tell me what—"

"I do not owe this to you!"

The bottle slipped out of her hand and fell to the floor. It was thick glass, handmade in some Scottish village, and managed not to crack. But its contents began spilling out. I went to pick it up, but Ms. P waved me away.

She carefully knelt down, righted the bottle, then grabbed a towel from the trolley and began sopping up the spilled wine. As she worked, she talked.

"I owe you many things, Will. But not this. We are both grown women and we are allowed our secrets. For example, you did not tell me about being attacked at Coney Island and I did not ask. I trusted you were keeping it secret for a reason."

My guts started sliding into a sinkhole.

"How did you—"

"Because I am not blind," she said, raising her head from her scrub work. "Sand on your skirt and sweater. A fresh lump on the back of your head. The deflated tires on the car— I assume because the keys were stolen rather than lost down a grate. And I have not seen you carrying your new pistol in several days. What that has to do with the Mafia and why you felt compelled to confront a mob enforcer, I do not know."

I opened my mouth to ask the obvious question but, again, she beat me to it.

"Brynn Suilebhan has long been an informant of mine," she said. "He owes me more than he can ever repay, and he hears much from his position behind that bar. He called as soon as the FBI left. I assume their raid was courtesy of Agent Faraday. Now that I can spare a moment to think about it, I will also assume it was part of a charade. Done in service of pressuring this Russo person to give you the name and location of your attacker."

She slowly got to her feet and dropped the wine-soaked towel into the ice bucket. I didn't need a mirror to know my face was burning bright red.

"I am not angry that you did not tell me," she said. "You

have your reasons. I am not insulted that you keep your secrets. I am insulted that you think I wouldn't know. This disease may be robbing me of my balance and my strength and even sometimes my speech. But it has not taken my goddamn mind!"

I took an involuntary step back. My knees hit the back of my desk.

"I still have my mind," she repeated, her voice hoarse and shaking. "And, for now at least, I have my dignity. I will not let Jessup Quincannon take that."

She stood in front of her desk, looking up at the painting on the office wall. She placed her hands flat on the oak and leaned forward, like she was anticipating something. Like she expected that girl under the tree to turn around and show us her face.

For a moment I felt like an intruder. A peeping tom caught stealing an intimate moment that wasn't meant for me.

The moment passed and she straightened back up.

"Please leave, Will."

Not an order. Or a request. Only a tired plea.

I left the office, closing the door behind me. I told Mrs. Campbell to stand down and pack everything away for later.

"If she gets hungry, she knows where to look," I told her.

I went upstairs to my bedroom. I kicked off my oxfords, took off my jacket, undid the holster and put it on my nightstand. Then I sat on my bed and thought about crying.

Thought about it, but couldn't. I felt drained. Dried out.

Who could blame me? The last six hours felt like six days.

There was the boondoggle with Russo; the drama with Lazenby and Whitsun and Staples; then Quincannon and Ms. Pentecost and finding out she'd known about what happened at the beach this entire time.

I felt stupid. Stupid and guilty and ashamed.

Ashamed for not telling Ms. P when I had the chance.

Ashamed I'd gotten found out. Ashamed I'd fallen for Casper and his girl's ploy in the first place.

"So stupid," I said to my bedroom ceiling. "You are so incredibly stupid."

I turned my head to look at the window. Still light out.

"I just want it to be over," I said to myself.

Which is one of the nicely consistent things about bad days. If you just wait a while, eventually they end.

CHAPTER **36**

Ms. Pentecost and I didn't see each other for nearly forty-eight hours. How did we manage that, considering we share a home and office?

Through a considerable amount of mutual effort.

Ms. P spent the rest of Monday in the office, emerging, I assume, for bathroom breaks and hopefully to get some food. I didn't know, since I spent the rest of the day in my bedroom, going downstairs only for dinner, which I took back to my room.

When I got up the next morning, Ms. Pentecost had made it to her bedroom. I thought about knocking, but it was far too early for her, and I had the feeling the request to leave her be was open-ended.

My first stop was my desk, where I placed a call to a locksmith, who said he'd be by later in the morning to change the locks on the front door. I also resolved to get the Caddy into the shop as soon as possible to switch out the ignition. No reason to take chances.

I moved on to the kitchen, where I settled myself at the kitchen table and dug into a plate of eggs and the day's edition of the *Times*.

There was a short piece—page three, below the fold—on the Bodine case. It was basically ten inches of "the police are hot on the trail but they won't say who or why or how."

Two details stood out. One was that there was no word about Bodine owning the building. Staples was running a tight ship.

The other interesting detail came in the first sentence of the third paragraph.

"Forest Whitsun, famed defense attorney and friend of the deceased, presented himself to the police yesterday to assist with the investigation.

"'Vera Bodine's death is a tragedy,' Whitsun declared in an exclusive interview with this reporter. 'Not only is it a personal tragedy, but it's a tragedy for the city of New York, that an elderly woman living alone should be preyed upon like this.'

"The man called 'New York's real-life Perry Mason' added that he had every faith in the investigators to find the person responsible.

"Police continue the hard work of clearing out Bodine's apartment. Bodine, a hoarder and virtual shut-in . . ."

And so forth.

"God, he's good," I mumbled through a bite of egg.

Mrs. Campbell, who was in the pantry taking inventory, poked her head out.

"That's what they say."

"What?"

"About God."

"I'm talking about Forest Whitsun," I said, holding up the paper. "The man is served a warrant, gets practically dragged out of our office. Somehow he spins it so the papers think he went on his own. To graciously lend the police his assistance."

Mrs. Campbell laughed.

"Sounds like something you would do."

"It's different when I do it. I do it with grace and subtlety. And I never, ever give them a personal quote. That's just grandstanding."

"If you say so."

I was going to elaborate, but she'd already stuck her head back into the pantry to tick off bags of beans.

I looked back at the article, making note again that Whitsun had said "investigators" rather than the police. That, I had to admit, demonstrated a certain amount of grace.

None of the press had picked up on the fact that Whitsun was our client. Now that the *Times* had him in the mix, that wouldn't last long. That discovery would push the case back to the front page again.

I wondered what Whitsun had told the police, and what they might have let slip to him. I could find out with a phone call. But a phone call wouldn't get me out of the house.

I wasn't ready to see Ms. Pentecost again. That feeling of guilt and shame was still too close at hand.

The clock chimed nine. Even defense attorneys should be in their offices by now, I thought.

I asked Mrs. Campbell if she'd mind fielding the locksmith. She said she wouldn't, though when she asked why we needed the locks changed, all I told her was I lost my keys and was playing it safe.

"I don't blame you," she said. "As my mother used to say, the world's full of saints, but the sinners and snakes have them sorely outnumbered."

"Amen," I said.

Then I left to visit the serpent's den.

I'd never seen Whitsun's professional digs. The picture I'd painted in my head was a smaller version of Boekbinder & Gimbal. The closer I got to the address, the more I began to suspect my vision was way off.

Whitsun and Associates was a storefront operation on the corner of an unremarkable intersection deep in the Bronx. The firm had its name etched on the glass, but the sun-bleached outline of the letters above the door advertised the ghost of Donger and Sons Butcher's.

No bell announced my arrival.

Where there was once a display of the day's selection of fresh cuts, there was now a waiting area showcasing the wide breadth of humanity the city had to offer. There was a Puerto Rican family huddled together talking anxiously. I didn't speak Spanish, but I knew what *desalojo* meant. There was a white-haired Negro gentleman in a pair of carefully patched overalls, his arm in a sling and a bandage barely covering a nasty gash on his forehead. There was a slope-shouldered hulk of a man with forearms half the size of my torso taking up most of a corner. I might have mistaken him for a holdover from the butcher's shop if it wasn't for the stack of union pamphlets piled neatly in his lap.

There were half a dozen others, but that gives you the feeling. Replace the fellas with gals and it could have been our Saturday open house.

A door opened and a secretary with a clipboard stepped out: about my age, Negro, wearing a navy-blue pinstripe suit, the skirt of which had a tear along the seam that had been quick-fixed with a trio of safety pins. Her hair was curled and pinned into victory rolls that doubled as a resting spot for a pair of cat-eye glasses. She retrieved them, settled them into place, and glanced at the clipboard.

"Mr. Washington, you can head on back now. First door on your right."

The man with the busted wing heaved himself up with a grunt and limped through the doorway. The woman with the clipboard saw me and walked over.

"Can I help you?" she asked, setting her glasses back on top of her head.

"Is Forest Whitsun available?"

"He is, but he's awfully busy at the moment. I'm his associate, Pearl Jennings. What do you need to see him about?"

This was the woman Whitsun had told me to call when he got nabbed.

"I'm Will Parker. I'm from Lillian Pentecost's office."

I couldn't quite pin down the look she gave me. I'm going to go with "intrigued."

"Forest has told me a lot about you," she said.

"Uh-oh."

"Most of it was very complimentary."

"Well, lawyers get paid to lie," I said. "No offense."

"Some taken. You need to see Forest?"

"If he's free."

"I'll see if I can pry him away."

Pearl went back from whence she came. I passed the time eavesdropping on Whitsun's clientele, and then the man in question came out. He had his jacket off, his shirtsleeves rolled up, and his tie was at half-mast. Other than that, everything was properly combed, shaved, and ironed.

"Let's talk outside," he said. "Every room has a client in it."

He led me outside and down the block a ways before finding a patch of sidewalk he liked.

"You've got news?" he asked.

"I was going to ask the same thing. You're the one who spent the night with the cops."

"Hardly. Pearl made some calls. I was out by dinnertime."

"One of those calls being to Roberts at the *Times*? That was a neat trick."

He gave me a self-satisfied grin.

"As if your boss hasn't used the papers to her advantage," he said.

I wondered what he'd think if he knew Ms. P was the one who'd leaked Bodine's memory magic to keep the case in print. I didn't intend to find out.

"So what's the deal?" I asked. "Staples seemed pretty keen to break out the hot pokers on you. Was he just whistling Dixie?"

"Oh, no, Detectives Staples was definitely looking to take me out behind the woodshed," Whitsun said, looking up one end of the block, then down the other, like he expected Staples to come sprinting around a corner, cuffs in hand. "That was four solid hours of questioning. A lot about dates and times and alibis. Where was I when. Which is ridiculous, since they've got no idea the exact time of death. If he asked about Vera's will one more time, I think I might have slapped the son of a bitch."

A passing woman pushing a baby carriage cringed and gave him a wide berth. Whitsun smiled and nodded at her and kept swearing.

"Except the bastard didn't ask. He never asked. He phrased it like 'It's strange that this woman you were good friends with never told you she was naming you her sole beneficiary.' Then a nice big pause to give me time to incriminate myself."

This time it was me who looked up and down the street.

"So just between you and me, and with no boys in blue in earshot, did you know about the will?"

His hands went flying in the air.

"God dang it, woman, just when I think I'm starting to like you, you ask some fool question like that."

I decided to count to five before pointing out that he had not actually answered my fool question, but he beat me to it.

"No, I did not know about the will. And before you ask, I think she didn't tell me because I would have told her I didn't want it."

"You don't want a big hunk of Manhattan real estate? Three hundred grand?"

"Hell, no! If I want to collect that money, I'll have to give the boot to everybody in the place. I'm the guy you come to when you're getting evicted. I don't push papers under doors."

It was a good speech. Unrehearsed enough that I believed him.

"Well, it would have been nice to know what was in the will before the cops came knocking," I told him. "You'd think your old boss would have given you a heads-up."

Whitsun shook his head. "This wasn't John's fault. He'd fight a warrant tooth and nail. But on my way into the station, I passed Ken Devine. He's the one who gave the police the will, the smug son of a bitch. Maybe he really thinks I had something to do with it. Or maybe he just wanted to get under my skin."

If the steam rising from under Whitsun's collar was any indication, I think Devine had succeeded.

"Then on the way out, Staples had the gall to tell me they were starting to empty out Vera's apartment. That the city considers it a health hazard and, besides, it's the only way they can properly search the place. I said like hell they were, but he reminded me the will's not executed yet. Probably won't be for a while, especially while I'm a suspect, so I don't get a say."

From over Whitsun's shoulder I saw the office door open. Pearl poked her head out, spotted us, then came hurrying up the sidewalk.

"Looks like you're about to get called to the bench, counselor," I said. "Sorry if I was rude. The questions needed to be asked."

"I don't know if they did, but I accept the apology. Now I've got a question for you," he said. "What's your boss doing on the federal front? Does she have a lead on who this FBI asshole is?"

I wanted to congratulate Whitsun. Usually someone had to be in the same room with Faraday to peg him as an asshole. But I didn't know how much about that Ms. P wanted spilled. Even to our client.

Especially to our client.

"Ms. Pentecost is working some very promising leads."

Pearl sidled up to us.

"I need you back in," she said. "Mr. Washington's shift starts at noon and I'm pretty sure the Rendozas have their granddaddy watching the baby. He's been known to have a few beers for breakfast."

"Shoot. All right. I'm going," Whitsun said, already moving back down the block. He looked over his shoulder. "Tell your boss to work those leads faster. Or I'm gonna have to make another call to the *Times*."

Then he dashed into the office like Clark Kent into a phone booth. It was a good two blinks after the door swung shut that I realized Pearl was still standing there.

"Was there news?" she asked. "About the case, I mean?"

I shook my head. "Nothing worth printing. I wanted to make sure the police didn't rough him up."

"I think they wanted to. The way some of those officers looked at him."

"He's a defense attorney. Probably have his picture nailed up in every precinct. Right below Ms. Pentecost's and right above mine."

I meant it as a joke, but Pearl wasn't smiling.

"You know they don't have to prove it, right?" she said. "They just have to accuse him. Long enough and loud enough. That'll do the job. That's why you and your boss need to get this settled. The worst thing would be if this went unsolved."

"I figured the worst thing would be if he got arrested."

Now she gave me a smile. Just a small one.

"Oh, no. We can win in court. But if this goes unsolved and he's still a suspect? There's no chance to fight. No chance to win. It'll hang like a millstone around his neck."

She turned to go back to the office, but I stopped her.

"You mind if I ask you a personal question?"

"Depends how personal."

"Pretty personal."

She gave me the nod to go ahead.

"Whitsun—he made his bones fighting for the little guy.

But his biggest headlines came from representing Barry Sendak, a man who put the torch to three apartment buildings in Harlem. Seventeen dead."

"You're asking what's a smart Negro with a law degree doing working for him?"

I shrugged. "Pretty much."

"You know how he got saddled with Sendak?"

"Something about the former mayor asking?"

"That's right," she said. "The fire chief called the mayor and the mayor called Forest. Asked him personally to take the case. Really impressed on him the importance, you know?"

I did. Fiorello La Guardia asks a favor, you say yes.

"Besides," she added, "it's not like he tried his best."

"Excuse me?" I said. "I might have been in the cheap seats, but from where I was sitting, he was swinging for the bleachers."

She laughed. It was a nice laugh.

"Honey, I've read the transcripts. That part right before Sendak snapped? Where Lillian Pentecost cut his balls off in front of the jury? Do you think my boss didn't tee that question up for her? I mean, my God, Forest practically gift-wrapped it."

She smiled and pivoted on her patent-leather pumps.

"Nice to meet you, Will Parker," she called back as she walked away. "I hope you bring us some good news soon."

CHAPTER 37

Another thing to peck away at my brain. Did Whit-sun throw the Sendak case? Did Ms. Pentecost know he did?

It had been a very long year since that trial. I tried to remember that moment. Whitsun had asked a perfectly reasonable but very stupid question. It was stupid because he didn't know the answer and it opened the door for Ms. Pentecost to flip Sendak's emotional levers. Sendak snapped and the jury got to see the monster beneath the milquetoast.

Did Whitsun know what he was doing when he asked it? Or at least suspect?

Returning to the Caddy, I got in and slammed the door.

"Goddamn it," I said. "Maybe he's not a snake."

Since I had learned nothing useful, I saw no reason to hurry back to the brownstone. That's what I told myself anyway.

How to keep occupied? I could go to the Museum of Modern Art and poke around the Fennel case. If her colleague's suspicions were correct and Julia Fennel was seeing a woman, I might be able to sniff something out where Whitsun had failed.

But Whitsun would almost certainly be upset if I nosed into his case without permission. Which would probably make my boss upset.

More upset than she already was, I mean.

So I went back to the Baxter Arms. I wanted to press Vera's

neighbors about strangers again. If, as we suspected, the killer had come back multiple times to search Vera's apartment, what were the chances he or she wasn't seen coming or going at least once?

Unless the killer lived in the building. Another good reason for me to return to the scene.

I did a quick drive-by first. There were a pair of police cars parked out front. Unlikely that either belonged to Staples. A lead detective doesn't hang out at old crime scenes.

To be safe, I parked a couple blocks away and approached on foot. As I passed the right-side alley, I saw that it was blocked by a massive, open-topped Department of Public Works truck.

The truck was positioned directly beneath the fire escape, and thus directly beneath the kitchen window of Bodine's apartment. As I watched, a beefy cop, his uniform unbuttoned to reveal a stained undershirt, squeezed through said window and tossed a load over the edge.

I recognized Bodine's record player as it plummeted the three stories to land in the back of the truck with a tremendous crash. Once the dust settled, I hopped onto the back bumper and looked into the truck bed.

When Staples told Whitsun they were emptying the apartment out, he wasn't kidding. There was a mountain of clothes, empty cans, and newspapers. In one corner a pile of Kewpie dolls stared up at me, blank-eyed and broken. There were enough books to start a library, covers torn, pages soaked in filth from fresh garbage. Pizza crusts and apple cores and empty bottles stinking of sour beer.

It seemed that the city was keeping the truck there until it was full or the apartment was bare, and neighbors were taking advantage. In one corner was a pile of women's clothes that were too fashionable to have been Bodine's. Peeking out from underneath were a bunch of loose photographs. I eased my way in that direction so I could grab a handful. A woman's face—soft features framed by a blonde bob, always with a manufactured smile—looked back at me from most of the snaps. Nobody I recognized. Just more of somebody else's trash.

"Hey, lady! Watch out!"

I leapt down and barely missed having a pile of records land on my head.

I was about to yell something decidedly unladylike when I heard a man's voice echoing up the alley. It was faint, so I only caught every third word or so. But it was familiar.

"Can't . . . anymore . . . dangerous . . . no . . . to stop . . . police everywhere."

I squeezed past the truck and edged toward the back corner of the building. I peeked my head around. The rear alley was empty.

Then I heard a woman's voice. Also familiar.

"Hardly everywhere, Clark. There's only a few, and they're all up on the fourth floor."

"But, Esther . . ."

"You know I can't stand it when you whine like that."

The voices were coming from one of the first-floor windows. I pressed against the wall on the off chance Esther or Clark glanced out into the alley.

"I told you at the beginning of this, there couldn't be half measures," Esther said. "We started . . ."

I didn't hear what they started. They must have moved into another room. Then suddenly I caught up to Clark mid-sentence.

"—wonder where I am."

"You're a partner. Act like it. You promised me lunch at Keens. I'm not spending another day eating canned soup and that Italian slop from around the corner."

A door opened and closed.

I hurried around the far corner and got to the mouth of the alley in time to see Boekbinder & Gimbal's second fiddle open the door of a cab for the widowed former schoolteacher in #102, Diane Murphy, who apparently answered to Esther.

What the hell was going on there? An affair? Clark Gimbal didn't seem the type to go in for nooners, and the way Murphy talked to him didn't ring postcoital.

And why worry about the police? Murder was definitely not a half measure. Was that what she was referring to?

A whole lot of questions, and no answers. But I knew one thing for sure: Keens didn't do a quick lunch.

I ran back to the car and grabbed my set of picks out of the trunk.

The lock on #102 was a lot flimsier than the one on the back stairs. It took me all of thirty seconds to get into Murphy's apartment.

Again, I was struck by the lack of furniture even though she'd been there for months. I had chalked it up to a recent widow still learning to do for herself. Not wanting to settle in, because settling in meant moving on.

Now I wondered.

Her bedroom was like the rest of the house. A slim twin bed. No paintings. A closet with a sparse collection of clothes.

No diaries tucked under the mattress. No collection of fake IDs taped behind the headboard. The bathroom was clean, too.

In the kitchen, I found an unhealthy amount of canned soup and a mostly empty fridge. The only oddity was a large metal toolbox tucked under the kitchen table.

I opened it, hoping for I don't know what. A hidden stash of heroin or money or a bloody length of pipe.

Nope. Only tools. No lead pipe. A couple wrenches that could have done the job, but close examination found no blood. Only the usual grease.

I spent another fifteen minutes in the apartment. I shouldn't have. Keens might have been full. Gimbal could have changed his mind and brought her back. But my luck held. To a point, anyway: The fifteen minutes yielded me nothing.

On the way out I glanced at the empty cage on the floor. Mr. Whiskers must still be out chasing rats.

I hoped he was having better luck than I was.

Usually I would rely on Ms. Pentecost, telling her what I'd uncovered and letting her fill in the blanks. But when I got back to the brownstone, I found that she was still in bed. Or in bed again.

"She came down to get lunch, then went back to her room," Mrs. Campbell informed me as she passed over the new keys to the front door. "Said she wanted to spend the day reading."

Spend the day reading. Certainly not unusual for my boss. Just not when we had a murder to solve. At least she was eating.

"I guess I'll go check on her," I said.

I went upstairs and, again, got to within a knuckle's width of knocking and stopped.

She didn't need checking on. She'd told us very clearly what she required: to be left alone.

Still, I hesitated, listening for a long minute before finally turning away and going back downstairs. I typed up my report on what I'd overheard at the Baxter Arms and placed the pages on Ms. Pentecost's desk, where they would be waiting for her when she was ready for them.

Then I went to a movie. I can't, for the life of me, remember what I saw.

That night I woke to the sound of footsteps in the hall, then descending the stairs. I squinted at my clock. The morning was in the low single digits. I thought about getting up, but decided not to.

If she needed me, Ms. P knew where to find me.

I woke again a little later. Now the thumping was coming through my ceiling. That familiar two-feet, one-cane rhythm. The footsteps were interrupted by a low, drawn-out rumbling. Was Ms. Pentecost moving furniture around?

I had my feet on the floor, ready to go upstairs and assist, when the rumbling suddenly stopped. I held my breath and listened. The occasional footsteps. The occasional tap of her cane.

I swung my legs back up under my covers. Again, if she needed me, she knew where I was.

At least she was up and about. And hopefully on the case.

CHAPTER 38

On the case, yes. Where exactly in the process, I had no idea. By the time my alarm jolted me awake at seven o'clock, Ms. Pentecost was back in her bedroom. Sound asleep, if the snores I heard through the door were any indication.

I went to the third floor.

In the middle of the room, right in front of the single arm-chair, was a portable chalkboard—this big thing on wheels Ms. P had rescued from a university lab that was being torn apart for renovations.

While my boss can hold a seemingly infinite number of facts in her head, sometimes I needed a little help visualizing the essentials. Apparently, she needed some assistance this time as well. Specifically in regards to Vera Bodine's movements leading to her death.

Ms. P's scribbles took up both sides of the chalkboard.

On one side you had the big picture.

Began working at Boekbinder & Gimbal as personal secretary to John Boekbinder (December 1919)
Moved into apartment at the Baxter Arms (1934)
Urged Forest Whitsun to take on Father Carlyle case (August 1938)

Purchased Baxter Arms (April 1940)

Retired from Boekbinder & Gimbal
(February 1941)

Whitsun first visit. Bodne's hoarding is not noticeable
(summer 1941).

Bodine is approached by the FBI. Shortly after, she
begins work identifying Nazi collaborators (March
1942).

The FBI discontinues the project (summer 1944)

Whitsun visits Bodine for the first time after discharge
from the Army (December 1946)

On the other side of the board were more recent events.

Diane Murphy moves into Baxter Arms (June 1947)

Bodine told by Barbara Johnson about Danberry Group
offer (mid-July)

Julia Fennel found dead (August 4). Front-page article
appears (August 8).

Urges Whitsun to take on Ramirez defense (August 8)

Seen leaving apartment in morning by Rodney
Camper (several times between August 11–15).
According to Lt. Lazenby, Bodine was not
witnessed habitually leaving the building prior
to this.

Asks Sgt. Grady about reporting a crime (August 18)

Whitsun visits. Bodine presses him about defending
Ramirez (August 18, 2 p.m.).

Bodine seen leaving the apartment building clad in
professional attire by Daniel Snejbjerg (August 18,
5 p.m.—last known sighting)

Whitsun visits and finds Bodine "missing"
(September 1)

Will discovers body (September 3)

Printed at the bottom was some chicken scratch that I deciphered into a series of comments and questions. Some I understood, some I didn't.

—**Where was she going?**
—**What crime did she consider reporting?**
—**Final trip? Afternoon? Did this incite something?**
—**No bowls on the floor**
—**Did Teetering know?**
—**Worried about her memory**

On the seat of the chair was the brittle, now-blank clipping I'd found in Bodine's pocket. Beneath it were other clippings—all from our files. I fanned through them. A few were on Bodine. But most were from the Fennel case.

I went downstairs to the office. No instructions on my desk, but my report from the day before, outlining my eavesdropping and subsequent breaking and entering, was gone.

"She was about to head to bed when I got up," Mrs. Campbell said when I walked into the kitchen. She was standing over a frying pan, attending to some discs of batter so perfectly round Archimedes would weep.

"I don't suppose she told you anything about her plans for today."

"Not a peep," she said as she flipped a flapjack. "She was just hanging up the phone when I saw her."

"The phone? When was this?"

"Oh—six o'clock or so."

Who the hell was Ms. Pentecost calling at six in the morning? And for what? I thought about the order of events on the chalkboard. The list of questions that needed answering.

Who would Ms. P call who could provide the answers?

My flapjacks arrived before the answer did.

The difficulty here was that I didn't know what wheels my

boss had put into motion. Which meant I didn't know what I could do that wouldn't get in the way of them.

Instead, I turned my attention back to my own problem: tracking down Manny Casper. I started with the phone book. I'd already checked, and there were seventeen Caspers listed, none of them named Manny or any derivation thereof.

I started down the list anyway. I put on my sweetest "gal looking for her long-lost guy" voice and asked anyone who picked up if Manny was there and that they should tell him it's Lola looking for him.

I got four immediate hang-ups; three who said there was no Manny there and when I asked the follow-up said they didn't know a Manny Casper; one woman who cursed me out for waking the baby; and one guy who said I sounded cute and why don't I forget this Manny jerk and come over and visit.

One woman said she thought she had a second cousin named Emanuel, but she'd never met him and her mother was dead and she was the only one who'd have known for sure.

No one answered at the other seven numbers.

Oh, well, I thought, that would have been too easy.

I left a note for Ms. Pentecost and went out. Russo had described Casper as a two-bit punk. Which meant he might have a record. I hit all the precincts nearest Coney Island, as well as chasing down some beat cops I had a decent working relationship with.

My story was that Casper was a possible witness on a case and I needed to ask him a few questions. None of the precincts had a record on him, but one of the beat cops recognized the name.

"I've seen him in one or two bars around the boardwalk," the cop told me over a roast-beef-and-onion sandwich that I was paying for. "Always on the edge of things, you know? Not at the table with the serious crooks, but perched nearby."

That paired with what Russo said. Unfortunately, that was about all the cop could give me.

"I've seen him around the neighborhood a bit."

"How much is a bit?"

"I don't know. Two, three times. Walking down the street."

"Alone or with a girl?" I asked.

"Once with a girl."

"You remember what she looked like?"

"I remember she had nice legs—that's about it."

I spent another half hour driving aimlessly around the Coney Island area, slowing down for every pedestrian who came within spitting distance of Casper's description. No luck. Eventually my own stomach started rumbling and I drove back to the office. I pulled up to the curb in time to catch a reporter-turned-librarian limping down our front steps.

Hollis Graham had taken a fall over the summer and broken his ankle. His story is he tripped over a box of *Life* magazines. I think he was out jitterbugging and tried to do a split. He might look like a modest academic, with his pressed slacks and natty cardigans and the pile of gray curls that were always threatening to tumble down his forehead, but I knew he had a wild side.

After the accident, there was some rumbling from his employers about him retiring. But then there was some counter-rumbling from Hollis about seniority and pensions and how he was only winged, not mortally wounded. So he'd spent the last few months seeing to the archives at the main branch of the New York Public Library, wielding a pair of crutches, which were now noticeably absent.

"When did you toss the drumsticks?" I asked, hopping out of the car.

"Last week," Hollis replied as he carefully navigated the steps. "Damn things kept knocking into the shelves."

"Probably bunched up the sleeves of your cardigans."

"That, too."

"Sorry I was out," I said. "What do you need?"

"A warm beer and a masseur with very firm hands," Hollis said, hitting the sidewalk and taking a breather against the railing. "Your boss needed some back issues. Called me this morning at an ungodly hour. Thought I'd swing by on my lunch break. Got to go up to the third floor. The sanctum sanctorum. Utter shambles of a filing system, but still very impressive."

That Ms. P had Hollis's home number wasn't a shock. He had been her contact before he had been my friend. That there was anything urgent in the works was a surprise, though.

"What back issues?" I asked.

"Some copies of the *Free City Press,* the *Enquirer,* and a few of the other smaller rags. All around a two-week period in August."

Interesting.

"I better go in and see if the boss needs a footstool. Are you okay on your own? Need me to run you down a cab?"

"I've got a bum leg, not two broken arms. I'll be fine," he said. "Go do your job. I've got to get back to mine."

I paused in the doorway long enough to see Hollis make the corner, then went inside and climbed two flights. I found my boss where I usually found her, though at least this time she was in the chair and not sitting toddler-style on the floor.

She was dissecting a newspaper with the precision of a butcher picking apart a bird.

I stayed in the doorway for a long moment, considering my approach. Do I pretend the last two days hadn't happened? Ask her how she's feeling? Apologize for not telling her about the mugging? Or just dive in and start picking apart newspapers?

"As Mrs. Campbell would say, hovering in doorways invites in trouble," Ms. P said as she discarded one paper and picked up another.

I approached, but with caution.

"Find a match?" I asked.

"Not yet. You saw Hollis?"

"I did. He told me about the errand you had him run. I'm assuming you're looking for something that matches what I found in Bodine's pocket."

She nodded.

"Vera Bodine was seen leaving her apartment at least three mornings the week following the Fennel murder, two of them consecutive. This is suggestive, but not conclusive."

"What tips the scales?"

"Nearly every newspaper I saw at her apartment was the *Times*," Ms. P said. "She clearly had a subscription. But in her kitchen, I distinctly remember there being a copy of the *Free City Press*. And I believe one of the *Enquirer*. I was more concerned at the time with finding any personal correspondence. I neglected to examine the newspapers."

"Let me see if I've got this straight," I said. "She finds out about the Fennel case in the *Times*. She takes an interest. So every morning—or at least several mornings—she ventures out into the great wide world to see what the other papers have. Why? What did they get that the *Times* didn't?"

"That," Ms. P said, "is what I am attempting to discover."

She tossed one paper aside and picked up the next.

"I take it you've read my report on the Gimbal-Murphy incident," I said.

"I did. Actually, it was that which started me on this track."

"You think Gimbal's involved in the Fennel murder?"

"I think . . . I think the conversation you overheard provided the answers to a few of the outstanding questions. Enough that I could see the puzzle a little more clearly."

I was about to ask her what questions she was referring to when her eyes lit up. She took Bodine's clipping and placed it next to the open newspaper in her lap.

"Eureka!" she shouted.

"I didn't know people actually said that."

"Hush. Look here."

I looked. The article was deep inside the August 18 issue of the *Free City Press*. It was a jump from a story that had started earlier in the paper. It was the exact shape of the clipping I'd pulled from Bodine's pocket.

My boss took a pencil from behind her ear and made a circle where Bodine had done. I peered over her shoulder and read.

"'A gold bracelet with a flowery mother-of-pearl inlay,'" I read aloud. "She was interested in the jewelry Ramirez got caught pawning? Why? The *Times* had that from the start."

Ms. Pentecost shook her head. "The *Times* merely said that it was a gold bracelet with Miss Fennel's initials inscribed on the inside."

"So the reporter at the *Free City Press* is more meticulous than the rest. Good for him. Why did Bodine care? Did she recognize the description? And from where?"

If Ms. Pentecost heard the question, she didn't acknowledge it. She was tracing the penciled circle with one carefully shaped nail, over and over, round and round, like she was casting a spell.

I stopped talking. Maybe even stopped breathing. I kept my eye on her finger, circling those ten words. I didn't check my watch, but we'd long passed the minute mark when . . .

Her finger stopped.

She tilted her face up to meet mine.

"Call Mr. Teetering," she said. "Tell him Lillian Pentecost requests his company at her office tomorrow morning at ten a.m. Tell him that if he chooses not to attend, my next call will be to the authorities. Tell him this, and only this. Give him no further information other than our address. If he asks why I wish to speak with him, refuse."

"You think the Nazi did it?" I asked.

"I think I'd like to speak with him. Here. Tomorrow morning."

"Why not tonight?"

"There are preparations that need to be made."

"We really calling the authorities if he doesn't show?"

She did that thing with her one eyebrow that I absolutely never practice in the mirror.

"All right. Nazis for brunch it is."

Abracadabra.

CHAPTER 39

I was half a flight down when Ms. P called out.

"What time is it?"

"Twelve forty-two and some amount of seconds," I called back. "Want me to see about lunch?"

"No, I can attend to that myself. Once you've called Mr. Teetering, there is a phone number written on a pad on my desk. Call it at one o'clock."

"And who exactly am I calling?"

One breath, two breaths. No answer. I continued down.

I reached Teetering at his store and relayed the message from Ms. Pentecost word for word. He asked the expected question.

"What does Lillian Pentecost wish with me?"

To which I repeated the request and the follow-up threat of contacting the authorities again.

"Can we expect you?" I asked.

There was a long pause and then the click of a receiver. Whether that was a yes or no, only time would tell.

Since that telephonic errand took only a few minutes, I had a solid ten to ponder my second. There was indeed a phone number written on a pad on Ms. P's desk. Not one I recognized. It wasn't local—that's all I knew.

While I waited, my eyes wandered to the painting on

the wall. Ms. P hadn't mentioned Quincannon and I hadn't brought him up.

That couldn't go on for very long. She was allowed her secrets, sure. But Quincannon was dangerous. He had cops and judges and who knows who else in his pocket. He could make life difficult.

If we were in some kind of war with him, I wanted to know the lay of the land.

At one o'clock and some seconds, I dialed the number on the pad. It rang only one and a half times before a man's voice answered.

"Cappachi's Wet and Dry. This is Tom Cappachi speaking."

"Uh . . . hello? This is Will Parker calling from Pentecost Investigations in—"

"It's her!" he shouted. "Sorry. I wasn't yelling at you, Miss Parker. . . . Here you go. I'll be stocking the shelves if you need me."

There was the sound of the receiver being handed off and then—

"Will? Is that you?"

"Holly?"

"Yes! Hello."

My heart performed one of those maneuvers you usually only see with skywriters.

"What . . . How did you . . . ?"

"Tom—that's Mr. Cappachi. He owns the Wet and Dry. Its slogan is 'Wet your whistle while you get your dry goods.' He thinks it's very clever, but I feel there's a missed chance at more alliteration. Anyway, he drove up to the cabin about half an hour ago. He said he received a call at his home this morning from Ms. Pentecost asking if he would drive me to and from his store so I could be there when you called. I suspect she's paying him, but he wouldn't confirm that. I was barely awake when he got there and— Is something wrong? Are you sick?"

"No," I said, wiping my cheeks. "My eyes are just leaking. Keep going."

"What was I saying? Oh, that's right. When he got here I was barely awake. Wearing a pair of overalls and this ratty red flannel shirt. My hair is—I think bird's nest is too kind. Rat's nest? Possum's nest? Do possums have nests?"

I didn't know and I didn't care. I just wanted her to keep rambling. On and on until she used up every word in the dictionary or Ma Bell decided to call it a day.

Eventually, Holly ran out of steam, capping it with "How have you been? I imagine not well. Otherwise, Lillian wouldn't have gone to all this trouble."

"Where do I even begin?" I said.

"I find it helps to start at the beginning, though I know other writers work out of order."

So I started with my encounter with Casper and his girlfriend under the boardwalk. Then moved on to getting hired by Whitsun, rooting out the FBI connection, discovering the body, breaking into a maybe-German-spy's house, getting a knife pressed against my nose, getting caught in the dustup between Lazenby and Staples, and ended it with our visit to Quincannon's and the ensuing fallout with Ms. P.

"That all sounds terrible," Holly exclaimed when I was finished. "Are you all right?"

"Oh, I'm fine. I've had disagreements with Ms. Pentecost before. Eventually she'll see reason and tell me what Quincannon has on her."

"I was actually talking about you getting robbed and knocked unconscious and then—"

"I wasn't unconscious. Just a little dazed."

"And then having someone threaten to cut your nose off."

"I've been in worse spots," I assured her. "I had my hand on my gun. The FBI was outside."

"Well, it sounds terrible to me."

"All that matters is I track this pair down before they make any other plays using my ID or, God forbid, my gun. If that Beretta hasn't been sold or used by now, it'll be a damn miracle. Really, what I need is advice on how to approach this thing with my boss. I mean, do I push now or wait until we wrap up the Bodine case, however long that takes?"

No words on the other end of the line, but I could hear Holly's fingers fidgeting against the receiver.

"What are you thinking?" I asked.

"I was thinking that man Quincannon is so very awful," she said. "Except *awful* doesn't really do it. A string of rainy days is awful. That man is . . . a cancer."

"Yeah, and cancer kills if you give it time. I should do something, shouldn't I? I wish she wasn't being so . . . Is *obstinate* the right word? *Recalcitrant?* I want something stronger than *stubborn*."

More fidgeting.

"I wouldn't say she's stubborn. Or any of those other words," Holly said. "I mean it really makes sense, doesn't it? Whatever Quincannon's dredged up in her past, it makes her feel . . . helpless. She probably doesn't want to talk about it because she doesn't want to feel like a victim."

Then she added, "Like you with the mugging."

"What do you mean?"

"I mean, that's obviously why you didn't tell Ms. Pentecost about it. You were taken advantage of and hurt and you were probably ashamed and you didn't want to think about that, so that's why you didn't tell Lillian. That way you didn't have to relive it."

"No, that's . . . We picked up the Bodine case. And—and we already had these other things and I didn't . . . I didn't want to bother her. That's all it was. I mean . . ."

Something unpleasant was happening in my chest and I could feel my face getting hot.

"Look, I've been hit before," I said.

"I know."

"Worse than that, and by worse people. I have the scars to prove it!"

I was shouting now. But Holly didn't rise to meet me.

She just repeated calmly, "I know. I know, Will."

My hands were shaking and I had to get a two-handed grip on the receiver.

I took a breath and opened my mouth to yell something . . . but what?

Holly knew I'd been through worse. I'd shared things with her I'd never told anyone else. She knew about my childhood. The things I'd survived before I ever met Lillian Pentecost. The things I'd survived since then.

So what was I going to yell at her?

That I wasn't a victim? That there wasn't a part of me that didn't still flinch every time I thought of lying in the sand, helpless, listening as Casper found my pistol and wondering if he were going to use it on me? That I hadn't been focused on finding the pair and getting my gun back because I was pretending that if I could do that I could erase the whole thing from ever having happened?

"Will?"

I had been quiet for a long time.

"Yes?"

"Are you okay?"

I took a pair of deep breaths. In through the nose, out through the mouth.

"Not so much, no."

"I'm sorry."

"It was . . . It was just so stupid," I said. "The whole thing. That I fell for the setup in the first place. That they got the drop on me. I mean, for God's sake, I chase criminals for a living. It was . . . stupid."

"It could have happened to anyone," she said.

Then she added, "No, no. I take that back. It couldn't have

happened to anyone, because not everyone would have run in there. Not everyone would have heard a woman cry out and dashed in to help. So, no, it couldn't have happened to anyone."

"Lucky me."

"No," she responded. "It's everyone else who's lucky. That there are people like you. People who will dive into danger without thinking of themselves. I love you for that."

Love.

We'd said the word before, but it had always been in the bedroom during moments where lots of interesting things get said.

I thought about saying it back. But just like when my hand was raised to knock on Ms. Pentecost's door, I hesitated.

Instead I said, "I'm lucky, too."

"How do you mean?"

"I'm not used to dating girls who are smarter than me."

Laughter down the line. I loved her laugh. There was the scrape of a lighter and the sucking in of a Chesterfield.

"If I was so smart, I'd have figured out the end of this book already."

The conversation slid into fictional problems and how to fix them. Or not. Holly liked what she referred to as "unresolved notes."

I wished her luck, and she did the same. With great reluctance on both ends of the wire, we said our goodbyes.

After hanging up, I spent ten minutes or so sitting at my desk getting my feelings together. When I felt properly stable, I went back upstairs.

Ms. Pentecost was perched on her chair, leaning forward, resting her chin in her hands and staring at the chalkboard. She'd revised the order of events to reflect what we knew now about Bodine's reasons for leaving her apartment.

"How'd you know?" I asked. "I mean, I know how you knew about the . . . that I was attacked. How did you know I needed Holly?"

"You seemed distressed and . . . Well, when you spend time with Miss Quick you seem . . ."

Lillian Pentecost doesn't get flustered much, and it was actually kind of adorable.

"I get it," I said, saving her from having to find the end of that sentence. "Anyway—thank you."

"Of course."

She turned her attention back to the chalkboard. This time I decided to knock.

"Holly says I shouldn't push, so this isn't me pushing," I told Ms. P. "I just want you to know that when you're ready, I'll be waiting."

For a moment, I thought she was going to ignore me. Then she nodded. One small nod, but it was enough.

"How did your call with Mr. Teetering go?" she asked.

I told her, both of us happy to move on to other things.

"So it's a coin flip whether we're having a Nazi over," I said. "I mean, a coin flip whether he's coming, then another for whether he's actually a Nazi."

"We should prepare, regardless."

I asked what kind of preparation was needed.

Turns out a lot.

CHAPTER **40**

By 9:30 the following morning, we were ready: freshly coiffed, wearing our sharpest suits, fed on bacon and buttermilk biscuits, and prepared for anything.

Or nothing.

I'd been wondering how long we would give Teetering. Until 10:10? 10:20? Do I call again? Follow-up threats are never as good as the original.

Turns out, I needn't have worried. At 9:52 there was a knock on the door. Two raps so quick I might have imagined them.

The first coin landed heads.

I found the store owner waiting on the stoop, also dressed in his best: black suit, white shirt, black tie. His left sleeve hadn't been tailored and the empty cuff drew attention to his missing hand.

His remaining strands of hair had been carefully combed, his wire-rimmed glasses polished, his mustache waxed. He gave a pair of quick blinks when I opened the door. That was the only acknowledgment that he recognized me as the pearl-clutching auntie.

"I am here to see . . . I have an appointment with Lillian Pentecost."

"Right this way."

I led him into the office and placed him in the seat of honor. He didn't drag his feet, but he wasn't beating any records. He had the demeanor of a man who was here to arrange a funeral. Very possibly his own.

Ms. P didn't rise to shake his hand, and he didn't insist. The articles about Bodine's death were lying out on her desk, headlines turned to face our guest. As far as I could tell, his eyes didn't linger there any more than they did on anything else in the room.

I did not take my usual place at my desk. Instead, I took a seat on the sofa under the window. I slipped my Browning Hi-Power out of its holster and rested it on my thigh, finger off the trigger but loitering nearby.

I'd asked Ms. P if it wouldn't be easier to frisk the man when he got here. She said that would have been rude. He was, after all, an invited guest.

Rather I merely kept a loaded semi-automatic pointed at his back. Much more polite.

As for the gentleman in question, he was sitting ramrod straight, elbows resting on the arms of the chair. And as to what his face was doing, I would have to ask Ms. P after the fact.

"Mr. Teetering. Thank you for coming."

"I don't understand what I'm doing here, or why you wish to see me."

Ms. Pentecost raised a finger and waggled it at him.

"No, no, Mr. Teetering," she said. "I'm afraid it's too late for that. If you were truly oblivious as to why I summoned you, you wouldn't be here, now, at a time when you should be manning your store. At the very least, you would have asked to speak to me rather than my associate and demand to know what I wanted. Or you would simply have ignored the summons. It's a long drive from Danville to Brooklyn, especially in morning traffic. But you came."

Teetering looked down at his lap. The gesture revealed the back of his collar, and I saw a dusting of talcum along the freshly scraped neckline. He'd wanted to look his best.

His head came back up.

"Several years ago, the FBI came to me," he said. "Questioned me. Accused me of things. I told them they were mistaken. That they had the wrong man."

Ms. P placed both hands flat on her desk and leaned forward. "I do not get wrong men, Mr. Teetering. I do not call men to travel to my office on a whim."

She moved the news clipping aside to reveal a photograph, one of the two that had been slipped through our mail slot the week prior by Faraday or one of his minions. She slid it toward Teetering.

I would have given everything remaining in my bank account to see his eyes. As it was, I was left to look for tell-tales in the curve of his back, the way the fingertips of his remaining hand dug into the arm of the chair.

As for my boss's fingertips, she used one to tap the chest of one of the German officers in the photo. The one with the obscured face and the scar on his hand. Twice she tapped. Like it was a door and she was expecting somebody to open up.

His breathing changed. It got faster, shallower. Fear? Or was he revving himself up for something? To make some desperate move on my boss?

I straightened the barrel of the Browning just in case.

He reached a hand toward the picture. He didn't touch it. His hand hovered there, like he felt some kind of warmth coming off it. Then he drew his hand back.

"That is not me," he said.

"I did not ask if it was."

The way she said it, he knew he'd stumbled. You don't answer questions you're not asked.

"There are other photos, of course," she continued. "The

creation of smaller, portable cameras made photography much more accessible to amateurs, even by soldiers fighting in the Great War. Miss Parker has taken up the hobby herself and has been very instructive on how even these amateur photos contain exceptional details when enlarged."

That was a bluff. There were no other photographs. Except Teetering didn't know that. At the mention of my name, he turned and looked at me, clocking the gun while he did so. He stiffened and slowly turned back to my boss.

He found her sitting forward, enough so the light coming in the windows fell across her eyes. She caught it at an angle, so it glinted off her good eye and reflected flat off her glass one.

It made her look like some old-world god climbing down to pass judgment. Which is how a lot of people have come to see Lillian Pentecost over the years.

Divine reckoning in a three-piece suit.

"Let me be frank with you, Mr. Teetering," she said. "I came across you during the course of another investigation. Your secrets and your past are not my concern. Treaties have been signed. The war is over. I am inclined, as they say, to let sleeping dogs lie.

"However, crimes committed on American soil are a different matter," she continued. "I do not know you. I do not know what you have done in the years that you have been in this country. What crimes you have committed, who you have hurt, what you have done to maintain the identity you wear. This is my dilemma. And yours."

"I have hurt no one," Teetering said.

"You will need to convince me, sir."

Teetering squirmed, or at least it seemed like that from behind. He shifted from side to side before glancing over at the door to the dining room, then behind him at the door to the hall, and at me.

"Will, please open the doors and leave them that way."

I did as instructed, revealing nothing so disturbing as the coatrack and our dining table.

"There are no hidden police," Ms. Pentecost assured him. "No one is here but us. Miss Parker is taking no notes. If I am satisfied with your answers, whatever you say in this room will go no farther."

I don't know if I'd say he "heaved" a sigh, but he certainly picked one up and put it down again.

We had him.

"Why don't we start with your name?" Ms. P suggested.

"Durchdenwald," said the man who wasn't Teetering. "Colonel Hans Durchdenwald."

Lillian Pentecost: When did you come to America?

    Hans Durchdenwald: I arrived here in the spring of 1924.

LP: You were sent here?

    HD: No, no. I came of my own volition. I wanted to begin a new life here in America.

LP: But you arrived under a false name.

    HD: I wanted to free myself from who I had been. I wanted to forget the war. Everything I saw there.

LP: And did you?

    HD: For a time. Then I received a letter. It was written as if from a cousin in Berlin. But I have no cousins there. No family.

LP: When was this?

    HD: May 1938. Examining the letter, I discovered it contained a code. One that we used to pass messages during the Great War. It told me that I would have a visitor. That I should make a sign in the window of my store. An *X*, using soap. That would tell him it was safe to enter.

LP: You met with him?

    HD: He came as a traveling salesman. Of radios. He gave me a message from a man I knew when I was in the Deutsches

Heer. This man had been my subordinate then. We had been friends, I thought. This man—this salesman—

LP: What was his name?

HD: He did not give it and I did not ask. He passed on a message from Dietrich. This was my friend. I was to collect messages and pass them on by short-wave radio. He gave me the equipment and the codes. The messages would come hidden in the invoices of goods that were sent to my store.

I told this man, this salesman, that I wouldn't do this. I said that I was no longer a soldier, no longer a citizen of the fatherland. I was American. I wanted to live my life and have nothing to do with Hitler's Germany.

He told me I had no choice. That a soldier is always a soldier, even when he puts on the mask of a merchant. I did as he instructed. I set up the radio in the basement of my house. Soon the messages began to arrive.

LP: What did these messages say?

HD: There were initials and numbers. The names of cities. Sometimes there were words like "munitions" and "steel" and "ships." But mostly numbers.

LP: How often did these messages arrive?

HD: Perhaps once a week. Sometimes less.

LP: And you never met the people sending them?

HD: I did not.

LP: Did you keep the invoices?

HD: The invoices? . . . No. No, I did not.

LP: Are you sure? You kept none of them?

HD: I burned them. After I sent the message out on the radio, I burned each one.

LP: How long did you continue in this way?

HD: For three years. Three years huddled in my basement. Living in fear. Fear that I would be caught. I was sure I would be. But I was even more afraid of what would happen if I stopped. All they had to do was to send a letter to the newspaper or to the authorities and my past would be found out.

Then I read in the paper—this was in the summer, 1941—I read that a ring of German spies had been arrested. Dozens of them. And very nearby. They had a radio, too. The FBI had known about them all along.

LP: *But you kept sending the messages.*

HD: I did. For a time. I kept waiting for a knock at my door. But it did not come. Those months were hell.

Then the attack came on Pearl Harbor. Suddenly we were at war. America was at war. Children I had seen grow up were lining up at the recruiting office.

I'd seen war. I knew many would not come back.

I decided I was done. Let them send their letters. Let them come for me. I destroyed the radio. Dismantled it and threw it in the Sound. When messages arrived, I burned them without reading them.

LP: *Were you contacted? Because you had stopped your transmissions?*

HD: No. I was not.

LP: *And there was no reprisal from your German contacts?*

HD: None.

LP: *This radio salesman never returned?*

HD: He—

WILL HERE: At this moment the phone rang and two out of the three of us jumped. I hurried to my desk, picked up the receiver, said, "Call back in half an hour," to whoever was on the other end, hung up, then turned off the ringer on both our phones. A little out of breath from the maneuver, I retook my rear-gunner position.

LP: *I'll ask again. Did this radio salesman ever return?*

HD: He did not.

LP: *Did you find this strange?*

HD: I found it fortunate. It was God's grace. I prayed that in the chaos of war they would forget about me. And they did.

LP: Still, you took precautions. Drastic ones.

    Your hand.

    HD: Yes. The scar. I received it early in . . . in my military career. An incendiary ignited too soon. The mark was distinctive. I was afraid . . . As you say, I took precautions.

    But this—this is proof of how far I am willing to go to cut ties with my past.

    Yes, I did things. I had no choice.

    But I am no longer the man I was. I am Leonard Teetering. I spend my days selling comic books and sewing kits. I am a deacon. I am . . . I am a good man. I mean no one any harm. I mean my country—this country—no harm.

    I wish only to live the rest of my days in peace.

LP: Perhaps you will have that chance. I have only one last question. This picture here. Do you recognize the person in it?

    HD: No. I don't believe I know him.

LP: Not the man. The woman.

    HD: I don't believe so. Perhaps I knew her when she was young, but I can't say.

    I'm sorry. Who is she?

LP: No matter.

    What does matter is that I believe you. You are not the person I am looking for. You are free to go.

CHAPTER 41

He went. He didn't ask questions. He didn't plead. He took my boss at face value that he wasn't our target and left.

I wasn't so sure.

"This guy's been living a lie for decades," I said once he was gone. "Calling himself a made-up name with a straight face. I think if he had any tics he rooted them out years ago."

"Perhaps," she said. "Though I think I have some skill at gauging reactions, however smothered. Still, I will not discount Mr. Teetering—Colonel Durchdenwald—for certain. Not until we know for sure."

"Let's hope that comes soon," I said. "You remember to turn the tape off?"

"Ah, no, I didn't."

Ms. Pentecost reached under her desk and flipped a switch. There was a faint click from the bookcase. I got up, removed a section of books from the third shelf down, and slid open the back to reveal a reel-to-reel magnetic tape recorder.

I flipped a switch and rewound the tape most of the way back into the reel, then flipped another and listened as voices emerged from the tiny speaker.

"—crimes you have committed, who you have hurt, what you have done to maintain the identity you wear. This is my dilemma. And yours."

"I have hurt no one."

"You will need to convince me, sir."

I stopped the playback, relieved that the setup had worked, and rewound the tape the rest of the way.

These were the preparations Ms. P had been referring to yesterday. The tape recorder, we already had. We'd splurged on one as soon as an Ohio company started selling them to the general public earlier that year.

There had been at least one instance in relatively recent memory where someone had confessed to a crime in our office and we were left with no proof other than our word that the confession occurred. We thought the device might come in handy.

However, as of the previous day the machine had still been in a box in the basement. It had taken a bit of experimenting to get it functional. The microphone came included, but the remote on/off switch with the five-foot cord hadn't. Luckily, I knew a photography studio in Harlem that sold me a remote shutter release with an extra-long cable that I managed to rig to work with the recorder.

The hidden compartment in the bookcase had been there since Ms. Pentecost had arrived at the brownstone, and I occasionally had fun speculating over what it had been used for.

Anyway, the whole hidden tape-recorder setup had been inspired by a previous case, and it looked like it had worked.

"I can listen to the full show later," I told my boss.

"No," Ms. P said. "I would like to listen to it now. To make sure nothing was missed."

We listened to the whole thing. She at her desk, me at mine, Teetering present only through magnetic tape.

A few syllables were lost to scratches and warbles, but otherwise the whole interview was there. When it ended, I rewound the tape again, and removed it from the machine, slid the panel back, and began replacing the books.

"We're going to have to call the manufacturer. See if they have a remote cable that actually attaches properly," I said as I placed the reel of magnetic tape back into its box for safekeeping. "That reminds me . . ."

I turned the ringers on the phones back on and then sat back down at my desk.

"We'll have to figure out a better route for the cords, too," I added. "There are a couple of inches peeking out from under the rug where they go up beneath your desk."

Ms. P nodded. "I'll leave that to your discretion. I don't want to make a habit of surreptitiously recording interviews. It comes close to betraying our guests' trust. However, it could be useful again in the future."

"You want this in the safe?" I asked, referring to the tape.

"I want you to package it for—"

The phone rang. I answered.

"Pentecost Investigations. This is—"

"Get me Lillian Pentecost."

Before I could tell the caller that only one person gave me orders, he added, "Tell her this is Brynn Suilebhan. I got news."

I put my hand over the receiver.

"It's your bartender friend. He says he has news."

Ms. P picked up her phone, then gestured at me to stay on the line.

"Hello, Brynn. You have something to report?"

"Jesus H. Christ. I've been calling every five minutes for the last hour. If this comes too late, it's not on me."

"What is it?"

"You wanted me to keep an ear out for anything related to Donny Russo or Manny Casper. Well, I got you a twofer," he said. "Russo was here this morning. He'd been stewing. Real pissed at what happened the other day. He figured to blame Casper. He asked some of the regulars if they knew where his mother's living these days. One of them did. He left to go visit her about an hour and five minutes ago."

"He intends her harm?"

"I don't know what he intends, but he was snorting on that

Benny inhaler the whole time he was standing here. He was so wired, he was vibrating. If he starts something, I don't think he'll stop."

Ms. Pentecost asked Suilebhan for Mama Casper's address. Turns out she was Mama Bellucci, which was why I never found her in the phone book. She'd dumped her husband's last name after the divorce and now lived in a place up near Bronx Park.

I had to rely on Ms. P to relay this last bit because I was already moving, grabbing my holster, Browning, jacket to cover the holster, etc.

As I moved, I repeated a single word over and over, and you can probably guess what it was.

"This isn't your fault," Ms. P said when she was off the phone.

"Oh, it absolutely is," I argued. "I went in hard with Russo and put him onto Casper and now some poor old lady is gonna pay the price."

"Perhaps we should call the police?" Ms. P suggested.

It wasn't the worst idea. They could get there quicker than I could. But there was a problem with that.

"If Russo is really ramped up and cops go knocking on the door, he's liable to do something dramatic. Like cut off an old woman's nose, or slit her throat. I've never met her, but I'd like to get Mama Bellucci out alive. How I'm gonna do that, I'll figure out when I get there."

I had the office door open and one foot out into the hall when I turned.

"But if you don't hear from me in an hour, call the cops and tell them to go in hard."

CHAPTER 42

I hit every damn light and then some, so the drive to Mama Bellucci's place ate up most of that hour. I had time to ponder the concept of irony again. I was a little hazy on the dictionary definition, but I thought me rushing to save the mother of the man who mugged me probably qualified.

Mama Bellucci lived in an apartment building not too different from Bodine's. The front of it faced a busy street. Lots of businesses: a bakery, a bank, dueling grocers. Plenty of people on the sidewalk.

That was good. If I could get Russo outside, he'd be less likely to start slicing or shooting. I hoped.

There was also a fire escape in case I needed another way to get in.

I wedged the Cadillac into a space and hurried into the small lobby. There were names on all the mailboxes, and I confirmed Suilebhan's information that Bellucci was in apartment 319. That put her on the front right corner of the building.

I started working the angles.

I'd spotted a pay phone on the corner. If it had a phone book and Bellucci had a phone and was listed, I could call her and confirm that Russo was there. I could come up with some story that would get him outside, run up the fire escape while he was going down the stairs, get into the apartment. Then I'd be waiting, gun ready, when he came back.

That was tight. A lot of moving parts and very little time to squeeze them in. This was all assuming Russo was still in there. Maybe Bellucci knew where her son was and had given him up. I'd met a lot of mothers who would. Russo could already have come and gone.

Either way, I couldn't dither forever. While I'd been standing in the lobby, three people had come in. The first two—both elderly men—gave me curious looks as they headed up the stairs. Probably because I was mumbling under my breath about pay phones and potshots.

The third person to come in was a young woman—a girl, really, barely out of high school. She had jet-black hair styled in a tight coif, was wearing dungarees rolled up to the knees and a men's blue flannel shirt, and was carrying a brown paper bag.

She started in the direction of the stairs, then saw me and stopped. She did an elaborate show of patting her pockets and mumbling, "Oh, my key. I left it at the shop."

I almost let her get to the door. Luckily my brain caught up in time for me to grab her arm and yank her back.

"Hey!"

I didn't slam her against the wall of mailboxes, but I did press firm.

"Hey yourself," I said. "Why, I do believe it's Willowjean Parker. Or so thinks the staff of First National."

"What are you talking about?" she said, trying to squirm away. "Let me go."

"You ditched the falsies, but you can't do much about the shape of your face."

You want to gauge how sharp a person is, time how long it takes them to discard a lie that isn't working. By that measuring stick, this girl was sharp as they come.

"You'd be surprised what you can do with a little Max Factor these days," she said, her voice calm as a summer's day.

She stopped squirming but kept her eyes pointed toward the front door.

"What's the deal?" she asked. "Are you working with Russo?"

"No," I said. "I'm here to make sure he doesn't cut your boyfriend's mother's nose off. What about you? You working with him?"

"Hell, no," she said with a convincing sneer. "He called Manny and said he wants his money or else."

I glanced at the paper bag in her hand.

"Is the money in there?"

She opened it enough for me to glimpse the modest mound of greenbacks. Nowhere near the five grand Russo said he was owed.

I looked to the door.

"Where's your beau?"

"He's . . . We figured it was smarter if I came. He and Russo, they don't get along."

That was an understatement.

"You dress like a kid, so you think he'll treat you with kid gloves?" I asked.

Now that I had her up close, I could see the age on her. The cracks and the lines. Still younger than me, but definitely out of grade school.

"Manny thought that I could explain how we're getting the money. I'm good with people, you know? Besides, Manny says guys in the crew don't hurt women. It's against the rules."

Maybe I was wrong. Maybe she was in grade school. Then again, I'd known plenty of women, and a few men, who let a guy talk them into making some dumb mistakes.

She must have seen the judgment in my eyes.

"I know it's not the smartest play," she said. "But Sofia's really sweet and . . . I just don't want her to get hurt."

The subtext being that her boyfriend didn't give two shits about his mother, or was too chicken, or both.

That was neither here nor there. I could use this, I thought.

"I don't suppose you have any of the getup you used to impersonate me at the bank stashed nearby," I said.

She looked confused. "Yeah. It's in the car, but—"

"Show me."

With me keeping a firm grip on her arm, she led me out into the street and around the corner to a Packard convertible—a shiny burgundy number that looked fresh off the showroom floor.

"Did you steal this, too?" I asked.

"Nope," she said. "Bought it right off the lot."

"Hang on. You owe the mob money and you're out buying Packard specials? Is this how you spent the five hundred dollars you conned out of my bank account?"

She rolled her eyes at me, and I seriously considered slapping her.

"We put down two hundred and set up monthly payments," she explained patiently. "But Manny knows a guy who will buy it now for two grand. We sell it, skip on the payments, and we're up another eighteen hundred."

Not the worst con in the world. Again, it took a second for my brain to catch up.

"Hang on. Whose name did you finance it under?" I asked.

She got very busy fishing her keys out of her pocket and opening the trunk.

"Look, if you want the car, you can have it, okay?" she said. "We can find another way to get the money."

"Let's get your boyfriend's mother out of harm's way, then we'll talk about what I want."

She lifted the trunk lid to reveal the floor of a Bloomingdale's changing room: skirts and blouses, bras complete with falsies, a dozen pairs of shoes, and a mound of wigs, including one of close-cropped red curls.

In a corner of the trunk, I spied a very familiar purse. I snatched it up and pulled out my wallet. No cash, of course, but my identification was there. So were my keys, as well as the leather slapper that had been turned against me.

"Where's the gun?" I asked.

"What?"

I got my nose as close to hers as I could without giving her the wrong idea.

"The Beretta that was in my purse at the time you clubbed me on the head and snatched it."

"We tossed it down a sewer grate."

My skepticism must have showed.

"Manny wanted to keep it, but I don't like guns," she said. "You bring a gun, someone's gonna get shot. I made him throw it out."

I didn't know her well enough to tell whether she was lying, and I didn't have time to grill her further. I needed to make a decision, and quick. Could I trust her to carry off her part of my half-baked plan to break Mama Bellucci loose?

The thing that tipped me in favor of trust was that she'd shown up in the first place. Yeah, her boyfriend had probably manipulated her, but she was here. She was willing to walk into a room with a mobster because, as she said, her boyfriend's mom was "really sweet."

"What's your name?" I asked.

"My name?"

"Yeah. I can't keep calling you 'Hey you.'"

"Colleen. Colleen Lighthead."

That name sounded familiar and I wondered why. Had I seen it somewhere in the third-floor files? Again, there was no time to dither.

"All right, Colleen, here's the plan. But first . . . can you do voices?"

CHAPTER 43

I had to hand it to her. Colleen could pull off a mean Willowjean Parker. The wig was a little too long and the wrong shade, and the suit seriously needed tailoring, but from a block away and three flights up, it would do.

I was lying belly-down on the fourth-floor fire-escape landing—one floor up from Sofia Bellucci's window. Colleen was dropping a nickel into the pay phone on the far corner.

I'd gotten to my perch by going up the stairs as far as they went, picking the lock for roof access, then heading across and down. This way I could get into Bellucci's place quick while still having a line of sight on Colleen Lighthead.

One hand was flat on the metal grate. The other was gripping my now-retrieved purse. It contained everything it had before, along with a few items I grabbed from the Caddy, as well as the keys to Colleen's Packard.

I trusted her to work the con, but not enough to stick around after.

From across the street, I saw her mouth start moving. This was the first of two calls and pretty straightforward. She had to sound breathy and frightened, with just the suggestion of a quivering bosom.

She clicked the receiver and dropped another coin. This was the tricky call.

Her mouth started moving again. We'd spitballed some lines and settled on a handful of possibilities. Even from my perch I could tell she was getting into it—sneering and snarling at the handset.

Below me, I heard a man's voice shouting. Then the window slammed open. Through the grate of the fire-escape landing, I saw a head poke out.

The Will Parker counterfeit gave a dainty wave that she snapped into a one-finger salute. Russo screamed an appropriate response, then jerked his head back inside.

I counted one, two, three, four—then heard a door slam. I gave Colleen a thumbs-up and she ran into the nearby bakery, pulling off the wig and jacket as she did so, while I shimmied down the fire escape and leaped through the still-open window.

Sofia Bellucci—at least that's who I assumed the middle-aged woman in the flower-print housecoat cowering on the sofa was—screeched so loud I was afraid Russo would hear her even from the stairwell.

I put a finger to my lips.

"Ditch the slippers for some shoes and head down the fire escape. Colleen's waiting in the bakery across the street."

The woman looked at me like I had two heads and both were speaking Esperanto.

"Your son's girlfriend? She's waiting for you."

Her eyes lit up.

"Right. Colleen," she said, grabbing a pair of house slippers and pulling them on. "What about that gangster? Isn't he going outside?"

"In about two seconds, he's going to be running back up here. Go, go, go!"

She got, got, got, crawling out the window and starting the three-flight trek down the fire escape, her slippers slapping madly against the metal.

I ran out the door of the apartment, flung open the door to the stairwell, and shouted down.

"Hey, Russo! Too slow!"

There was the squeal of shoe leather failing to grip tile.

"You bitch! I'm gonna f—"

Frown? Filet? Faint dead away? I didn't stay in the stairwell to hear. I ran back to Sofia Bellucci's apartment, slammed the door, and set the lock. Then I got some distance, drew my semi-automatic, and waited.

Not much time for second thoughts, but I still managed them.

If everything went to plan, which it hardly ever did, the police were on their way. They'd gotten a breathy call from a woman who lived down the hall from Ma Bellucci telling them how a man named Donny Russo was banging on the door and threatening to kill somebody. Screaming about how the police are after him and he has nothing to lose. When Russo actually did bust in, I'd be there, gun in hand, to hold him until the cops arrived.

The doorknob rattled and Russo began shouting obscenities from the other side.

My second thoughts revolved around something Colleen had said.

You bring a gun, someone's gonna get shot.

What were the chances Russo would stand still and wait for the cops to show? Slim enough that I wouldn't bet a bankroll on it.

He'd make a move and I'd have to shoot him. Maybe I could wing him. Catch him in the thigh and put him down.

The grizzled Irishman who'd taught me to shoot had always said, "You pull the trigger, you aim to kill. Aim for an arm and you hit air."

So, yeah, if Russo came at me, I was aiming to kill. And he was almost certainly going to come at me.

There was a "Hiyah!" from the hall and the door shuddered in its frame.

All these thoughts led me to the conclusion that what I was really doing was lying in wait to kill a man.

Another "Hiyah!" There was the sound of wood cracking, but the door still didn't give.

I'd killed men before, but always in self-defense or in the defense of others. What I was doing now didn't feel the same.

Sure, I could justify it and the cops would buy it. But it gave me the same queasy feeling in my stomach that keeping secrets from Ms. Pentecost did. It was a bad idea, and I was going to regret it, and I knew it.

"Hiyah!" A louder crack. One more kick would do it.

Diving out the window wasn't an option. That would leave Russo loose, and I figured Ma Bellucci wanted to sleep in peace again someday.

I shoved the Browning back in the holster, retrieved my purse from where I'd dropped it, and pulled out the leather sap. Then I flattened myself against the wall beside the door.

"Hi—"

I reached out and twisted the deadbolt.

"—yah!"

The door exploded inward, followed quickly by Russo. He was off-balance and bent over. The back of his head might as well have had a bow on it.

I brought the sap down, giving it that little flick on the end. Russo dropped like a discarded marionette.

I knew from recent experience that he wouldn't be out long. I reached into my purse again and brought out the pair of police-issue handcuffs I'd grabbed from the Caddy. I cuffed Russo's hands behind him. I considered a moment and also tied his shoelaces together.

Better safe than bull-rushed by a handcuffed mobster.

The sound of police sirens began wafting through the window.

"Perfect, fellas. Just past the nick of time."

I went back into my purse, pulled out a notebook and pencil, tore off a page and wrote, "Donny Russo. Open warrant for assault in Westchester County."

I removed one of the bobby pins keeping my curls in check and used it to pin the note to the back of Russo's shirt collar. I didn't know if that was necessary, but I always try to underestimate the police. I'm less disappointed that way.

I went to the window to flag Colleen and Bellucci to let them know the excitement was over and the coast was clear. The two were supposed to be waiting out the excitement at the bakery across the street. I had my arm halfway up when I noticed the empty parking spot.

The burgundy Packard was gone.

"Of course she knows how to hot-wire a car."

Russo groaned.

"I wasn't talking to you."

A police car pulled up and a pair of uniforms stepped out, stood for a minute to get their bearings. One of them began counting off the street numbers.

I was glad I left the note.

Finally they found the right building. I waited until they were inside the lobby, then slipped out the window and began making my way down the fire escape.

On the way, I thought about choices and trust and what I was going to do when I got my hands on Colleen Lighthead again.

CHAPTER 44

I used the pay phone to call Ms. Pentecost and let her know how things had turned out.

"Colleen got away, but nobody had anything important cut off, so I'm going to chalk this up as a win," I told her.

She grunted in approval and said she'd see me soon.

However, I didn't want to leave until Russo was officially carted off, and apparently cops don't believe just any old note left on an unconscious gangster.

Somebody must have eventually called Westchester, though, because after an hour of dragging their feet, they brought Russo out and tossed him into the back of the cop car.

I was standing in the doorway of the bakery at the time. We caught eyes and I toasted him with my bagel.

He said something witty in response, but the window of the patrol car was up so I missed it.

Pity.

By the time I got back to the brownstone it was going on evening and the office was empty. I fell into my chair and was reaching for the phone book on the very, very off chance I would find Colleen Lighthead inside, when I saw the note.

It started with "Will" and ended with "L.P." In between was a list of instructions. I glanced through them, then went back and read them again. Then a third time for good measure.

I sat down at my desk and thought for a while. I'll never be as smart as Lillian Pentecost, but give me enough clues and I can usually get there. The instructions on the list were clues. Combined with what I already knew, it painted a picture of who killed Vera Bodine and why.

Now we just had to prove it.

I went upstairs and knocked on my boss's bedroom door.

"Come in."

I did.

Ms. Pentecost was sitting in her armchair by the window, her book in her lap, the Dutch dictionary open on the table in front of her.

"Did the police arrest Mr. Russo?"

"They did," I said. "To make sure he stays arrested, I'm going to place a call to the Westchester DA's office to let them know he's been picked up."

"Excellent. I'm sorry you were not able to keep hands on the woman who robbed you."

I shrugged. "I shouldn't be surprised. I heard a story about a scorpion and a frog that applies. At least the sting didn't cost me this time."

"Indeed."

I held up her note.

"About this list."

"You have questions."

I took a seat on the edge of her bed.

"A few," I said. "Not about the frame we're building. I see what you're getting at, and I have to admit it all fits. My questions are mostly procedural. The errands for me are straightforward enough. Same for the one we're asking Whitsun to run. It's the requests we're making of Faraday that have me worried. That's going to take some manpower on his part. I might have used up any goodwill with him on that Russo stunt."

"I understand if it might take some persuading," she said. "Tell him about our meeting with Mr. Teetering. Offer to give him the tape of the interview in exchange."

I wasn't expecting that.

"We told Teetering he wasn't on our to-do list," I reminded her. "Doesn't this fall under the heading of betraying our guests' trust? Or didn't you believe him when he said he'd gone straight?"

"I did believe Mr. Teetering when he said he abandoned his homeland and that the mission was forced on him," she said. "Although I do wonder about his statement that he was never contacted again. That this traveling salesman never showed up to find out why he had ceased his transmissions."

"What are you thinking?" I asked.

"I'm thinking that perhaps Agent Faraday should look under Mr. Teetering's back porch. The one he was building when he purposefully cut off his hand."

I'm the suspicious sort and tend to see murderers behind every rosebush, but even I hadn't considered that.

Something suddenly occurred to me.

"This list of instructions," I said. "The questions you're having us fetch answers to. Most of these you must have gotten from that newspaper clipping and from what you already had on the chalkboard. Right?"

"Correct."

"So did you ever really suspect Teetering? Or did we get him here and get him on tape for the sole purpose of having leverage with Faraday?"

Ms. Pentecost cocked her head from side to side. It wasn't a yes, but it was close.

"It was something that needed to be ruled out," she explained. "Better sooner than later. And, yes, I was thinking of how we might entice Agent Faraday to help us with our cause."

Lillian Pentecost was never cold. But, damn, could that woman be calculating.

"Let's say there's a skeleton under Teetering's porch swing," I said. "Even then, that skeleton belonged to a Nazi spy. I know it's your call, but I'm inclined to say, 'No big loss.' Why don't we see if we can get Faraday to help us without handing over the recording?"

She shut the book in her lap and set it beside the dictionary on the table. For the first time, I caught the title of the Dutch tome: *Het Achterhuis*. Above it was a name.

Anne Frank.

"I might consider that," she said. "If it were not for the photo."

"Which one?" I asked. "There are a couple in this caper."

"The photo of Colonel Durchdenwald. It was taken in Belgium in 1914. How familiar are you with the events of the First World War?"

"I know most of the cast of characters and that the good guys won. That's about it. It was a little before my time."

She drifted for a few seconds, her eyes going to the book on the table.

"I was young," she said. "Most of the people around me treated it as something happening in another world. One that did not affect us. My father used it often in his sermons, but as fodder for crafting a larger metaphor about good and evil. Rarely did he speak of it as something concrete and real, something that was happening to actual human beings. He was . . . he is a great believer in human salvation. He does not like to dwell on the cruelties of man."

I could actually feel the undercurrent beneath Ms. Pentecost's words. Like whatever Quincannon had on her was just beneath the surface, and if she went too far in that direction the riptide would snatch her away.

She took a deep breath and yanked herself back.

"However, there was a train that came through our town. Riders would discard newspapers, even foreign ones. The conductor allowed me to retrieve the discards, so I had a window into the world beyond our small community.

"I remember very clearly reading about the German invasion of Belgium," she said. "The destruction of churches, the burning of libraries. The indiscriminate murder of civilians. Thousands died during the invasion and in the months of famine and disease that followed. They would eventually call it the Rape of Belgium. It was the first time I'd heard that word used in that way. I remember very well the feeling it instilled in me. The horror. And rage."

She was quiet for a long minute, her face turned to the window and the last sliver of sunset. It gave the illusion that she was wearing a mask of blood.

Finally, she looked back to me, away from the dying light, and the illusion vanished.

"Mr. Teetering was an officer," she reminded me. "He would not simply have been following orders. He would have given them. He would have had a direct hand in these horrors."

I nodded. "And some things can't be forgiven."

"Oh, no," Ms. P said. "Anything can be forgiven. But we are not the ones who can grant that forgiveness. History might not have as complete a memory as Miss Bodine. In fact, it rarely does. But some crimes should not be forgotten."

I managed to get hold of Faraday that evening. He demanded the tape first. I demanded the favors first. We went back and forth like that for a few rounds. He eventually caved when I reminded him that Lillian Pentecost always made good on her deals, and if she said the tape was good, it was good.

Before we ended the call he said, "I heard your bent-nosed friend got scooped up by some public officials this afternoon."

"You hear a lot of things."

"Kind of my job, Parker." I swore I could hear a smile in his voice. "That warrant in Westchester isn't gonna hold him long. You're going to have to keep a sharp eye out."

"Yeah," I said. "But that's kind of my job."

After I hung up on Faraday, I dialed Whitsun and gave him his marching orders. We needed him to go to Rikers tomorrow and ask Mr. Ramirez a question.

As expected, Whitsun had questions of his own.

"What's Pentecost on to? Where the hell does this get us?"

"Hopefully to the murderer," I said.

"Who is it? I'm the one paying your damn fee. I demand that you tell me who you're looking at."

He was a paying client, which is why I didn't use the first seven words that came to mind.

"Look," I said. "If this pans out, you'll have a front-row seat. If it's a dead end, it's better you don't know about it."

"You don't trust me not to jump the gun?"

"I barely trust you to ask your client the question. Don't prove me right."

I hung up before he could begin a cross-examination.

With our two hounds given their respective scents, I started planning out my own assignments.

Tomorrow was going to be a very long day.

CHAPTER 45

The next day was so long, it stretched into two.

I stumbled back into the office a little after six p.m. on Saturday, exhausted. I collapsed at my desk, kicked off my two-toned oxfords, pulled off my socks, and gave my toes a stretch.

I'd spent all of Friday running hither and thither, come back and slept for about five hours, then gone out and done it again. My outfit—a white blouse and teal slacks designed to give me an air of cheerful approachability—was smudged, stained, sweaty, and impossibly wrinkled. If you were going to approach me, it would be to give me a nickel and send me to the nearest drop-off laundry.

I needed a shower. Scratch that—a long, hot bath. But first I needed to give my boss the news. I'd come in late the night before and gone out early that morning and had possessed neither the time nor the energy to type up a report.

Hearing a rhythmic thwacking emanating from the rear of the brownstone, I padded barefoot through the kitchen and went out the back door to find the other two ladies of the house in the rear courtyard.

Mrs. Campbell, taking advantage of the cancellation of our usual Saturday open house, had spent the day catching up on chores, and was in the midst of her bimonthly beating of the rugs. She had rigged a clothesline from one wrought-iron gate to another to hang the rugs from while she went at them with a broom, her tight gray curls flinging back and forth with each swing.

My boss was dressed in her rattiest ensemble: a men's sleeveless undershirt, sweatpants that had been cut off at the knees, and a pair of Keds that looked like they'd enjoyed a former life as a dog's chew toy. She was running through a series of fencing moves using her cane as a stand-in for a sword, and, from the sweat dripping off her, she'd been at it a while.

She was transitioning to the rhythm of Mrs. Campbell's broom-beats, and my arrival didn't even make her stutter.

"Mr. Whitsun called shortly before lunch," she said in the breath between returning to a neutral stance and starting the circuit again. I'd seen the routine enough that I'd picked up the terminology.

"I took notes during the conversation," she added. "They're on your desk."

"I missed them. I was too occupied with staying upright. Want to give me a preview?"

"Mr. Ramirez's answer confirms my theory."

Salute. En garde.

"Agent Faraday may take a bit longer to respond. His errands are less straightforward."

Short lunge. Recover. Parry. Riposte.

"How did yours fare?"

Medium lunge. Recover. Parry. Riposte.

"My first two errands were as smooth as Lauren Bacall between silk sheets," I said. "Only had to try seven newsstands before finding our guy. As for the doorman, the answer was yes and he's willing to testify to it."

Short lunge. Recover. Parry. Riposte.

"And the other two?" Ms. P asked.

"Digging up the answer on Gimbal took a bit more doing. There are some rooms in the Hall of Records that desperately require ventilation."

"The result?"

I told her.

"Excellent." Parry, riposte. "And the last?"

"That's where I hit a snag."

I gave her the rundown and she continued the circuit. Short, medium, short, medium. Eventually she got up the nerve to go for a long lunge.

Halfway through the maneuver, she lost her balance and toppled forward. She managed to catch herself with her off hand, but it was hardly elegant.

I moved to help her up but she waved me off.

"I'm fine. That's the fourth time I've fallen. I've gotten used to it," she said, taking a handkerchief out of her back pocket and wiping the blood off her knuckles.

"Maybe you should skip the big lunges," I suggested.

"Maybe I should," she admitted. "I might also avail myself of your target range in the basement. I don't believe I can rely on swordsmanship for self-defense."

"My basement is your basement. Literally."

We sat on the back step and thought about next moves.

"The problem," I said eventually, "is that even if Faraday comes through big, it won't be enough. Not to prove it beyond a shadow of a doubt. Like Pearl Jennings said, if we don't prove somebody else did it, people will always assume it was Whitsun and think he got away with it."

We sat with that for a minute, the silence punctuated by the continued battering of the rugs. Between swings, Mrs. Campbell called over to us.

"Why don't you get 'em all together and press 'em?"

"Press who with what?" I asked.

She walked over, broom still in hand.

"Like in the movies," she explained. "Get all your suspects in a room and start showing them what you know and grill them. Get them to crack."

Ms. Pentecost shook her head.

"I'm afraid that technique, while dramatic, is rarely effective, Eleanor. Spontaneous confessions are difficult to elicit. Especially without an eyewitness."

"Well, it was just a thought," Mrs. Campbell said, turning back to the rugs.

"Actually," I said, "that might not be a bad idea."

Both women looked at me expectantly.

"Getting an eyewitness," I clarified. "I think I know where we can find one."

CHAPTER 46

It wasn't everyone we'd come across during the course of the investigation, but it still made for a full office. There was me, of course. And Whitsun. He'd taken the nicest of the guest chairs, which was his prerogative, being the client.

Boekbinder, Gimbal, and Devine had been directed to the sofa. When Boekbinder tried to get up and claim a chair of his own, I had to stop him.

"Assigned seating," I explained.

Whitsun confronted Devine about handing Bodine's will over to the cops, to which Devine replied, "Some people actually respect the police, Forest."

I stepped in before it went any further.

Whitsun's associate, Pearl Jennings, was perched on a chair by the door. Across the doorway from her was Diane Murphy of #102, the frizz of her pith-helmet bob framing her head in a halo of light.

Between them, his bulk barely contained by the doorframe, was Lazenby. Behind him in the hall were a pair of his favorite sergeants. We'd considered inviting Staples, since it was technically his case. But Lazenby had been good to us, and we wanted to return the favor.

Also, we needed a little official juice to make sure all our guests arrived at the appointed hour, and Staples wasn't likely to play along.

It was Monday evening, two days after our conversation in the courtyard. Not much time to write, produce, direct, and cast our little stage show, much less rehearse it.

Command performance. One night only.

As soon as everyone was settled, I gave Lazenby a nod. He passed it on to one of his sergeants down the hall, who passed it on a third time.

The door to the dining room opened and the star made her entrance.

Ms. Pentecost was costumed in an English wool two-piece that must have been dyed twice to get it so black. With her white silk shirt, blood-red tie, and matching silver stickpins (one for the tie, one skewering the center of her braids), she looked like the Grim Reaper if he had a better tailor.

Her only props were a handful of newspapers that she laid out very precisely on top of her desk before taking a seat. I had argued for starting off with a long stretch of silence, slowly sweeping the room with her trademark piercing gaze.

Ms. P nixed it as overindulgence. Speed, she contended, was our ally. As soon as her posterior hit home, she was off.

"Thank you for coming," Ms. Pentecost began. "I know you all are very invested in discovering what happened to Perseverance Bodine. Who killed her and why. By the time we leave this room I hope to have answered those questions."

Diane Murphy chimed in from the cheap seats.

"I'm terribly sorry for what happened to Miss Bodine, but I don't understand why I'm here. I was practically dragged out of my apartment by this officer."

She gave Lazenby a less-than-kind look.

"There was no dragging," he rumbled. "I said that you were not required to attend."

"When a police lieutenant says you should be somewhere, you tend to assume there will be consequences if you decline," Murphy snapped.

No riposte for that, since she was right.

"You're quite correct," my boss said. "There would certainly have been consequences. But I have no reason to leave you in suspense. Let's shed some light on your role in this affair now, shall we?"

"My role? I had nothing to do with this mess. I never even met the woman."

"This mess," Ms. P said, feeling the word out in her mouth. "It really is one, isn't it? There's been quite a lot going on at the Baxter Arms. So, why don't we clear away some of it, Miss Gimbal."

I had a good view of everyone's faces, so I got to watch her and Clark Gimbal's eyes go wide, while everyone else did a blinking double take.

"That's . . . I'm sorry—my name's Murphy," the first-floor tenant said. "Mrs. Diane Murphy."

"Yes, it is," my boss said. "And you are a recent widow trying to make ends meet. The best lies are the truth, aren't they? But before you were Mrs. Diane Murphy you were Miss Diane Esther Gimbal. Clark Gimbal's sister and co-owner with him of the Danberry Group, a company created expressly for the purpose of purchasing the Baxter Arms."

Lazenby looked confused. "We looked that up," he said. "I thought the Danberry Group was owned by some South African company."

"On paper, yes. But only on paper," Ms. P explained. "Over the years, I imagine Mr. Gimbal has become exceptional at these kinds of clerical machinations. If you go digging very deep in the Hall of Records, you will find his and Miss Gimbal's signatures. Miss Parker can show you the way."

The other lawyers in the room were looking at Clark Gimbal in confusion and disgust. The man did not hold up well under scrutiny. His balding pate was covered in flop sweat and he was hunched so far forward in his chair he could have kissed his knees.

"Clark, is this true?" Boekbinder asked. "Were you trying

to get Vera to sell to you? Why not just make an offer? Why all this?"

Gimbal didn't answer quick enough, so my boss did it for him.

"Because Miss Bodine didn't want to sell, and Mr. Gimbal knew it. She had bought the building in the first place because she wished to own one small corner of the city that she could control. She could keep it safe. Unchanging. Mr. Gimbal knew this, so he had to resort to more clandestine methods. Thus, the Danberry Group, bribing tenants to leave, and placing his sister in Apartment 102."

She focused her attention on the woman sitting at the back of the room. She was holding up a lot better than her brother. If she was sweating, it was somewhere I couldn't see.

"You moved in last June," Ms. P said. "Shortly after, the other tenants began to experience a variety of problems with their apartments. Issues that would weigh in favor of them taking the offer and moving out. Pipes started leaking. Electrical sockets failed. Light bulbs in hallways went out. All caused by you, of course. Your brother essentially managed the building for Miss Bodine, so he would have had access to the master key.

"Then there were the rats," she added. "People thought they were drawn by Miss Bodine's hoarding, but no. You brought them. In a cage."

Which covers the "Bowls on the floor" note Ms. P had scribbled on the chalkboard. No, there hadn't been a bowl of water or milk on the floor of #102. Nothing to suggest she'd been waiting for Mr. Whiskers to return.

"It was the timing that gave you away," Ms. P explained. "That and the chance occurrence of Miss Parker being in the back alley when your brother visited you last week. She heard everything."

Esther Gimbal Murphy's eyes went wide at that, but she very quickly got her face under control.

"That's hearsay," she said. "Isn't it, Clark?"

Clark was too busy withering to respond, so she continued alone.

"And so what if we formed a company? So what if we offered to pay people to leave? All legal," she said. "That stuff about light bulbs and rats: I'd like to see you prove it."

"But why?" Boekbinder asked the pair. "Clark, you're a partner. You get a fine salary."

"Not managing partner salary," Clark's sister answered for him. "Not managing partner prestige."

"He said he didn't want to be managing partner. He said he was happy."

Esther Gimbal snorted. "Does he look happy?"

The heap that used to be Clark Gimbal glanced up briefly.

"She talked me into it."

"Oh, grow a spine," Esther snapped. "You're the one who was always talking about how much that building was worth. How you were always telling Vera Bodine she could sell it and live anywhere she wanted, and how she always refused."

"So you killed her for it?" Boekbinder exclaimed.

Both Gimbal siblings jumped out of their chairs.

"No! Never!"

"I never even met the woman!"

"We had nothing to do with that!"

"Sit down!"

That last was from Lazenby, who had a bellow that could fracture plaster.

Once everyone was settled, the Gimbal in the dress said, "I never met her. Clark warned me not to let her see me if I could help it, because he didn't know if maybe she'd seen a family photo or something and would remember me as his sister. So I never saw her, never spoke to her, and certainly never killed her. I'd never do anything like that. Neither would Clark. My God, look at him. He barely had the guts to do this."

"It's true," Clark added. "Vera was off-limits. Esther never went near her. Vera was . . . I would never harm her."

"You son of a bitch." That came in stereo from Whitsun and Devine, who had taken a break from staring daggers at each other to throw them at Gimbal.

"I was doing her a favor," Gimbal whined. "She needed to be free of that place. To get out of there. It wasn't healthy. We should all be ashamed of letting her get that way. A shut-in. My God, you saw how she lived."

"The great humanitarian," Devine sneered.

"She trusted you," Whitsun spat.

"Gentlemen, please." This was from my boss. Everyone turned back to her, waiting for a verdict.

Finally Ms. P said, "I believe you. Not that either of you is incapable of murder. I find most people are, given the right circumstances. But Miss Bodine's death does not get you closer to obtaining the building. Your plan was working, after all. Tenants were beginning to leave. Vera Bodine would likely have eventually been forced to sell. Also, her homicide, if unsolved, would delay the execution of the will and leave ownership of the building in a legal limbo. That's why you came to me asking if I was still investigating the case, Mr. Gimbal. You wanted it solved and quickly. No, no. I don't believe you murdered her."

Whitsun threw up his hands. "Well, then, for Christ's sake, who did?"

Ms. Pentecost leaned forward in her chair and surveyed the room.

Here we go, I thought. Everything up until now was the overture. Now came the show.

"There has been a constant refrain since the beginning of this case. Miss Bodine was a shut-in. Mr. Whitsun impressed that upon us when he first procured our services. Mr. Gimbal repeated it just now. The headlines reporting her death proclaim it for everyone to see."

She looked down at the newspapers oh-so-carefully arranged on her desk.

" 'Elderly shut-in found murdered.' 'Shut-in discovered in trunk.' 'Pentecost seeks killer of shut-in.' "

She looked back up, shaking her head.

"But she wasn't, really. A shut-in is somebody who has closed the door between themselves and the world. Who has turned inward. Vera Bodine was anything but that. Yes, she was isolated. Yes, she protected herself from the world. But I don't believe she had abandoned it. On the contrary. Throughout her life she worked in the interest of fairness. For her friends, her fellow employees, the tenants of her apartment building, and in service to her country. That impulse never ceased—that desire to make the world a better place. She never stopped caring about justice."

I hadn't been able to get tickets to Sir Laurence Olivier's *Oedipus* the year before, but I can't imagine he'd held an audience any tighter than Lillian Pentecost was managing to with her opening speech.

"Perhaps it was because of her memory. We are able to continue living because the small injustices are forgotten. And the large ones dim with time. We are able to fool ourselves into believing that the world is right and fair. But Vera remembered everything, so she knew the truth. Mrs. Murphy, may I see your keys?"

The whiplash turn sent everyone's eyes to the saboteur sitting in the back of the room.

"My keys? What do you need my keys for?"

"Indulge me."

Lazenby leaned over her shoulder.

"How about you give her your keys? I'll keep it in mind when I'm adding up how many crimes you might have committed."

That got her fumbling in her purse. She pulled out a small

ring of keys. She handed them to Lazenby, who delivered them to my boss.

"Thank you, Lieutenant."

She placed the keys on top of the newspapers and continued the soliloquy.

"People who knew Miss Bodine, including people in this room, said she rarely left her apartment. But our investigation has recently uncovered that between August ninth and August eighteenth, she left every day. Every single day for ten days."

Ms. Pentecost reached into the inner pocket of her death-black suit and produced the clipping from the *Free City Press*. It wasn't the one I'd pulled out of Bodine's pocket. This one was fresh and dry and had all its ink still attached. We'd re-created the circle Bodine had drawn around the words. We used red pencil, which was a guess, but an educated one.

Ms. P held the clipping up for a long moment, then placed it next to the keys. While she did that, I kept my eyes on another pair of peepers in the room.

Not a tic, not a twitch. The first doubt that this was going to work began squirming in my stomach.

"On August eighth Miss Bodine read a story in *The New York Times*. It described the murder of Julia Fennel and the subsequent arrest of Nicholas Ramirez for the crime. It caught her attention. The next day she went out and walked to a newsstand on Seventh Avenue to purchase a copy of every paper that covered the murder. She did the same thing the following day. And the next."

That was errand number one for me. Canvas the newsmongers around her apartment building until I found someone who remembered Bodine. Bad odds, considering the foot traffic a newsstand gets in a given day. But Bodine stood out.

"She seemed like a real worried lady," the vendor told me. "Like it was real important she get those papers."

My boss continued. "On August eighteenth, she found an

article in the *Free City Press* that described in greater detail the bracelet that was supposedly stolen by Mr. Ramirez. A gold bracelet with a flowery mother-of-pearl inlay. The initials J.F. inscribed on the inside."

On the end of the couch, Devine angrily uncrossed one leg and crossed the other. "Come on," he grumbled. "Spit it out."

The smile Ms. Pentecost gave him was like a late-September breeze. Pleasant at first and colder the longer it lasted. By the time she turned her attention away from Devine, he was shivering.

"She had already suspected the truth. Dreaded it, perhaps. Ever since she saw the first article on Julia Fennel's death. She asked Mr. Whitsun to take on the case, but refused to tell him why. She needed to be certain. Then the other story, the mother-of-pearl inlay. She pushed Mr. Whitsun again, and again he said no. Still she wouldn't say why she wanted him to represent Mr. Ramirez. She believed in justice but . . . she was also loyal.

"The afternoon of August eighteenth, she left her apartment one last time. Not to buy papers. She'd already found what she was looking for. Once I saw the pattern, I knew she could have only one destination. Will, what did Mr. Francis Mejia tell you when you spoke to him?"

This was errand number two.

"Most of you probably know him better as Frankie," I told the room. "At least that's what you call him when he holds the door for you. I asked him if he'd seen Vera Bodine since she retired. He said he held the door for her the afternoon of Monday, August eighteenth. This was around six o'clock. He remembered the time because he was about to clock out for the day."

"And her demeanor?" Ms. P asked.

"He said she looked very grave. His words. No pun intended."

"Vera came to the office?" Boekbinder asked. "Why? What was she doing there?"

Ms. Pentecost turned to him, and if you thought her look was cold before, now it was positively arctic.

"I imagine, Mr. Boekbinder, that she was there to ask if you had killed your mistress."

CHAPTER 47

If you guessed Boekbinder was the killer because there were only so many people in the room, what can I say? Our office isn't that big and we had to be choosy.

The patrician lawyer reacted exactly like you'd expect an innocent person accused of murder to react. With a look of stunned shock, followed quickly by some indignant ejaculating.

"Excuse me? Miss Pentecost, making an accusation like that is—it's beyond theater. How dare you—"

"I dare because it is true," Ms. P declared.

Boekbinder was quivering with the perfect amount of outrage. Again, I started to doubt. But I kept in mind what I said about lawyers when we began this case. They're the best liars in the business, because it's their business to lie.

"It's true that Miss Bodine came to your office. It's true that she showed you a clipping. The bracelet. She remembered it. Those initials. That piece of jewelry. One gift among the hundred that she was tasked with purchasing the final Christmas she worked for you. You likely would have thought nothing of it. Slipping that gift in with those for employees and clients. A present for your mistress."

Boekbinder jumped to his feet.

"That is slander!"

Everyone flinched. Lazenby took two steps forward to get in range in case the lawyer leaped. My boss didn't even blink.

"Miss Fennel's co-workers said she always denied having a suitor, but they doubted her. There was suspicion her lover was a woman and that was why she kept her romantic life a secret. They neglected the more obvious answer. That her lover was married."

"I'm finished with this," Boekbinder said, turning to the door. Whitsun got up and stepped in his path.

"Not yet, John."

For a moment, I thought Boekbinder was going to get physical. Lazenby must have seen it, too. He took a third step into the room, looming over Whitsun's shoulder to let Boekbinder know that if he got past the defense attorney, he'd have heftier problems to deal with.

"Did she ask you to leave your wife? Or perhaps you made promises earlier in the relationship?" Ms. Pentecost asked Boekbinder's back. "Mr. Ramirez was hired to double the size of Miss Fennel's closet. But according to him it was barely two-thirds full. Of course, if she expected you to leave your wife and move in with her once you retired, she would need the space."

That was Whitsun's errand. Asking Ramirez about the contents of Julia Fennel's closet. Which understandably confused him. Now I watched as Whitsun's eyes went narrow and hard.

Boekbinder turned back to my boss.

"Did you tell her that your retirement would be the spark that ignited a new life?" Ms. P continued. "One where you and Miss Fennel would no longer need to hide? Or did she merely assume it?"

Boekbinder opened his mouth but Ms. Pentecost waved a dismissive hand.

"No matter," she said. "All that matters is that you informed her this was not the case. That's why she told Mr. Ramirez to cease his work and paid him for his services using a gift you had given her. That sounds like a very angry woman. Angry enough, I imagine, to threaten to finally tell your wife herself. How you reacted is laid bare by the evidence. An attack fueled by rage and fear, and then the calculated covering up. Making it look like a robbery, perhaps even with Nicholas Ramirez in mind. Did Miss Bodine get this far in her deductions? She was, by all accounts, a very sharp woman, above and beyond her memory. As your assistant for many years, she would have been intimately familiar with your predilections and tastes. I doubt Miss Fennel was your first paramour."

This time she actually gave Boekbinder a gap to slip in a response. I had to give him credit. The man must have had ice water pumping through his veins. Ms. Pentecost barreling down on him; Whitsun behind, looking like he was ready to go for the throat; his associates on the couch, mouths open in shock.

But somehow he managed to quell the shaking, jack his chin up, and speak like he was addressing opposing counsel in the highest court of the land.

"This is the most fantastical, disgusting conjecture. I will take great satisfaction in suing you for slander."

Ms. Pentecost blinked once, twice.

"Conjecture? Ah, yes. The evidence. Will?"

I picked up my notebook, but before I could start, Lazenby came forward and put a hand on Boekbinder's shoulder.

"Why don't you take a seat? You're making me nervous."

He directed Boekbinder to take the chair that Whitsun had vacated. Then Lazenby and Whitsun stepped back to flank the door.

I couldn't have choreographed it better myself. Off his feet, Boekbinder lost something of his dignity. And now he was surrounded.

I flipped a page and began talking.

"Jacques Gagnon operated a jewelry store on West Forty-seventh Street from 1932 to 1946. Now his son runs it. Junior said he thought that bracelet looked like his dad's work. Dad was famous for his mother-of-pearl, apparently. Gagnon senior's still around, by the way. He moved back to France after the war to help rebuild. His memory isn't anything like Vera Bodine's but according to the cable he sent yesterday, the bracelet is his design. Made as part of a big Christmas order in 1940. For Boekbinder and Gimbal."

I'd never been to a wax museum, but Boekbinder was giving me a preview. Ms. Pentecost gave me the nod to continue.

"Woolworth's, August twenty-third, one dozen lavender sachets. Glibb and Sons Housewares in Staten Island, August twenty-fourth, two dozen. Hoboken Home Goods—that's in Hoboken, in case you're curious—August twenty-fifth, another two. There's five more. You can see the list. Guess Vera was getting a little ripe, huh?"

That earned me a single twitch of Boekbinder's cheek. I took it as a victory.

"Spreading out these purchases was an excellent precaution," Ms. P said. "However, we have certified statements from store employees identifying you from photographs," Ms. P added.

The jewelry and department stores were what we'd traded our conversation with Teetering to Faraday for. I don't know how Faraday explained the use of manpower, but he'd gotten the canvassing done in two days flat.

"All of this is circumstantial," said Pearl, piping up for the first time from her seat by the door. "A good defense attorney will take it out like clay pigeons. If the case even gets to court."

I didn't mistake the comment as a defense of Boekbinder. It was clearly a question: What else did we have up our sleeve?

Ms. Pentecost gave a slow nod, like she was just now, in the moment, pondering the problem of hard evidence. Then she flicked her eyes to Boekbinder and latched on.

"Mr. Boekbinder, may I see your keys, please?"

That elicited a full-out flinch from the lawyer.

"My keys? No. Why?"

"I was wondering if you were still carrying this key."

She picked up Mrs. Murphy's key ring and sorted through it until she found the one that wasn't like the others.

"The master key to Miss Bodine's apartment building," she explained to the class. "The one that allowed you access to the back stairwell. A number of residents said they heard rats moving in there at night during the last couple weeks. But it was you. Going up to Miss Bodine's apartment. That's who Mr. Wocjik heard walking around during those days following Miss Bodine's death. It was you searching for this clipping. It was in her pocket, by the way. You should have searched her before putting her body in the trunk."

Boekbinder didn't shiver, but everyone else in the room did. He, on the other hand, was starting to sweat. He gave the least natural shrug in the history of shoulders.

"Of course I have a copy of the key to Vera's building," he said. "I dealt with her management company when Clark wasn't able."

On the couch, Gimbal and Devine exchanged a glance. They knew Boekbinder's answer was bullshit. That didn't matter, though. It was what a jury would consider reasonable doubt that counted.

"You never personally used it?" Ms. P asked.

"Never."

Ms. Pentecost smiled. There was actually some warmth in this one. Not because her feelings toward murderers had changed. She simply smelled blood.

"Will, would you invite our guest in, please?"

I got up and opened the side door. Our guest was sitting where we'd left her, patiently waiting at the dining room table.

"We're ready for you, Mrs. Culligan."

She stood up with a groan, pressing her hand into the

small of her back, and followed me into the office. She took a spot between Ms. Pentecost's desk and mine, looking around the room with a mixture of curiosity and apprehension.

She looked out of place in this company: stringy gray hair pinned up in a utilitarian bun; a paisley-print dress that might have been pink a hundred washings ago; hands clasped to her chest, fingernails bitten to the quick.

Ms. P gave the woman her full attention. She didn't look it, but Mrs. Culligan was our eleven o'clock number.

"Mrs. Culligan, thank you so much for being here today."

"My pleasure," the woman said, in a way that suggested it absolutely wasn't.

"Could you tell everyone where you are employed?"

"I work a couple jobs. I do some washing at the veterans' hospital. Sheets and gowns and the like. That's on weekends. I do some sewing for people around the neighborhood. Mostly I work for Cramer."

"Cramer?" Ms. P prompted.

"Cramer Cleaning Services. I clean office buildings. Vacuuming, dusting, emptying the waste bins. Windows, too. But only in the private offices. They want all the windows done, they'll have to pay extra. That'd take a lot more time, and my time ain't free."

With that last bit, some of the apprehension disappeared and was replaced with a kind of homespun dignity.

"Which office buildings do you clean in your job at Cramer?" Ms. P asked.

"It depends. They rotate us around. Since the beginning of August, I've been at the Hibbert Building. Me and three other girls. Three nights a week. We start at six p.m. and go until we're finished."

"This is the building that shares a rear alley with the Baxter Arms, is that correct?"

That last wasn't a question, but the old woman answered it.

"Yes, ma'am, it is. Though I didn't know the Bodine lady.

And I don't read the papers," she said. "Terrible thing. What a terrible thing. I live alone now since my Patrick died and it sets your mind running, doesn't it?"

"It certainly does," Ms. Pentecost agreed. "You had cause to notice the apartment building before, didn't you?"

"I don't know about cause. But I noticed it, sure. If you're talking about the man I saw going into it at night."

Everyone still sitting leaned forward in their seats, me included. Everyone except for Boekbinder. He sank back.

"You saw a man going into that apartment building at night? Through the door to the back stairwell?"

"Sure," she said. "Couple of times. He just seemed out of place is all. Since nobody else ever went that way that I saw. And the way he acted. Real nervous. Like he was afraid he was going to get mugged."

"You noticed all this from a high office window at night?"

"Well, it wasn't that high. I've got floors two through six. And there's a light right over that door."

"Is that man in the room today, Mrs. Culligan?"

Without a bit of hesitation, the old woman nodded at Boekbinder. "Sure, that's him right there. Can't mistake that hair. It practically gleamed in the light, it did."

That broke him. His shoulders sank. His hands started shaking. He turned to the sofa, searching for any hint of support from his colleagues. Nothing doing. Devine and Gimbal were a united front of disgust and disappointment.

"She was already dead," Boekbinder said. "I swear. I went up to talk to her and she was already dead. She must have fallen and hit her head."

He was really sweating now. Practically panting like a dog.

"All right, there's interfering with a body," he continued. "Making a false statement to the police. Maybe breaking and entering, but I had a key and . . . I didn't murder her, and you can't prove I did!"

Ms. Pentecost stood up. She wavered for a moment before grabbing her cane to add an extra buttress.

"Perhaps I cannot, Mr. Boekbinder," she said. "That will ultimately be up to the district attorney and, later, a jury. However, I do believe that with a little added focus the police will easily be able to prove that you were Miss Fennel's lover. There were many fingerprints found in her apartment. I'm sure one or two belong to you. And it's unlikely that you were in a relationship for so long without being seen together. With that proven, I believe a jury might find its way toward a conviction. Unless you have a good defense attorney. I'm afraid the very best is unavailable."

Boekbinder turned and found Whitsun's eyes.

"Forest, I—"

"Go to hell, John."

There was no anger in his words. Only sadness.

Ms. Pentecost nodded to Lazenby, who began issuing directions to his pair of sergeants. The first took hold of Boekbinder, who allowed himself to be ushered out. The other rounded up the Gimbal siblings.

"I don't know what charges will stick, but we'll find something," Lazenby told the pair.

While they were doing that, I ushered our star witness out the side door and up the stairs. I installed her in my room, where we spent some time chatting.

By the time I got back, the only people left were my boss and Lazenby.

"—going to need to re-interview everyone who was here. Everyone in her building," the lieutenant was saying. "Signed depositions all around. Including from you and Parker. I'm not sure how much we'll actually need you for the Fennel case, but we'll definitely need you for Bodine."

Lazenby looked toward me.

"Mrs. Culligan will need to come with me," he said. "I

don't want to let her out of my sight until I've got her statement typed up."

"Right," I said, running a finger under my collar. "Mrs. Culligan. Bit of a problem there."

Lazenby's brow dropped to half-mast.

"What kind of problem?"

I yelled over my shoulder.

"The coast is clear!"

The woman who stepped through the door bore a passing
resemblance to Mrs. Culligan but only if you squinted. She'd
rouged her cheeks and put on lipstick, ditched the gray wig to
reveal henna-wash curls, and traded the wash-worn dress for a
fashionable purple number that cinched nicely at the waist and
left her arms bare.

Nobody was mistaking Maeve Bailey for a cleaning
woman.

"I haven't had that much fun in years," she crowed. "Not
since Benny Higgins and I worked cons at the Haymarket.
Although I was fifteen at the time, so my idea of fun was a little
unrefined. Hello—Maeve Bailey at your service."

She extended her hand. Lazenby stared at it, and her, like
they might be venomous. He looked at my boss, then at me.

"There's no Cramer Cleaners?"

"Oh, there is," I said. "They didn't see squat. When you
have the lights on in an office building at night, you can't really
see outside very well. All you get is your reflection. And the
angle in that alley is a little too steep. Boekbinder might have
figured that out if we hadn't set him up for it so well."

"Oh, the look on his face," Maeve purred. "Adoration is
always nice to see on a man's features, but I highly recommend
fear. Let's try this again. Maeve Bailey, spiritual adviser, for-
merly of Hart and Halloway, currently of Coney Island."

This time Lazenby took the cue.

"Lieutenant Nathan Lazenby, New York City Police
Department."

Maeve gave a long, lingering shake and I kept a close eye on her fingers and his watch.

"So, there's no eyewitness," he said when she disengaged.

"I'm afraid not," Ms. P told him. "However, we have an excellent audio recording of the events of this evening, including, I assume, of Mr. Boekbinder's declarations at the end."

Lazenby's frown didn't let up.

"Without an eyewitness, nailing him for Bodine might be tough."

Ms. Pentecost shrugged. "True. But what I told Mr. Boekbinder was not a bluff. I believe if you focus your attentions on Miss Fennel, you will find evidence of his relationship with her. They were lovers for years. They would have been seen. His fingerprints will be there somewhere."

"You should check behind the headboard," Maeve suggested. "Oh, don't give me that look. They weren't meeting up to play pinochle."

Lazenby wasn't a wasteful man, so he didn't spend any more breath on arguing.

"All right," he said. "I'd better get to the station house. Once Staples hears about this he's going to try and swoop in. Damned if I'm letting him. You better come with me, Mrs. Bailey. I'll still need a statement from you."

"It's Miss Bailey," Maeve told him. "Usually I don't go strolling with cops, but for you, I'll make an exception."

She tucked her arm through his, and the pair headed out the door. On the way I heard her say, "Now, Nathan, how does your wife feel about you spending your days chasing murderers?"

"I'm not married."

"Oh, what a shame."

When they were out the door, I turned to my boss.

"That could be a problem."

But she was only smiling.

"There are worse problems to have."

Ain't that the truth.

CHAPTER **48**

The next couple of days were spent as most cases are once the cuffs snap shut. With the trimming of loose ends.

The first thing I did as soon as we had our office to ourselves was give the newspapers a call and get Boekbinder's name out there as the guilty party. I played up the "Lillian Pentecost Solves Two Murders with One Stone" angle in the hopes that big headlines would usher Mr. Ramirez out of prison faster.

Later that evening, I played courier, delivering two incriminating audio reels. The first went to Lazenby, who was still writing reports and barely even looked up from his typewriter.

The second audio reel went to our favorite FBI agent.

I met Faraday a little after midnight across the street from the White Clover. He'd instructed me to park a couple blocks away and walk. In the trench coat and fedora, he looked every bit the cliché. Which, by now, I knew he wasn't. At least not entirely.

"I've got the dagger if you've got the cloak," I told him when I walked up. "We could have done this inside. The rest of my night's free. Watching Rosa work the stage is as good a way to spend it as any."

"Rosa's not on tonight."

There was something off-key in the way he said it.

"What's wrong? You two on the skids?"

He shook his head.

"Look," I said. "I might ask questions for a living, but it's after hours, so cut me a break."

"She's visiting family in Brazil."

"I thought her family was from Puerto Rico."

"She doesn't talk to that branch. She has an aunt in Brazil, though. Never met her, but they've exchanged letters. She'll be safe there."

I was about to ask what he meant when a parade drove past. No candy-colored floats. Just five police cars and a pair of paddy wagons. They had barely come to a full stop in front of the White Clover when about thirty cops poured out and charged the front door.

The bouncer put his hands out, like he was planning to single-handedly block the entire battalion. The cops practically trampled him in their rush to get inside.

"Jesus Christ," I said. "Did somebody forget a bribe?"

Faraday shoved his hands in his trench coat and pulled it tight around him.

"Somebody wrote a letter," he said.

"A letter?"

"Oh, you know. Moral degeneracy and filth and won't somebody do something about *these people*."

Right. A letter.

"They sent a plainclothes in tonight," he added.

That was how the police usually worked. Send somebody in to scope the scene, take notes, see what was shown onstage, who in the crowd was clinching who. Then make a call when the place was at maximum moral degeneracy.

"I thought they knew all the vice-squad guys."

"They borrowed someone from the Bureau. I've met him. He really looks the part."

I looked at Faraday in surprise.

"How far ahead did you know this was coming?" I asked.

No answer from the special agent. Faraday kept his mouth

shut and his eyes fixed on the busted-open door of the White Clover.

"Far enough to make sure Rosa was nowhere near here," I answered for him. "Though why you sent her all the way out of the country, I don't know."

"She's safer there."

The way he said it, it was like he was trying to convince himself more than me.

I was about to ask him a follow-up when the first cops started coming out the door, shoving their prisoners in front of them or dragging them behind. Men in black tie, band members in their spangly jackets, waiters barely old enough to buy the drinks they were serving. Some were sobbing. Others were yelling, threatening the cops with lawsuits.

A drag queen tripped over the hem of her long white gown and went sprawling. She grabbed on to a police officer's leg trying to get back up.

He snarled and pulled his leg back, then he sent a kick right into her down-turned face. Blood and teeth went flying.

Suddenly there was a series of white flashes, and every prisoner to a man and woman turned their face away. The cops had brought along a photographer. I recognized her as a stringer who sold work to half the city's papers. She'd asked me out once. Now I was glad I'd turned her down.

"Judas," I hissed.

Faraday must have thought I was referring to him.

"If I warn them and it gets traced back to me, I'm done," he said. "Besides, if they dodged tonight, the cops would only try again."

I looked to Faraday and was shocked to see tears in his eyes. One escaped down his cheek. He didn't even bother to wipe it away.

Of course he was sad, I thought. His marriage was freshly over, Rosa was off for who knows how long, the place where he could sit in the back and feel safe and comfortably anonymous was being shuttered.

He'd had a life. One that probably made it at least a little bearable to be a homosexual sporting a badge.

Now it was gone.

I reached out and gave his arm a squeeze.

He jerked away.

"Recording," he snapped.

I reached into my bag and handed him the reel. It disappeared into the folds of his trench coat.

"Don't call me for a while, Parker."

He walked away. I had a feeling the former Colonel Durchdenwald was about to be the recipient of a whole lot of pent-up rage.

I spent another minute watching the horror show at the White Clover. I wasn't alone. Dozens of people were lining the sidewalk now, wide-eyed, laughing, jeering, spitting curses at the men and women being shoved into the paddy wagons.

"Look at that. They're finally doing something about those queers."

I turned around. There was a woman standing in a doorway in a housecoat and slippers. She could have been Mrs. Campbell's American cousin.

"They should lock 'em all up," she added when she saw she had my attention. "Lock 'em up and throw away the key."

I could tell she was waiting for a response. I had a few. Some of them you could even print. But it would have been nothing for her to yell over to the cops.

"Hey, over here! You missed one!"

So I said nothing and walked back to the car, feeling the woman's eyes burning a hole between my shoulder blades every step of the way.

The next morning, Ms. Pentecost took a crack at smoothing over my feelings.

"There was nothing you could have done," she assured me.

"I don't know about that," I said. "I could at least have told that woman what I thought of her."

"You bore witness and you survived and kept your freedom. That is a victory. And far more than a Pyrrhic one."

I made a note to look the word up later and let the conversation end at that.

We were both seated at our respective desks. Ms. Pentecost was proofing our report on the case. I was adding up our bill, which I would deliver to Whitsun along with the report later that day.

Ms. P had been thinking of offering a discount, having heard of Whitsun's storefront shop and the clientele he was bringing in. I reminded her that not only was he the proud owner of a Manhattan apartment building, but he was eyeing what was left of Boekbinder & Gimbal for a million-dollar civil suit on behalf of the Bodine estate.

One partner tried to swindle her; the other killed her. I liked his chances.

"He can afford the full Pentecost price," I declared.

As I added up expenses, I also tallied the number of sighs and grunts coming from my boss.

"What's the matter?" I asked.

"Unanswered questions."

"Such as?"

"Miss Bodine's comment to Mr. Whitsun that she was worried she was losing her memory, for one."

I shrugged. "She was getting up there in years. Everyone worries about their memory a little at that age, perfect recall or not."

"Then there's her question to Sergeant Grady asking how she would go about reporting a crime."

"Where's the question there? That was right before she went and saw Boekbinder."

Ms. Pentecost shook her head. "She didn't ask how she

would provide information about a known crime. She asked how she should report one."

"Look," I said. "Maybe Grady got the phrasing wrong. Or maybe he didn't, and she just fumbled the question."

Ms. Pentecost considered it for a moment, then gave a grunt and went back to proofing the report.

Those kinds of loose ends bothered her. Me? Not so much.

At the end of a case, there are always unanswered questions. Scattered like bread crumbs that lead you nowhere but in circles.

Besides, I figured she was really worried about other things. On the corner of her desk was a stack of files—everything related to Quincannon. I might not have fully understood what he had on her, but I knew she was looking for a toehold on him.

I was ready to lend a hand. Just as soon as she was ready to ask.

CHAPTER 49

That afternoon, after dropping off the report and the attached invoice to Whitsun, I hopped on the subway and traveled to East Harlem to clear up a loose end of my own.

My destination was a flophouse south of Jefferson Park. It was the kind of joint that probably aspired to charge by the hour, but johns were willing to pay the extra buck elsewhere so they didn't walk away with lice.

The front door didn't have a working lock. Not that anyone who rented here had anything worth stealing. I found the room I was looking for on the basement level. I knocked once. Twice. When a full minute went by without an answer, I went at it with my picks.

Once inside, I gave it a quick toss. It was a one-room number with a shared bath down the hall, so it didn't take long.

Then I sat on the busted-spring Murphy bed, got my Browning out, and waited.

It wasn't long. About twenty minutes later, I heard footsteps—a single pair wearing heels—followed by the jingle of keys. The door opened and "Colleen Lighthead" stepped in.

Again, she was sharp. She saw me, tensed to run, then saw the gun pointed in her general direction and cut the impulse short.

"Why don't you close the door, Sally. We need to have a talk."

She did as instructed. I nodded at the wicker stool in the corner—the only other piece of furniture in the hovel. She sat.

"How'd you find me?" she asked.

"Your agent," I told her. "It took me a minute, but I eventually twigged that Colleen Lighthead was the name of the girlfriend in *Riviera Sunset*. I happened to see that show, so I knew you didn't play the part. But I thought maybe you'd auditioned for it and that's how you remembered the name. The casting agent recognized you from the short list. Gave me the name Sally Madder. That got me to your talent agent, which got me to you."

"That no-show audition I spent an hour waiting for?"

"Yeah, that was me," I admitted. "I thought it'd be nice to have the place to myself for a few minutes. Didn't find my Beretta. You really toss it in a sewer?"

"That's what I said, isn't it?" She actually sounded offended, like she didn't tell a hundred lies before breakfast.

I asked where I could find this sewer grate and she gave me directions. My piece had probably been swept away, but it was worth checking.

That bit of business taken care of, I asked, "Where's your boyfriend?"

She shook her head. "I don't know. Not here. Not for days."

"I'm not playing," I warned her. "Russo might be in the clink, but his boys aren't. Manny's gonna want me to find him before they do."

"I'm telling you I don't know where he is," she said. "When I brought his mother back here, he was gone. All his clothes, too. I mean, look around. He packed up and ran."

I'd noticed that. Not a pair of skivvies or a safety razor in sight.

"So Manny ditched you? Didn't even wait to make sure his mom was okay?"

She shrugged, making as if she didn't care, but she hadn't rehearsed it and it fell flat.

"We talked about L.A.," she said. "He told me I was more Hollywood than Broadway. Knowing him, he'll get off the bus in Cincinnati, get into a dice game, and lose his shirt."

"Speaking of modes of transportation, you sell that Packard coupe yet?"

She shook her head. "No," she said. "I tried, but you took the key and this guy didn't like that it was hot-wired. I gave him a story, but he didn't bite. It's parked around the block."

A tear started to leak out, but she set her jaw and willed it back.

"Are you gonna turn me in?" she asked.

I sighed. This one was a heave.

I'd been thinking about it the whole ride over. If I'd found Casper with her, calling the cops was a near-sure thing. He'd be safer in jail than on the street. Besides, I'd remembered the sound of him hitting Sally when I was lying dazed under the boardwalk.

The two needed splitting up.

Now that he'd done the splitting for me, there was only Sally. Sally, who had played the role of bait so I could get mugged. Sally, who had walked into First National and talked them out of five hundred dollars of my hard-earned money. Sally, who had swindled the Packard dealership using my name.

But it was Sally who'd shown up to help Casper's mom while he cowered back home and packed a bag.

She'd played it cool when she'd impersonated me on the phone to get Russo out in the open. Yeah, she'd pulled a runner, but what did I expect? In her shoes, I'd have done the same.

"I don't know what you're like as an actress," I told her. "That casting agent I talked to called you a perennial also-ran. But as a con woman, you're not half bad. Which ain't necessarily good. You know just enough to earn yourself a nickel in the House of D."

I was referring to the Women's House of Detention in

Greenwich Village, which did a great business in chewing women like Sally up before spitting them out.

"A girl's got to earn a living," she said.

"Russo called you a junkie. Heroin?"

"I haven't touched it in six months," she said.

"You sure about that?"

She held her chin high.

"You searched the place. Did you find anything? Any works?"

I hadn't. Also, nothing about Sally suggested she was still on the nod.

I slid the gun into its holster, then reached into a pocket and pulled out a piece of paper. I handed it to her.

"What's this?"

"It's a phone number."

"No shit."

I ignored the attitude.

"The woman at the other end is expecting you to call," I told her. "You pass muster, she'll take you on."

"Take me on as what?" she asked.

"Right now, she'll probably play you off as some kind of spiritualist in training. Maybe say you can talk to ghosts. But that might not fit in with her new con quite so much."

The Murphy bed's springs gave a relieved squeal as I stood up.

"She'll find some use for you," I said. "Pay attention and you should learn a thing or five. Meanwhile, I'm gonna take the Packard. I'll head over to the dealership tomorrow and see if I can't get them to take it back without asking too many questions."

Sally squinted down at the number on the paper like it was hieroglyphics. She looked back up at me.

"Why are you doing this?" she asked.

"Someone pointed out to me recently that there are some

crimes that shouldn't be forgotten," I said. "Five hundred bucks and a knock on the head? I probably won't forget that anytime soon. But I can forgive it. You read me?"

Her nod was uncertain. If I were her, I wouldn't have trusted me, either.

"If it makes you feel any better, you're going to owe me," I told her. "You're gonna owe me big."

With that last loose end neatly trimmed, I walked out.

CHAPTER 50

Except it wasn't the last.

I told you that unanswered questions don't bother me, but apparently they do. This was exacerbated by the fact that three days after being arrested, Boekbinder was still pleading, "She was dead when I got there," to anybody who would listen.

On Thursday, Lazenby called Ms. Pentecost with the update. Boekbinder's prints were indeed among those collected from Fennel's apartment. Including a freshly lifted set from the top edge of the headboard.

Score one for Maeve.

People in Fennel's building had seen Boekbinder around, and once the attorney's picture hit the papers, waiters at three different restaurants had come forward swearing they'd seen the pair together, huddled close in booths, sharing kisses, hands on knees, that sort of thing.

All the restaurants were twenty blocks or more from Fennel's place, which is why the original canvas had come up empty.

The witnesses were just the icing. A search of Boekbinder's house turned up a cache of letters and love notes the pair had exchanged over the years. Very steamy reading. In one of her last letters, Fennel mentioned the museum soiree she'd been planning to attend the weekend she was killed. She said it would make an excellent place for them to debut publicly as a couple, and that if Boekbinder demurred she might have to consider finally introducing herself to his missus.

And while he'd tossed the shirt he'd been wearing when he bludgeoned her, he'd kept the cuff links. Apparently he hadn't noticed the blood smeared on one of the posts.

A mountain of evidence was piling up, all on the Fennel side of the equation. None for Bodine.

"The DA is talking plea," Lazenby told my boss. "Figures a trial will be long and expensive. Boekbinder's got deep pockets and a lot of friends. Though fewer than he had a week ago. They'll probably throw in Bodine's murder. Make him plead guilty to both for a reduced sentence."

I could tell Lazenby didn't like it. Neither did I.

Which is why that afternoon I went over to Bodine's apartment to take one last look around. Maybe we'd missed something. Maybe I'd missed something. I really don't know what I expected to find.

The truck was still in the alley. I peeked in. Not as full as it had been, so it had been emptied at least once. I did a circuit around the building, thinking I might find Commander Cody hunting rats, remembering too late that it was a school day.

I went up the three flights to Bodine's apartment. We still had the key Whitsun gave us, so I let myself in.

It was empty. Or nearly so.

The sofa was still there. The kitchen table and chairs and the Frigidaire. The armchair in the sitting room. The bed was still in the bedroom. The trunk was long gone, having been confiscated by the police as evidence.

How many truckloads had it taken? I wondered.

Had Whitsun been cleared soon enough to oversee any of it? Had he been able to comb through, looking for photos or diaries?

I hadn't thought to ask when I'd dropped off the bill. He and Pearl had been too busy sorting through clients to chat.

Did that mean I needed to go trash picking? See if there

was anything in the truck in the alley that we might have missed? Personal items Whitsun wanted to keep?

I hoped not. Just because Murphy wasn't around anymore to hand-deliver rats didn't mean there wasn't a homegrown supply nesting at the bottom of that truck.

I figured I'd better give Whitsun a call. Whitsun or my boss or both.

Some bright light had decided Bodine's phone was junk and tossed it, too, so I started downstairs, planning to hit the sidewalk in search of a pay phone.

I was passing the second floor when I noticed that the door of #201 was open and there were cardboard boxes piled up outside it.

I went over and poked my head in the door.

Half the apartment was in boxes. The other half was in the process of being packed, disassembled, or both. A man was sitting on the floor using packing tape to carefully seal a cardboard box.

What was his name? Carter? Carver? All that came to mind was "Model Train Guy."

I knocked on the doorframe.

"Excuse me."

Startled, he looked up, peering at me through his army-issue specs.

"Oh, hello. Can I help you?"

"Do you mind if I use your phone?" I asked. "I'll only be a minute."

"Sure, sure. It's on the wall in the kitchen," he said. "Don't mind me. I'm just trying to get the ketchup back in the bottle."

Again, he was the only one chuckling at his jokes.

I found the phone where he said, tucked the receiver between shoulder and ear, and dialed Whitsun's number. I let it ring a dozen times before hanging up. If Pearl and Whitsun were jammed with clients, there'd be no one to answer the phone.

I decided to count to fifty and try again.

"So you're leaving?" I asked. "Even with the extra three hundred out of the picture?"

That was common knowledge now. Gimbal's real estate scam hadn't been as big a headline as ATTORNEY SLAYS LOVER, SECRETARY but it was still twisted enough to make the front page.

"Yep. That sure was disappointing," he said. From his tone, I suspected there was a "very" missing. Maybe even an "exceptionally."

"I put a down payment down on that house in Jersey City. Did it right before this all hit the papers," he explained. "They won't take it back. I signed a contract. They say if I try and back out, the penalties will cost me more than the three hundred, so . . . ketchup back into the bottle."

One of the kitchen drawers had been emptied, its contents piled on the counter beneath the phone. Half a dozen pencil stubs, a pile of paper clips, a few business cards, a grocery list so faded by time that I could barely read the word RUTABAGA.

A small black-and-white face peeked out from beneath the grocery list. I moved the list aside to reveal a string of tiny snapshots taken at a photo booth. It showed two teenage girls, laughing, smiling. Both of them blond and pretty in a way that suggested blood relation. Sisters, probably. The one on the left looked familiar.

"Is your . . . uh . . . is your wife around?" I asked. "Or is she still on that birthday cruise?"

From the living room came the sound of tape ripping.

"Oh, no, no. She's already in Jersey City. Getting the house ready, you know? Lots to do. Lots, lots, lots."

What was my count at? Fifty? Sixty? I started dialing again. As I spun the dial, I asked, "What was her name again?"

"My wife? Rhoda."

Rhoda. Of course. I could see it typed out in front of me.

Rodney Camper (DOB: 7/11/1909)
Occupation: train repairman
Rhoda Camper (DOB: 2/22/1912)
Occupation: homemaker

Rodney and Rhoda. Who could forget a pair of names like that?

But it was the date I remembered now. Her birthday. All those twos.

Then it came to me. Where I'd seen that photo-strip face before. An older, wearier version of it. Looking up at me from the top layer of garbage in the truck in the alley.

I sure would like to have a film reel of my face in that moment. Because I've had eyes on Ms. Pentecost when she's working a puzzle, and I can always tell when the pieces fall together. There's a sort of slackness that comes over her, like all the tiny muscles in her face have been given permission to relax.

Then the smile. That barely there Pentecost grin.

I did not smile.

I didn't smile when I remembered those photos in the truck. Scattered right beside a pile of clothes that almost certainly belonged to Rhoda Camper. I didn't smile when I thought about how Rodney had been going around telling everyone his wife was on a birthday cruise when her birthday was in February. Not something his neighbors would catch, seeing as how no one in the building socialized.

Unless you were the old lady on the top floor with the perfect memory. The one who'd seen all of the rental applications, including tenants' dates of birth.

I definitely didn't smile when I remembered the first time Ms. Pentecost and I had visited the Campers' apartment. Rodney on the floor with his train set.

It runs better on a hard surface.

But no rolled-up rug in sight. Nope. Because that rug

was probably wrapped around his wife's body wherever he'd decided to dump it.

"The phone working okay?"

My skeleton nearly departed my skin. Camper was standing next to me, his body filling the kitchen doorway. It was all I could do to keep my hand from moving toward my holster. I was a quick draw, but not that quick. And Camper might have been doughy, but he was big.

I willed myself not to back away. Tried to keep the knowledge out of my eyes.

"Phone's working fine, but nobody's answering. Guess I'll try later."

I smiled and moved as if to leave.

"Thanks again," I said.

He stepped back and moved aside to let me pass.

"Sure. No problem."

I started toward the open front door and freedom.

"Good luck with packing and—"

His hands swung down over my head. Something bit hard into my throat and I was pulled backward off my feet, heels scrabbling at the hardwood floor.

I went for my gun, but before I could get a good grip, Camper swung me around and threw me. I landed on a freshly sealed box. There was the sound of exploding crockery as it crumpled beneath me. The Browning went flying out of my hand and across the room.

Then Camper was straddling me, his full weight pressing down on my rib cage. He got a grip on the long strip of packing tape that he'd used to garrote me and wrapped it twice around my throat.

He began pulling it tight, tight, tighter, cutting into the carotids on either side of my neck and hijacking my brain of blood. Desperately I tried to get my fingers between the tape and my neck. The edges of my vision began disappearing into darkness. My thoughts turned thick and slow.

This was how I was going to go out? Strangled on the floor of a shitty apartment? Taken out by some wife-killing mug because I was a second too slow?

Hell, no.

I stopped panicking and remembered what I'd told my ladies last time we were in the basement: When a guy's on top of you, the first step is to make life difficult for him.

I went for his eyes first. My nails skittered off the lenses of his glasses, but the move caused him to rear back. I bucked as hard as I could and he lost his grip and teetered to the side.

The tape didn't loosen all the way, but it was enough. Fueled by a burst of fresh blood to my brain, I scrambled backward through broken dishes.

Still on his knees, he tried to leap back on top of me, but I managed to bring my legs up in front of him. He plowed forward anyway, and I ended up with my legs wrapped around his waist.

He was a big guy, plenty of reach. Even trapped between my legs, he was easily able to lean forward and reach my throat. And this time he wasn't bothering with the tape. He wrapped his fingers around my neck and went to work.

Camper probably didn't know a carotid from a katydid, but he was perfectly happy to crush my trachea, which is a much worse way to go. I could feel my eyes bulging, my lungs burning, straining.

It was so unpleasant I almost forgot what to do next.

I crossed my arms over his, got a hold of his elbows, and squeezed. That took the power out of his grip and gave me a trickle of air. It also locked his arms to my chest.

I unwrapped my legs, swung them up and onto his shoulders, crossed my feet, then thrust my hips into the air. His upper arms went one way while his lower stayed glued in place.

There was a wet, gristly snap. A shard of broken white bone jutted out from above the soft meat of Camper's right elbow.

He stared at it in horror and began to scream, long and loud.

But instead of falling off me and clutching his broken wing, he shrugged my legs off his shoulders and jumped forward, landing hard on my sternum. My stolen air burst out of my mouth.

Still screaming, he pulled his left arm back and curled his fingers into a meaty fist. Then he brought it down like a hammer aimed at the side of my head.

He missed.

Maybe it was because he wasn't a lefty or because his glasses were askew or because of the pain. Whatever the reason, his fist slammed into the hardwood at an angle right next to my ear. Perfect for hearing the sound of his pinkie cracking.

The fresh pain caused him to suck in air and cut off his train-whistle wail.

Camper looked down at me in bafflement. Then ignoring the blood and broken bones, he raised both fists in the air. No way I could dodge this. He bared his teeth in a grisly smile.

Suddenly there was a dull thump and Camper plummeted forward, sprawling chest-first across my face.

A hand reached down, grabbed Camper's broken arm, and rolled him off me. Sergeant Grady looked down at me and his unconscious neighbor. In one hand he held a baton. The other was gripping the bathrobe he hadn't bothered to slip on.

Grady, it turns out, sleeps in the nude.

But he didn't seem shy, and frankly I didn't care.

"Goddamn it," he muttered. "Guess this means my shift starts early today."

CHAPTER 51

Turns out, Rodney's wife hadn't been as keen on moving house as he was. He wanted to take the money and move to Jersey City. Find a better house and a cushier gig. Rhoda liked the apartment, liked the neighborhood, liked being able to walk a few blocks and catch a show. Rodney wasn't so much of a theater guy. They argue, tempers flare, or at least his does. He shoves her, she falls, hits her head on the edge of the coffee table, end of Rhoda. So he rolls her up in the rug, lugs her out in the middle of the night, tosses her in his truck, and drives her out to the Meadowlands. He drops her in a sinkhole, figures the mud will suck her down, but the Jersey cops found her in a thatch of cattails."

"They found her in what?" Holly asked, shouting the question into my ear so I could hear it over the roar of the wind and the engine.

"Cattails!" I shouted. "You know. With the long stems and the—"

"Oh, cattails!"

We were whipping along the winding stretch that led up through the forest to Brent and Marlo's cabin. We'd just picked up supplies from Cappachi's Wet and Dry, where I got to meet Tom in person and thank him for fetching Holly for that much-appreciated phone call. When he asked, I said I was her cousin, because Holly liked him and I didn't want to test it.

I continued the tale.

"Anyway, he comes up with the story of her going away on a birthday cruise. He didn't think it through much. But nobody knows her; she's a loner, no regular friends. She's got a sister, but they haven't talked since they were in high school. Nobody to question it."

"Except for Vera," Holly said.

"That's right. Except for Vera Bodine. Maybe she caught the birthday on their rental application. Maybe the mail she accidentally got from them included birthday cards for Rhoda. She worried it was her memory finally going. The first crack in the dike. But it got her thinking. Wondering why Camper might want to make up a lie to cover his wife's absence. It bothered her enough to ask Grady about reporting a crime. At least that's what Ms. Pentecost figures. On account of how she whispered the question to Grady. She didn't want Camper to overhear. Though I still think it could have been the Fennel murder she was talking about.

"Either way, she might have been whispering, but Grady wasn't. And Fridays were Camper's day off, so he was home to catch Grady asking her what crime she was talking about. He figures she's talking about him. That evening he goes up carrying a plate with a towel over it. 'Hey, Miss Bodine, my wife came back and she made these cookies fresh from the oven for you.' Instead of cookies on the plate, it's a wrench. He hits her, closes the door, and walks away. She's a shut-in, after all. He figured it would be weeks before anybody noticed. Didn't count on Boekbinder showing up later that night to try and talk her out of coming forward about Fennel. Boekbinder probably thought he'd hit the jackpot. Dead Vera meant no worries. Except she'd had that clipping and he didn't want anyone—Whitsun, especially—to come across it. So he searched, couldn't find it the first night, came back the next night, and the next, working through the apartment, eventually put Vera in the trunk, and so forth and so on.'"

A squirrel darted out into the road, and I swerved in a tight half-circle to miss it. The Packard handled like a dream.

"Camper told you everything?" Holly asked. "Right there to you and his neighbor? I thought people never confessed like that."

"Well, he was concussed at the time."

"He was what?"

"Concussed!" I shouted. "Severely."

Which would probably get the statement he made to Grady and me tossed out of court. Not that it mattered. There was the body in Jersey, blood on the corner of the coffee table, and the bloody wrench tucked in the back of his truck. You don't throw away a good wrench.

Camper was going away for life. Or death. Whichever the D.A. decided. Maybe he and Boekbinder could be cellmates. Neither could handle being disagreed with and three women were dead because of it.

Holly draped an arm across the back of the seat and brushed her fingers against the bruises that ran like a purple and brown choker around my throat.

"So Ms. Pentecost was wrong," Holly said. "About Vera's murder."

I shrugged. "She knew something was off. I mean, that's why I went there. Too many loose ends."

"Too many what?"

I smiled and shook my head. I'd tell her the whole thing again when we were back at the cabin. We had plenty of time.

After the ritual giving of the statement, a visit to the hospital so a doc could peer down my already-bruising throat, and the return to the office to fill Ms. Pentecost in on the events of that afternoon, I requested some time off.

"I was thinking two weeks," I told her. "We've never talked vacation time, but then again I've never asked for it. With five years under my belt, I figure I have at least that much saved up, but I can probably do with only one if you think I'm indispensable."

"You are absolutely indispensable, Will," she said. "But I think I can survive for two weeks without you. In fact, why don't you make it three. We have no active cases at the moment."

"Except for Waterhouse. And Quincannon, if you want to call that active. Think you can take the needle off those for the time being?"

"I think . . . We could all use a break. Now the question becomes wherever will you go?"

The query came with the Pentecost version of a mischievous glimmer.

"In a perfect world, the Bahamas," I told her. "But I've got enough freckles for the season, and besides, the beach doesn't have the company I want. So a mountain getaway will have to do."

"I'm sure you'll have a lovely time," Ms. P said. "Please give Miss Quick my regards. Work can wait until you return."

Thanks to the lack of a phone, my arrival was a surprise to Holly. Despite her earlier invitations, she was initially a little skeptical that she and I could spend three weeks cooped up in a cabin together. If I hadn't known her so well, I would have been insulted.

"I have writing to do, you know?" she'd told me after I'd pulled up in the convertible, its trunk filled with three weeks' worth of sundries. "I'm on a real roll, but I've got two more chapters to go and then at least one more revision before I'm through. Not to mention, I have that story for *Black Mask* that I need to polish off. I have deadlines, you understand. This is my job. You can't be—"

"I can't be what?" I asked, throwing my arms around her neck.

"Distracting me."

"I promise," I whispered in her ear, "I'll be a good girl."

She pressed a palm into my chest and pushed me away.

"See? That's what I mean," she said, readjusting her glasses. "I can't concentrate when you get how you get."

"How *I* get? Madame, you have a very selective memory."

"I don't know what you're talking about," she said with an adorable little huff. "Now I suppose we better bring your things in and unpack. There's not much drawer space."

I popped the trunk on the convertible, revealing the massive suitcases.

"Oh, good lord," Holly exclaimed. "What all did you bring?"

"Just clothes," I said. "Shoes. A few hats. The essentials."

"You shouldn't have packed so much," she said. "There's no reason for so many clothes."

"There isn't?"

"No."

"No reason at all?"

"Well, I mean there's nowhere to go around here, so you don't—"

"Hey, no, I understand," I told her. "You think I've got too many clothes. I'm not gonna lie—I think you're right. I mean seriously, who needs this? All that time spent ironing and all it does is collect coffee stains."

"What are you doing?"

"And who the hell invented bras? Not a woman, I'll tell you that."

"Will, put that back on."

"And pants!" I shouted out into the forest. "What bastard decided these were essential?"

"Willowjean Parker!"

"Holly Quick!" She stopped, mouth open in a frozen *o*. I reached out and drew her close. "I love you.

"Also," I said, finding the first button, "you seem to be terribly overdressed."

———

A little while later, we were sprawled in the front seat of the Packard. We were still sweaty, but our breathing had returned to a steady pace. Holly was leaning back into me, using my thighs as armrests.

Her skin, a tawny brown in winter, had grown several shades darker in the intervening weeks. Apparently there was a natural spring a little ways up-mountain where it was possible to sunbathe in private. I resolved that we would be spending a lot of time there.

As we lounged, Holly traced the outline of my tattoo with a ruby-lacquered fingernail.

"Does it still hurt?" she asked.

"Not anymore. It itched for a day or two, but now I don't feel a thing. I mean I feel things. I feel what you're doing right now, and I'm not complaining. I just mean . . . you know."

"Can I ask you a personal question?" she said.

"Considering our arrangement, I think personal questions are on the table."

"Why did you get it? Men get tattoos to show them off. Girlfriends' names. Mermaids on their chest. That sort of thing. No one's going to see this."

"No one?"

"Hardly anyone."

I thought about that as her fingernail did another circuit of the dagger and rose.

"I guess I wanted a reminder."

"Of your friend?"

"Sure," I said. "A reminder of her. But also of a particular place and time and how important it was to me. And how far it is from there to here."

Holly nodded like she understood, and I think maybe she did.

We were quiet for a time, heads tilted back, staring up at the branches and the leaves and the sky above. A breeze came through and rustled the trees and picked up the black wave of Holly's hair so it tickled the underside of my chin.

She rolled over between my legs and pushed herself up so her face hovered above mine, her hair falling over both of us like a veil. Her glasses had tumbled off at some point and I had a clear view of the flecks of amber and green swimming in the brown of her eyes.

"Will?"

"Yeah, Holly?"

"I'm really very cold."

"Yeah, me, too," I admitted.

"I know pants are the devil's work, but I think I want to put mine back on."

"I guess we should."

"Are you pouting?"

"I guess I am," I said.

"Well, how about we throw some clothes on. Then we take your new car—"

"Only my car for two more weeks. Then it's back to the dealership."

"Take your new car down to the Wet and Dry and get something nice and hot for dinner. You can tell me all about how things wrapped up, and after we get back and have eaten dinner and built a fire, then we can lay out that bearskin rug and . . ."

She leaned down and growled the last bit into my ear. She was very, *very* precise with her language.

There was no question as to what I did next.

CHAPTER **52**

I blinked and the time was gone.

Because Marlo's family was apparently well off, I'd assumed the cabin would be a rich girl's idea of rustic. But it was made of honest-to-God logs and was a tight two stories—bedroom and office upstairs, den and kitchen downstairs. The only toilet was an outhouse, and bathing was done at the aforementioned natural spring, which we visited as much as we could until it got too cold.

Cleanliness is neighbors with godliness, after all.

There was no phone and there wasn't a New York City newspaper within fifty miles. It was glorious.

Each day was blissfully boring. We would wake and eat breakfast and take a long walk in the woods, or go down to the spring to wash up. Then I'd read a book and Holly would look over what she'd written the night before, then we'd fix lunch and Holly would hole herself away in the cabin's office, which was little more than a closet with a typewriter, and pound away on the portable Remington while blowing cigarette smoke like a freight train out the window.

And, yeah, there was a lot of distracting done, on and off the bearskin rug. But not enough. Time always seems to move fastest when you most want the clock to stop.

Soon we were heading back to the city. The top was up on

the Packard. While we were in the mountains, autumn had finally descended on New York, and the air had a bite to it.

I dropped Holly and her one modest suitcase off at her place in Morrisania. Inside the suitcase was her novel, complete with ending.

She'd allowed me to read it, and I told her it was good. Better than good—it was one of the best detective stories I'd ever read, and I've read a lot. I think maybe she even believed me.

Then I directed the Packard over the 59th Street Bridge in a relaxing loop down through Queens and into Brooklyn. I had decided, at Holly's urging, to keep the Packard. She pointed out that I made a healthy salary and had few expenses, save for clothes and the occasional Broadway show.

I liked how the coupe handled. And if Holly and I wanted to spend a weekend or two out of town, it would be nice to have an automobile of my own.

There were certain things you just couldn't do in your boss's car.

I planned to visit the dealership the next day and ask to get the bills sent to me. The real me. I'd explain the situation as best I could, but I figured as long as they were getting the payments from somewhere, they wouldn't ask too many questions.

I was a block away from the office when I noticed the police cars.

There were four or five parked on the street outside and a flurry of men going up and down the steps.

I stopped the Packard in the middle of the street. A terrible coldness flooded through me.

She was dead.

Someone had gotten to her. I'd left her unprotected and look what happened.

I stepped out of the car on wobbly legs and managed to start moving toward the open front door.

I heard a woman's voice shouting from inside.

"You stop that! You stop that right now!"

Mrs. Campbell. I'd never heard her so upset.

A patrolman stepped in my way.

"Sorry, miss, you'll have to go around."

"This is my house" is what I wanted to say. "This is my house and my office and I work and live here and I demand to know what's going on."

But then he'd tell me. I was sure to my bones that his answer was going to be "There's been a murder."

The question needed to be answered, though, and I had my mouth open to ask it when a pair of figures stepped out of the open doorway and onto the top of the stoop.

Lillian Pentecost, followed closely by a cop in a sergeant's cap.

"Boss!"

I couldn't keep the relief out of my voice. The relief and joy. Not dead! Not murdered while my back was turned. Very much alive and well.

Ms. P blinked, looking as surprised to see me as I was to see her.

"Will?"

The cop nudged her down the steps and I noticed for the first time that she didn't have her cane. She wouldn't have been able to use it anyway, because her hands were cuffed behind her back.

"What's going on?" I called out.

"Call Mr. Whitsun," she said as she was moved into the back of an unmarked sedan. "Tell him I am in need of his services."

The sergeant slammed the door shut. I pushed past the uniform guarding the street and pressed my forehead against the window.

"What's going on?" I shouted again. "What's the charge?"

The sergeant slapped the roof of the car, but Ms. Pentecost managed to shout back the answer before it sped away.

"Murder," she cried out. "The charge is murder!"

WILLOWJEAN PARKER
LEAD INVESTIGATOR
PENTECOST AND PARKER INVESTIGATIONS
NEW YORK CITY

ACKNOWLEDGMENTS

I know—a cliffhanger. Please don't hate me. But there was no other way to do it. The stakes are about to get raised for our heroines, and I hope you'll stick around for the ride. Which is why my first thanks go to you, my readers, for your passion, your praise, and your love for these characters that, if the messages I get are to be believed, rivals my own.

And as always, special thanks go to:

My agent Darley Anderson and the rest of his all-star team: Mary Darby, Georgia Fuller, Rosanna Bellingham, Rebeka Finch, and the rest.

My editors Bill Thomas and Carolyn Williams for their belief in this series and making sure this latest installment is worthy of its leads. And to the rest of the folks at Doubleday who helped get this book into your hands. Those include, but are not limited to, Elena Hershey, Jillian Brigilia, Monica Brown, Maria Massey, Maria Carella, and Michael J. Windsor.

Jay Ferrari, who taught me (and by proxy, Will Parker) how to snap an attacker's arms.

Jessica Spotswood, who remains my first and best reader, and who always reminds me that while Lillian and Will might make their living using their heads, what's happening in their hearts can be just as thrilling.

And to the booksellers and librarians across the country who have taken the time to hand-sell this series while also standing as a bulwark against hate, censorship, and general villainy—you are appreciated and loved.

Thank you all.

About the Author

STEPHEN SPOTSWOOD is an award-winning playwright, journalist, and educator. As a journalist, he has spent much of the last two decades writing about the aftermath of the wars in Iraq and Afghanistan and the struggles of wounded veterans. His dramatic work has been widely produced across the United States and he is the winner of the 2021 Nero Award for best American mystery. He makes his home in Washington, D.C., with his wife, young-adult author Jessica Spotswood.